Bud Harrison

5-9-52 —

4908 Maine View Dr.

Ma. 1652 —

MIGHTY

MOUNTAIN

ARCHIE BINNS

BY THE PACIFIC

BINFORDS & MORT : *Publishers* : PORTLAND, ORE.

MIGHTY
MOUNTAIN

New England Remembers the Sea

O<small>N HER VOYAGE</small> *home from the Northwest coast, the* Maid *was in a collision at Buenos Aires. The other ship was to blame, though even then they might have got clear with a sober mate and a New England crew. But things are the way they happen. What was not the fault of Captain Wallace was his misfortune. He stayed to settle the matter of damages, which dragged out nearly a year. Because of yellow fever, which was always about, and because of school which waited for young John at home, Deborah Wallace and her husband were parted.*

Almost a year after she returned to Fairhaven, Deborah had a letter in her husband's careful logbook hand saying he would sail that April, thriftily, in the homeward-bound whaler, Sea Queen, *Captain Ely. April was already long past and, a few doors away, Mrs. Ely waited for her husband. Her wait had been longer than Deborah's; she shared it with the five-year-old son her husband had never seen.*

A month after the letter, the Sea Queen *was in port. Deborah did not see the ship ghosting in from Buzzards Bay or warping to the dock. She heard of the arrival from her neighbor, who heard it from the butcher's boy. It is not seemly for a captain's wife to go out of her way to watch incoming ships, however much her heart is looking seaward from the hill.*

Even when the ship was in, she did not go down to the dock. The wife of a New England captain does not do that, though the mask that hides her eagerness is thin as charity. She sat at the parlor window, sewing. The docks were only a few cables away, but it was a long wait. A captain does not rush home on foot, any more than his wife hurries down to the shore. He waits for the "captain's hack."

In the late afternoon she heard the slow roll of wheels and the creaking of the loaded conveyance. She heard it, sewing swiftly, stitch after stitch. Then she saw the gray, black-harnessed horses, and the hack itself. It passed the gate without stopping. Deborah had done all that should be done of patient waiting. She had done nothing to displease the fates or upset the delicate balance of the world's machinery. Now she saw the machinery failing her and going wrong. The hack rolled past without stopping and went away into silence. Later she saw dark figures returning. Two old captains, with their stovepipe hats in hand, were coming up the walk. She put her useless sewing aside and got up, to be on her feet when they brought the news that she was a widow.

Things end sharply in this world. Only one does not always know until afterward when a part of life ends. Afterward, Deborah saw that several parts of life ended when

4

the Maid *was rammed by a Peruvian barque. That mishap was the end of her resolve to sail with her husband wherever he sailed. It was the end of all sailing for both of them, unless one counted her voyage home with the children and his final voyage, which was not the one he planned. Captain Ely said something of the sort. Near the end of a three-day* pampero, *dying of yellow fever, John Wallace had seen his voyage coming to an end at sea—or stretching away into eternity—and he whispered that he was in the wrong ship, bound for the wrong port.*

So several parts of life ended for Deborah, who was twenty-eight that June and not much more than a young woman. Out of the wreckage she salvaged enough to buy a grocery store in New Bedford, where she set about raising her boys and making ends meet.

Once a summer woman from Brooklyn observed to her that New Englanders are restrained. Deborah did not see how people can be anything else. But she was sorry for the woman if she thought New Englanders did not have imagination. If all their memories and dreams were put together, they would make a complete picture of this earth, and all the far corners of the sea, ice-studded and wrapped in fog, and bathed in bright tropical sunshine.

In her own right Deborah had clear memories of places which were now as distant from her narrow street as some lost star. Her husband and his ship were gone the way of flesh and blood and New England oak, but they had had their moment of immortality, when they matched themselves against the stars and great winds and the ocean that keeps its youth through all time. And she had shared that moment.

One of the things she remembered best and saw most clearly was the Northwest coast. The Maid *had spent a year carrying timber to San Francisco, and trading on Puget Sound. She remembered Mount Rainier, towering up into the sky to the southeast of the Sound; the base of the mountain dissolved in the haze of distance, while the dome of snow and ice appeared to float in the upper air, detached as the moon. It had the ghostly whiteness of the moon at dawn, near its setting, and no one had ever climbed to its summit. The whites had not attempted it, and the Siwash Indians were afraid. They believed the gods lived up there and only came down to walk the earth at night. The Siwashes were content to live at sea level and let the gods alone.*

Deborah remembered the countless canoes of a people afloat, moving lazily on the flood tide of summer, the paddlers singing the canoe song, which at first had seemed tuneless and harsh. Afterward she became used to it. And, long afterward, she liked to call up the song in her mind's ear. It seemed right then, and simple with meaning. With every few strokes the Indians kept time to their song by striking the sides of the canoe with their paddles. Listening to the song in memory, she waited with a thrill for that throb of paddles against hollow cedar, across clear water. It was something like a drumbeat, and something like the half-resigned cry of a people who passed their lives at sea level, but were never allowed to forget the great white lodge which the gods had pitched in the sky; it was visible from every reach of the Sound and looked down on them wherever they went.

In her mind, Deborah had a picture of the Maid *in Cormorant Passage, with the lights of Steilacoom astern, standing in toward Nisqually Reach. She remembered the jungles of great evergreens coming down steeply to the edge of still dark waters at night. Deep waters full of stars. She remembered the ship ghosting through those waters with the profound tide and a breath of night air that drew in from the Strait. Above the cold fire about the cutwater of the ship she saw, gleaming, the figurehead which was a mystery because its features were hers, and what it had been she had been. They were both gone, one of them under the sea and the other cast up on dry land. That other self of hers was something which strangers in her store could not be expected to guess: a woman in white, with a star in her hand, gliding over the sea.*

That part of her life was over. But she remembered it as one would remember a voyage to the moon. And she sometimes thought of Elmer Hale, who had gone out there in the ship. Elmer was a promising boy and Captain Wallace had sworn to make a man of him if he stayed with the ship. But Elmer had a dubious old uncle who had gone out to the Oregon Country years before, and was ending the bright promise he had shown at Harvard in the company of a squaw. There was also a young woman whom Deborah did not like. So, one way and another, Elmer had not been ready to return with the Maid, *and they had a Sandwich Islander in his place.*

Deborah counted on talking with Elmer when he came home. She had been hurt by his leaving the captain who planned to do so much for him. But it may have been that

7

time and the West had made a man of him. And Elmer would see her as something more than a widow storekeeper. They would talk about the Northwest coast. He would bring news of people she had known out there and fill in her picture of the country. On shipboard, she had seen only the edge of things, and Elmer had explored the dangerous interior.

But Elmer never came home to Fairhaven. She was not quite sure whether he made out well or badly in the New World. All she was sure of was that the voyage in the Maid *had changed everything for him. His life was not what any one would have foreseen for a boy born on a New England hillside farm. Inside the gateway of the far western world he found a different kind of life altogether.*

CHAPTER ONE

THE GATEWAY of the far western world was not easily entered. A hundred and seventy-two days out of Fairhaven, the barque, *Maid,* rolled up the coast of Washington Territory with a light southwesterly on her quarter. Near midday she raised Cape Flattery as a blue island which slowly joined hands with the mainland. There was the smoke of Indian fires from the mainland beach, and smoke from the Indian houses on high Tatoosh as it bore abeam in the afternoon. On first look, Elmer mistook the Makah village for a white settlement, because of the plank houses with peaked roofs. With land to be had for the asking, it seemed odd for settlers to choose that barren block of stone, with the surf pounding white about its dark foundations. He wanted to ask old Tom, who was their expert on far western matters, having been in a whaler that put into the Strait for water somewhere near the beginning of time. Before Elmer could ask, all hands were called to braces and sheets. The foreyards were sweated over and the main checked as they whirled over of their own accord. And the *Maid* rounded Tatoosh and stood into the Strait of Juan de Fuca with the wind on her other quarter.

The boy thought it a fine moment, this swinging in through the gateway of a strange, new world with a wind tailored to order. Captain Wallace must have thought so, too. He was walking the weather side of the poop—a fine figure of a man, with big shoulders and a brown beard. His wife and son were aft by the cabin skylight, Mrs. Wallace sewing, and young John, still in dresses, looking through a toy spyglass covered

9

with red leather. In less ambitious moments, Elmer told himself he would be satisfied to reach the age of thirty-four, part owner of as good a ship, and with as fine a wife. Coming from a penniless young foremast hand who was never quite without ambition, it was a tribute to a man's achievement, and to the woman who sailed with him.

Helping Tom coil down the weather main brace, Elmer said comfortably, "It's no trick getting into a strait like this!"

"Maybe," Tom said. "If they want us to pass—" He stopped to open his silver tobacco box, and bit off a piece of pigtail.

The whaleman's doubts and the opening of the box were like bad magic. The wind flawed, suddenly, and the swelling sails went flat. All at once the air was warm and scented with evergreen smoke. Overhead, the mainsail filled with a loud bang, and fell slack again. From everywhere aloft there were other sharp reports. Then all the sails were flapping senselessly, as if they had just shot themselves. Captain Wallace shouted orders to wear ship, and the first mate was tailing onto a fall behind Elmer. He was cursing as if the watch were to blame for the wind suddenly changing from southwest to east. Aloft, everything was shaking, with sheets rattling and blocks kicking. The boy had never seen a ship taken aback before, with all her sails turned inside out. For all he knew, it was the end of everything, with the barque starting to make sternway toward the white wreath of breakers about Tatoosh Island.

But things quieted aloft as they wore around. The mate, no longer blaming the crew, wiped his forehead and said, "I'll be blowed!" He had hardly said that when the sails were slack against the masts again. The wind was suddenly cold, blowing off the sea, and everything threshed and banged aloft as they were taken aback for the second time. Caught between the easterly blowing out of the Strait and the southwesterly blowing off the Pacific, the bewildered *Maid* found headwinds in both directions and was taken aback each time she wore around. And while that was happening, Tatoosh Island and the Cape were gliding away to the south as if they had gone adrift.

When the wind became reasonable again and gave the *Maid* something she could understand, she was close-hauled on the port tack, standing up toward the Cape which was a long way to windward. Astern, the high mountains of Vancouver Island were coming out clearer, lifting details of forests and ravines out of the blue haze. In one place there was something like a pillar of snow against the land. A waterfall, Tom said.

They set the main and main-topmast and mizzen staysails and drove the *Maid* through the long Pacific swells. She sailed bravely, but in the lap of some enchantment which kept her from going anywhere. The Cape did not come any closer, and the mountainous shore and waterfall astern did not go any farther away. They were in the grip of a strong current which set north toward the forbidding island.

It was not the same thing as romping through the Strait toward Puget Sound, this being thrown outside for an inconclusive tussle with the sea. At twenty Elmer was young enough to feel a personal disappointment which was quite detached from the dangerous position of the ship. He found what comfort he could in the Biblical prophecy of the time when "there shall be no more sea." And he thought unfavorably of his old watchmate, Tom. Tom was a better sailor than whalemen are reputed to be, and he was a good friend. But after a voyage of six months, there were moments when the boy could find unreasonable fault with him. He did not like the fact that Tom was about five feet high, with almost as much beam. He did not like the strip of woolly white beard which cradled Tom's face, from ear to ear, like a loosely-slung hammock. He did not like Tom's friendly old eyes, because they encouraged him to forget disappointments, which was like reminding him he was due for plenty more. It was also irritating the way he spoke of this as a short voyage, though that is all you could expect from a whaleman, used to being gone four or half a dozen years at a time. But the most annoying thing about Tom was his attitude toward life. All he asked for below was a few hours of sleep and enough salt horse, with a little knitting or sennet work for his spare hours. On deck, his wants did not seem to go beyond occasionally having his hands free to give his breeches a hitch, and to open his silver tobacco box. On a fine night in the tropics, he might like to yarn about a white whale named "Mocha Dick," who was older than sin and would never be caught. That was because Mocha was really Neptune. He got himself up as a white whale to plague stingy New England captains into forgetting their profits and chasing something rare. It was a tiresome story that had no end because there were any number of stingy whaling captains, who were devilish stubborn in what they undertook. And they could never catch old Mocha Dick because it was the sea itself they were pursuing. Tom really believed the yarn, or wanted to, which was worse. One way and another the boy found him thoroughly irritating at moments toward the end of a half-year's voyage. But Elmer was generous enough to see it was not Tom's fault. Tom was past sixty, and it was all you could expect of an old man who had nothing more to live for. If the *Maid* failed to weather the mountainous, blue-green shore under her lee, if she piled up on the rocks near the foot of the snowy waterfall, it could make no real difference to an old man like Tom. It would only remind him, with an apologetic start, that his life was over long ago.

With Elmer, such a mishap would be a different matter. He had never known a woman, or anything but poverty and a good home. He required years to manage a very necessary triumph. Not exactly revenge, but a lesson to life. If this voyage ended on a hard lee shore, the breakers which would end Elmer would not end his need. He was convinced of that. He would die without fear, but with a vast sense of unsatisfied longing and injustice. He would leave a kind of vacuum to trouble the world forever after. There was a certain satisfaction in the thought. It would be no small potatoes to discomfort the whole world with his passing. . . .

"THAR SHE BLOWS!" Tom's voice was like guns, booming in his weather ear. The old man was pointing eagerly to windward. "Sperm whale, and a monster!"

Elmer expected a whale as big as an island, but there was only a distant, dark line in the rolling sea, and a weak fountain of spray.

He saw the rest of the watch looking intently to windward, some of them broadly amused. At the break of the poop, Captain Wallace was acknowledging the hail with a grim smile. His smile said plainly that if you take a whaleman to sea, what else can you expect?

The *Maid* was not a whaling ship. Sperm whales meant less to her than mackerel, which they might catch by trolling. Still, it was something to look at. And there was some satisfaction in seeing the old whaleman yanked out of his perpetual calm.

Tom was prancing like a racehorse at the post, moving his raised right arm back and forth. His closed, hairy fist held an imaginary harpoon. He was testing its balance and getting the rust of disuse out of his arm. "There's a thousand gallons of oil," he said, "floating on the sea in nature's casks, and whalebone for my lady's corset!"

"It may belong to some one," Sam said. "I think I saw a brand on that big one marked 'a hundred gallons.'"

Elmer was smiling, but he shared Tom's feeling for a fortune going to waste. "Don't you reckon we could get one, Tom? There's a harpoon in the lazaret."

"Aye. If there's a will, there's a way." Then Tom looked sorrowful. "I've done my duty," he said, virtuously. "I reported the whales. The rest is up to the Old Man." He canted his head toward the captain, who was young enough to be his youngest son.

"Stand by to go about!"

They tacked ship again, with the white waterfall as plain as ever, hanging down the side of the blue-green forest on their quarter, and the Cape as far up to windward as it had been an hour before. Elmer stared disconsolately at the distant houses on the square mass of Tatoosh. They were houses, all right, but there was a bleak strangeness about them. Probably because they were unpainted and without windows. They did not seem to have chimneys, either, though smoke was coming out of one peaked roof.

"Those houses," Elmer said, "who lives there?"

"Savages," Tom said; "sea-fishing savages."

Elmer said doubtfully, "Indians don't build houses."

"It's a curious thing," Tom said. "These ones do. The time we watered in the Strait, we saw one of their houses twice as big as the Mariners' Home. It had planks three feet wide, as nice as you ever saw."

Elmer did not know whether to believe any of it or not. He looked at Sam and saw him struggling over a witticism which was never said. A hundred yards to port, a dark mass rose suddenly, with the sea lacing white along its side.

"*Thar she breaches!*" Tom's roar was unnecessary. The whale was so dismayingly large that no one could have escaped seeing it. And they were close enough to feel the great, dull, snoring sound as a fountain of water went up and blew away to leeward.

"Oh, Jesus!" The old whaleman was prancing again, and working his harpoon arm. "What's the profit in going to sea in a ship that isn't fitted to catch whales?" The squared-off head sank under a long gray swell and was gone. Tom stared after it. "Safe as a church!" he muttered. "And this ship out of Bedford Harbor!" But instead of dwelling on his shame he turned to philosophy. "It's a curious thing," he said, "the way the world's sinless in all places, in some ways. I've seen places where you could go naked without ever being cold or bitten by as much as a midge. And there's places where a virgin could sleep outdoors, unharmed. And there's places where you could carry gold in an open basket, without being robbed." He took out his silver tobacco box, and bit off a piece of pigtail, with a sigh. "But I never did see a place where a naked virgin could sleep outdoors beside a basket of gold and not suffer some kind of loss or inconvenience."

"Hell's fire!" Sam said. "What kind of a world would it be where you could advertise for every kind of trouble and not come by any?"

Elmer did not know which of them was right, but it developed that even here a whale was less safe than a church. Watching for another one to hulk up suddenly beside the ship, he saw something quite different. A twenty-foot form shot clear of a long swell and seemed to poise for a moment in the air; twenty feet of speed and power, brilliant in black and white, with a dorsal fin like a long, curved sword. The thing poised for a moment, then turned sideways in the air, curved from head to tail in a clean arc. When it struck, the solid, booming impact of the blow was enough to make you think the sea was hard as oak. Then there were two more, falling through the air, with their curved sides down. They were not falling into the sea, but onto a dark, disappearing mass. Fathoms away from where they struck, the great fluke of a whale smashed through the sea and disappeared.

"There's blood!" Sam said.

Elmer thought he saw red in the foam, then the next swell moved serenely over the place of battle, and washed it clean.

"The devils!" Tom gripped the bulwark and stared into the sea. "Oh, the devils, the devils!"

"What are they?" the boy asked. "Sharks?" Though he had never seen black-and-white sharks that did tricks in the air.

"Killers," Tom said. "Sharks are lambs to those! They're killer whales. Likely, there's a dozen, taking turns, dropping on that sperm's head, and stripping the blubber off him. They've no conscience and no fear. They're born mad, wanting to kill and tear and destroy. They'll follow that whale all day and all night, stunning him when he comes up to breathe, tearing him to pieces under the sea. Killing's their joy."

Sam said, "There's nothing like a Yankee for running down his competitors." He pointed seaward. "There go your profits!"

At sunset they could still see the clean shapes of killer whales leaping up and falling with the wild tirelessness of the sea. The Pacific was an old, savage place, all right, full of death and loneliness.

Almost at the beginning of the dog watch, the *Maid* gained the shelter of Cape Flattery and began beating up into the Strait against a light southeasterly. It was a matter of a change in tide, and skill had nothing to do with it, but both watches took credit for the victory, and there was enough for both. Inside the Strait they were no longer at sea, but in the arms of the earth. The land breeze was soft in their faces and perfumed with the sweet smoke of evergreens. To a boy who had his moments of homesickness, the breeze had the smell of coming home. It suggested human habitation and growing things. And only one who has been at sea for the first time, for half a year, can know what it means to be homesick for the earth.

Elmer stood at the starboard bulwarks and looked hungrily at green, growing things. The shore toward which they were beating was abrupt and high and wooded with immense evergreens. Beyond that high foreshore, the land went up in swell after swell, hill after hill, until it piled up into mountains. And nowhere was there any sign of earth or rock. Only the great forests billowing up and away, green and gold-green and blue at sunset.

Standing beside the boy, Sam Cutler said, "It's like Maine all over, only spread out and piled up higher."

Elmer said, "Yes," though he had never been in Maine.

"It'll be nice for you, having kin out here."

It was a warming thought, finding one of your own family in a world where everything else was new. "If I can find him," Elmer said.

"You know where he lives?"

"He was at Nisqually the last time we heard." That had been three years ago, maybe more.

"Nisqually. Is that a town?"

Elmer said, "I don't know."

"You'll find him," Sam declared. Then he said, "I wouldn't mind seeing Jarvis, myself. Not that we were ever real cronies."

"I never knew him very well, either." Elmer had been about eleven when Uncle Jarvis buried his second wife and went out to Oregon. Before that, he might have seen his uncle half a dozen times. Jarvis belonged to the fortunate side of the family, while Elmer's people never had any luck.

Sam said, "I wonder what Jarvis does with his education, out here in the woods?"

"I don't know what he does."

The lean and speculative seaman went on as if he had not heard. "I never rightly figured what he did with his education at home." He bit a fresh chew of tobacco. "Jarvis always was a deep one."

The boy was silent because he did not really know his uncle either. At home, family portraits were apt to be tantalizingly incomplete. Because he never heard any ill spoken of his own kin, he assumed it was the family policy to mention virtues and let other matters go. Like his second cousin, Jonathan. When Elmer asked what Jonathan died of, his mother explained that he was found dead in a house in Boston. When he asked what Jonathan had been like, she recalled, triumphantly, that Jonathan had been good to his mother. That was a family portrait, as complete as many others. As a background, night in the great city of Boston. In that night, a young man with curly hair was lying dead in a mysterious house. And, like an epitaph, there were the words, "He was good to his mother." The weeding out of all but virtues gave his portrait great simplicity.

That ignorance was partly Elmer's fault. He had not thought of Jonathan since childhood. He thought of him now only because of this mysterious night which was settling over the Strait of a new world. It was the same unknown, mysterious night that made a background for the portrait of Jonathan. What he knew about the young man was what a child was told. If he could ask his mother now, or his grandmother, he might learn much more. He had left home almost at the moment of discovering how to learn the meaning of things you see and hear in childhood. If you could know in time, if you could remember to keep going back to the same things as you grow older, you might reach majority with a good idea of the way things and people are. Elmer had perceived the method just too late for it to do him much good. At the moment of kissing his mother good-by on the wharf, he had had the unsatisfactory realization that he knew less than he might have known. It was much as if his mind were still wearing some of its swaddling clothes. He had failed to protest because he was used to them, and his parents had been too busy to notice that he was growing up and needed something more suitable. So he had gone away, a tall and strong young man with an unsuitable baby's bonnet on his mind. At the moment of farewell, he thought, his mother was uneasily aware of the bonnet, but it was then too late for her to remedy it. So it had been left for him to get rid of the thing as best he could. . . .

Through the dark web of memories and thoughts, he heard
Sam Cutler ask, "Be you planning to settle out here, Elmer?"
He was dimly shocked by the thought of staying so far from
home and his own family. "No," he said, "I wouldn't do that.
I'll stay with the ship." Staying with the ship, he would never
be altogether away. In the ship he was with people from home;
people who knew his people. The ship was a part of Fairhaven,
and after a while it would take him back. "I'm going to stay
with the ship," he said. The ship was homelike and real in the
growing dark. The new land, walling the Strait, was mostly
an idea. There were great forests and streams of water, and
game and fish. But, as yet, he had no contact with those things.
In the *Maid,* they trusted to the shelter of New England oak.
At supper they had eaten salt horse and sea biscuits bought in
Fairhaven. When Elmer drank at the scuttle butt, he was drinking water from a stream at home.

Elmer was silent and full of thoughts, while the new land
made other people more talkative. At the beginning of his
wheel watch, Captain Wallace and his wife were on deck, talking together in quiet voices. Twice the cow mooed insistently
from between-decks. The first time Captain Wallace said,
"She smells the land." The second time Mrs. Wallace said,
"Poor Bessie! Do you think we can manage to give her shore-
leave in a field?" The boy did not hear the words of the captain's
answer, but his voice sounded indulgent and amused. After
that, young John's voice trailed up from the yellow-lighted
cabin skylight: *"Ma-ma! Ma-ma, I want a drink of wa-ter!"*
On *"Ma-ma!"* and *"wa-ter!"* his voice went up and down like
the call of a phœbe in the springtime at home. Mrs. Wallace
got up, still talking as she gathered her cloak about her, and
went below. The captain told the second mate when to go about,
and to call him if there was any question. He was to be very
careful because everything was so peaceful and easy. Everything was peaceful, but it was a hundred miles to anything like
a white settlement, and there was nothing like being careful.
The captain did not really talk to the second mate; he only gave
instructions. But his voice was friendly and his instructions

seemed longer than necessary, as if he wanted to go on talking to some one.

When Captain Wallace was safely below, the second mate talked to Elmer, at the wheel. He did not exactly talk, but made friendly remarks in a subdued voice whenever he paused to look into the binnacle. It was the effect of their landfall at the end of a long voyage, the boy decided. Friendliness was being passed about the ship like rum served to all hands. Elmer felt a little sorry for the second mate, whom the captain called "Mister," and the crew referred to as "Jones." Mr. Jones had a lonely life on board, not being quite an officer or one of the crew. Aft he was only a second mate, and forward some of the men knew him ashore. They sometimes made jokes about him and his wife. Mrs. Jones was a shrew who led him a dog's life ashore, and made him help with the housework, so it was said. Perhaps he made long voyages to be rid of her, but he was not quite rid of her when he was sailing with his neighbors. With his eyes on the luff of the dim main course in the dark, Elmer pondered the difference in wives. Mr. Jones was separated from his wife by twenty thousand sea miles, and she still lessened men's respect for him. Mrs. Wallace had been with her husband for those same twenty thousand miles, under the critical eyes of the crew, and she had done nothing to make him seem any less a man.

"Like harbor sailing, isn't it?" In the dim glow of the binnacle light the boy saw the second mate's face beside him. The face was almost young, a little haggard and a little lost.

"It's fine," the boy said, with his eyes on the luff of the sail, and the dark, high wall of land which did not seem much farther off than the end of the bowsprit in the dark.

"We'll have two hundred miles more of this," Jones said, "going farther inland all the time."

The boy said, "M'm," and gave the wheel half a spoke. He wished Jones would not talk to him. The night had come down very dark and without stars, and dew was settling on the cool, smooth spokes of the wheel. There was just enough wind to keep the sails asleep, and it seemed to him the tide had turned and was going out. Against the shadowy wall of land ahead, the *Maid* seemed to be making more leeway. Abaft the break of the fo'c'sle, near the fore hatch, a pipe made a faint, pulsing glow, lighting up the smoker's face, but not enough so it could be recognized. Farther aft, near the main hatch, there was a sudden burst of laughter from the watch. Elmer wondered if it had been caused by the distant Mrs. Jones, and he felt sorry for the second mate, who was walking the poop alone. Not really alone, and that was the misfortune of his life. Whether he knew it or not, a shrew walked with him and made him something less than a man.

"That's right, Elmer, keep her full and bye." Mr. Jones was standing beside him again. "Full and bye's the word."

Elmer was keeping her full and bye, so he did not feel called on to answer. If he had said what he wished, it would have been that the shore was looming very close ahead.

Even the imagined remark was unnecessary. Considering the two kinds of darkness ahead, Jones asked, "You'd think that shore was close, wouldn't you?"

The boy said, "Yes, sir."

"It's a good two miles, with no outlying dangers." Then he added, indulgently, "One like that fools you. It looks like it's on board you while it's still far off. And when a shore's that steep-to you can sail within a biscuit-toss."

"Yes, sir."

Jones walked the poop again, with his invisible nemesis, and Elmer wondered if they weren't within a biscuit-toss already. It seemed to him that now he could smell the land. Not just the evergreen smoke which had been in the air ever since they entered the Strait. Now it was more like the smell of earth, and of dew on green leaves. It was a good smell, and he did not mind steering for it. The second mate had assured him everything was all right, and he steered with a will. Afterward, he wondered if he hadn't steered a little fuller than full and bye. But at the time he was not conscious of doing that. He was only conscious of the ship stealing through the dark night and the calm sea, and of the heady smell of the earth from which he had been separated for so long. . . .

"All hands to go about!" The voice roared through Elmer's pleasant intoxication and sobered him in a moment. Captain Wallace, bare-headed, in his shirt sleeves, was asking the second mate, "Where the devil d'ye think you're going?"

Jones said, "I thought, sir—" and at that moment the ship lifted under their feet as to a gentle sea, slid forward with the sound of a long sigh and stopped, immovable. Somewhere at the moment of grounding, the boy had been brushed away from the wheel, which the captain spun uselessly, and then let go. For a little bit of time, the silence on the poop was broken only by the rippling splash of the outgoing tide. The smell of land was strong about the ship, and the land itself loomed close and high in the darkness. From the land there came a sound like falling water and the long, freezing cry of some animal, hunting or hunted. The ship had made land beyond a doubt, on a savage and unpremeditated shore.

CHAPTER TWO

ONE OF Elmer's schoolmasters had liked to point out
that soil should only be called "dirt" when it is out of place.
What would Schoolmaster Pearson have called the sandbar on
which the *Maid* rested, with two feet of her boot top showing?
The sandbar was earth out of place, at least in relation to the
grounded barque. "Grounded" is a comforting word to hear,
just as "stranded" is a terrible one, even to think. A stranded
ship stays until it is broken up, while a grounded one gets off
on the next tide. At first the boy had visions of the barque
becoming a total loss; of the captain ruined and his wife and
child captured by savages. And he had visions of going through
life with some of the guilt on his own head.

The shadow of terror did not begin to lift until they were
carrying out a kedge in the longboat. The first mate was in
charge of the boat, and he was in good humor, partly, at least,
because the mishap had not occurred in his watch. When they
were clear of the ship, the mate said cheerfully, "It's not the
first ship that's grounded, and it won't be the last." The way
he spoke made it sound as if this were no great matter, and he
was a fine fellow who was cooler than his own captain in
emergencies.

Sharing the same thwart with Elmer, Sam Cutler asked as
they pulled on the oars, "It's not serious, be it?"

The mate said, "I should think not." He said that just as the
oars dipped, and the relieved boy pulled with such a will that
the cold green sparks of phosphorus boiled about his oar. "Not
in this millpond, at half tide."

Now, Elmer thought, it would not be so bad if they went under the *Maid's* bow again. The first time, when they were taking the kedge into the boat, he had looked up and seen the white figurehead leaning forward above him in what seemed an attitude of suffering and reproach. He had lowered his eyes, and was afraid to look again. Partly that was because the wood carver had made the figurehead look like Mrs. Wallace—more beautiful, maybe. Or maybe it was only because the figurehead was always alone above the sea, away from the small things of daily life on board. The figurehead had gently swelling breasts, like a curved sail divided by its buntline, while Mrs. Wallace's modest dress did not suggest such things. But that part must have been right, or the captain would not have let the wood carver present her that way. With one arm upraised, the figurehead was holding a star in her hand, while Mrs. Wallace's hands were more apt to be busy with sewing. Maybe it was she, cleared of the cobwebs of small duties and other people's ideas of how a woman should conduct herself, and what she should do and say. He had thoughts like that when they were getting the kedge into the longboat, and he looked up and saw her, white, above them, just outside the little room of light the lantern made in the dark. She was leaning forward above them, in an attitude of suffering and quiet reproach. She was saying they should have been more careful, so near a strange, unlighted shore. They must do their best now, because her heart was in the ship, and she wanted to glide on forever above the sea. The boy had looked down in shame and fear because he had not been as careful as he might, and there was no telling what ruin might come of it. Now, with the mate making light of their grounding, he felt less guilty, and he had more hope that his life would not be permanently blighted.

"Avast rowing," the mate said. Astern, the manila cable rose to the surface of the water, dimly lighted with phosphorus, and stopped the boat with its elastic tug. The mate took a sounding with the hand lead. "And a half five." His voice was satisfied, and he coiled in the wet line, with sparks of cold fire clinging to it in the dark. "Lay out on the bow oars, while we get this overboard." Sam and Elmer tugged at their oars, and the others wrestled with the kedge. "Watch yourselves!" It went with a dull, churning splash, and the longboat was suddenly in trim again and buoyant, like the buoyant hope of escaping disaster this time.

"Kedge is laid in five and a half fathoms!" the mate sang out. An echo came back, from the ship or the shore—"*and a half fathoms!*"

The mate seemed startled. "Who the devil was that?" though it was apparent to any one else that it was the echo of his own voice.

"Come back on board!"

"Aye, sir!"

"*Aye, sir!*"

Sam remarked, "There's a good echo." Tactfully, he was answering the earlier question, though the mate must have known as soon as he asked. At the moment, he probably had his ears so tuned for the captain's expected voice that he did not recognize his own—or else he was more nervous than he seemed. He did not seem at all nervous, and he let the boat drift a few seconds before giving them the order to row back. "There ought to be fish here," as if he would like to make a holiday of their trip. Then he looked toward the ship and remarked, "You'd hardly see her, except for her light."

That was true. All that was real about the ship was a section of rigging lit up by the anchor light. Her hull was only a deeper darkness in the night, and the spars and clued-up sails were shadows against the shadowy land. It was a dark, cool night, alive with the smell of the new land and the damp northern jungle.

The mate was going to tell them to row back to the ship. He cleared his throat with a grunting sound that lingered oddly because he did not give the order. Instead, he waited, with his shadowy head on one side. "D'ye hear anything?"

They listened, dutifully. At first, there was nothing to hear. Then an impatient voice blasted across the water: "Boat ahoy! What are you waiting for?"

"Coming, sir!"

"Coming, sir!"

As they were rowing back, the mate said, "I could have sworn I heard the sound of oars." Maybe he was nervous, after all.

The *Maid* had gone aground in the last half of the ebb tide. Allow, say, two more hours of ebb, perhaps a little for slack water, and three hours of flood tide to float her. She would be afloat by daybreak, barring bad luck. And their luck did not threaten to be bad. The flat-floored barque sat on the sandbar on an even keel, with the pump sucking dry at the first turn of the handles. The sea was calm as the Acushnet River, and the light easterly showed signs of dying out.

At midnight they were allowed to turn in; only the watch stood by. Elmer went below with his watch-mates, then came on deck again. He was wide-awake and restless, and the fo'c'sle did not feel right. With no motion to the ship, it was disconcertingly steady, as if everything had ended. And it did not help to see Mr. Jones morosely arranging his gear in John Stirling's locker. John had taken his sea chest aft, exchanging places with the second mate. The fo'c'sle did not feel right because of the change in officers and men. And its ominous steadiness was as unsuitable as the rocking of a house in an earthquake.

On deck there was the reassurance of the calm night. The boy found satisfaction in the thought that when he slept again the ship would be safely afloat. His staying on deck was a willing kind of penance. He would have liked to work with the watch, but things like that were not done, unless it was a case of "all hands." And there did not seem to be much to occupy the watch. Four of them were standing by in the waist of the ship, waiting for some change or some idea on the part of the captain to give them occupation. On the fo'c'sle head, Elmer found the fifth man: a shadowy figure seated on the windlass. He hoped it was some one with whom he could visit, but he was disappointed. The shadow was Ezekiel, who was so miserly with words that no one knew him. He acted as if talking were some new and undignified fashion which went against his grain. Still, in being near him, there was a kind of companionship, however ghostly. Elmer seated himself on the stock of the port anchor. "Watching the kedge line?" he asked.

Ezekiel answered, "Aye."

They sat in silence while Elmer considered the position of the ship. It was impossible to judge distances on so dark a night, but they were farther from shore than he had first imagined. Maybe it was a quarter of a mile; maybe twice that. Mr. Jones had been right, in a way, but he had also been wrong. The outlying sandbar had spoiled his theory that you can sail right up to any steep-to shore. "Tide still going out?" Elmer asked.

The answer was a gesture overside, inviting the boy to look for himself.

He looked, dutifully, and could not make up his mind. Then he saw a black shadow off the port bow: a log with three bristling stubs of broken branches. It did not seem to be moving, though he hadn't noticed it at first. Then it slipped gradually out of his range of vision, under the bow. The tide was still going out, but with such a slow, half-hearted drift that you expected to see the flotsam recalled any minute. "We'll get off all right, won't we?" the boy asked.

Ezekiel said, "When she's afloat." There was not much comfort in him.

It was a fine idea, sitting up with the ship until she was out of danger, but it was a long night, with nothing to do. At first there was the excitement of being close to a strange, new coast, but after a while the excitement ebbed away. There were only the still ship and the dark flood of water and the darker shore, and the breeze, which had grown cold. Elmer drew his jacket closer about him. In spite of himself, he yawned.

Ezekiel stirred on the windlass and said, "Better turn in," with the words far apart and clear.

The advice was kindly, but the boy could not take his advice. He shook his head to rouse himself. "I'd rather not."

Ezekiel said nothing more, but the boy decided to compromise between his own resolve and good advice. He settled down on deck and rested his back between two of the iron bands on the wooden anchor stock. It was not too comfortable, but that way he was able to fold his arms around his shins and rest his head on his knees. He rested that way for a minute, then looked up in the darkness and shook his head because he had almost dozed and was in danger of falling asleep. He rested his head on his knees again, and dreamed that he was at home. It was a winter night and the covers had slipped off his bed, and he was not awake enough to do anything about it. . . .

He woke with a start and saw Ezekiel looking over the side. There had also been voices, but that must have been in his sleep. Now the ship was silent, but uneasily awake. He got up stiffly and asked in an undertone, "What is it?"

In answer, Ezekiel made a short gesture toward the sea.

Elmer heard nothing except the murmur of voices aft, and saw nothing but dark water and driftwood. A tree trunk with curved stubs of limbs glided into his range of vision from under the bow. He must have slept for a long time. The tide had turned and was coming in. Then there was the sound of a quick, firm splash. It sounded close by the ship and farther aft. There were voices from on board.

"There it is again!"

"I saw a streak in the water. By that driftwood."

There was no use trying to learn anything from Ezekiel. The boy climbed down from the fo'c'sle head and hurried aft. The watch was lined up along the bulwarks, on the port side. There were other figures on the poop, leaning over the rail. Elmer stopped by the first seaman. "What is it?"

"Something in the water, swimming."

"Can you tell what it is?"

"No. It keeps out of sight in the driftwood."

"Do you think it's big?"

"Pretty big."

The man beside them said, "It has plenty of power when it makes a stroke." Proving the statement, there were two quick, firm splashes, as if a big fish were swimming on the surface, with its tail partly out of water.

"Over there!"

"D'ye see it?" Among the black driftwood there was a dying streak of cold green fire.

It was uncanny, but it was also a little absurd. The day before they had seen whales and killer whales, with hundreds of times more power than whatever was lurking among the driftwood. And they had thought nothing of them. Now, the officers and the watch were all upset over something that was probably no bigger than any one of them.

Elmer had not thought of Mrs. Wallace since he woke. If he had thought of her, he would have taken it for granted that she was quietly asleep below. He was surprised to hear her voice from the poop. Her voice was not loud, but each word was distinct: *"John, there's a boat close on the other side!"*

The quiet voice struck like a bolt of lightning. The thing in the driftwood was forgotten as they scrambled across the deck.

"What in hell is it?" a scared voice asked.

Another man said, "Jesus!" wonderingly, and there was the "clack" of a locust-wood belaying pin drawn from the rail.

They did not know what to make of the high, black shape which had drifted down on the ship out of the darkness and was close on board. It might be some kind of boat, but that was hard to believe. It had come down on them without a sound, and its whole fantastic shape was motionless. Elmer decided it was a great tree trunk, with branches and a mass of upstanding roots that somehow gave the appearance of men.

On the poop, the captain's voice said, "Steady," and a match spluttered. Then he said, "Watch yourself!"

The night air seemed to catch fire as the flare hissed and burned away the darkness. In its blinding glare, the tree trunk became a great boat, filled with beings out of some fantastic dream. The boat was a canoe, more than half the length of the ship, and it held at least sixty men. Sixty men and women and creatures that seemed to be half-men and half-beasts. Some of them had the bodies of men and the heads of birds with long, sharp beaks, while others had the heads of snarling animals.

From the poop, Captain Wallace gestured with the hissing flare and shouted, "Keep off!" Then he said more quietly, "Mister, call all hands." Even for sober New Englanders, the boatload alongside was disconcerting company on a dark night.

There is a natural explanation for everything. Even though you can't find it, it is there. That was part of Elmer's faith. By looking long enough, he convinced himself that the men with heads like birds and beasts of prey were wearing masks. Only the things were so finely made that it was hard to say where the imitation left off and the real commenced. And when a man with a bird's head addressed the others, his foot-long beak opened and closed so naturally that some of the sounds of speech were made by its clattering.

At first, the borrowed heads took all your attention. But as soon as you decided it was a trick, however fine, it became less interesting than the undisguised men. They were big, athletic fellows, with a kind of quick, reckless grace that you had to admire while you were afraid. Some of them had thin beards on their chins, and thin, drooping moustaches, like Chinamen in pictures. Most of their faces were painted with curved horizontal bars, sharp at one end, and broader at the other. In the matter of dress and undress, there was great variety. Some wore jackets covered with close-set rods of wood, and shin-guards of the same material. Others were naked except for a blanket of skin. About the only uniformity seemed to be in head-dress. Except for the bird and animal helmets, most of them wore conical straw hats which were squared off at the peak.

"*Keep off!*" the captain shouted again.

Twenty or more paddlers were backing just enough to keep the great canoe clear of the ship. No one on board knew what they meant, or who they were, only they did not have the look of being up to any good. Both watches were on deck, and the new second mate was passing out rifles. In memory of his late position, Jones was questioning the old whaleman. "You've been on this coast before, Tom. What kind of Indians are these?"

Tom said, "They're not the kind we saw in 'thirty-eight. I

never set eyes on their like before," then he squinted more closely and qualified, "unless it was on the China Coast."

Sam Cutler said, "If those are Chinamen, they're a long way from home."

"No farther from home than we are," Jones said unhappily.

Certainly the conical hats and drooping moustaches gave the strangers an oriental air. Chinese pirates might have looked like that. Elmer fingered the rifle which had been put in his hands, and studied the mysterious, insolent faces. Whatever their race, they had the air of reckless pirates, and the air of enjoying themselves immensely.

On the poop, Captain Wallace lit a second flare and dropped the burning stick of the first between the ship and the great canoe. *"Keep off!"* His tone would have made any white man jump to obey, but the canoe kept its place alongside. And yet the order was understood well enough. A man with a fat, oval face and flat eyes stood on an after thwart and translated it to the others. In answer, the canoe was swept by a wave of ribald laughter which came rolling back from the shore as if the coast were joining in. One man in the canoe, and then another, spoke up, apparently suggesting replies to the captain's order. After each suggestion there was a roar of laughter. Without understanding a word of what was said, you understood the meaning of that laughter and knew the suggestions were indelicate.

The laughter brought smiles to the sober New England faces that lined the bulwarks, but it did not bring relief from uneasiness. The second mate declared the men in the canoe were drunk. Likely enough they were, and there was no comfort in the thought of being overpowered by a drunk and reckless crew of savages.

Elmer clung to his rifle and studied the natives earnestly, hoping for some sign of friendliness; some sign that they would go their way in peace. He found no such sign, but he found something else. Watching them, he forgot a little to feel for the ship and for himself and his own skin. Instead, he was feeling something of the way the savages felt, or the way he supposed they did. They weren't bothered with things like consciences or pity. There was a kind of reckless swing in the way they talked and moved, as if they knew nothing about going back in their minds the way people with consciences do. For them, he thought, living was one reckless adventure from which they never turned back, even for a minute in their minds. They found it good to be alive and strong, with enemies to overcome. Seeing and hearing them, you couldn't help feeling that forward swing to their lives. They went into life as if it were an arena, and if they died, they died fighting what was before them. They never fought themselves with their consciences.

"Elmer, don't stand there mooning!" The voice of the new second mate tramped into his reverie. "You hold that gun as if it was a mop! You look like a housemaid mooning after a parade of soldiers."

"Yes, sir," Elmer said. He was startled because Stirling had never spoken like that before. Until that day they had been fellow-seamen and the Penobscot man had never been less than civil.

Even now, he might be trying. "Look, Elmer," he said, "we're supposed to keep them from boarding us. You're huddled up here beside Tom as if he was your mother, and there's hardly any one for'ard! Now, stir your stumps."

Elmer said, "Yes, sir," and started forward toward where their line thinned out to nothing. The canoe alongside was fully seventy feet long, and the line was thin at best.

Stirling went with him, part way. "Look alive," he said pleadingly. "We don't want those savages to think we're a lot of gander-legged dressmakers, do we?"

At his new station, by the light of the flare, Elmer saw women in the bow of the canoe, and then he saw only one, because she was too lovely to let his eyes travel any more. She was standing on a rough wooden chest, unconcerned with all the uproar about her; unconcerned by the ship and its armed crew, but interested. Except for her standing on the chest, Elmer might not have seen her, and she would have seen very little. She looked small and delicate, and her face troubled him pleasantly. It was familiar but strange, oriental, but not Chinese. Chinese are supposed to have faces like masks, and this golden little face was full of life. Chinese have flat eyes, turned up at the corners. This girl had flat eyes but they did not turn up at the corners, and they were lively and full of agreeable wickedness. The wrong kind of wickedness could not have anything to do with her childish grace and sweetness. In the midst of the heathenish uproar in the canoe, she was standing on a wooden chest, looking the ship over while she chewed a dark strip that might have been smoked meat.

The girls Elmer knew at home ate either with unimaginative heartiness or painful restraint. He had never thought eating could be attractive. Now he saw it as a romantic occupation. He held his long rifle like a housemaid's mop and leaned over the side, looking earnestly at the girl. Aft, there was a good deal of shouting between the ship and the canoe, but it was only a far-off din in his ears. The girl stood on the big wooden chest, gnawing daintily at her strip of smoked meat and looking at the ship. Except for a skirt of soft, woven grass, she was naked and unashamed. In the light of the flare, her breasts looked as if they had been carved out of gold.

Elmer stared until the girl met his eyes and smiled. Her mouth was rather large, and her chin shaped to a delicate point. Her smile gave things a sharper, sweeter flavor, and she held up the scrap of food, offering him a bite. He smiled and shook his head, and kept on smiling, earnestly. She called something in an unknown tongue, and he answered with regret, "I don't know!"

She pointed at him and held an imaginary rifle, then touched her naked breast with one childish finger, looking up appealingly. Asking if he meant to shoot her.

He laughed and shook his head. His conscience was clear because he could not imagine harming such a lovely and trusting wild thing.

She took him at his unspoken word and did not pretend to be afraid any more. Indicating the ship, she asked "Boston men?"

He was agreeably startled. "No, we're from Fairhaven."

The name did not mean anything to her. She looked puzzled, then asked, "King George men?"

He shook his head. Perhaps she was asking if this was an English ship. "We're Americans," he explained, "from Fairhaven, Massachusetts."

She answered with a look which said the world must be a large place, with parts she had never heard of.

Elmer pointed at the girl and the reckless crew about her. "Where are you from?"

She seemed to understand, but her answer was in a foreign tongue which told him nothing. Then she indicated herself. "*Tillicum!*"

That, he judged, was her name.

"*Tillicum!*" he repeated. She nodded and looked pleased. It was a romantic night.

"Tillicum my something-or-other," an unfeeling voice said beside him. Stirling was there, lowering a lantern over the side. He made the lanyard fast and addressed himself to Elmer. "The Old Man isn't burning any more flares. Keep your eyes open, and don't let them savages touch the lantern, or try to come on board."

"No, sir," Elmer said earnestly. He was being very wide-awake and alert.

The second mate looked down at the canoe. "The lantern will give you enough light."

"Yes, sir."

"If you keep your eyes off that little hussy down there." Overnight, Stirling had changed from a friendly shipmate to a disagreeable officer. But when he was gone, the boy kept better watch. He knew in his heart that he had not been sufficiently partisan for the safety of the ship.

The flare sank and went out. It was like darkness until his eyes accustomed themselves to the change, and then there was the light of lanterns. They were just enough to show the immense canoe hanging close alongside, and its restless, wild company. He was more aware, now, of the immense darkness outside the lantern light. In that darkness the rippling splash of the incoming tide was sweet music.

"Tillicum!" the girl called from the canoe. In the light of the flare, she had appeared golden, with black shadows. Now, by lantern light, she was tenderer and more shadowy; somehow farther away. Her voice was pleasant, calling to him in the half-dark, but he had heard of other sweet voices that coaxed sailors to their death on a savage shore. He was uneasy, and he paid more attention to his rifle than to her.

He thought he felt the grounded ship stir under his feet. Then he decided he must be mistaken, because no one else seemed to notice. Then some one passed him and went forward. After a minute, he heard the *quack, quack* of the windlass, and again he felt the ship coming to life under his feet. There could not be more than two men forward, he thought, but the windlass worked with surprising ease. It chattered away, *quackety, quack,* as if the whole crew were pumping it. And the savages alongside could not have suspected that the ship was being kedged out from under their noses. Different ones were shouting comments, and each one was answered by a burst of ribald laughter.

"Laugh away, you hyenas!" some one said, grudging them their fun.

They laughed away, with or without permission, and the windlass quacked steadily. The only trouble was, the ship did not seem to be turning. And the windlass worked too easily. It quacked faster, as if there were no limit to its possible speed. Then it stopped altogether, and there was the droning scrape of cable being pulled in by hand.

"Mr. Holbrook, what the devil is going on up there?" The captain's voice was impatient.

"Kedge seems to be gone, sir!"

"Get the cable on board, and lay aft! Lively!" The captain had once made a fuss about a silver spoon which went overboard with the dishwater. Now he accepted the loss of the kedge as if it were nothing. And they were depending on it to get them off the beach, out of bad company. Elmer could not accept the loss so readily, and he was in a mood to fight, at last. All of him understood what he should have known from the beginning: they were in a well-rigged trap, and even now they could only guess at its extent. Also belatedly, he was beginning to be afraid. And he did not want to look at the men with the heads of long-beaked birds. They were as real as if they were real, and the ship was beset by savage and cunning birds of prey.

Forward, the droning scrape of cable stopped short with a curse. There was a consulting pause, then the mate's voice: "Captain, the cable is fast to a log!"

"Cut it, and lay aft!"

Fast to a log! That was unpleasantly strange. It was just possible that the manila had fouled a log, with so much drift-wood about, but it was not probable. More likely, it had been tied there by whoever cut it from the anchor, and it was all part of the same plan.

Under foot, the ship was coming to life, bumping gently on the sand, The bar seemed to be nudging her keel, warning her that she had no business there. Some one was running aft along the deck, and Stirling was coming forward with new instructions. As he passed along the line, one rifle after another was raised and rested on the bulwarks. Then his instructions got ahead of him. The rifles were all bristling over the side before he reached Elmer, at the end of the line.

"Keep them covered," Stirling ordered, "but don't shoot unless they try to board us."

Things were coming to a head, and it was time to look alive. More men in the canoe were standing, some in the bottom, and others on thwarts and chests. They were yelling derisive, harmless insults, but they made a kind of screen on the near side of the canoe. What went on behind their backs might be less harmless.

The ship was stirring and touching lightly on the sand. Halliard blocks creaked from aft, and footsteps throbbed by and died away forward. The girl in the canoe called, *"Tilli-cum!"* She looked strangely sweet, but the boy could give her only a glance. He was busy trying to see what went on behind the careless, yelling human screen. All he glimpsed for certain was a naked man sitting on a thwart, with water dripping from his hair. Until then it hadn't occurred to him that these savages might be good swimmers who were taking turns reconnoitering in the water about the ship; finding a way to board her, unnoticed—if there was a way. . . .

"She's swinging!" some one yelled.

The ship did not seem to be doing anything. The canoe was in the same position. Only the paddlers were no longer backing water. Their paddles were motionless. Then they took a deliberate forward stroke.

"Watch the devils!"

Out of the corner of his eye, Elmer saw one of the lanterns fall from the side of the ship, a streak of descending light which ended in the sea.

"Who did that?"

In answer to Stirling's outraged shout, the lantern below Elmer made a sudden *smash,* like a start of surprise, and went dark.

"Shoot if they touch the side!"

From forward there was the surging rattle of a headsail on its stay. From farther aft, another lantern gave a surprised *smash* and went out. How were you going to tell, for certain, the moment they tried to board the ship? Elmer wondered if he shouldn't pull the trigger the next time a lantern went out. There were only two left, and the canoe was riding as close to the ship as if it were her shadow. Forward, canvas slatted and quieted. Then another sail made a surging rattle on its stay.

Smash went a lantern.

Then the night seemed to catch fire again as a flare burned away the darkness. The immense canoe was close alongside with men standing, poised, blinking in the sudden glare of light. Others held rifles, half raised. Forward, one more sail slatted and quieted.

"Keep off!"

There were derisive yells in answer, but the canoe sheered off a little grudgingly. The night breeze was now in the faces of the men along the bulwarks. Overhead the weather mainbrace fell slack. Behind them, on the port side, they were sweating the yard about to the starboard tack. There could not be many of them, with most of the crew on guard, and some one at the wheel. At least, the first mate was on the brace tackle, panting, "Heave, heave!" as if he were tearing his lungs out. Then Stirling's voice, gaspingly, "Sorry! Did I step —on your foot?" The politeness was bewildering until a woman's voice panted, "It don't—matter."

"*Tillicum!*" a voice cried from the canoe. The voices rang strangely in the boy's head. The voices of two women, both mysterious in their way. One panting in the dark, "It don't matter!" as if pain were nothing, and the other crying a strange name. His mind confused them with the voices of good and evil.

The main course came down with a soft, sliding rumble as the clew lines were let go. It shook, slapped out and quieted as it filled. The *Maid* gathered weigh, borne up by the tide and steadied by her sparse sails. The men in the canoe were paddling faster to keep alongside. All at once they began dropping astern. They were not paddling any more, only brandishing their weapons and yelling. Their yell was something like a cheer. Maybe they saw they were fairly beaten, and had no hard feelings. Maybe the encounter was a drunken joke, and they had never meant any real harm. One could take his choice.

By daylight the *Maid* was under full sail again, beating up into the sunrise, past the great forests of the shore. The tide was at its flood, brimming over the beach, so that the sea and the forest met. And the shore no longer looked savage in the light of day, only fair and green with the promise that soon they would be able to set their feet on land. They all felt good and admitted to each other that they knew a thing or two about fighting Indians. No one had been hurt, and the ship's damage amounted to the loss of a kedge and a few broken lanterns.

That was all so far as any one but Elmer knew. Looking to make sure there were no savages lurking under the bowsprit, he found at least a trace of them. It looked as if there had been more than one canoe, or maybe a bowman on a drifting log. Loosening the headsails, Ezekiel had not realized his lucky escape. The arrow had stuck fast between the swelling white breasts of the figurehead. For a moment, the boy thought he should report his find. Then he wondered if the captain wouldn't consider it a bad omen. Certainly neither of them would want Mrs. Wallace to know. He tried to withdraw the arrow, but it broke and he dropped the feathered shaft into the sea. Then Sam Cutler came to use the head, with a handful of oakum in his hand. The boy gave his breeches a hitch, as if he had been there for the same purpose, and he climbed on deck, leaving the arrowhead buried between the gentle breasts.

When he went on the poop for his wheel watch, Mrs. Wallace was there as usual, with Master John. He was looking at the shore through his red telescope. "I see trees, Ma! It's a green land."

"It's a lovely land, Johnny." She caressed his hair. "Soon we'll go ashore and see it, close." It was plain the boy knew nothing of what had happened during the night, and his mother wasn't going to say anything to make him afraid. She was rather pale, but Elmer felt proud of her because she had helped work the ship, and he decided she was beautiful. Only one thing troubled him, and his eyes were drawn unconsciously toward her breast. There was no wound, of course.

CHAPTER THREE

AT STEILACOOM, the *Maid* was surrounded by Indian canoes. Several were paddling alongside before her anchors were let go, and after that they approached from all directions. A whole fleet of canoes, but with a difference. Here, they were in a center of far western civilization, under the guns of an American fort. Civilization's center was a village of log cabins and frame houses without paint, and the fort was a mixture of both, recognizable because of its tall flag pole and wooden bastions. Indians were nothing to fear, with the *Maid* lying off a fortified town on a summer afternoon, and a brig from Salem anchored near by.

As a point of fact, this would be no place for any one with an aversion to Indian canoes. The only civilized small boat in sight was the gig riding astern of the black Salem vessel. The Indian canoes had triumphed on the water, but the men in the canoes were a compromise of civilizations. There were Indians in native nakedness and Indians in American clothes. Some of the canoes were paddled by Indians, with bearded white passengers. Others were paddled by white men, and when they climbed on board it was noticeable that most of them wore moccasins, as if they found the native method of travel best, both on water and on land.

A New England ship does not travel twenty thousand miles for nothing. Before the first traders and Indians were on board, the main hatch was uncovered and the crew was hoisting goods out of the hold. There were hardware and drygoods and rum, on consignment and on speculation. Once or twice in the friendly uproar, Elmer tried reminding himself that this was the ship which had been his home for half a year, but he could not keep the idea in mind for more than a minute; it seemed too improbable. Partly it was the sight of rum barrels coming out of the hold, confused with the recollection that Captain and Mrs. Wallace were teetotalers. But mostly the sense of strangeness came from the crowd on deck which had always been a quiet place, except for weather and the sea.

Elmer had the job of helping Sam pile cargo on deck beside the hatch, and of seeing that no one removed anything without authorization. He made out as best he could among the white men who had been roughened or made more gentle by the wilderness, and the Indians who had lost some of their wildness through contact with white men, and who were buying or begging rum to get back something they had lost. Elmer was reasonably busy trying to distinguish friends from birds of prey, and potential customers from diddlers. Here, as elsewhere, it seemed that men who shine before strangers do so because they have no friends. Gold is displayed less conspicuously. Here was a humble Indian in a dirty blanket, whose English vocabulary consisted of "rum." He repeated it in a begging tone and might have been brushed aside if he had not opened his hand. In his brown palm there was an eight-cornered slug of gold which made him a customer worthy of being escorted to the mate. Here was an Indian who must be a chief, at least, dressed in broadcloth trousers and frock coat, a bell-topped hat and checked shirt and moccasins, carrying an umbrella and an official-looking document.

"Teapot!" the Indian said, and put the document firmly into Elmer's hands. He struck his chest. *"Hyas teapot; hyas Salmon Charlie!"*

The "teapot" proved to be a letter of recommendation, written in a clear hand and workmanlike English:

"To whom it may concern:

"Salmon Charlie has been in my employ in the capacity of boatman. I take pleasure in recommending the old scoundrel to Perdition. In the matter of sobriety, he is ordinarily too drunk to distinguish his Posterior from his Elbow. In the matter of honesty, it is my belief that he is capable of telling the Truth if it suited his purpose,

but no such occasion arose while he was in my employ.
Like the Three Graces, his Talents go hand in hand:
to Drink, to Piss and to be Quarrelsome with other indians. If the subject of this Recommendation be wearing
my Pearl Studs which disappeared while he was in my
employ, the Reader will do me a favor to strip the same
off him.
                          "Joshua Lynch, Master,
                    "Brig *Sarah Lord* of Boston."

Appended, there were briefer comments:

 "Salmon Charlie has been in my Employ for one Ca-
lamitous Day. While I do not question the Good Faith of
Captain Lynch, I have not found the Bearer as reliable
as his Recommendation led me to believe.
                    "James Williams, Master,
                    "Barque *Twin Brothers,* New York."

 "The Bearer of this recommendation has been em-
ployed by me as Guide. (I could get no other.) I am
most grateful to him for not causing my death, the only
misfortune which did not befall me during our Journey.
                          "Daniel Horn,
                    "Pike County, Missouri."

There were other comments, some almost illegible, others
quite unprintable, but all attested to the worthlessness of Salmon Charlie, and they did it with reasonable good nature.
Somewhere behind the blasphemous recommendations, you
suspected, there was something likable about the preposterous
Indian. Undoubtedly, he had a genius for being of no use,
and genius had been recognized.

It was only after the native was gone that Elmer realized
the document held enough humor to be shared with the whole
crew. "You ought to have seen that paper, Sam——"

Sam did not hear him, being occupied with an interview of
his own. He was talking to a sturdy young woman in old-
fashioned clothes, and enjoying himself, teasing her. The first

Elmer heard of their conversation was the girl saying, "We don't *want* a mermaid! We came here for a keg of nails."

"Mermaids is more romantic," Sam insisted.

The young woman did not look like one who would be tempted by romance. She was sturdy and businesslike and awkwardly dressed. Elmer took her to be a spinster of about twenty, until he saw her face, then he decided she wasn't more than sixteen. She had black hair and eyes, and red cheeks, and she wouldn't have been bad looking except for her sullen expression. It cast a shadow over her face the way her homely clothes blighted the rest of her. "You Yankees can't sell us a mermaid when we want nails to build a house. Anyway," she said, "I don't know what to believe of that truck about mermaids and flying fish. I never seen the sea before, I never saw a ship, except steamboats on the Missouri." She looked up, speculatively, at the maze of spars and rigging against the warm sky. "I never did see anything like this." There was a note of wonder in her sullen voice. After all, the visit on board seemed to mean more to her than a keg of nails.

Elmer warmed toward her a little, out of pity for one whose opportunities had been so limited. "We're six months out of Fairhaven, Massachusetts," he said casually. Six months sounded impressive, he thought, though the voyage would have been more to boast of had the time been less.

The girl did not seem to hear him. She was looking about with practical interest. "Steamboats have roofs over them," she said, considering the open deck. "It must be hard, doing your chores when it's raining."

Elmer could not help smiling, but Sam was all gravity. "Well, now, it ain't bad," he said, "you get used to it. Of course, we always carry umbrellas when it rains."

"What if it's windy?" she asked. "I'd think the umbrellas would blow away."

"They do, ma'am." Sam spoke as if that were the end of it.

"Then what, pray?"

Sam considered. "Well, of course, a sailor's supposed to

hang onto his umbrella, and tuck reefs in it when the wind pipes up. But if he loses it in a good cause, working aloft or steering, well, he just goes to the Old Man and asks for a new one. The Old Man don't like to do it, but it's cheaper than having his sailors down with pneumonia."

The girl seemed to notice Elmer for the first time. "What are you laughing about?" she asked.

"Nothing," he said, feeling guilty and not wanting to laugh any more.

She turned her attention to the ship again. "What do you do when you're on the ocean and it gets dark? You haven't any place to tie up, have you?"

"Only when we're near the coast," Sam told her. "On the ocean we anchor for the night, and go to bed."

The girl thought it over. "I suppose that's why it took you so long to get here," she decided.

Elmer laughed again, and the girl did not reprove him. Maybe she understood he was not laughing at her. He was laughing at Sam for lying himself into a corner that rubbed his professional pride.

"Well, now," Sam labored, "six months ain't bad for a little barque like this——."

"It ain't little; this is a big ship." She turned to Elmer for confirmation. "Ain't it?" Her eyes were nice and deep when they weren't sullen.

"Yes," he lied. "She's one of the biggest afloat."

Sam swallowed and went on. "Six months ain't bad, even for a big ship. Of course, anchoring nights and Sundays draws a voyage out; holidays, too. With one thing and another, six months ain't bad. And I'm thankful we didn't have to brave the perils of the hundred-and-eightieth Meridian——"

The black eyes glowed with interest. "Is it very dangerous?"

"Well, now," Sam answered cautiously, "I wouldn't say that. Sometimes it's nothing. But, again——" He shook his head, darkly.

"What happens, sir?"

"There was one ship," Sam recalled. "I won't mention her

name. She reached the Meridian on a Sunday morning and anchored for the day——." He made a gesture of finality. "And there she was."

The girl looked blank, waiting. Then she asked, "Why couldn't the ship go on?"

"It was the Sabbath," Sam reminded her. "The crew was pious men, like us, and they couldn't travel or work the ship on Sunday."

"Why didn't they go on the next day?"

"They couldn't, ma'am."

"Why couldn't they?"

"That was Sunday, too."

"What?"

"Don't you see, ma'am? They anchored on the Meridian on a Sunday. That meant it was Sunday as long as they stayed there. And they couldn't leave on the Sabbath."

"I don't believe a word of it," the girl said, "go on."

"There ain't much more to tell." Sam appeared disinclined to tell even that.

"What did they do?"

"What could they do but keep the Sabbath? The Old Man read the Divine service every day, and the crew sang hymns. Men who were on passing ships told me that by the third week of Sundays the noise down there was something terrible, because the sailors was getting impatient——"

"If it was Sunday, like you say, why didn't the other ships anchor?"

"Ha!" Sam looked triumphant. "It was only Sunday for the ship that anchored on Sunday. Say two other ships passed each other near the unfortunate *Prudence*—but I won't mention her name. If it was Thursday on one ship, it would be Friday on the other. That's because the ship going west would have two Thursdays that week, and the ship going east would have Wednesday one day and Friday the next——"

"I don't believe a word of that nonsense!" the young woman said. She turned to Elmer for confirmation. "There's no such place as he's talking about, is there?"

"No," Elmer lied. "Sam was joking." He saw his friend

swallow, while the young. woman looked more tolerant. Inconsistently, she asked, "What did they finally do?"

"You wouldn't believe me."

"No," she admitted, "but I want to hear."

"Well, they finally drew lots, and the losing watch turned heathen and sailed the ship out of danger. They calculated it was better for half of them to burn in hell than for all of them to rot in the Pacific."

"A very likely story!" She made it sound more likely that all sailors would burn for liars. Then she asked, "What's the price of nails?"

"I couldn't tell you, ma'am, except that we're selling them at a bargain. I'll ask the mate."

"I'm not buying the nails," she said. "I only wondered."

Elmer asked, "Where are you building your house?"

"We don't just know," she said. "We've only got here."

"Did you cross the plains?" The thought made her more interesting.

"We crossed last year and settled in Oregon. But there's chills and fever in the Willamette, like they told us there wasn't, so we came up here."

"What's it like, crossing the plains?"

She answered darkly, without looking at him, "It ain't anything I want to talk about."

"*Hey, Liza!*" a voice called.

"Good-by, sirs," the young woman said. When she was not being rude, she had a kind of old-fashioned politeness.

"Good-by," Elmer said.

"Good-by, Eliza."

She answered Sam with a sullen look. "My name ain't Eliza, it's Lisette."

"That's a funny name."

"I expect it's no funnier than I am," she said defiantly.

Elmer knew how she felt. He knew what it was like to be in town and hear snickers at forgotten hayseeds on his miserable clothes. "You aren't funny," he said. She was, in a way. He meant that he knew how it stung to look funny.

She looked at him, less defiantly, and he had a feeling that her trust in him had gone beyond anything that had been said. He thought she wanted to thank him for something, but there wasn't time or opportunity.

"Hey, Liza!"

Elmer had a glimpse of the man who had called: a lean, medium-old man with weak blue eyes and a discouraged stoop. Beside him, Tom was hitching a line to the purchased keg of nails, ready to deliver it over the side. He had that glimpse, and then his attention was demanded by a sling of goods coming up from the hold. *"Avast heaving! Lower away! Gently, now!"*

When he and Sam had guided the load to the deck and unhooked the tackle, the young woman was gone.

Sam laughed, "They don't often come that green! 'It must be hard, doing our chores, when it's raining!' "

"She didn't believe anything but the lies," Elmer recalled.

"You were worse than I was, Elmer. You contradicted every true thing I said."

"I know." He couldn't explain it, but he had contradicted his friend because he wanted the girl to hear things that were true. But everything had been so mixed up that only lies sounded like the truth. "I didn't mean it that way." It wasn't right for the girl to visit a ship for the first time in her life—and go away knowing less than she did before.

He pondered it in greater security after Sam Cutler had been sent to settle some confusion in the hold. Sam was replaced by the silent Ezekiel, who had no experiences to relate, and apparently no interest in the Indians and settlers and traders who made a new world of the deck. If he saw them at all, you'd think, he saw them as flitting shadows which he endured with patience, knowing they would go away again and leave him with the realities of the ship and the sea.

The boy started under the blow of a heavy hand on his shoulder. Beside him he saw moccasins, thick-legged blue jeans, and, as he looked up farther, a faded hickory shirt open over a tremendous, gray-haired chest. Still farther up, there was a bushy gray beard, warm gray eyes and a headland of untidy hair jutting out into a big, half-bald forehead. Elmer was six feet tall in his shoes, but the man beside him was six feet four in moccasins. The four inches made as much difference as a score of years. Elmer felt like a small boy again. "Uncle Jarvis!"

Shaking hands powerfully, Uncle Jarvis said, "You weren't expecting to see me, h'm?"

In that respect, at least, Uncle Jarvis had not changed. After almost everything he said, he shot you a warm look from his gray eyes, and said "H'm?" Encouraging you to agree, but giving opportunity for contradiction. In other ways, he seemed to have changed a great deal in eight years. But, as they talked and the strangeness wore away, the difference seemed less, until the boy was not sure he had changed at all, except in his dress. And that had always tended to be untidy.

Elmer said, "I was going to look for you, as soon as I could get ashore."

Uncle Jarvis said, "Well, the mountain came to you." He was so big and thick-bodied that it was something like being visited by a mountain. And though he was interfering with the work about the hatch, it did not seem to matter. A peevish housewife may kick a cat out of her path, but when a man finds a mountain in his way, he goes around and does not feel ill used. "Your mother wrote that you were coming out in the *Maid*," Uncle Jarvis said. "When I heard she was expected today, it seemed a good idea to come up, h'm?"

"I'm glad you did, Uncle!" He felt warm and alive and strong, standing with one of his own kin. "It was good of you."

"With this light easterly," Uncle Jarvis said, "I gave you a week from the Cape. You made it, even with running aground in the Strait, h'm?"

Elmer said, "Yes." Then he wondered. "But how did you know all that?"

"From the Indians," Jarvis said. "Their canoes are everywhere, and word passes along. It's a rare thing in summer for a ship to reach here before the news of her." Then he asked, "Can't we talk without people getting in our way?"

"I'm supposed to stay by the hatch," Elmer apologized, "When it's my watch below——"

"Work can always wait, h'm?" Uncle Jarvis had the lordliness of a man who has never had to work for other men. Something in him had never been tamed by that experience. In that way, he was younger than his nephew. "I spoke to your captain," he reassured. "I can remember picking him up out of his cradle, and getting wet for my pains." Lest Elmer might think less of his captain for that, he added, "Without a bladder, he'd never have grown up, h'm?"

"No, he wouldn't."

"Let's find a place, out of this infernal noise, where we can unburden our related hearts."

"I'm not sure I should. All this stuff about——"

"You have your mother's conscience, Elmer. I foresaw that; I warned John not to expect anything of you while I was about. I served notice that I would take you away." As they were walking forward, Uncle Jarvis said, "Your mother's letter didn't tell much. How do things go on the fa'm?"

Elmer said, "Crops aren't selling very well. And Norway's shipping ice to Europe cheaper than we can. It's hurt business around home. This seemed the only way I could earn cash money."

"I never thought you'd turn out to be a sailor."

"Neither did I. Ma didn't want me to go." Elmer's oldest brother, Charles, had been swept from the deck of the *Stag Hound* into the China Sea, as many another farm boy had been lost from the hard driven clippers. Elmer and his uncle stopped near the break of the fo'c'sle head and leaned over the bulwarks. The channel between the mainland and the islands was sparkling blue in the sunshine and there was a blue haze over the land. The air was nice with the smell of sea salt and evergreen smoke. They seasoned the soft warmth of the breeze and gave it a gentle sting, like some half-remembered pain, or a bereavement that does not hurt any more.

Uncle Jarvis said, "If it weren't for this haze, you could see the mountain."

"What mountain?"

"Rainier, if you like your mountains named after British admirals. 'Tahoma,' if you don't. That isn't a name; only the

Siwash word for 'mountain.' When you're in sight of the greatest mountain of all, you don't have to call it by name. When you say 'the mountain,' every one knows what you mean."

"What is it like, here?" Elmer asked. "Is it as fine as people say?"

Uncle Jarvis laughed at the size of the question. "I suppose not," he said. "But in some ways it's finer. You've had your first sight of it the wrong way, though. You'll never see it quite as you should."

"How is that?"

"It's too late, now," his uncle assured him. "You'll never look on it again for the first time. To properly appreciate it, you should cross the plains by ox team, half a year of that, say. Then from The Dalles to the mouth of the Cowlitz by bateaux and portage. Up the Cowlitz for a hundred miles by Indian canoes, and then walking or driving over the worst road the devil ever invented, with a stop at Hard Bread's by way of luxury. Reaching Puget Sound that way, you swear never to travel another mile on the earth's surface. You're prepared to stay even if it were the devil's own country. When it turns out to be worth staying for on its own merits, it seems like Paradise, h'm?"

The boy thought of their own difficulties on the way. "Are the Indians friendly here?"

"They're my brothers," the untidy mountain of a man assured him. "I am a member of the Nisqually Tribe."

"It must be queer, living with an Indian tribe." Exciting, too. This was something to write home.

"No," Uncle Jarvis said. "I've never felt more at home."

"The Indians we met in the Straits weren't very brotherly."

"I heard about your brush with the fierce, sea-roving Haidahs."

"What kind of Indians are they?"

"Queen Charlotte Islanders," his uncle explained. "But they're only there in winter. The rest of the year they rove south, plundering more peaceful tribes, capturing slaves and raising hell for the love of it."

"They had the biggest canoe I ever saw. It must have held sixty people."

"Some of them hold a hundred, and they make as long sea voyages as the Vikings did."

"Some of them had bars across their faces."

"Curved, and pointed at one end, h'm?"

"Yes. What did they represent?"

"The dorsal fin of the killer whale."

"We saw some killers, off the Cape, attacking a whale. I never saw anything so fierce——"

"Then you know something about the Haidahs, who use the killer's dorsal for their emblem, h'm?"

"Do you suppose· they really meant to capture the ship?"

"After all, I wasn't there," his uncle reminded him. "They might have been drunk, or feeling good after a raid on one of our tribes, h'm? All I know for a certainty is that if they'd thought it worth their while, you wouldn't have stood any more chance than a whale against a school of killers."

Elmer had felt something of the sort. "I'm glad I won't meet those Indians again!"

His uncle looked surprised. "You may meet them anywhere down here."

"How do you mean?"

"Why, you might meet them ashore there, on the street. Maybe we'll find them camped on the beach in front of my house. Or you may work beside the warriors in a timber camp."

"I thought they were savages!" Elmer was faintly disappointed.

"They are," Uncle Jarvis assured him, "but they're damnably adaptable. They're always ready to turn an honest penny, or a dishonest one. Summering down here, they rent their women out to bachelor settlers for housekeepers. If raiding's unprofitable, the men go to work in a timber camp or sawmill. There's nothing Haidahs won't do."

Elmer remembered the girl. "Some of their women are kind of good-looking," he said.

"You weren't too scared to notice that, h'm?"

"I guess not." Growing bolder, he said, "I didn't think Indian women could be so pretty."

"More than one white man has broken his heart over a Haidah girl."

The boy glanced up at the big, bearded face, wondering.

"I'm not one of them," Uncle Jarvis reassured him. "I'm a simple fellow about women. They don't bother me much, that way." After a minute of musing over his good fortune, he gave his nephew a shrewd, good-natured look. "So you saw a pretty one, h'm?"

"Her name was 'Tillicum'." Elmer confided that fine secret, and was immediately abashed by his uncle's laughter. "Is that a funny name?"

"It isn't Haidah, and it isn't a name. 'Tillicum' is jargon for 'friend'."

"Oh!" The boy felt more green than disappointed. The girl had told him she was his friend. That meant more than telling her name. And now it appeared that he might meet her again, as likely as not. "I'd like to learn jargon," he said. "Is it hard?"

"It's as easy as sin. Three hundred words, and no grammar. And some of the words are English. You could pick it up in a week."

"I would like to learn it," the boy said earnestly.

"You'll learn," his uncle said. "You'll learn." Then he asked, "Think you'd like to try your luck in a new country, h'm?"

"I couldn't do that," Elmer said. "I'm signed on for a three-year voyage." It was something to which he could cling. The barque linked him with home and his family. It was at the end of a thread which had been stretched out to twenty thousand sea miles, but had not been broken. His mother had come down to the pier to see him off. She would be there to meet him when he returned. That way, the thread would never really be broken. . . .

"Three years," Uncle Jarvis said. "That's a pity. In three years here you'd be prosperous."

"Would I?"

"Not in money, but in everything else. You can still take up a five-hundred-acre preemption claim. I have one picked out for you. You could take up a thousand if you were married——"

"Really?"

"But you'd have to woo fast, h'm? This fall claims will be cut to a quarter section for a man, and a half section for a man and wife."

Elmer had only dimly heard the part about a wife. He was not thinking of that. His mind was busy stretching itself, trying to encompass the thought of five hundred acres of land for the asking. "Couldn't I take up a claim while I'm here? When I went home, maybe I could get the family to come out——"

His uncle looked reprovingly. "There are obligations, mostly to yourself. You have to prove up on a claim, h'm? Make improvements. You have to build a cabin and clear land. It's only reasonable, when the improvements are for yourself. And when you brought your family out, you'd want something to bring them to, h'm?"

"Yes." Elmer's hope for five hundred acres was gone, or almost gone. You can spin out an unbroken thread for twenty thousand miles, for half a year, or a year; the human heart can do wonders, but even it cannot spin out the same thread forever, in a new place. Somewhere the thread is certain to break or dwindle to nothing. Then you find yourself alone at the beginning of your own life, in a strange country. "I'll plan to take up land the next voyage," he decided. "This time, I'll get leave to look around."

"We'll go ashore now," his uncle said. "We'll have supper at my place; it's only twenty miles by water. I've already asked for your leave."

Elmer felt the stir of adventure in his unexercised young heart. Then he had been free from the minute his uncle had climbed on board! "You mean I can go now?"

"Approximately," Uncle Jarvis said. "But there are formalities. Your captain wants to see you before you go."

"All right."

"You'll hear words of wisdom from a sincere man."

"Captain Wallace is wise; he's a good captain."

"While you're listening, remember wisdom isn't always right."

"How do you mean?"

"You'll hear about the wisdom of staying with the ship; the future you'll have at sea. You'll hear about all the keels that are being laid, from Baltimore to Searsport; the masters needed to command them——"

"There are an awful lot of ships being built," Elmer said. "Boston is turning out clippers now. More every year——"

Uncle Jarvis said, "I know. You can almost hear the hammers and caulking mallets from here. Our merchant fleet is blowing up like a balloon, h'm? But the thing's already punctured."

The boy's mouth opened. "Why?"

"It's only an opinion. As I see it, man's a land animal, and ships are only to take people places. America has arrived and gone ashore."

Elmer said, "I don't understand."

"What I'm trying to say is that it's the rocky island and the starved shore that breeds sailors. Where there's a land of plenty waiting for the ax and the plough, young men aren't going to eat hardtack on the sea, h'm?"

Now the boy was beginning to see the shape of the idea. "I hadn't thought of that before. I suppose not."

"With five hundred acres of land for the asking, a man's not going to be content with straw in a fo'c'sle, and the trampling waves of the sea in place of multiplying cattle."

"No, he wouldn't." The judgment was sincere, but it wasn't for himself, who was duty bound to complete the voyage.

Uncle Jarvis took his arms from the bulwarks and towered upright, running his fingers through his graying tangle of hair. "Young America's reached its destiny and is going ashore."

"Yes," Elmer said. It did not quite apply to him, who was going only to see the land, but the thought gave him a certain feeling of pride.

CHAPTER FOUR

TOM LOWERED the boy's sea-chest into the big dugout canoe, kindly, but with no more thought than if it had been a keg of nails. And Jones, the unsuccessful, appeared briefly beside the old whaleman. His look said that he did not expect any good to come of the expedition ashore, and it also suggested that he had half a mind to go along, because no good had come of his own life afloat.

The old man and the failure were the only ones to salute Elmer's portrayal of Young America going ashore to the rich lands of the West and leaving Yankee ships to their fate. He departed with the feeling of a truant from a busy school. But he had the comfort of knowing that his stay ashore would not be permanent. He was to rejoin the barque after she made a voyage to San Francisco with timber and returned with more goods for trading on Puget Sound. Meanwhile, he had sixty dollars, which was half his pay, and a new country to explore.

Captain Wallace had observed that the arrangement was generous, and Elmer agreed. He had also listened earnestly while his captain spoke of the glorious future of the American merchant marine, and assured him his destiny was on the sea. That was as Uncle Jarvis had predicted, and the boy found himself a battleground where the two men fought each other politely. In some ways the captain had the better of the argument because he had started at sea as a cabin boy, and prospered steadily. Jarvis had been born with a silver spoon in his mouth, and had not exactly turned it to gold. But Captain Wallace did not use that argument directly. He only suggested that Elmer weigh facts rather than words and decide how much his uncle had prospered in the new world.

That was something the boy still had to decide. Now, while he paddled near the bow of the fine dugout canoe, his uncle was only a big voice booming from aft. And the new world was slipping by in the shape of a high shore and opening away ahead and to starboard in a blue and sunlit inland sea, filled with high timbered islands and headlands. Nowhere did the boy see a farm or clearing, or any sign of life except a column of blue smoke from the beach of a distant island, and canoes moving lazily on the incredible waters. Everything was new and fresh-smelling and clean. The islands and headlands were rugged and forested with tremendous trees, and the water was cold to the touch and very deep, but there was no look of harshness anywhere. Cool waters and warm sun balanced each other, and everything was seen through soft blue haze that touched the world with gentleness.

Ahead was a narrow, sharp-pointed island, crowded with big fir trees. The vista narrowed as Uncle Jarvis turned the canoe into the passage between the beaches of the island and the high mainland. "Cormorant Passage," his voice boomed softly. "Ketron Island over there. When the tide's in it looks rather like a ship. It's supposed to have been a big canoe that was taking young saplings to some treeless place. The gods objected and ran it aground there, and the saplings grew into trees."

Having explained the most immediate scenery, the big voice said in a different tone, "How are all our many relatives, Elmer? How do they stand the years?"

While the boy was wondering where to begin, the big voice rumbled on comfortably, above the dips of paddles, "People make a bad habit of relationships, h'm? A man should be like a bull moose that goes through the woods without thinking too much about the health or whereabouts of his maternal grandfather or third cousin or unmated aunt. I'm like that, mostly. Only now and then I have memories. Then I wonder: 'What ever became of my star-gazing brother? Into what well did he fall at last?' or, 'How does Emily spend these nights on earth, and did she ever achieve that simple experience which too much thinking made so difficult for her?'"

Elmer said, "Uncle Joshua is poorly. He's having trouble with his rheumatism again."

"As I remember, he had a pretty wife. Dorothy, wasn't it?"

"Yes." Though Elmer could not think of his aunt as pretty.

"Have they any children?"

"Ten."

"That's one way of counting the years. Now she's not so pretty, h'm?"

"No. She had to have most of her teeth pulled." When his uncle did not ask anything more, the boy remembered brighter news. "Aunt Caroline had a new cupola put on her house. It was finished the fall before I left."

Uncle Jarvis snorted. "It was too God-damned civilized already. I remember cold afternoons after a sleigh ride, with all of us waiting our turn at the privy and trying to be polite." Boastfully he said, "Wait till you see my place! A man can let fly out of any window in the house."

Their talk about relatives was not much of a success. Elmer was not used to talking above the dip of paddles to some one he could not see, and Uncle Jarvis soon lost interest in the family. Paddling in silence, Elmer was able to pay more attention to what he could see of the big, high-stemmed canoe. The only dugouts he had ever seen at home were crude, half-hearted things. But this one was as true of line and smoothly made as any planked boat he had ever seen. It was large, even for two paddlers, but it was light and handled beautifully. With the aid of the incoming tide it was already racing out of Cormorant Passage, with a world of islands and headlands opening away ahead and to the north. And it was overhauling a larger craft which had been far ahead.

"You have a good canoe!" the boy said over his shoulder.

Uncle Jarvis rumbled cheerfully, "You can't see her lines when you're sitting on them, but they're worth looking at: hollow entrance and flat floor and rounded bilges and long clean run."

"Clipper lines!" the boy said.

"You notice that, h'm? Pook or Webb might have copied her for his latest."

"Where did the Indians get the lines?"

His uncle's voice said, "I calculate they were using clipper lines while we were building apple-bowed butter tubs!"

Elmer asked, "How did they know? How did they find the perfect lines?"

"Lazy," the big voice said, as if that explained everything. "Laziness designed these swift canoes, and greed designed the clippers. Men progress by their vices, h'm?"

The boy did not know what to say to that because it was contrary to all he had ever learned. At least he had the reassurance that laziness was not triumphing in the canoe ahead. The four half-hearted Indian paddlers in the larger canoe were being overtaken steadily. Now he could hear the hollow, drumlike sound of their paddles striking at intervals against the sides. He could hear their indolent, harsh voices, punctuated by the beat of wood against hollow wood. Over his shoulder, he asked, "Why do they hit the canoe with their paddles?"

"That's music to the trained ear," Uncle Jarvis said. "They're beating time to their canoe song."

Elmer had not realized it was music, and he had not guessed they were singing. But listening with the facts in mind he perceived that they were singing a kind of tuneless chant. The throb of paddles on hollow wood forever called their wandering voices back to reality. And it was the authentic voice of the canoe joining in the imperfect song.

There were a man and two women and a young woman in the Indian craft. They looked more content than clean, and their broad, homely faces were wreathed in smiles as the overtaking canoe drew abreast of them. Klahowya!" they called, and "Tyee Jarvis" and other things which the big man answered in the same language. Elmer was introduced and greeted with more wreathing smiles and more Klahowyas, and the Indian canoe dropped astern as the more ambitious white men dug the water with their paddles again.

Elmer's impression of the Indians was that they were short and squat, with broad, flat faces that were oriental in an unpretentious way. They did not have the physical magnificence of the fierce Haidahs who had threatened the Maid, or any of their reckless arrogance, and there was no feeling of any forward swing to their lives. They had the air of a gentle, lesser people who had settled down in comfort and would never trouble any one. Over his shoulder, he asked, "What tribe are those, Uncle?"

"Nisqually canoe Indians. We're coming to their territory now."

"They're friendly, aren't they?"

"The most genial in the world," his uncle said. "The only fault ever found with them is that they smell too much of their diet. Other peoples have their stink of tobacco, garlic, sweat, horses, h'm? These have fish." Then he said, "D'ye see that bluff to larboard?"

Elmer could not help seeing the sheer, yellowish bluff. The foot of it was on the gravel beach, a hundred yards away, and its top was three or four hundred feet higher, crowned with fir trees that raised it to a six-hundred-foot wall against the sky.

"In the old days, the Nisquallys used to roll their traitors from the top, and gravity did the rest, h'm? A man who survived was innocent."

Looking up at the dizzy height, the boy asked in wonder, "Did any one ever survive?"

"Justice was infallible," the big voice said.

Elmer looked back toward the indolent canoe. "They seem gentle for that sort of thing."

The voice behind him chuckled. "You'd never find canoe Indians that far above their element. But there are horse Indians in the tribe, like people of a different race. They have herds of cattle and horses on the big prairie back of here, and they live in good plank houses."

The canoe had been in deep water off the steep-to bluff. Now Elmer saw flounders ghosting away over a bottom of shoaling sand. The bluff was turning inland past low country channelled with watercourses. There was a wooden pier, reaching the edge of the water at half-tide, and a substantial warehouse beside it. Elmer paddled more gingerly, afraid of running aground, but the big voice reassured him. "I'll keep us off. We're over the Nisqually Flats. There, ashore, is the Nisqually Valley; the cradle of white civilization in this territory. That pier's the Hudson's Bay Company's naval depot. They landed at that spot in 1830. There's a road back to the big prairie where they have their establishment, Fort Nisqually, and their farms and herds."

Elmer said, "I thought the Hudson's Bay Company was only for furs."

"Not where other things are more profitable," his uncle said. "They saw the end of the fur trade at the beginning, and went in for stock and agriculture. They have thousands of head of cattle and sheep on the Nisqually plain. One of their big items is supplying butter to the Russians in Alaska. And they raise a deal of potatoes and grain."

"I thought this was American territory," Elmer said.

"It is, but the Company was here earlier. It claims all of Pierce County. The Indians, who were here first, claim it, too. And the American settlers who are squatting on it."

Paddling, Elmer said, "That must be confusing: three peoples claiming the same land!"

"It's very simple, because each is sure that he is right."

"Who's going to win?"

"We are," his uncle said, "because we have the settlers here, and thousands more coming, h'm? Their wagons are rolling on both sides of the Platte River. The drift is all our way. Sailors leave from every ship and take up land, and soldiers from the military posts, when they've finished their enlistment. Even the Hudson's Bay employees. When they've finished their term of service, they become American citizens and take up claims, sometimes on Company property. The magnet of success, h'm? It draws the very nails from the Hudson's Bay ship."

Elmer asked, "Will they make any trouble over the land?"

"I'd think not," the big voice said. "The Company has a government, and so have we. It'll be settled by litigation, h'm? The Company's chief factor here, Doctor Tolmie, is a gentleman who can read handwriting on a wall. He was trained to heal wounds, and he still follows that pattern. He's been here since 'thirty-three, and seen the rise and decline of the Nisqually establishment. He knows well enough that the interests of a company, however powerful, can't stand up against the needs of a people, h'm?"

"What about the Indians?" Elmer asked.

"They too have needs, h'm?" Then Uncle Jarvis said, "I don't know. They're reasonable people. It depends on whether our people are as reasonable." A mile ahead there were high bluffs again, following the salt water and turning inland to mark the far side of the Nisqually Valley. But now the canoe was gliding through shallow water, past the lowlands. And by the sound of the big voice, the conversation, too, was in shoal water. "Some men look on Indians as an inferior people."

Paddling carefully, Elmer asked, "Don't you?" He'd been brought up to believe they were.

His uncle said, "I don't know that there's such a thing as a superior people, except for individuals, h'm?"

"What about the government?" Elmer asked. "Or is there one?"

"We're not heathens, boy." His uncle chuckled. "We have a territorial government, quite complete, with a legislature that meets in Olympia. As a home touch, we have a governor from Massachusetts; from Andover, to be exact."

"Who is he?"

"Isaac Stevens."

The name was new to the boy. "What's he like?"

"Pint-pot size and full of energy," the big voice said. "That's about all we had time to observe. Stevens was here only for a few months last year. One of his several jobs is the railroad survey: bringing the Great Northern out here from the Missouri. He'd hardly arrived when he got wind that Jefferson Davis was trying to scrap his survey for a southern route. And he raced back to Washington without leave."

"We won't run aground, will we?" Elmer asked. The canoe was gliding past the lowlands with hardly a foot of water under it, and the big man's voice sounded as if he were more occupied with the halls of Washington than the Nisqually Flats.

But it was intentional, after all. "There are no rocks," Uncle Jarvis assured him, "and if we run aground we can push off, h'm? A friend of mine is camped hereabouts?"

On the low shore, where there was no sign of any farm or house, or any life except white seagulls flying, and walking on the narrowing beach, the boy saw a rounded hut, and he glimpsed what seemed to be a man, running into the hut on all fours, like an animal. "Was that a man?"

"It was." His uncle had stopped paddling, with the canoe drifting opposite the hut, a hundred yards away. He put down his paddle and roared through cupped hands, *"Yanatco! Klahowya six!"*

In answer, there was the long-drawn, dismal howl of a dog. It gave the boy a feeling of the uncanny: seeing a man run into the hut, like an animal, and hearing only animal sounds from there.

His uncle tried again, roaring, *"Yanatco! Nika Jarvis!"*

The only answer was a long, blood-freezing howl.

"We'll go on," Uncle Jarvis said. "It's no use trying to see him when he's like that."

Elmer looked at his uncle's regretful, shaggy face. "Who was that?"

"Yanatco. One of the Nisquallys' leading citizens." The big man took up his paddle. "But he won't see any one when he's in that frame of mind."

"Is he insane?" the boy asked, paddling.

"No," Uncle Jarvis said. "He's a gentleman of the old school who's suffered humiliation; one of the mighty who's fallen. According to custom, he runs on all fours and howls to signify that he's been debased to a dog's estate."

"What happened to him, anyway?"

"Nothing directly to him," his uncle said, "but Yanatco has some uncommonly fine children. One of the girls married a lieutenant at Fort Steilacoom, maybe two years ago, and that was a feather in the old man's hair. It was an Indian marriage, but that was marriage as he saw it, h'm? It's binding enough to keep an Indian as faithful to his two wives as an American is to one. But a few days ago the lieutenant was transferred to another post. By our laws, he wasn't married, and while he could live in sin he couldn't travel in that state. He had to go through a Christian marriage or give her up, h'm? So he sent her home to her father, like something he'd borrowed."

Elmer said, "That was a low trick!"

"Thoughtless, anyway," the big voice said, "and unfortunate that it was this fellow's daughter. Yanatco's a Nisqually of the old school, with puritan ideas. His family's the most important in the tribe. One of his sons, Leschi, has more influence with the tribes of the West than any other man, red or white. He's befriended honest settlers from the beginning, and made allowances for the Pikes."

"What are Pikes?"

"It's an Indian term we've taken over," his uncle explained. "The first party of ruffians who came in here were from one of the many Pike counties in the States. While they made life disagreeable for the Indians and other settlers and stole Hudson's Bay stock, they boasted about how things were done in Pike County. The Indians assumed that was some barbaric country to the east and named them for it, h'm? Now all uncivilized Americans here are called Pikes."

The canoe was almost past the lowlands. Ahead and to port, the wooded bluff went up high and steep from the floor of the valley, and a flood of water, a quarter of a mile wide, flowed past the foot of the bluff into salt water. They boy was puzzled by the second, broader river sharing the same valley with the Nisqually. "What river is this?"

His uncle's voice chuckled. "It's a creek, Elmer; Shonadaub Creek. It's only two miles long, but it picks up a volume of water, h'm?"

"I should say so!" Elmer said, paddling through the roiled flood of fresh water that was quarrelling with the salt. "I'd have sworn it was a river."

"It shows we have some rainfall, h'm?" Then the big voice said, "Medicine Creek joins it about a mile inland, but neither of them's over two miles long. D'ye see the farm upstream?"

Elmer saw the big cabin on a point of land, a mile or so up the flood of water, and the roofs of companion buildings.

"That's where the creeks join," his uncle said. "Jim Mc-

Allister's claim's between the two, on the Nisqually council grounds."

"You mean he took up a claim right in the middle of the Indians' land?"

"By invitation," his uncle reassured him. "McAllister had the advantage of coming early. He and his party were the first American settlers on this side of the mountains, and they were welcomed like kings. Leschi and a party of his braves met them on the Cowlitz River with pack horses loaded with food and presents. That was ten years ago, and Leschi was a young man. He brought the McAllisters home to his tribe and settled them here with the backing of old Yanatco."

"The man we heard howling like a dog?"

"Yes."

They passed the valley and were opposite a high wooded shore again, in deepening water, with the strong tide helping the canoe. By now the sun had gone behind the forests on the near shore, and they were in green shaded waters, deep and cold to the touch and profoundly clean to look at, and smooth-rippled. Away to starboard the sun was still strong and golden on blue water and narrowing beaches and high, wooded islands and great headlands towering above the sea beaches and the sea.

"On a rare day when it's really clear," his uncle said, "you can see the great snow peaks going away to the south: Rainier and Saint Helens and Mount Hood in Oregon, a hundred-and-fifty miles away."

"A hundred-and-fifty-miles!" Elmer hardly knew whether or not to believe it.

"They're all volcanic," the big voice said, "dead or dying for centuries. Saint Helens was in eruption a year ago, and on summer nights we could see her fires. The Indians call her Looit the witch woman. She was the most beautiful woman in the world, h'm? Jealous gods turned her and her lovers into mountains and covered them with snow to keep them from loving too hotly. Judging from last year, Looit's still unreconciled to cold serenity. In the sky at night we could see fire bursting from her peak of snow. A triumph of woman's persistence, h'm? And terrifying to a man of imagination. Those fountain bursts of flame, climbing the sky and sinking back and climbing higher before dying away in lightning flickers on the mountain. The supreme rebellion, h'm? Supreme defeat. . . . The death of love. . . ." Uncle Jarvis's voice became a mumble in his beard, and stopped. Then he said, "Women never bothered me that way."

They had been paddling for a long time, and they paddled for a long time more without talking much. The helping tide slackened and stood still, brimming the beach along the high shore where boughs of evergreens and great maples swept down over the calm flood that was loaded with driftwood and yellow foam. Under the branches the shore had almost the darkness of night.

While Elmer paddled in silence, wearily, the near land came to an end. He felt the light of sunset on his face as the canoe rounded a point, forested with tremendous fir trees. Uncle Jarvis said, "This is our bay, Elmer. We're almost home."

The canoe was standing into a reach that was about half a mile wide, and it went so far inland that the boy could not be sure where it ended. It gave him the feeling of paddling up a great river, except that the water was motionless with the slack of the tide, and mirror-smooth. He sampled the water with his hand and it was cold, with a bitter pure salt taste. Because of the forest, it was dusk on the western side of the reach, while the sunset light was on the low, yellowish bluffs and great trees of the opposite side. That enchanting light gave it the look of a golden shore.

As if he had been following his nephew's eyes, Jarvis said, "That's your side of the bay."

"Mine?"

"If you decide to take up a claim," the big voice explained. "I have one picked out for you, across from mine." Then, as if that might sound inhospitable, he said, "There's land on my side, too. But I think relatives shouldn't tempt Providence by being too close, h'm? With the bay between us we'll not interfere with each other's privacy or have quarrels that can't be mended."

"That's right," Elmer agreed. "Though I really can't take up land this time. I promised to go back with the ship." But he kept his eyes on the golden shore which already belonged to him a little in fancy. And his uncle held the canoe closer to that side. Across the water there was a clearing and a cabin with blue smoke going up in the dusk, but Elmer was more interested in the bright shore which might have been his life, except for the fact that he was going back with the *Maid*.

His uncle's voice said, "It wouldn't do any harm to step ashore, h'm?"

"I'd like to!" Elmer said eagerly.

The canoe turned in toward a little point of land where tropical-looking trees leaned out over the water; trees with long oval glossy leaves and bark that was red and satin-smooth in the sunset light. Before there was time to ask about them, the canoe rounded up behind the point and grounded on a narrow wedge of beach in a little cove. Beside them a stream rattled down to the beach in a little waterfall, and ahead was a rough, steep path leading up the bank.

Elmer stepped ashore, stiffly, but with a feeling of lightness and excitement. It was his first step ashore in the new world, and it was on land that belonged to him a little because it would be his if he were staying.

They drank from the falling stream, out of cupped hands, and after Fairhaven water, six months in the keg, it tasted fine and cold.

"Indians used to camp here in summer," his uncle said. "They used this stream and made this path. That was before my time, but they must have burned their camp site over more than once. There's open land enough for a small-sized farm." Elmer followed him up the steep path to level ground.

Near the edge of the bank the land was open except for the few tropical-looking trees with naked-smooth reddish bark. The ground was grassy or overgrown with creeping vines that were warm and sweet-smelling from the afternoon sun that had been lying there for long hours. It was a beautiful, lonely place, with nothing frightening about its loneliness because it looked out on good salt water.

Uncle Jarvis said, "It's too late for exploring today, h'm? But there's about two acres here with nothing bigger than brush or second-growth timber that's the right size for building a cabin. Back of that there's the true forest, with firs and cedars six, eight and ten feet through and up to three hundred feet tall. And there's fallen seasoned cedar for all the boards and shakes and fence rails you'd ever care to split. For canoes, too, if you want to try, but I'd advise you to leave that to the Indians. I have a smaller dugout that's yours for the taking."

They went back to the little wedge of beach, where Elmer's sea-chest was waiting with innocent patience in the big canoe. And Elmer felt a little like the chest that different people wanted to establish in different places. When they were pushing off, he said: "It's beautiful here, but I don't see how any one could clear enough land for a farm; not for one big enough to make a living."

His uncle said, "People here live mostly on salmon and potatoes and venison. In the fall the streams are so full of salmon that you've only to lift them out with a pitchfork. On the big prairie the herds of deer wander like tame cattle. And every beach is full of clams. There's a saying, 'When the tide's out the table's set.' For a mere living you don't need much more than a potato patch. But if you're ambitious it's only a matter of harvesting the crop that's on your land. There's a fortune in timber there at the water's edge; on my land, too. I've got along well enough without logging, but it's an urge that sometimes comes to a man from Maine, h'm? We might log in partnership."

Elmer said, "I'd like that, if I stayed." He wanted to talk about it more and find out what his uncle meant by a fortune, but he wasn't given time.

"First, though, you'd have to make your improvements, h'm? Build a cabin and clear and fence some land and make a garden. That wouldn't cost you anything but hard work. I've tools enough, and we can swim a yoke of oxen across to haul the logs for your cabin.

Elmer said, "You're very kind." If his uncle had been embarking on money-making logging at once, he would have been inclined to go ashore for good. But it was put off to the vague future, beyond building and clearing. He was a little discouraged by the realization that in eight years his uncle had done nothing toward harvesting his money crop which was already centuries old; and he did not seem to have progressed far with his farm. Ahead, on the western shore, it was already night in the forest of great trees. And out of the forest and the night there was carved a clearing of four or five stumpy acres where it was dusk. Close to the shore there was a log cabin with an addition which might have been a kitchen, and to the left there was a large shed or barn. Beyond the buildings and a zig-zag rail fence, there was the impression of a few spotted cattle and a gray horse, and a few fruit trees were in bloom near the cabin.

Behind Elmer, the big voice said, "It's a fine place."

"Yes," Elmer said.

Then the voice said, "I've been happy here."

The boy knew that it was a fine place indeed. Paddling through twilit water, mirror-smooth, and looking with different eyes, he felt the peace of a new, uncomplicated world, where everything was calm and silent and sweet-smelling.

Reassuring him against hunger, his uncle's voice said, "Mary is baking *kalse* in your honor."

Both Mary and *kalse* were new to Elmer. He'd never heard of his uncle remarrying, and assumed that he lived alone. "Mary?"

"My wife," the big voice explained. "You may have language difficulties at first, but I think you'll like her."

"Is she foreign?"

"Native," his uncle said. "She's a Nisqually woman."

Elmer didn't know what to say. Aunt Harriet had been a Cambridge blue-stocking who once had an essay published in the *Atlantic Monthly*. Now Uncle Jarvis was married to a squaw.

The big voice rumbled cheerfully, "When you've been married a few times you'll perceive that the most you get's a woman, h'm? Happiness is when you get a woman who doesn't kick up dust between you and the world you're trying to see."

Then the voice said, "You can avast paddling now." The tide-narrowed beach was close ahead, and Elmer saw a woman and two big dogs waiting there in the dusk. They waited in silence until the canoe grated on the beach and Elmer stared up. Then the dogs were rampant against the bow of the canoe, rending the peace of the new world with their savage clamor. Uncle Jarvis was roaring at them and the woman was beating them with a stick and scolding, "Wolf, Caliban! *Klatawa! Cult-a-mana! Klatawa,* you brute!"

When the dogs drew back a little, snarling, Uncle Jarvis said, "They're native dogs, savage but useful. It's safe for you to get out now."

Reassured, Elmer stepped out onto the beach, with his uncle following him. The dogs were silent and the woman dropped her stick and took the boy's hand. "Elmer," she said, *"Kla-howya!* Excuse the *cultus* dogs. You are good to see." She was small and sturdy and dressed like a white woman except for two braids of hair, and her voice was gentle and sincere. In the dusk her Indian face was not beautiful but it was comforting to look at. The boy liked her and felt at ease with her, and none of his other aunts had ever made him feel more welcome. And while he tried to tell her how truly glad he was to see her, his uncle stood by, gigantic and genial in the dusk, balancing the sea-chest on his shoulder with an air of triumph.

CHAPTER FIVE

SOME PEOPLE do not really need sleep. At least they do not let sleep get any strong hold on their beings. A man like that takes sleep like a drink, which he can also let alone. He takes it like a drink, and when the cup is empty he is in full possession of his faculties and ready for other things. A man of that kind opens his eyes at the break of rosy dawn, leaps up, whistling, and washes in ice water. He does not feel the unpleasantness of things at that hour any more than a donkey feels the unpleasantness of eating thistles. There are many such men; stories are full of them; they are heroes.

Elmer was not a hero. The little acorn of his daily effort was produced by a great oak of sleep, rooted solidly in the rock of universal foundations. On board ship it had been four hours on and four off, with his brief naps forever at the mercy of the cry, "All hands!" In the security of his uncle's cabin the boy soaked up nourishment from inexhaustible oceans of sleep. Now he was beginning to be filled up a little. He found luxury in opening his eyes to see the color and shape of things in the cabin, then closing them and sleeping again. Like flirting with the world from a cave until he was ready to come out.

This morning he had been awakened in grayness by the fierce barking of the dogs. He had gone away to sleep again and left them barking. After that he had come back because of voices in the next room: the slow, rumbling voice of his uncle, and the clear, earnest voice of another man. Elmer let his eyes close, and when he opened them, there was fire in the grayness and a strip of sunlight was scalloped on the opposite wall. Under the tawny Hudson's Bay blanket, his bunk was warm with the warmth of his body, and a fire crackled in the next room. The chill of morning was in the air and the world was nice with its layers of warmth and chill and promised warmth. There was a good smell of frying bacon, and the boy's uncle was in the room, lifting a rifle down from the wall.

When he saw that his nephew's eyes were open, Uncle Jarvis asked, "Be you ready to roll out, Elmer?"

Elmer answered with a luxurious yawn.

Uncle Jarvis pulled his shirt tail out of his jeans and wiped the rifle barrel till it shone. "We're going visiting as soon as we have breakfast," he said.

Elmer sat up in bed and looked vaguely for his trousers. This was the day they were going to explore one of the islands. Visiting suggested a change in plans, but he was not awake enough to think clearly.

Uncle Jarvis returned his borrowed shirt tail to its proper place and looked at the rifle's priming. "If you're like your Ma, you believe in Temperance and Abolition and all that, h'm?"

"In some ways, I think, Ma's too strict. But I believe in Abolition."

"You think the joys of Temperance are overrated, h'm? But I judge it wouldn't be against your principles to call on a nigger?"

"A Negro, here?" Somewhere, he had heard they were forbidden in the Oregon Country.

"If we look sma't, maybe we can find one in this western woodpile."

Elmer knew his uncle was feeling good when he said "Be you?" and dropped his r's, the way Maine people do. A man of his education knew better than that, and Harvard had never taught him to clean a rifle with the tail of the shirt he was wearing. He acted that way because he was feeling good, and it had something to do with the coming visit. Asked too much, he would tell very little. So Elmer only remarked, "I didn't know there were any Negroes about."

"There's one ten miles south of here." Uncle Jarvis tucked the rifle under his arm. "We won't be his only callers."

Lacing his second shoe, the boy asked, "Has the rifle anything to do with it?"

Uncle Jarvis looked grave. "Justice has to be done." Then he said, "Sometimes I think a rifle's overrated as an instrument of justice. Still, it fits the shoulder and cheek nicely. This one's for you, and it's loaded."

"All right," Elmer said. But he was going to use his own judgment.

"Breakfast will be ready by the time you wash. We're having corn slappers."

"All right," Elmer said.

"Maybe you don't like them." Uncle Jarvis seemed disappointed.

"I like them fine," Elmer said. "I haven't had any for a long time." He hadn't sounded appreciative because he had been wondering what kind of visit they were going on, with loaded rifles. That had kept his mind off corn slappers and breakfast. When he took his mind off the visit, he couldn't think of anything better than corn slappers and bacon and coffee. "I like them fine," he said. "You'll see!"

Two miles south of Uncle Jarvis's claim the narrow road joined a wider one, like a creek flowing into a river; a narrow and crooked creek flowing into a river of roots and holes and ruts and dust. The road could not have been much worse, but on a dry spring morning it was passable; the horses were used to that kind of going, and Uncle Jarvis seemed to think highly of the thoroughfare. Riding beside his nephew on his big brown gelding, he boasted, "This is the most famous road in America, and the longest."

"Where does it go?"

Uncle Jarvis said, "To Olympia, the way we're going. The other end is at the Missouri River."

Elmer blinked and stretched his mind to fit the information. The Missouri River—. "You mean this is the Oregon Trail?"

"Why, yes. It don't look like much, h'm?"

Discreetly, he said, "Somehow I expected to see lots of wagons and cattle."

"In the spring?" Uncle Jarvis asked. "No, you won't see

emigrant trains until fall. The ones who'll pass this year are back along the Platte."

"I suppose lots of them stop in Oregon."

"And some along the way. Two years ago, six thousand died on the road."

Elmer had heard of that disastrous year. "Cholera, wasn't it?"

"Cholera and bad management and too many trains. They ate off the grass faster than it grew. And in some places the traders' burned off what grass there was and bought cattle cheap."

"They must have had a terrible time."

Uncle Jarvis said, "Watching these emigrants come in, I saw that flesh is a luxury. It's the bones that matter. When flesh gets to be too expensive a luxury, the skull comes out in the face and takes charge. It's the skull and some dream burning in it that keeps the leg bones stalking on, and the wrist bones cracking the whip on galled skeletons of horses and cattle that must not be allowed to lie down because they would never get up again."

Elmer stirred uneasily in the saddle. "I don't wonder this country looked like Paradise to them," he said. "A place where they could stop at last."

"Getting here wasn't everything. They had to keep on living, and they were badly prepared for that. Most of them didn't have a week's food left. They reached here in the late fall with their first harvest a year off. Most of those who started with grain for seed had eaten it on the way."

"They must have had a bad winter," Elmer said. Or was it other pilgrims who suffered so during their first winter in a new land?

Uncle Jarvis caressed the stock of his rifle. "There's a story to think about," he said. "The misfortune of thousands is always the opportunity of one man to get rich. It was this time. Most of us didn't have anything more than our own garden patches; most of us hadn't cleared more than enough land for that. But one man was farsighted. He'd settled on a fertile little prairie, away from salt water, where land needed only the plough. And he'd foreseen the big migration. That fall his claim looked like the Land of Canaan. Acres of wheat, corn, potatoes, beans, pumpkins, everything. 'Rush's Folly,' some of us called it, not believing there would ever be a market for so much. When Leschi saw the autumn rain clouds making up, he remembered his neighbor with the big crop and he sent a dozen of his braves to help. Without them a good deal of the crop might have spoiled. But the tide was with Rush. He made a clean harvest before the autumn rains. And the rains brought him customers, even more than he expected; all needing food at once and for the winter, and seed for their planting." The big man chuckled and looked down at the boy from his high brown horse. "Like a Yankee's dream of Heaven, h'm? The right crop at the right time, and enough of it, even at the market price, to keep a man for the rest of his life."

Elmer was playing with the idea of doing the same thing, for some other great and providentially timed migration. "He must have made a fortune!"

Uncle Jarvis said, "He didn't make a dollar."

"Why?" Elmer was almost as outraged as if the fortune had been snatched from his own hands. "Why didn't he make anything out of it?"

Uncle Jarvis said, "Remember, before the crop was harvested, we called it 'Rush's Folly.' You can still call it that if you like. But remember what those emigrants had gone through, and the shape they were in. Fifty or a couple of hundred dollars was about all they had left for starting in a new country."

"I see." He'd forgotten that part of it.

"When Rush saw how things were, he said something like this: 'Gentlemen, I've never seen any of you before, but we are going to be neighbors and share this country together. This is a good time to start. Take what you need, and pay me back when you have crops of your own and can afford it.'"

"That was fine of him!" Elmer said. When he wrote home, a good part of his letter would be about a man named Rush, whom he had never seen. It deserved to be recorded.

"And that's the story of 'Rush's Folly,'" the big man said. The boy said stoutly, "I wouldn't call it folly."

"I haven't made up my mind."

"Why?" His surprise left an aftertaste of annoyance. All along he'd been sure of his uncle's admiration for the great-hearted Rush. Now his uncle wasn't sure but what the man had been a fool. A fool because his dream of the Promised Land had made it real for others! "Why haven't you made up your mind?"

"It depends on whether they pay him back, h'm?"

"Don't you think they'll pay him back?"

"From what I know of people, some will and some won't. It only depends on how many. If one out of ten remembered, I'd say it was a fair proportion."

Elmer's feeling of irritation returned. "You don't think much of people, do you?"

"I'm prejudiced enough in their favor to make a distinction between ingratitude and the lack of grateful demonstration. Time won't always stand still while poor people go back along the way to thank some one for a kindness. It's easier to let it slide, and maybe help some one else, h'm?"

That didn't help much, Elmer thought. Older people, like his uncle, had a way of making everything so unsatisfactory. They took something which should have been clear-cut, and made it complicated and unsatisfactory. And they appeared to be satisfied with it themselves. He couldn't believe they really were. But if he pressed the point, he would get no satisfaction from that, either. It would be better to talk of something else. In the fo'c'sle of the *Maid*, he'd learned that men may fight like enemies on one subject, and meet as friends on another. So when you feel it getting muddy and trampled underfoot, it's a good idea to shift ground. There was another part of the story which had stuck in his mind and started growing: a chief who watched the gathering autumn clouds and thought of a white neighbor with his harvest still in the field. "Leschi must be a great chief," he said.

"Leschi isn't a chief," Uncle Jarvis said. "Officially, he's just a citizen of the Nisqually tribe, with no more authority than any one of a thousand others. Unofficially, he's consulted in everything—unless it's something he's suggested, and then it becomes law."

"Do white people trust him, too?"

"Those who know him," Uncle Jarvis said. "I told you about his bringing the McAllister party here; the first American settlers. Later, when they were building the Military Road over the Cascades, he contributed horses for the work. He helped make this road we're on part of the Oregon Trail."

"That was fine of him!" Elmer said.

"It don't give you much idea of Leschi. Nothing I could get out of this chest of mine would do that, except saying that he inspires confidence."

"You think Leschi is a great man?"

They had turned off the main road and were riding over a narrower one, through country that was open except for groves of smaller firs. Deliberately, Uncle Jarvis said, "Leschi has greatness. That is enough for any one."

"Don't you think there are any great men?"

His uncle answered with a shrug. "When I was your age, I saw any number of great men. As I got older, I saw fewer and fewer."

Elmer asked again, "Why?"

"My eyesight, I suppose."

"Your eyesight don't seem to have failed."

"No. Perhaps it has improved." Then he said: "There it is."

Ahead, on a green prairie dotted with islands of fir trees, there was a big log cabin with smoke rising from the chimney; the snowy loom of an orchard in blossom; farm buildings covered with shakes of split cedar, and zig-zag rail fences around prosperous-looking fields. Saddle horses were waiting beside the log cabin, and there were men in the yard. Off to the right there were Conestoga wagons and the smoke of a campfire. Two black-bearded men were chopping a log and women moved about the campfire.

"That's the lay of the land," Uncle Jarvis said. "Be you ready for trouble, Elmer?"

The boy had a sudden feeling of hollowness in his well-filled stomach. "What kind of trouble, Uncle Jarvis?"

"I told you we were calling on a nigger."

Elmer had almost forgotten. It had been a long time ago, before he was really awake, and he was going to use his own judgment about what he did. "Is that where he lives?"

"Yes. This is George Rush's place."

"The man who gave his crop to the emigrants when he could have made a fortune?"

"Rush of 'Rush's Folly,' " Uncle Jarvis said. "Today he gets repaid for his crop, if he ever does."

It was like a lifting fog, with things beginning to loom up suddenly and take shape. But everything was far from clear. At home, Uncle Jarvis had said something about rifles as an instrument of justice. "He's going to be paid with rifles?"

"If they sprout in his fields like dragon's teeth, h'm?"

Off to the right, a whip cracked and curses were shouted. Oxen emerged from a grove: a yoke of red oxen and a yoke of red-and-white ones, pulling a log. The tall, black-bearded driver was lashing them with his long whip and blasting them with his great, profane voice.

Elmer said, "Is Rush in danger?"

"You can judge for yourself." Uncle Jarvis pointed with a long thick arm. "Those Pikes have filed on his claim, and now they're starting to prove up on it."

The feeling of chill had gone from the boy's stomach, and his veins were growing hot. Men, in broad daylight, trying to rob a man who might have been rich, but chose to help others. "They can't!"

"I'm not sure of that." The big man's voice was troubled and quiet.

Elmer was not annoyed with him now. It was the trouble that was complicated. Uncle Jarvis was not trying to make things difficult, but thinking of a way out. "There's the law," he suggested hopefully.

"That's the thing that worries me most."

"Why, Uncle Jarvis?"

"Because anything we do in the way of stopping those Pikes will be against the law."

"How can it be against the law to stop them from robbing a man who's done so much good?"

"Rush is only a squatter. Those Pikes had the legal right to file on his land. They have the legal right to put him off, and the law's supposed to protect them."

The shoe was on the other foot, savagely. "Why hasn't Rush ever filed on his claim?"

"I told you he's part Negro. That makes him a nigger, with no rights on American soil. He's never filed on his claim because he can't."

Elmer thought a long time, then he said, "All those people Rush helped—I'd think they'd come and drive the Pikes out before they knew what was happening!"

"Too much enthusiasm won't do, either."

They were close enough to hear the voices of men in the yard, and still Elmer didn't know what was expected of him. "How are we going to manage the Pikes?"

"*Hi, Jarvis!*" a voice called from the yard.

"*Hi, Bob!*" Then he said to his nephew, "I don't know what we'll do, but take it easy. Maybe we'll have to side with the others."

"With the Pikes?" Elmer was aghast until he saw the reassuring grin. "Only enough to prevent a runaway that would throw us all out."

In the yard there were two sunburned young men and a spry, older man with bright eyes and a thin, drooping moustache. Horses were tied to the long hitching rail, and rifles leaned against the wall of the cabin, with powder horns and flasks and bullet pouches beside them on the ground. The young men were Bob and Paul Porter, and the spry, bright-eyed man was their father, Levi. Uncle Jarvis shouted in his ear, "*This is my nephew, Elmer Hale! I kidnapped him from a ship!*"

Shaking hands, Levi shouted, "*I'm pleased to meet any kin of Jarvis!*"

The shouting brought another man from the cabin. He was medium in height and age, strongly built, with a look of dignified friendliness. Elmer was not sure he was a Negro until he had been introduced as George Rush. He was no darker than the sunburned brothers.

"It was good of you to come," Rush said. "I value this. Come in, Jarvis. You, too, Elmer. If I know your age, you can stand a bite after your ride."

"How's Mrs. Rush and the children?" Uncle Jarvis asked.

"They're visiting the Jameses," Rush explained. "They didn't want to leave, but I packed them off. I didn't want them underfoot if there was going to be trouble." He didn't look like a man expecting trouble. His only concern seemed to be for the comfort of his guests. "There's some food on the table," he said; "if you'll help yourselves, I'll bring you coffee." The table was made of long, rough planks, laid on three trestles, but their host had understated matters when he said there was some food there. At a glance, Elmer saw baked hams and a saddle of venison, and venison liver and bacon, with heated stones in the basket to keep it warm. There were loaves of bread and bricks of butter, pies and jugs of milk and cream. By way of replenishment, there were pots and kettles at the big fireplace, and a whole sheep roasting on the spit. A man with a wide hat far back on his head was crouched by the carcass. Elmer mistook him for some one who was helping prepare the feast, but he turned out to be another guest. After a minute he came lurching toward the table, with a slice of hot meat in the dancing fingers of one hand and a butcher knife in the other. Seeing the newcomers, he paused to put the meat on the point of the knife, and wiped his right hand on the front of his checked shirt. "Howarya, Jarvis?" he said, shaking hands. He was Bill Slocum, and he settled himself on the bench beside Elmer with a bump that made the boy reach protectively for his coffee mug. "Mutton's my meat," Bill explained, cutting a slice of bread. "I'd turn wolf for it." Then he added mournfully, "Dolly can't abide it; she says it tastes of wool."

"The coffee's hot," Rush said. He set down a half-filled mug with a carefulness which suggested that it should be picked up with equal care.

Uncle Jarvis asked, "Didn't you know before you were married?"

"Ha, if I could only remember!" The flushed face was solemn. Then it relaxed, and he shook his head and drank. "Before we were married, it seemed she liked everything I did. Now I think: 'What were all those things she liked that I liked?' Can't remember one." He sighed.

"Probably what she meant was that she liked you," Uncle Jarvis suggested.

"I don't know," Bill said. "Maybe she likes me, maybe she hates to be alone. D'ye know what? This morning she didn't want me to come here. Said I'd only get drunk and get in a fight, but I could see through it. D'ye know what I said? I said, 'No, sir! Not after what he done for us! If George Rush gets put off his place, I get put off, too. Nigger or no nigger—" He coughed apologetically, "Asking your pardon, Mr. Rush."

Rush said, "It was kind of you to think of me."

Elmer had become used to his drunken neighbor on the bench, and was filling himself with dried apple pie and coffee. After a while Bill got up and wandered out, leaving his mutton and bread half-eaten on the table, as if his appetite had suddenly failed.

Jarvis stretched his enormous arms. "An expedition's really started when you begin to worry about the drunk in your own party, h'm?"

"I never saw Bill drunk before this year," Rush said.

"Has he any more with him?"

Rush glanced under the table.

Jarvis reached down and brought up a quart bottle, half full. "We ought to put this where he can't find it."

"You hide it," Rush said. "I'm supposed to keep an eye on it."

The big man wiped the neck of the bottle on his sleeve before offering it to his host.

"Thank you," Rush said. "I don't care for any."

"Elmer?"

The boy shook his head. "No, I thank you."

His uncle drank, and put the empty bottle under the table. Rush poured himself a cup of coffee and sat down. He looked tired. "I never saw Bill Slocum drunk when he came here first. He worked hard and made a good start on his place."

Jarvis said, "It's some trouble between him and Dolly. A woman would find out in five minutes, h'm? Men aren't good at that sort of thing. But Bill ought to know he can't float himself out of his troubles on whiskey."

New voices sounded in the yard, and one man was already in the room, standing behind Uncle Jarvis. Now he gave him a thumping blow on the back. "Jarvis, you old temperance-lecturing hypocrite! I bet there's whiskey on your breath right now."

"We're drinking coffee, Adam." Jarvis held out his cup.

"Let me pour you some," Rush said.

The newcomer was a healthy-looking man of forty, with red cheeks and a pleasant air of confidence. His name was Adam Stark, and he took a seat on the bench beside Uncle Jarvis. "I've wronged you this time," he said, "but what can you expect when you've wolfed so much whiskey?"

Jarvis dismissed the matter with a generous wave. "How many recruits have we now?"

"Nine," Adam said. "Albert Green came with me from the Fork."

"Not enough." Uncle Jarvis shook his head. "This is an old settlers' picnic, and we're going to make it a day of pleasure."

"How many Pikes are there?"

"George counted eight men. There may be more. I think it's time to do a little scouting."

"I thought of something like this . . . "

Elmer wanted to hear the plan, but his attention was drawn toward Bill. The drunk had come in with a gaudy, smooth-shaven young man who wore his hair long and stepped lightly in beaded moccasins.

"You wait," Bill said. "You taste it, and then tell me what!"

Elmer felt guilty for his kinsman, but Uncle Jarvis was absorbed in discussing plans with Adam. Bill lurched against the table and reached down, groping.

Uncle Jarvis suddenly noticed him. "May I help you, Bill?"

"Left my powder flask," Bill mumbled.

"I think you have the right idea." Jarvis was talking to Adam again. "Appeal to their nobler selves. We can always beat hell out of them as an afterthought, h'm?"

"Gone, by God!" Bill was holding the empty bottle, with a stricken look. "I've been robbed!"

"That's the damndest powder flask I ever saw."

Bill ignored the jibe, eyeing Rush with sad anger. "And I trusted you!"

"You can trust me," Rush said. "I didn't touch it."

"I trusted some one I shouldn't!"

The roar of male laughter carried the boy back to the fo'c'sle of the *Maid*. It was the kind of laughter a woman never hears, except at a distance. And then it is only the echo of a world she cannot enter.

Bill laid the bottle to rest on the table. "No one will bother you now," he said sentimentally. "Albert, the invitation to a drink is put off, pending an investigation."

Albert was quite disinterested, tossing back his long hair before a poised wedge of pie. "Thank you, Bill. I didn't really want a drink."

"That leaves only one of us," Bill said. He looked about the table, with flushed dignity. "Who robbed me?"

Uncle Jarvis looked up, mildly. "I hate to accuse any one, Bill, but I think I did."

There was another roar of laughter and Bill shook his head. "You can't fool me, Jarvis; you can't throw me off the scent." He looked crafty. "I'll find the guilty conscience out there in the yard."

When he was gone, Adam said, "Jarvis, you old hypocrite, I apologized to you, and your breath is like a mountain still!"

"I confessed."

"You didn't sound convincing."

Uncle Jarvis looked perplexed. "I always confess that way." While the others were laughing, he suddenly became grave. "While we wait, some one should be looking over the Pikes' camp, h'm?"

"I'll go as soon as I finish this pie," the gaudy young man offered. It was a large piece which might have helped put off the evil moment, but he stuffed it all into his mouth. "I'll ged my rible."

"No, Albert," Uncle Jarvis said. "You look too wise."

Adam said, "You'd get to frolicking with the Pike women and forget to come back."

"Have they any pretty ones?"

Uncle Jarvis said, "See? Disqualified."

Rush cleared his throat. "I saw only one young woman, and she was not pretty."

Albert made a show of hesitating. "Only one?" he said. "Hardly worth the ride."

"There's Bob, or Paul——"

"They work best together," Uncle Jarvis said. "It's a team that shouldn't be divided."

"That's right," Adam said. His clear eyes swept about the room, through the open door, into the yard, and back again, to rest on Elmer. "What about your nephew here?"

The boy's heart gave a thump of startled protest and the last crumbs of pie stuck in his throat.

"He's our man," Uncle Jarvis agreed. "He has the right look of innocence and he fits nicely into bad company. Want to do some scouting for us, Elmer?"

Elmer swallowed and stood up. "I'll get my rifle," he said, as Albert had done. His voice was not very loud.

"No rifle, boy," Adam said firmly.

"You'd be sure to get hurt that way," his uncle added. "Going unarmed, you have a chance of coming back with a whole skin."

"All right," Elmer agreed. "What do you want me to do?"

"Ride into the Pikes' camp and pay them a call. Find out anything you can that might be useful to us, and come back."

Elmer swallowed resolutely. "What shall I say about the crowd here?"

"Nothing unless they ask you. Then you can say it's a picnic. But if they ask, you needn't deny that we're tough."

"All right," Elmer said. They were stepping out into the

bright and noisy yard. From the Pikes' camp he could hear the sound of axes, and the great, angry voice of the driver, shouting curses. Behind him was the log cabin where he had once sat at a table in comfort, eating a second breakfast. That had been so long ago that he couldn't remember what he had eaten. Only it seemed that he had eaten too much, and he felt like a lamb fattened for the slaughter.

CHAPTER SIX

*E*LMER'S COURSE lay through a sea of waving bunch grass that came to his horse's belly and threw out a continuous spray of grasshoppers. At the end of a quarter mile, he came to the Pikes' camp. Three Conestoga wagons, their gray tops patched with white, were drawn up in a quarter circle, with the outside toward Rush's cabin. Beyond the wagons were two campfires, with women around them; picketed horses and grazing cattle. Near the second fire, two tall, black-bearded men were notching a log, while a third stood by. The new cabin had already risen to the height of three logs, and a narrow gap in one wall showed where the door would be. The profane teamster was going away toward the grove where axes rang. As Elmer looked, a tree swayed, tottered back from its companions and fell into the open with a sigh of air rushing through its branches and a crashing thud which knocked the wind out of it.

Unchallenged, Elmer rode up to the nearest fire. In the bright morning, the camp had the clean smell of horses and cattle and dry grass and wood-smoke. A circle had been dug around the fire, and the grass burned off. A woman in brown calico sat at one edge of the circle, with her dark head bent over some work. Beyond her, a thin woman in faded red calico was churning and singing. The dasher, going up and down, kept time with the lament which she wailed with unmistakable relish:

"*Ma-ny are the complaints that a woman suffers from.*
Ma-ny are the pains that hide behind a smiling face——"

84

The boy blushed for the female secrets which he felt were about to be revealed, but he was spared. Song and dasher stopped, while the woman eyed him sharply. "Well, Stranger, what have you got to say for yourself?"

"Good morning," he said. "I just thought I'd pay you a visit."

"There's visits and visits," the woman observed. "Light down, if you ain't too proud."

"Thank you, ma'am." He lit down.

"Liza, bring the stranger some coffee."

Elmer looked quickly at the young woman in brown calico. She was the one he had seen on the deck of the *Maid*. He had rescued her from Sam's yarning with probable-sounding lies, and she had trusted him. Her name wasn't Liza, it was Lisette. That was all he knew. "Good morning," he said.

"How do you do, sir?" He couldn't tell if she remembered him. Her still face and sullen eyes didn't tell him anything. She took a cup from a cloth spread in the grass, and went over to the fire, where she knelt awkwardly, pouring coffee. Her hair was black and very thick.

"You live around here?" the woman asked.

"I'm visiting my uncle. I just got here from Massachusetts."

"Your uncle don't live there, does he?" She inclined her sunbonnet toward Rush's cabin.

"He lives on the Sound," Elmer said, "near Nisqually."

"Have some coffee, sir?" Lisette held out the cup.

"I thank you." The cup was very hot, and the coffee looked as black as her hair.

"I'll fetch milk and sugar," she said.

"There might be some doughnuts, Liza."

Between friend and foe, Elmer was getting pretty well filled up.

"I'll get to my churning," the thin woman said, "before the cream goes back."

So far, Elmer decided, he was making out all right. He was alive and well in the camp of the enemy, with a cup of coffee in his hands, and his horse grazing a few yards away, with the bridle reins trailing. No one had molested him and he was only troubled by the embarrassing hospitality of the Pikes.

The young woman brought sugar and milk and a plate of doughnuts. "Don't you want to sit down, sir?" She pointed to the ox yoke, where she had been peeling potatoes.

"You sit down," he said.

"I can find somewhere else."

"No," he said, drinking his coffee, standing.

She hesitated, frowning at the yoke. Then she looked past him defiantly. "There's room for two."

Sitting beside her, he thought there was some superstition about a young man and woman sharing a yoke together, but he couldn't remember it. He looked at the girl, who was peeling potatoes again. "I saw you on the ship at Steilacoom."

"Yes." Then she asked, "Is your coffee all right?"

"It's fine," he said.

"It isn't fresh."

"I like it this way."

"I was rude to you," she said.

"You were nice," he insisted. She had not been very nice, but he thought she wanted to be friendly when she found he wasn't laughing at her. "I liked you."

She did not answer, and there wasn't much more he could say. Talking to her was difficult. He ate a doughnut, which he did not want, and looked at her, sideways. He could see her full breast rising and falling rapidly as her hands worked with the potato and the knife. Her hands were large and rough, but their shape was smooth, and she had long fingers. When she knew he was watching her, she finished in haste and folded her hands in her lap. "I was very rude."

"No," he insisted.

She turned and faced him squarely. "Why did you come here?"

"To visit," he said. But he knew that wasn't any good.

"You didn't know I was here!"

He was startled, without knowing why. "No," he admitted.

"Why did you come?"

"I'd never seen an emigrant camp before," he said. "I wanted to see what it was like."

She lowered her voice to a husky whisper. "Are you one of those Pikes?"

"Pikes?" He did not have to pretend dismay.

Lisette looked doubtful, as if she might have made a mistake. "That's what they're called here—isn't it? I mean the lawless ruffians who want to put us off this land."

"I'm certainly not a lawless person," Elmer said.

"Why did you come here?" When he did not answer, she lowered her voice, "Did you come from the cabin?"

"Yes," he said, and braced himself to meet her angry outburst.

She sat perfectly still and did not say anything.

Elmer had never known any one who could make him feel so uncomfortable. "I'm as much of a stranger here as you are," he said. "I came over with my uncle, and I didn't know what was going on until I got here."

She said, "Your uncle knew. He's one of the Pikes, and you're his kin. You're helping him." She made each statement feel like a nail going into a coffin.

Thinking of a way out, he saw that there was nothing else as ingenious as the truth. "My uncle came to keep the peace," he said. "People trust him, and he has a lot of influence. Uncle doesn't want anything lawless to happen. He said we might have to fight on your side. That's a secret, though." It was also a secret that he had said it would be only enough to keep the settlers' enthusiasm from running wild.

The girl looked more friendly, but she did not seem any happier. "I hope there won't be any fighting," she said.

"I hope not."

"Dan's boys are powerful fighters." She looked toward the new cabin, where the black-bearded men were lifting another log into place. "There's seven of them, awful handy with rifles and bowie knives, and old Dan was a champion. They wouldn't stop at anything in a fight."

He said, earnestly, "I hope there won't be any fighting."

"Do you think your uncle will be able to stop those men?"

He had tried to convince the girl that he was on her side. Now he had succeeded, and it only made him sad and uneasy. "I don't see how we can stop them."

"Why not?"

"There's a dozen of them up there now, and there'll be more." He glanced toward Rush's cabin, which he could not see because of the intervening wagons. He could not see the cabin, but there were three men riding at a gallop along the road. The fields were sprouting dragon's teeth, all right.

"I'll get you some more coffee," the girl said.

He watched her cross the blackened circle of ground and kneel by the fire, and felt at a loss. He didn't see why he couldn't decide anything about some one who was so definite. He couldn't even decide about her person. She looked so strong and well-made, but she moved as if she were chained. Maybe that was because of her clothes, and her heavy cowhide shoes, which she tried to conceal, but all of her was like that. Whether it was an angry outburst or the beginning of an apology, it stopped with a kind of jerk, as if her mind had been brought up in chains.

When Lisette came back with his coffee, she said, "I don't see why there has to be trouble. The nigger has no right to be here. He's breaking the law, and it looks like other people want to break the law to help him. Why? Do they think more of a nigger than of white people?"

Elmer said, "They think a lot of Rush; he's their friend."

She looked at him with sullen curiosity. "You like him, too," she said.

"Yes."

"Why?" she demanded. "Why do they stand up for him against white people?"

He told her what Uncle Jarvis had told him about "Rush's Folly."

When he had finished, she looked at the ground and said, "I see." Then she said, defensively, "Dan offered to pay for his improvements."

Elmer had not heard of that, but he wasn't going to argue

the point. "He don't want to be paid; he wants to keep his land."

"He ain't allowed to have land."

For a minute the boy had forgotten that. He didn't answer. "Your uncle thinks a lot of this Rush, too, don't he?"

"Yes," he said, unguardedly.

"If you're through with your coffee," she said, "maybe you'd better go back. I expect we can get along better without the kind of help we'll get from you and your uncle." She spoke so quietly that it was like a cut which does not begin to sting until the knife leaves off.

Elmer got up, feeling hurt. "You're wrong about my uncle." The girl's look was withering, but she did not answer with words. He became aware of the half-filled coffee cup in his hand, and felt foolish. Finishing it would be poison, and handing it back to her would be an insult in return for hospitality. Since neither of them could touch the cup without being degraded, he set it on the ground beside the ox yoke. "I'm sorry," he said vaguely.

On the other side of the fire, the woman in red calico brought a tin dipper and poured a dash of water into the churn. She didn't seem interested in anything except butter, but she was. She straightened up, and looked sharply at Elmer. "Liza, is he one of those Pikes from the nigger's?" The dipper in her hand caught the morning sun and blazed light at him, like a flaming sword.

Under her breath Lisette said, *"You go!"* The two husky words were like the push of strong hands, urging him out of the camp.

Elmer walked over to his grazing horse and picked up the bridle reins. The gelding had gone on enjoying the Pikes' hospitality after his master was no longer welcome.

"Liza, is he one of those Pikes?"

"I think so, Ma." The girl was looking at him, sullenly, with her hands clenched. He could see the white bumps of her knuckles standing out on one red hand. The older woman had withdrawn the dasher from the churn, and looked as if she had a good mind to use it for a weapon.

Beyond the pair, Elmer saw a third woman approaching from the other fire. She looked as tall as Uncle Jarvis, and there was a mean cut to her old sunbonnet. Her faded calico dress ended a foot short of her thin shanks and the men's shoes on her feet. She was smoking a pipe, and in her arms she carried a long rifle as familiarly as another woman might have carried a baby. Elmer knew when it was time to go. He swung into the Mexican saddle, which had a reassuring feel. "Good-by," he said. The two women did not answer, but the third, drawing near, shifted her rifle handily and plucked the pipe from her mouth. Elmer rode away before she had time to speak.

Elmer was not satisfied with his scouting, but the scene at the cabin reassured him. The long hitching rail was blotted out by horses, the way a vine disappears when the leaves come out, and the yard was black with men. As he rode up, the last few were emerging from the cabin, with their rifles in their hands. Some were untying their horses, and others had already mounted. For a minute he was the center of attention, answering questions about the lay of the land and the number of the enemy, also the number of his conquests, and the likeliness of the women. Adam and Uncle Jarvis were more interested in the temper of the Pikes, and in what Elmer had told them. Uncle Jarvis enjoyed the account of the long-shanked female with the rifle, but Adam was disturbed. "What the devil would you do if a woman took a shot at you?"

Uncle Jarvis said, "Mourn for the unlucky bystander, h'm?"

But Elmer thought the old lady had a sharpshooter's eye. Anyway, she would derive equal satisfaction from hitting any one of them.

Standing beside the two leaders, Rush said softly, "I don't want any of you to get hurt." His face was gray, and he looked worried.

"We'll be all right," Adam said.

Rush said, "I'd rather lose everything I have than see one of you shot."

"There won't be any shooting," Uncle Jarvis said. "Those

Pikes didn't come all this way just to commit suicide, h'm?"

Rush said, "I'd feel better if I was along. Then, if anything happened——"

Adam shook his head. "We think you ought to stay."

Uncle Jarvis said, "We're going to meet the Pikes on their own terms. They told you this is a white man's country. When we get through, maybe they'll wish for a country of some other color."

"They'll get a bellyful, all right." Adam untied his cayuse from the long hitching rail. Touching the split cedar with his hand, he said, "It comes in handy, George, this rail you put up for us poor devils who used to come begging that first winter."

Uncle Jarvis said, "There must have been dragon's teeth in the seed corn you gave them, h'm?"

Rush raised his voice, trying to answer Adam. "Nobody came begging! You offered to pay me! You have—" His voice broke, or was drowned out. At the Pikes' camp they were beating an alarm on what sounded like a tin pan. Near Elmer, a buckskin with a silver mane stood on his hind legs and pawed the air.

"Stay with him, Bill!" some one shouted. "He's still a-pawin'!"

Out of the edge of his eye, Elmer glimpsed a forgotten rifle leaning against the wall of the cabin, with a powder flask and bullet pouch beside it on the ground. Some one must have been considerably excited to forget his rifle. Then it dawned on him that his hands were empty, and the rifle was his own. He recovered it, contritely, as the troop was riding out of the yard.

No one had told Elmer the plan of action, or his place in the troop. He would have liked to ride with his uncle, but his uncle had important things on his mind, and Elmer might only be in the way of more experienced men. So he fell in near the end of the procession and rode beside the sunburned brothers, Bob and Paul, whom he had met when he first arrived at the cabin. They wanted to hear all about his expedition to the Pikes' camp, and looked on him as a kind of minor hero. And

Albert, of the long hair and gaudy shirt, dropped back to inquire if he hadn't really managed at least one conquest among the Pike women. When Elmer assured him he hadn't, Albert rode ahead again, after making the motion of pushing Elmer away for a lying and enviable young libertine.

Elmer was embarrassed, but he was also inwardly pleased by the misplaced flattery. Between the scandalous Albert and the blue-eyed, sunburned brothers, he felt he had made a place for himself in that company of strangers.

Bob, who was the older brother, said, "We live on Scatter Creek. Come over and go hunting with us when you have time."

Paul said, "We're from Colesville, New Jersey."

"I'd like to go with you," Elmer said. "I haven't been hunting here."

"We have smart dogs. They hunt by themselves. When they tree a cougar, one of them stays to keep it in the tree, and the other comes to get one of us."

"I have a dog at home," Elmer said. "He's good for birds."

"We have fun with the dogs," Bob said. "When one of them comes to get us, we pretend to go without a gun. If it's Spike, he gets in front of you and barks, 'No, no, no!' But if it's Lop, he just sits down and looks at you; just like saying, 'Are you *crazy?* Cougar hunting without a gun?'"

"We're about there," Paul warned.

Up ahead, the horsemen were in single file, swinging out to the south of the gray-topped wagons. Uncle Jarvis had stopped beside the moving column, with his big brown gelding turned at right angles to the line of march. He looked very big and resourceful, and not at all afraid of being picked off by a bullet from one of the wagons. If a real war happened, Elmer told himself, his uncle would undoubtedly become a famous general.

Uncle Jarvis spoke to the men who were about to pass him, and rode off to the right. The horsemen followed in single file, swinging around to the north of the wagons.

They swung well clear of the end wagon and rode into the camp, just as Adam's troop was riding in from the other side. At first Elmer did not see any of the Pikes. Then he saw them all at once, directly and indirectly. They had made a fortress of the partially built house, and rifles were levelled from loopholes between the unpeeled fir logs. Even for outnumbered men, it was a powerful defense, but it had been spoiled a little by the division of the troop. The walls had been raised only to the height of four logs, and from the back of a horse you looked down into the hollow square. You could not see the men who faced you, but the ones facing the other way knelt innocently in full view, and they were very big fellows whose broad backs would make good targets. It stood to reason that the ones facing you were equally exposed from the other side.

Something of the kind must have occurred to the Pikes by now. One rifle was withdrawn from its loophole, and the owner stood up. He was a white-haired, tough-looking old man with the face of a captured eagle. And, like an eagle, you'd expect him to be quick and fierce as long as he had a breath of life. "What in hell do you want?"

Uncle Jarvis said loudly and cheerfully, "I want to apologize."

"Eh?" The old eagle face looked puzzled, then it hardened. "Staying away wouldn't need no apology." Then he said, "Get it over, and get out."

"We would not have come at this time, had we known you were at prayer."

"Eh?"

"Aren't you at devotions?" Uncle Jarvis looked perplexed. "I see those young men in there, kneeling——"

A snicker went along the line of horsemen, and old Eagleface leaned sideways as if he might be giving some one a kick. The remaining rifles wavered and withdrew from between the logs, and their owners towered up from behind the bulwark of the unfinished house. Even with somewhat sheepish expressions, the young men looked more alarming than rifles poked through loopholes. They were all big fellows, with ominous black beards and unkempt hair. And they still had their rifles, which they fingered provokingly; all of them wore bowie knives in their belts, and at least one had a Navy revolver for luck.

"Good morning, boys," Uncle Jarvis said, "I see you're building a house."

"What's that to you?" Old Eagle-face had a savage, ruffled look.

Uncle Jarvis went on pleasantly, "Moreover, I observe you're trying the house on to see if it fits. That's a wise precaution. With all you big fellows, it would be easy to build one too small."

It was really flattering, because the hollow square was rather filled by nine men, and the great, black-bearded fellows had the look of spilling over the side. But old Eagle-face was not flattered. "You go tend your own house," he said, "and we'll tend ours!"

Uncle Jarvis looked distressed. "We old-timers are full of advice——"

"Keep it!"

From the other troop, Adam called harshly, "I'm going to give you a piece of advice!"

"Eh?" Eagle-face half turned, at bay between the crossfire of words.

"You've made one mistake," Adam said. "You've built your house on another man's land!" He did not have the patience of Uncle Jarvis, and his face was red and angry.

Eagle-face shouted, "You liar! Sassing me on my own place! Go to the land office! Could I file on it if it wasn't open?"

"Don't call me a liar!" Adam shouted. "Are you blind? Didn't you see buildings and fences and crops on this land? Didn't you think it belonged to somebody?"

"If it did," the old man shouted, "why hasn't he filed on it, hey?"

Adam was very angry because he had the worst of the argument. "He don't have to file on it! He earned this land. Didn't he, boys?" The roar of agreement put him in a better position, and his voice became less angry. "He earned this land, and we're here to remind you of the fact."

"Don't sass me; answer me! If it was his'n and he didn't file on it, it don't stay his'n long. Why didn't he file on it?"

"He don't have to!" Adam shouted stubbornly.

"Don't go sneakin' and shoutin' and not answerin'!" Eagle-face screeched. "You know why he didn't file on it; he couldn't! He's a runaway nigger——"

"He's a man!" Adam shouted.

"He's got no rights!"

"He has friends, hasn't he, boys?" The answering cheer seemed to shake the disputed earth.

"Niggers are agin' the law, here! We're law-abidin' men. We won't have niggers for neighbors!"

"We won't have you for neighbors, by God!"

"Get off my land, you lawless Pikes!" Eagle-face screeched. "Get off my land afore we start shootin'!"

"You Pikes get off this man's land before we start shooting!"

"You're breakin' the law, threatenin' us with guns on our own property!"

"You claim-stealing——"

"You law-breakin'——"

"Wait!" The roar of Uncle Jarvis's voice made every one jump, and the name-calling stopped. "There's a point of law here," Uncle Jarvis said. "Shouting won't settle it. Our good friend here—" He looked toward old Eagle-face. "I didn't catch your name."

"Sims, if it's anything to you; Dan Sims."

"Our good friend, Dan Sims, states that he has filed on this land in accordance with the provisions of the law——"

"That's right," Sims agreed. "I've the papers to prove it!" He started to reach inside his shirt.

"I won't look at them now," Uncle Jarvis said. "Your word is enough." His voice grew larger. "So, gentlemen, it appears that this is Dan Sims's claim. Before the law, nothing can interfere with his full enjoyment of his claim; nothing but the prior rights of a squatter, which might have to be paid for——"

"He's a nigger! He can't——"

Uncle Jarvis said reprovingly, "Now, Dan, you took the words right out of my beard. In this case, gentlemen, the squatter, George Rush, has Negro blood. That prohibits him from owning land, or even claiming a squatter's rights. True in the cholera year this Rush saved hundreds of emigrants from suffering, and certainly some of them from death. But that has no legal bearing. Fortunately for most of us here, the law did not prohibit this Negro from an act worthy of the noblest citizen living; it only prohibits him from enjoying rights that are free to the meanest——"

Elmer felt the angry tears start to his eyes, and a growl of protest ran along the ranks of horsemen, like summer thunder. "To hell with the law!" some one said.

Uncle Jarvis went on, "So, gentlemen, it appears that Dan Sims will be in full legal possession of this land when he proves on it, and George Rush is an outcast in the eyes of the law, without rights and without redress——"

Behind their barricade of logs, the black-bearded men looked sheepishly uneasy, while old Eagle-face glared. "Don't you go making me out a Pike!" he shouted. "I said I'd pay——"

"No, Dan, you don't have to pay. Rush can't sell what he don't own. And the only thing he has in this world you can't buy: a few hundred friends among the white settlers. Because we're white men, talking together, I exclude his friends among the Indians. If they were here, it might be hard to make them understand these fine points of law which, I am sure, are clear to all of us."

Old Eagle-face spat over the log barricade. "Don't go trying to scare us with varmint talk!" he warned.

"I wasn't trying to scare you with anything," Uncle Jarvis said. "I was only telling you and these gentlemen that this land is legally yours, to use and enjoy as you please."

"I knew that all along!" He looked suspicious, but relieved. Then he said, "Can't enjoy it while all these buzzards are sitting around with rifles."

Uncle Jarvis said, "I wouldn't enjoy it, either."

"Then get them to hell out of here!"

"It isn't my property," Uncle Jarvis reminded him. "You tell them."

"I'll tell 'em!" Sims turned toward Adam's troop, and he looked very much like an eagle, hopping about in his cage of logs. "You heard what the Judge said!" he shouted. "Now get to hell off'n my place afore we start shootin'!"

"The hell we will!"

"You get off!"

"Wait!" Uncle Jarvis roared again. "Dan!"

The old eagle face turned again, angry and ruffled. "You just told me the claim is mine, accordin' to the law——"

"Right," Uncle Jarvis agreed. "Don't forget the law. If you break it with any shooting, you won't have a claim, or anything else."

For the first time, Sims looked at a loss. He asked, plaintively, "How'm I going to get these buzzards off my place?"

Uncle Jarvis rubbed his beard, looking up into the sky. Then he looked down again. "I'd say it was impossible."

"Paw, he's sassin' you! He's sassin' you, and you don't know it!" The outraged scream cut short the snicker that was running along the line of horsemen. When they turned their startled eyes in the direction of the scream, which still went on, a woman in faded calico was leaning out of the back of one of the wagons. *"Paw, he's been sassin' you all along, you old fool——"*

"Set down, Maw!" the old man bellowed. *"And keep settin'!"*

The mean-cut sunbonnet disappeared, and every one breathed again.

Uncle Jarvis put on his wide hat, which he had removed at the sound of a woman's voice. "Most of us here have wives," he said, understandingly.

The old eagle was not appeased. Maybe the voice from the back of the wagon had reminded him how bitter defeat would be. "Get off my place!" he yelled. "Get off or we'll shoot you off, law or no law!"

From the other troop, Adam called, "Don't be a fool! When it comes to shooting, we have more guns than you!"

"That's a brave boast, ain't it?" The old man hopped with rage. "Anyways, we'll die shootin' and knifin'. And it'll look nice for those of you that's left, murdering innocent settlers!"

Elmer decided it would not look nice at all, and he was not alone in his feeling. Across the hollow square of the unfinished house, he saw Adam's worried look, and the anxious frowns of his men. You'd suppose all of them had the same uneasy thought: "What if the old lunatic means it? What if he and his bullies prefer bloody murder and suicide to admitting they're licked?" Elmer thought Adam was asking with his eyes for Uncle Jarvis to do something that would smooth matters over. But when he looked, Uncle Jarvis was shaking his head, rue-fully, as if he had run out of ideas.

Old Eagle-face said, "Joshua, you give me that watch!"

One of the black-bearded sons reached into his pocket, with an air of casual pride, and the old man cleared his throat, solemnly. You could see the watch was an important possession which made the Pikes men of substance and refinement.

Still solemnly, the old man laid the silver turnip of a watch on the top log of the barricade, rested his rifle beside it, and swung back the hammer. "Ready, boys!" The click of locks sounded inside the barricade and was echoed along the lines of horsemen outside. It was the end of words, or almost.

"Don't say you didn't have fair warning!" Eagle-face screeched. "I'm warnin' you right now! You got two minutes to get off'n my property alive!"

"Paw." One of the sons facing Adam's troop turned appeal-ingly. "Paw, how we going to know when the two minutes is up?"

"Squeeze your triggers a mite now. When you hear me shoot, your finger'll know what."

"All right, Paw."

"The two minutes has started."

You wouldn't think there could be so much silence anywhere. Everything silence except a horse shifting his weight to rest one foot, and the shrill sound of grasshoppers in the field of hay. A horse blew through his nostrils, as loud as a trumpet. Then there wasn't anything but the shrilling of heartless grass-hoppers. One of the Pikes had leaned his rifle against the unfinished wall, and taken out a Navy revolver. They shoot six times, and the range is point-blank. Elmer balanced his cocked rifle and sweated and thought dream-thoughts. Man is a reasoning animal. Chickens are birds of flight. They can fly over a hen-coop, and come down into the barnyard muck again. Two minutes must be about up. Where does silence come from?

Uncle Jarvis unexpectedly shifted his rifle to his left hand and leaned back in his saddle to pull out his watch. He opened the case and looked and held the watch to his ear. Then he asked, cheerfully, "What time have you, Daniel?"

Old Eagle-face glared his annoyance. "Six minutes to ten," he said. "We start shootin' in a quarter minute."

"Six minutes of!" The big man's voice was full of consternation. "Your watch is slow! It's a minute after."

Daniel said, "What's that to you? We're shootin' you by our time." He looked down at the big silver watch on the log.

"No!" Jarvis said, like a command. "That wouldn't be right. We've got to get this matter of time settled. Look, Dan!"

"I told you." But Daniel glared up, grudgingly.

"Look," Jarvis said, "Daniel, wouldn't it be a shame if twenty men were killed because of a mistake in time?"

"Your mistake was to come onto my property! Git ready, boys."

"We must get this business of time settled," Jarvis insisted. "Surely some one else has a watch! Hasn't any one the time?" He sounded so urgent that Elmer felt in his pocket for a watch he had never possessed.

"*Paw, you old fool!*" The rebellion from outside had blazed up again, and the mean-cut sunbonnet was thrust out of the back of the wagon. "*Paw, there's Indians coming, while he talks you outen your shirt!*"

There were a dozen or twenty Indians riding along the road at a hard gallop: buckskin and white and calico ponies, half-veiled by their cloud of dust. The leader stood out clearly against the dimmed press behind him: A big, heavily built man with a look of repose you could almost feel.

Elmer felt a nudge, and saw Paul leaning toward him. "*It's Leschi!*" He whispered it, but the name was like a great cry.

Elmer looked quickly toward the road again, but it was too late. His view of the leader was cut off by the Pikes' wagons. He was only in time to see the last of Leschi's followers: dim horsemen, flying like shadows through the dusty mist and disappearing behind the covered wagons. . . .

Uncle Jarvis was talking reasonably to Sims. "You see how it is," he said. "You have the whole country raised against you."

The stubborn old eagle was still holding out. "I'd die rather'n be beaten by a nigger!"

Uncle Jarvis laughed. "By God, Dan, I'd like to see any one man who could lick you! But when you throw in all the white settlers and the Indians, it adds up, h'm?"

"It adds up." Sims looked old and beaten. Then his defiance blazed out again. "What about the work we've done?" He gestured in both directions at the unfinished house about him. "We'd be a laughing stock!"

"Humph!" Uncle Jarvis snorted. "A few hours' work with your boys and two yoke of oxen! It wouldn't amount to more than ten dollars."

"You going to pay me the ten dollars?"

Uncle Jarvis winced. "I wasn't thinking of that, or I'd have said five!" Then he smiled like one who has been fairly beaten. "All right, Dan, I'll buy your improvements." He dismounted, with a sigh, and dug into his pocket. Elmer let down the hammer of his rifle, softly, and laid it across his saddle, as the others were doing. The black-bearded Pikes had leaned their rifles against the logs of the unfinished cabin, and were standing about with thumbs hooked through galluses. Sims looked at them, sharply. "Yoke up and get ready to strike out, boys. Tell your Maw to pack."

The young men obeyed sullenly and left the barricade. The gaudy Albert had drifted nearer the Pikes' wagons, and stopped. Maybe his desire for the Pike women was balanced by the fear of what he had glimpsed, and heard. Watching him, Elmer wondered if he shouldn't find Lisette, and say something to her. Only he didn't know what he could say. And he didn't think the eviction would sweeten anything she might say to him. He stayed where he was.

More happened that day than the sprouting of dragon's teeth
in Rush's fields. It was a day which brought three men closer
to the earth; at least, it brought them closer to the realization
of that bond. Actually, weeks before, in Washington, new
voices from the Far West had brought up the name of George
Rush, along with unanswerable questions. Months afterward,
news arrived in Olympia of a special Act of Congress. The Act
was in recognition of a man's service to a migration, and it
gave Rush and his heirs the right to hold land forever. But the
men in the hayfield had no way of knowing that. Warm flesh
and blood had filled the gap of the law's delay, until the law
caught up with them and made their judgment a part of America.

The second man who was drawn more closely to his native
earth was Leschi. Elmer had seen him in the process, without
understanding. That was after the feast in celebration of their
victory over the Pikes. Elmer and the brothers from New
Jersey lay in the shade, too full for anything but the bright,
impossible plans of youth. Occasionally, one of them raised his
head to look at the sunlit world, which, like the boys under
the tree, was in its youth. And everything in that young, victorious world was good: the Conestoga wagons of the Pikes
lurching away to the north, followed by big horsemen with the
loose stock; cattle and sheep grazing in fields which the boys
had defended; a cornfield, from close to the ground like a
Lilliputian forest, and three giants, clear-cut against the spring
sky, with their knees among the tree-tops of growing corn.

Uncle Jarvis and Rush and Leschi were making a tour of
inspection, as farmers do when they visit each other. From
time to time Elmer glimpsed them, and lost them, and saw them
again. Once he saw them standing at a fence, with their backs
toward him, looking at the grazing stock. Once he saw them in
the cornfield. Later they were in the kitchen garden, near enough
for him to hear their voices. He did not understand the language they were speaking, but he knew that Rush was explaining to Leschi how you care for a garden. Leschi asked about
everything, and sometimes Uncle Jarvis added some fine point.
The great Nisqually listened, with his piercing eyes fixed and
an unforgetting look on his splendid, homely face.

Once Rush knelt on the cultivated soil and scooped away the dry, loose surface to show the moisture underneath. Leschi and Uncle Jarvis squatted beside him; the Negro and the Indian and the white man. Each of them took some of the soil in his hand and looked at it; the earth of which all of them were made. And the boy, who was watching them, saw that the sun and the growing things and the earth knew no difference in the color of their skins. He was just as sure his uncle felt no difference, either, and he envied him that quality.

When every one else had gone home, the three friends went on with their talk beside the fire, and Elmer saw Leschi close. The Indian sat on the earth floor at the right of the fireplace, and Elmer on the left. Between them, the other two sat in chairs: Rush leaning forward, with elbows on knees, looking softly into the fire. Uncle Jarvis had taken off his moccasins and socks for comfort, and he sat on the edge of his chair with his naked feet extended and his shoulders back so he was all in a straight line. Stirring his gray tangle of hair with one hand and watching the starlike sparks of the fire, he looked like a Titan, launched feet-first through space and contemplating the universe as it went by.

Mostly the boy watched Leschi and listened to his voice. The Indian was not as big as Uncle Jarvis, but he was powerfully built, with a beautiful homely face and a great sloping forehead; the largest forehead the boy had ever seen. But that was only part of Leschi: a powerful body and a homely face you never tired of watching, and a huge brain. Behind those things was something you trusted as you would trust the earth.

Leschi did most of the talking that evening, and all of the talk was in Nisqually. It was a language the boy did not understand, but he found himself listening to everything the Indian said. And it was only true in a way that he did not understand. Leschi seemed to have some trick of using words so that they were less like words than the things they stood for. While he talked, he made a building motion with his hand, so you could almost see a structure taking shape. While new words were being added, like blocks of stone, you could still feel the presence of the earlier ones, as if no word were lost.

When they were riding home in the starlight, Elmer commented on the Indian's speech.

Uncle Jarvis said, "It's a gift, h'm?" Then he said, "You were listening to the greatest orator on the coast."

"Was I?" Though he was ready to believe it.

"Comparisons are never quite true," his uncle said, "but Judge Black in Olympia swears that Leschi is the best he ever heard anywhere. That's high praise from a man who's listened to Clay and Webster, h'm?"

Elmer thought it was.

"D'ye ever read Rousseau?"

He never had.

"Don't believe him, if you do. You can see him, with tears as big as horse-buns rolling down his cheeks, yearning for the life of the noble savage. Natives aren't noble savages; white men aren't either. But if you live long enough, or are lucky when you're young, you may find yourself in the presence of nobility, h'm? You were tonight, only you didn't understand the language."

"What was Leschi saying?"

Uncle Jarvis said, "He was making all of us the gift of peace. That's a fine thing in itself, but to properly appreciate the gift, you have to think over his experience with our alien tribe. Remember he met the McAllister party on the Cowlitz, with gifts, and persuaded them to come up here, and he helped build the Military Road over the mountains to make the way easier for new settlers, h'm? Well, there've been more settlers than he dreamed of, and the Pikes, whom he hadn't foreseen. Like Rousseau, in a way, he'd imagined all of us as noble savages. In return for his more than brotherly welcome he's seen the hunting and grazing lands encroached on, and enough of his people debauched. He's seen his fine sister used and thrown aside like a common whore. He's seen his father running on all fours and howling his mortification. It would be hard, you'd suppose, for a man to think justly while he listened to the howling of a dog that had once been a man who'd been his father, h'm?"

The boy shivered and looked up at the river of sky and stars that followed the Oregon Trail through the woods. "I don't see how he could think at all!"

"He was in a position where he had to think, and, out of filial respect, he couldn't very well shoot the old man, h'm?" After a while, he said, "You'll notice that Leschi is more mature than his father. Pinch a baby, and it'll yell and kick in all directions, but the mature man takes the knife out of his heart with no irrelevant gestures.

"Leschi has gone on from things as they are. He doesn't hate all of us because some of us have wronged him. And he still believes his people can learn from us. But, with another migration already on the plains, he knows it's time for someone's mind to scout ahead and keep all of us from going over the precipice. Since Americans have no taste for planning their future, he's done the scouting, and found a way around the precipice. At his own expense."

Elmer asked, "How do you mean?" He was getting sleepy, but he didn't want his uncle to think he had fallen asleep listening to his big voice in the wilderness.

"I mean the Nisquallys could lay honest claim to half a million or so acres of land, and make a good show of defending it. But, as Leschi said tonight, peace is as real as land, and without peace land is only a dream. He isn't concerned with the maximum of what his people can claim, but with the minimum of what they need. And so that all of us can go on in orderly peace, he's decided to put himself and his people on a reservation."

"A reservation!" Elmer said. "Is it necessary?"

"Probably not this year," his uncle admitted. "But Leschi is thinking of other years, h'm? He's too proud to use the word 'reservation,' but he's seen the handwriting on the wall. That's why he proposed giving up a whole county in return for title to a few thousand acres. As he sketched the reservation, it comes to about fifty acres of land for each Indian. That's modest, h'm, when a single settler is allowed five hundred?"

Elmer felt cheated. "Fifty acres." He said it in a tone of personal loss. "Will the Indians stand for it?"

"When Leschi proposes it, yes. Until now, they've only dug camas and wild sunflower roots. Leschi wants them to learn how to grow everything. That way, when the big prairie is ploughed under and the game killed, they'll still be able to feed themselves."

"I saw him going around with you at Rush's," Elmer said.

"That was Leschi's first lesson. In the fall, he wants one of us to teach him to hold a plough."

CHAPTER SEVEN

═══════

*T*HE THIRD man who drew closer to the earth was Elmer. That day at Rush's decided him. The day and the friends he found and the corner he made for himself in the minds of men who had been strangers. Next day he had gone to Olympia and filed on a claim across the Inlet from his uncle's.

Elmer was never the same person afterward. Whether he became someone else or became himself at last, he did not know, and he had no time to find out. He'd supposed that securing a claim was a disproportionate matter of receiving five hundred acres in return for a signature at the land office. He learned better, even while he was galloping home. Home? Even that had changed, along with everything else in his life. His home was no longer at his uncle's. It was across the Inlet, on his five hundred beautiful acres. And his house wasn't built, or land cleared for a garden and orchard. The place hadn't been touched since the beginning of time, and he had only a few hours of daylight to get home and make a start. While the gray gelding thundered over the bad road, Elmer mourned for the lost week of his youth, which he had spent in visiting when he should have been working on his claim. After a few minutes he forgot to mourn; he was lost in planning how he should make a start, and in reckoning how much he would have done by the time darkness overtook him. He urged the gray into a harder gallop, to help make up for the inertia of five thousand years of untouched wilderness.

So, at the land office, you give much more than your signature in return for your five hundred lovely acres. You give yourself, passionately, to the country and the earth.

Because he was living, now, Elmer had no time to think about himself. He no longer lay in bed in the morning, but dragged out his muscle-sore limbs as soon as he woke. Now he thought of food only at mealtime, and not always then. Twice in one day he was too occupied to see the flag hoisted on the other side of the Inlet, and he had to be reminded by the stern firing of a gun. Since then, he had taken a lunch with him in the morning, and tried to keep an eye open for the supper flag, which was always hoisted too soon.

This evening, though, Elmer mended his ways. Sawing a length from a fallen dead cedar, he kept his eye on the cabin across the Inlet. When he saw Mary come out with the night-shirt-flag in her arms, he left his saw in the cut and climbed down the high bank to his beautiful gravel beach. His saw was almost through the five-foot log, and a few more strokes—but he was on his good behavior. He eased the borrowed dugout into the clear water and pushed off. If he could have arranged it, he would have rowed to his uncle's and paddled back. Then he would never have to take his eyes off his new house. It was the most beautiful house on the Sound: twelve by sixteen feet, made of clean peeled fir logs. It had a cat-and-clay chimney, three windows and a door. Three windows were an extravagance, but the house deserved them, and there were other advantages. More windows meant shorter logs, which were easier to handle. Many of them Elmer had lifted into place without assistance; he could point out every one.

Looking back over his shoulder, the boy admitted that his house would look even more beautiful when it had a roof. But if any one criticized that lack, let him come around tomorrow evening! What about those poles, ready for shakes? What about that drum of cedar, almost cut from the big windfall log?

Elmer was going to supper on time for a very good reason. This was to be his first night in his own house. By getting to supper on time and hurrying back, he would have two hours of daylight to make his house even more beautiful and complete. From the first night he possessed his land, the boy would have slept there in a blanket, under what shelter he could manage, but Uncle Jarvis would not hear of it. He swore that the place was a wilderness of cougars, which was a great exaggeration; sometimes Elmer worked all day without seeing one. But when Uncle Jarvis said "no," it was like an elephant sitting down on you. Elmer agreed to sleep on the other side of the water from his desire until he had walls to protect him, and a door and windows to keep out wild beasts. Nothing had been specified about a roof over his head, so he won out on that point, with the provision that he take one of the dogs to make up for the temporary lack.

At his uncle's table there was boiled ham in place of dry and tiresome venison, and kalse roots which had baked underground for three days. Mary encouraged his appetite by stroking her hand downward along her stomach and saying, *"Muck-a-muck, Elmer!"* It was a good dinner and his appetite needed no urging, but his mind was never quite present, and the food he ate was shadowy.

He lingered a minute, out of politeness. Then he said, *"Spose nika klatawa. Klahowya,* Mary!" He was beginning to get the hang of Jargon through marriage with the land in which it had grown.

When he got up to go, Uncle Jarvis whistled for the dogs, and helped him carry his gear to the canoe. "You're so Goddamned energetic," he grumbled. "You'll ruin this country!" Then he said, "I'll be over tomorrow and help you make shakes. Maybe we'll get some of the roof on, h'm?"

"I thank you," Elmer said, putting things in the canoe.

"Here, Wolf!" The big mongrel jumped into the canoe and stood in the bow, with the alert air of a lookout. He was obedient only because he enjoyed travelling in a canoe. Wolf was a native dog and, like his kind, he had no sentimental or friendly traits. Perhaps, to be a success, he had to be a little more savage than the bear and cougar that he hunted. Uncle Jarvis said, "I'll put the bacon in the stern. The brute may not think it worth while to knock you overboard to get it. Think you'll make out all right?"

Elmer said, "I'll make out fine. If I need protection from your dog, I'll catch me a cougar!"

"Catch a big one!" Uncle Jarvis said, pushing off the loaded canoe.

Companionship was warming, but the boy felt no lack of anything as he paddled away from his uncle and the shore. His life was too full for him to need any one. Ahead of him, across the glassy water, he saw the unexplored, high shore of his own kingdom. The logs of his new house caught the sunset light and shone as if they were really made of gold. The great trees behind it were green-gold, like some enchanted forest, and above them, a few points to the south, an incredible dome of snow floated in the sky, pink in the sunset and touched with blue shadows. Mount Rainier would be there forever, and his relationship to that eternal landmark had been defined in the land to which he had come home.

When Elmer landed on his own shore, he felt even more content. The wolfish dog sprang out of the canoe without a backward look, and went exploring on his own. In peace, the boy lugged his supplies up to the house. When everything was inside, he latched the new plank door and hurried to the cedar log.

He counted twenty-one strokes of the saw, one for each year of his life. Then the severed block trembled and settled closer to the ground. He put his shoulder against the bleached, stringy bark, laughing silently at the lightness of the great cedar drum which he rolled out of the tree and upset among the ferns. The heart of the drum had been hollowed out by dry rot, but the rest of the dull, reddish wood was perfectly seasoned and sound. Four blows of the ax split the drum like a ripe pumpkin. A dozen more split it into as many convenient bolts. And each blow of the ax released more of the imprisoned fragrance of a thousand summers. He had never known such wood, and laughed at the ease of its splitting. At the same time, he was at a loss. The work he had expected to do in an hour hadn't taken ten minutes. The bolts were ready, and his uncle wouldn't be there until morning to show him how shakes are made.

He knew that shakes are made with the tool called a froe,

which his uncle had put in the canoe. He hurried to the house, where it was already dusk, and found the implement among the blankets and equipment on the floor. The place looked untidy, but while the summer daylight lingered outside he could not bring himself to put one thing in place. Housekeeping could wait. It was enough now to latch the door against Wolf's return.

The froe was an L-shaped tool, with a wooden handle for its vertical, and a steel blade with a wedge-shaped section for the horizontal. The blade's thick back was dented, showing how it had been used. Elmer set the blade near the edge of an upright bolt, following the grain, and struck its back with the back of the ax. The wood split part way and by prying on the handle he detached something that resembled a shake. But it was not a good shake; it was bulged in the middle, and of irregular thickness. The next bulged still more, and was spoiled by a dead knot which made a hole through it. The third was still worse.

It looked as if the art of making shakes required a teacher, but he must try once more. He set the blade across the grain of the wood, half an inch from the edge of the bolt, and struck it with the back of the ax. "Pop!" A piece of wood flew off as if it had never really belonged there. He picked it up and looked at it. He was holding a shake as flat as a board except for little crinkles on its surface. When the edges were trimmed, it would be perfect! He tried again: one blow, and a shake as perfect flew off the bolt. The third was the same, except that he had not set the blade quite true. The fourth was perfect, and he kept on until the bolt vanished into the summer air which was rich with the smell of cedar and trampled ferns.

He upended the next bolt, and attacked it with froe and ax while the shakes popped and flew and piled up about him. He went on in a kind of frenzy, attacking bolt after bolt. In the deepening dusk he had to peer down and feel to set the froe. The bolt he was working on split in two and vanished, and he had to feel with his foot for another. There was none. He was standing alone before a mountain of beautiful shakes, enough for a whole roof! Because he did not know how it had happened and could not quite believe it, he sat down suddenly. He was not conscious of having done any work, but he was panting and hot with sweat. Resting a minute, he put an arm on the fragrant shakes, and felt their even, crinkled surface with his hand. Undoubtedly, this miracle was in the wood, and he was no longer mystified by the plank houses of the Siwashes. It was no more than natural when they had great cedar trees which split, even and true, at not much more than a sharp glance.

In a minute he was on his feet again, wrestling with the desire to start putting on the roof when the moon came up. He gave up the idea, reluctantly, because his house deserved the best, and moonlight carpentry was sure to look less perfect by day. Then he found comfort in the fact that the shakes still needed their edges trimmed. That was something he could do at night. He gathered up a tremendous armful and stumbled carefully to the house, which he found in darkness. Beautiful, patient house, waiting for him in the dark. He tripped over something inside, and shakes fell, clattering, from the top of his load. His barked shin stung, but the mishap did not change his sentiments. It was his housekeeping and not the house which was at fault.

Everything went smoothly again when he had started a fire. He was able to see his way around the equipment on the floor. And, when he was outside, the lighted window guided him. Also, it was beautiful, shining for the first time. He stopped to admire it on each trip to the shake pile. "There is a new window lighted in the world," he told himself. "Some one has begun living." He even pretended to wonder who the fortunate person might be. Once he went to the window and looked in. He saw only the bright fire burning alone in the beautiful barren house, and the litter of belongings on the earth floor. It gave him a ghostly feeling, and he did not make the experiment again.

He carried all the shakes inside and piled them neatly against the wall. They deserved to be treated with respect, and he wanted to have them indoors in case of rain. Looking up, he saw stars between the bare poles overhead and the smoke from his chimney going up, innocently, into the dark sky. He'd forgotten for a moment that his house had no roof. As soon as the shakes were on—but it was the shakes he had planned to protect! Well, he couldn't think of everything at once.

Trimming shakes was a job which helped itself along. He sat on an upturned bucket near the fireplace and held each shake between his knees while he sliced the edges with his uncle's draw-knife. When the shavings got in his way, he gathered them up and threw them on the fire. The fire blazed up and gave him better light for the next batch.

He was content, working indoors, until the darkness outside the east window began to dissolve. Then he became restless with a strange, expectant delight, and put his work aside. That was an in-between while, with the square of window trembling between darkness and light. He could not yet do anything useful outdoors, and he was no longer satisfied with trimming shakes by the fire. He compromised by picking up his scattered belongings and arranging them neatly. When he found the hammer, he drove two nails in the log above the fireplace and rested his rifle in their square, rigid little arms. The place immediately looked more like home, and he hung up the powder horn and bullet pouch to keep the rifle company. Because of Wolf, who was barking distantly in the woods, he drove another nail, as high as he could reach, and hung up his slab of bacon. He hung the frying pan and skillet near the fireplace, filled the coffee pot with water from the bucket, and set it by the fire. Then he folded his blankets neatly.

All he needed now was a bed, and the magic splitting of the cedar had given him ideas for that. In another day or two he would have a beautiful bunk, made out of boards which he would make. It would have lockers, such as the officers had under their berths on board ship. All he needed tonight was a mattress on the floor.

East of the house there was a golden light, like a fire burning in the blackness of the forest. He stood, with the dew settling on his hands and upraised face, and watched the coming of the light. This belonged to his bargain with the land office; a bargain in which he received, and gave, so much more than was written. He had the assurance that, forever, the moon in summer would rise through this same part of the forest. And he would be here to welcome it as long as he had nostrils for the loveliness of the night air, and eyes to see.

While he watched, a shaft of moonlight found a straight path among the intricate trees. It reached the edge of his tiny clearing and glimmered on round, shiny leaves. Struck by that shaft of beauty, the coarse salal looked like a shrub of silver growing in the night. The rising moon found more loopholes and slanted down its paths of light on fallen trees and ferns and rhododendrons with long, polished leaves and clusters of pale blossoms.

Because he had come out for a purpose, the boy stirred and began gathering ferns for his bed. He combined beauty with usefulness, breaking off the tops of ferns that were growing in the moonlight and collecting their springy, branching leaves. Their cool enchanting fragrance filled him with a restless, unformed excitement. On such a night, and such a bed— But life was already complete.

When he went in, the fire on the hearth had burned down, but the room was not dark. Roofed with nothing but five naked poles, it let in an avalanche of moonlight which was not pleasing because it was unsuitable. It was moonlight out of place, and it suggested a house in ruins, with the roof fallen in. Elmer did not feel like lingering after he had spread the ferns near the hearth. He stayed only long enough to touch his stack of new shakes for reassurance, and he promised himself that the moon would never mock his beautiful house again.

Outside, where the moonlight belonged, he had no more resentment, and his eyes and swelling nostrils drank in the enchanted night. This moonlight and this part of the earth and these woods belonged to him. And he belonged to them and would keep faith with them as long as he lived.

He gathered more ferns, absently, with his earlier feeling of hurry gone. While he worked, he was under the spell of the dew on gleaming leaves about him, and pools of mysterious brightness in the woods, where Wolf's profane voice was baying, and where there was so much darkness, and so much light.

Carrying his second armful of ferns to the house, he froze at
a light, rushing sound. A spotted fawn bounded through his
clearing, alive with speed and wild loveliness. It was like one
flying glimpse of moonlight changed into young flesh and
blood; then it was gone into the woods on the other side. The
boy was still looking after it when Wolf came baying through
the clearing, a dark, evil beast, in hot pursuit. The boy shouted
and whistled after him, but the dog did not seem to remember
the voice of man, or recognize the clearing as anything but a
moment of open space in the savage wilderness through which
he raved. They were both gone, the hunted and the hunter, and
Elmer heard the sound of the chase dying away through the
moonlit woods.

"The beast!" he muttered, and went indoors with the ferns
for his bed. He was ashamed of the dog, but could not change
its wolfish nature.

The house was still full of unsuitable moonlight, which
shone on the earth floor and reduced the place to a lonely shell.
He spread his blankets on the ferns and built up the fire with
fir limbs, and went out. If the moon would not let him stay in
his own house, he would make it work for him outdoors. He
took a grub-hoe and began digging up the ground between the
stumps in the place he had chosen for a garden. Some day he
would dig and burn out the stumps themselves, so the ground
could be ploughed. But, until then, he would do as others did
on forest claims, and cultivate with a hoe.

Every blow broke land which had not been disturbed since the
beginning of time. Every root he grubbed out was a victorious
skirmish with the wilderness; a root that would never grow
again. He made certain of that by shaking the earth carefully
from each one. And when he had enough for an armful, he
carried them to the western boundary of his kingdom, and threw
them over the bank, where a high tide would carry them away.

"Don't you roots come bothering around my place any
more!" he warned them.

He was death on alien roots in his garden, and kind to the
earth. He cultivated deep, and when he could find no more
roots with the grub-hoe, he put his hand in the earth and felt

for strands he might have overlooked. Finding one and tugging it out made that part of his land more perfect forever. And, afterward, there was the satisfaction of moving his arm deep in the earth while the loose soil flowed past his hand, and the last damp clods crumbled between his fingers.

Several times he told himself he had done enough for one night, but he did not quit until the moon was setting behind the great firs on his uncle's shore. Then he realized he was tired. Probably he was very tired, but his time hadn't been wasted. From this night he had snatched a piece of cultivated land about twenty feet square. There were stumps in it, to be sure, but between the stumps the earth was tamed forever. From now on, Elmer would have the say about what grew there. "From now on," he told himself, stumbling to the house.

Wolf, too, had decided to call it a day. While the boy was coaxing the fire into life again, he scratched at the closed door and barked impatiently. Elmer let him in because he still had the habit, from shipboard days, of taking orders. A minute later he regretted it. Wolf drank noisily from the water pail, turned a complete circle on the bed and settled himself in the middle of it, with a dog yawn.

"Hey, that's my bed," Elmer said.

The dog ignored him.

"I'll be there in about one minute," Elmer promised him. He put more wood on the fire, and sat on the upturned bucket to take off his shoes. When he had them off, he was so stiff and tired that he could hardly get up again. Bed had never looked so inviting, and he wasn't going to be cheated out of it by a dog. "Wolf, get up!"

The dog opened his eyes and gave the boy a cold, unsympathetic look.

"Get out, you brute!" He gave the bed a push with his foot —and jumped back. Wolf had not got up, but lunged his head forward, snarling, with all his big fangs showing. He looked more like a mad wolf than a friend of man. But then, he was not a friend of man. He was a native dog, and he and man put up with each other to a certain extent because they found it convenient. Elmer had forgotten that for a minute, and he had forgotten the etiquette of ordering one of the brutes about. He opened the door and went back to the fire, where he picked out a fir limb with one end blazing and the other not too hot to hold. He put the firebrand in front of the dog's face, closer and closer. "Get out, you brute!"

Wolf got up, reluctantly, with his black lips clear of his fangs, and the light of murder glaring from his eyes. Snarling, he allowed himself to be backed out of the door, which Elmer slammed in his face.

"The brute!" Elmer put the brand back on the fire and crawled into his hard-won bed. "The brute," he said, and fell asleep.

He fell into the profound depths of sleep, and could not wake, even when the devil of a racket broke out wherever he was. He could not wake, though he could not help hearing some of it. It was Wolf, the brute, raving outside; trying to bark the door down. Let him bark. He was trying to climb up the side of the house. Let him climb, and break his neck! It sounded as if he had made it. The noise of his claws stopped overhead, while his barking raged on. He was going to jump down into the room. Let him jump, and try to get the bed! Elmer was ready for him, holding the blankets against all comers. Wolf had jumped. His tail slapped the boy across the face, like a soft rope, as he thudded down. He could stay inside if he found a bed of his own. Probably he had, because Elmer was undisturbed, except for the horrible din of noise. Wolf, the brute, clawing outside the door and trying to bark it down. No, Wolf's inside. Can't help it, he's outside, too.

Elmer had no interest in the mystery, but he would never be able to sleep in comfort, besieged by pandemonium. He made a supreme effort, and opened his eyes. He must have slept for more than a minute, after all. The fire had burned down to a few coals, and the room was in darkness, under the night sky. Wolf, the brute, was going mad outside. The part about his climbing the side of the house and jumping in had been a dream. One Wolf, inside or out, was too many. Have to stop his noise, somehow. Build up the fire. No kindling. Have to use one of the new shakes. Too bad, shakes.

He stumbled toward the pile of shakes, and was shocked by a spitting snarl that stopped his heart and nearly wrenched his ears off. That, and two glaring eyes that his fright enlarged to the size of moons. No shakes, with that crouching behind the pile! He backed away to the fireplace, with its few dying coals, and blessed himself for having put the rifle where he could find it. He cocked the rifle, and backed close to the door, with Wolf going mad on the other side. If the rifle misses fire, get outside. Better get out, anyway, as soon as the trigger's pulled.

It was too dark to see the sights, but at a distance of twelve feet he should be able to hit something. Then he made out the front sight against a glaring eye, and pressed the trigger. The rifle banged and kicked, and he threw open the door as the room disappeared in powder smoke. He threw open the door to get out, and was knocked down. He should have worried more about the dog, and less about the cougar, but he scrambled out, somehow, and began reloading his rifle. Shakes were clattering inside the house, and Wolf was making a worrying growl. The sound was reassuring. He was ramming a bullet home, when the dog came out quietly and stood beside him, as if to say everything was in order.

"Good dog," he said, and they went into the house together. They went into the house, but Elmer did not venture too near what had been the shake pile until he had rekindled the fire with one of the scattered pieces of cedar, and started a blaze in a pitchy limb. Then he saw there wasn't anything to be afraid of, and he pulled the cougar out into the room by the tail which had slapped across his face in his sleep. Its length was two thirds the width of the room, which made it about eight feet, and his bullet had gone through one eye.

They both looked at it for a minute, then Wolf lost interest, and turned away. Elmer looked at it a minute more. In the morning he would skin it and nail the hide on the wall to dry for a rug. Summer fur, but it was a fine big cougar, with a head like a great cat, only nobler and more graceful. The cougar was big, and it wasn't. Eight feet long, and about six inches wide. Lying dead on its side, it looked like something that had been planned in only two dimensions; a shadow thick-

ened as an afterthought. Studying it, he could see that it had
been planned as a kind of shadow. A shadow that could flit
through narrow places, silently, on great soft paws that made
no sound when their curved daggers were drawn in. A shadow
that could hide its eight feet of tigerish power and sharpness
behind a six-inch sapling. A beautiful, strange thing, with a
kind of trick to the planning of it. He would look at it again in
the morning. It must be nearly morning now. He was falling
asleep on his feet, and Wolf, who had seen any number of
cougars at close range, had taken the opportunity to curl up on
the bed.

Regretfully, Elmer went to the fireplace for another brand,
and held it under the dog's nose. Snarling, Wolf got up and
backed away, to settle himself sullenly on the floor. With that
truce arranged between them, the boy tossed the smoking stick
back into the fireplace, and crawled between the blankets, and
was asleep.

CHAPTER EIGHT

THE AUTUMN rains began the day of Elmer's wooing.
It was his own fault, in a way; he should have taken time off
earlier. But how was he to know? Wooing is one of those
things that happen. He hadn't known it would happen to him.
Or maybe he hadn't let himself know. Anyway, he'd made a
mess of it. Riding through the mud of the Oregon Trail, he
swore nautical oaths and made gestures of disdain to ward off
his humiliation from himself.

He'd expected to find the girl who was intended for him
some day, of course. As far back as he could remember, Elmer
had had the girl in mind, though he'd never seen her. Until he
made his voyage around the Horn, he'd assumed she lived in
Massachusetts. That must have been a mistake, though, since
he was destined to marry in Washington Territory. He couldn't
bring himself to admit that the change of location might also
have changed the identity of the girl. There could be only one.
And, wherever he was, she had to be the one he had dreamed
of in boyhood.

She was associated with wild white morning-glories. The
first time he ever saw her clearly was on a spring morning at
home. He was driving the cows to the pasture, and dew was
silvery on the grass, giving it a virginal sheen on which no
one had ever walked before. There were wild white morning-
glories growing on a stone fence. While he saw them with his
eyes, his mind saw the girl whom he would some day meet and
love. He saw her for only a flash of time, but he saw her
clearly and would recognize her when they met at last. She

was coming toward him, as if from a crowd, wearing a long white party dress. She had soft, dark brown hair and fair skin, flushed with pink, and dark, answering eyes. She had recognized him while she was in a crowd of people and was coming to meet him as she vanished, leaving nothing but a spray of wild white morning-glories on the stone fence of the cow pasture.

That is what you dream. The reality is something else. So far today, Elmer had asked four different girls to marry him. Not that he cared anything about them. To hell with them! He made a gesture of disdain, riding on through the mud and drizzle toward Olympia. Anyway, their refusal was no reflection on him. Two of them, he had learned, were already married, and the others were about to be. Under the circumstances, they had to refuse him. Their refusals had been tinged with regret, he was convinced of that. Sally Brown had said, "Oh, why didn't you—" and then put her hand over her mouth. You didn't have to hear the rest to know she had started to say, "Why didn't you come around earlier?" Which was just what he should have done. And the burst of family laughter he heard when he was riding away probably had nothing to do with him. Margaret Burton had said, "You poor boy!" Which was just like saying, "I wouldn't have disappointed you if you had come around last week!" It also showed she had a good opinion of herself. Well, she hadn't been asked for pity. She meant nothing to him, and, to hell with her! Probably, when he was riding away, he had only imagined the sound of laughter, though the imagination was enough to make his ears glow in the drizzling rain. And Elmira—. To hell with Elmira! He made such a gesture of disdain that the tired gelding looked around to see what he was throwing into the bushes beside the road. Constance—. He hadn't caught her last name. Constance whoever-she-was. He didn't have anything against her. She was just a scared little girl, waiting for the minister and the young settler who was going to marry her. And her widowed mother had been very nice to Elmer, making him comfortable and encouraging him to stay when there wasn't anything to stay for. When she was being sorry for him, she was sorry for herself, so he couldn't hold that against her. She had put her hand on his arm and said, "I know how you feel, with no one to hug at night. I'm only thirty-three. Most people think I look younger. Augustus was just your size. . . ." In that whirl of confusion, words had bounced off, with their meaning lost. But now he decided the widow had caught some of the excitement. Probably she was hoping some older man would come along in search of a wife. But that had nothing to do with him, and he had made a mess of things.

Elmer had made a mess of things because he didn't know himself well enough; he hadn't foreseen what he would do when the time came. At least, that was one of his stories. For weeks, he knew, young men had been scurrying about in search of wives. He had known that without catching the excitement; not until the inconvenient eleventh hour. He had told himself he didn't approve of marrying in haste for the sake of an extra few hundred acres from the expiring Pre-emption Claim Act. He had been scornful of a two-weeks' courtship—and was condemned to do his courting in a day. That was one of Elmer's stories. It was true, but it was not the whole truth.

The other story was that he intended all along to get himself a wife and the land to the south of his, but he had been in bondage to his house and the land he already had. His house had been like a first wife, demanding that he fulfill his promises to her before courting another, and when a house commands, you obey.

Obediently, he had built a wide berth out of split cedar boards, smoothed with a draw-knife. He made lockers under the berth, ship style, and furniture from more hand-cut boards. When that was done, his house demanded company: a woodshed, to warm its heart, and a barn for visiting or borrowed horses, and for the horse Elmer might buy. The barn was also to shelter the larger tools and implements to which the house objected.

Being feminine, the house accepted a lesser version of the fine things it had demanded. It was satisfied with a woodshed-barn, but it had other ideas. "If you expect us to be happy this winter," it said, "you must lay in a supply of food. And

not the kind you buy, either. Your uncle says the salmon will
be running before long. That means you must have a smokehouse ready. And while you are waiting for the salmon, you
might try curing hams of venison the way your Grandmother
Hale used to do with mutton hams." Now, Elmer had a tall
smokehouse, waiting for the salmon run. And, while it waited,
the smoke of green alder oozed out of cracks between the shakes.
Inside there were mellowing four venison hams which had been
pickled the proper length of time and rolled in coarse flour from
Crosby's Mill.

One way and another, the house worked Elmer like a slave,
when he might have been courting. He could not complain
because ·it was a beautiful house, with sound ideas, and for
everything he did for it the house repaid him in full. The
house was just, too. And it was not altogether just to say
that the house prevented him from courting. It delayed him
until he had done what was necessary, but it also urged him on,
slyly. The house suggested that the barn would not be much
use without a road, or at least a trail. That led him to hack a
trail along the Inlet to its head, where it joined his uncle's
road. That road, in turn, connected with the Oregon Trail,
which connects with all the highways of America. Cutting the
trail delayed his finding a bride, but it provided a means of
bringing her home. And the trail did more. It led him through
the five hundred acres which would be the dowry of his bride,
if he found one in time. It led him through fir and cedar timber,
as fine as his own, and rich alder-bottom land which would be
easy to clear and profoundly fertile. And it led him across a
beautiful little creek, bordered with salmon-berry bushes and
bleeding hearts and maidenhair ferns. The creek was ten feet
wide, and at the riffles it was only a few inches deep, but its
gravel bed and flowering banks were littered with the year-old
bones of fish half a fathom long. In a few more weeks it would
be choked with salmon driving inland to spawn. Before the
trail had reached the outside world, it connected him with a
great food supply which would be a part of his wife's dowry.

So, while house and land delayed his wooing, they finally
urged him on his way and sent him out with greater determi-

nation. The only trouble was that they were forgetful about time and left him only two days for wooing. Only one day, really. Elmer knew that if he went home tonight with his humiliation, he would not have the courage to start again tomorrow.

Except for pride, he would give it up and go home now. He would do that if he could wipe out the memory of his rebuffs. But the best he could do was to keep his humiliation at arm's length with disdainful gestures. And, if he could wipe those memories out of his mind, would the four young women forget? More likely, every time they saw or thought of him, they would say, "You poor boy!" If he didn't go home with a wife, he had better not go home at all. There wasn't anything for it but to go on.

Thanks to his house and land delaying him, Elmer had made a mess of his wooing, but he hadn't tackled the thing entirely without plan. In the morning he had gone to Nisqually, where he started proposing, and he worked southwest, toward Olympia. That way, as the day progressed, he moved nearer the land office. It was a good plan of campaign if it had worked. Even though it hadn't, he was condemned to follow it.

Elmer's next port of call was the Sawyer place, about three miles farther on. The Sawyers had plenty of daughters, four or five, Elmer thought, and some of them were of marrying age, if they weren't already married. He'd met Jane in Olympia with her father, and she looked nice. Probably the others were nice, too, if they weren't married. If they were, to hell with them. He made another gesture of disdain to ward off humiliation in advance.

There was nothing between here and the Sawyer place, and the afternoon was getting on. He touched the gray gelding with his heels, and sent him at a thudding gallop over the rough road in the drizzling rain. Nothing here; this part of the world is a blank. Whoa! Wait a minute! One eye had caught the naked flash of peeled logs which hadn't been there the last time he passed this way. Peeled logs and a glimpse of a new shake roof, and a curl of smoke in the wet air. Off to the right there was a new house which meant that some new family had settled there, and they might have daughters.

Elmer swerved his horse into the new little road that cut through Oregon grape and stunted salal. He was leaving no stone unturned today.

It wasn't a bachelor, anyway. With a clear view of the house he saw a woman in the yard. A young woman or a big girl, with her skirts tucked up, splitting wood. He couldn't decide much more about her, except that she had well-shaped legs, and they disappeared when she saw him riding toward the house. She shook the reef out of her skirt and petticoat and went on splitting kindling—more clumsily, he thought, than when he had first seen her. She seemed to become less as he drew nearer: less skillful, and no more well-shaped legs. She became just a woman in dark calico and a damp sunbonnet, splitting kindling.

He halted near the chopping block, and hoped she would quit working before she hurt herself. "Good afternoon," he said.

When she looked up, he saw the thick, black hair under her wilted sunbonnet, the flushed face and strange, sullen eyes. It was the Pike girl, Lisette, whom he hadn't seen since the battle on Rush's farm. She was thinking of the same occasion. "What do you want now?" she demanded, panting. "Are you going to put us off this place, too?"

"No," he said, wondering where the seven black-bearded brothers might be. If they were about, it would be safest for him to keep his horse under him.

She laid the ax on the wet ground. "Why did you come here?"

"I came to see you," he said.

Probably she knew it was not altogether true, but she did not contradict him. "Did you?" she was studying the chopping block so intently that he looked at it, too. The maze of ax-cuts on the block made him think of lines on the palm of a hand. Lisette was studying them as if she were reading some palm to foretell the future.

"I came to see you," Elmer said. He was beginning to believe it himself.

"Did you?" she asked the block.

There was no sound of any one else about, and he dismounted. "Yes," he said.

She looked up, with something distantly amused or mocking in her dark, sullen eyes. "It's a great day for visiting, ain't it?"

"Why?" This was not his first visit of the day, but it hadn't occurred to him that she might have had callers.

"You're the sixth," she said, looking at the block again. "There've been five other young men ahead of you."

"Oh, there have!" he was vaguely displeased, and something else. The insolence of five young men calling on Lisette! He had known her first, and seen her on board ship, before he ever stepped ashore in the Territory. "Five!" he said.

"Yes," she said. "They wanted to marry me."

"They did, eh?" The amount of competition made her strangely desirable, and it gave him a feeling of desperation because others had been ahead of him again. "Did you promise any of them?"

She shook her head, slowly.

He felt relieved, almost too much, and too suddenly. All day he had been battering against a stone wall. Suddenly the wall was gone from in front of him, and so was the ground. He stood, unprepared, at the edge of an abyss.

"I'm not promised to any man," Lisette said.

He said, "I'm glad of that," with his voice sounding strange to himself.

"Why?" It was a husky whisper, which he felt rather than heard.

"I don't want you to marry some one else," he said. "I want you to marry me."

She sat on the chopping block, in the drizzling rain, and looked down at her folded hands.

"I have a fine claim," Elmer said. "It's on salt water, with fine timber." Then he said, "I have a beautiful house, too. It's only a cabin, but I made it myself."

Looking down at her rough hands in her lap, she said, impatiently, "I don't care what you have!"

He made the gesture of disdain which had become a habit only this time it felt more like despair. "Why, Lisette? I've always liked you, and I'm sorry about last time. I couldn't help it——"

When she raised her head, her look was not scornful, but curiously complicated. "You ain't asking me just so you can get more land?" Her voice was pleading.

"I'm asking because I want you," he said. A few minutes ago that would have been a lie, but now it wasn't, altogether. He must have her for refuge against the humiliation and rebuffs of the day, when he had felt so much alone. He didn't want to be alone any more. He had set out to win her, and when he started something he never turned back. "I want you, Lisette."

Looking down at her hands in her lap, she said, "I suppose we might as well get started."

"Where?" He was made dizzy by plans going ahead before he realized he was accepted.

"We'll find a minister in Olympia, I expect."

He moistened his dry lips. "Yes."

"And maybe you'll want to fix things up about your claim," she suggested.

He felt dizzier, and fought with a desire to hug her, out of gratitude. But that would be all wrong. She knew about the five hundred acres; she saw through the whole wretched business, and accepted it. All she demanded in return was for him to pretend it was not so, and she was making it easy for him.

"Oh, I don't know," he said carelessly.

"You wanted to go today, didn't you?" She wasn't sullen any more, and they were friends.

"I think we might as well." Then he asked, "How old are you, Lisette?"

"Seventeen," she said.

"I'm twenty-one," Elmer said. He felt his courage rise. He wasn't alone any more, and he was ready to face the world, or the whole Pike tribe. "Where are all the others?" he asked.

"You mean Uncle Dan, and his boys?"

"The big ones, with the black beards."

"They went on to Eld Inlet, and we stopped here."

His courage rose still more. "Where are your folks?" He would ask for Lisette's hand in marriage, and if they didn't see fit to say "Yes," he would carry her off, anyway.

"You mean Ma and Pa Sims?"

"Yes," he said.

"They're in Olympia, getting married."

Elmer blinked, then he suddenly saw it was funny, and began to laugh.

"It has something to do with his claim." Then Lisette said, "I expect they were each other's punishment for living in sin. Anyway, it's not the way you think. When they were young, there weren't any preachers in Missouri, not many, anyway,. and they got used to doing without. And it didn't matter so much when they didn't have any children."

"What about you?" he asked.

"My folks died on the plains," she said. "The Sims took me in; they were in the same wagon train."

Elmer felt suddenly light, as if the world had just begun, and the troubling things in his mind were gone like a dream. Lisette wasn't a Pike, after all! "Lisette!" he said. "If I had known—" He didn't know what.

"Does it matter?" she asked sullenly.

He had no answer.

"I thought about telling you, that other time."

"You could have."

"No," she said. "It wouldn't have sounded right. It would have seemed like saying I was too good for the people I was with. You ain't ever too good for people who take you in when you haven't any one else."

He felt as if he had been spanked, but it was good to be in the company of passionate loyalty. "I like you, Lisette."

"I'll be ready to go with you when I get dressed," she said. "Better come in where it's dry."

"I thank you," he said.

"Will your horse be all right?"

"Yes." With the bridle reins trailing, the cayuse was as good as picketed. Elmer gathered up the kindling which she had split, and Lisette carried the ax.

When they were near the door, she hesitated. "There's only one room."

He said, "I'll wait outside." It wasn't raining very hard.

"No," she said, "you might catch your death."

"I never catch cold," he boasted.

"You might." She raised the latch with its thong. "You can look at the fire while I get ready."

It came to him, a little at a time, that this was an adventure. Before, he had been too hurried and bewildered to realize much of anything. Life had descended on him like goods dumped into the hold of a ship, with no time to check and stow them. The rush was over, now. He sat at his ease on a bench before the fire. The fire warmed him, and was good. Behind him, in the room which he had never really seen, he heard the rustle of clothes. This was his wedding day, and his bride was dressing to go with him. Lisette. He would have to ask her last name, since it wasn't Sims. There would be time enough for that on the way to Olympia.

Sitting on the bench, looking into the fire, he tried to accustom himself to the idea that he had a bride. Sometimes it seemed almost real, and sometimes it was like a strange dream. He remembered that a man is supposed to kiss the young woman when she says "yes." But it had not been like that— their courtship by the chopping block in the rain. And Lisette hadn't said "yes." She said, "I don't care what you have," which sounded like a refusal. Then she said, "We might as well get started." That was her acceptance. Instead of kissing her, as he should, he asked stupidly, "Where?" It had not gone the way courtships are supposed to, but when it all happens in a few minutes, you can't think of everything. He would remember to kiss her at the first opportunity. Or would she want him to? It sounded like presumption when you remembered he'd only seen her twice before in his life. But when you remembered they were going to be married that afternoon, the presumption seemed much less.

Lisette was a long time getting dressed, and they did not talk during that time. Perhaps she was afraid he might forget and look around while answering her, or maybe she did not feel that conversation was quite proper under the circumstances. And he did not intrude. She took a long time, but he did not mind the delay. His feeling of hurry was gone, and it seemed that he was accomplishing something in just waiting for her. Judging from the sounds, she washed, and spent time brushing her hair, and changed her mind at least once about what she was going to put on. There was also something to mend, he thought, and something that had to be looked for and something that did not go just right. Then there was the sound of firm writing, and at last her voice: "Elmer, what is your last name?"

"Hale," he said, looking dutifully into the fire.

"I thank you." There was more sound of writing.

"I don't believe I know yours," he said.

"Parker." The writing stopped after a few seconds more, and he heard her footsteps, which were strangely light. "I'm ready, now."

He got up and looked at her, dressed as he had never seen her before, in a silk dress and ribboned bonnet. She was perfect! Well, she looked fine, anyway. After his first moment of surprise, he realized the dress was old and not very fashionable. The bonnet wasn't so new, either. But there was a kind of bloom about her. All her life, maybe, she had planned that when the day came she would have beautiful clothes. It hadn't happened that way, but she had expected it so much that now you could almost see the fine things. They weren't there, but they were near enough for you to feel their spell.

"You're pretty!" he said.

"No." But she was pleased. And she did look fine. Her face was pale with excitement, and it made her thick hair and shining eyes look darker than ever. She was alive with a mysterious bloom of excitement which made him feel unimportant, though he had awakened it.

"You are pretty, Lisette!"

She shook her head. "I'm not pretty."

"You are." He put his arms around her and gave her a quick kiss. As a kiss, it was not very satisfactory, but he felt the surge of some response in her strong young body, and her mouth brushed the side of his face, unskillfully. He would have liked to try again, but she slipped out of his arms.

"Now we must go," she said. She put on an old gray pelisse and took up a carpet bag. "Will we be coming back this way?"

"Yes." He was wondering if he should try another kiss.

"Then we can hide this beside the road."

He was grateful because, that way, they would not have to stop at the house on the way home, for visiting and tedious explanations. She was already thinking about getting home to start their life.

At the door, he thought ruefully that Lisette looked ahead better than he. With forethought, he'd have brought a horse for her to ride. The idea was suggested by the sound of double hoof-beats, and a rider who had turned in from the main road, leading a saddled buckskin cayuse. It seemed a pity if any one so provident was still on the road in search of a wife.

The drizzle was growing heavier outside, and the young couple stood in the doorway, waiting for the caller. "Here's your seventh today," Elmer said. "Maybe you'll like him better than me."

"No." He felt the girl touch his hand. "I've promised."

The rider was a young man who had been at the battle on Rush's farm, though Elmer couldn't remember his name. He reined up near the chopping block, and looked at the two in the doorway, without dismounting; a pleasant-looking young man on a wet bay horse. "Hello." Then he said, "Looks as if I'm too late."

Lisette said, "You were too late a long time ago."

The young man bowed, and put on his hat. "I am sorry." Then he took it off again. "You don't happen to have a sister?"

"No, sir."

The caller put on his agile hat. "Then I am wasting your time."

"And yours," Elmer thought. But that riderless buckskin—.
"Excuse me," he said. "Would you rent me your extra horse?"

"Certainly not!" The caller looked, and sounded, offended.

But it was a serious matter of transportation. "You'll have
better luck without it," he argued. "People will think——"

"To hell with you!" The young man wheeled his horse
away from the chopping block, and touched his wet flanks
with the spurs.

Lisette and Elmer stood in the doorway and watched him
gallop back toward the main road, with his phantom bride
galloping beside him on the buckskin cayuse.

CHAPTER NINE

GOING to Olympia was important but not very sociable. Two people with only one horse makes conversation difficult, unless both walk. Lisette had suggested that, but Elmer decided they should take turns riding, with Lisette having the first turn. Under other circumstances, he would have suggested "ride and tie," which is the scientific method of two people sharing one horse. That way, one rides ahead for a distance, ties the horse and walks on. When the other comes up to the horse, he rides the same distance, passing his partner on the way, ties the horse and walks on. That is much faster than having the horseman keep pace with the one on foot, and it gives the horse periods of rest. But the day being what it was, God knows what might happen to a young woman walking alone, or a saddled horse unguarded by the road. So they kept together for protection.

They were to take turns riding on the way to Olympia, but Elmer convinced Lisette that she should ride all the way, and he would make up for it coming back. He argued the point after he had figured in his mind what everything would cost, and decided he would have enough money left to buy her a pair of shoes. Her shoes, he argued, were too thin for walking in mud. He said that, walking on the off-side near her right shoe, which was comparatively good. Her left shoe, which he had held while helping her onto the horse, was split along one side and mended with common thread. Her shoes, he guessed, were a great embarrassment to her, and she did not have any others except the heavy cowhide ones which she had tried painfully to conceal on other occasions.

Because Lisette was a woman interested in his welfare, she

argued against the unnecessary spending of his money. And because she was a woman and wanted to look her best, she finally agreed to the purchase.

At Sylvester's Store they found a pair of lady's sewed boots which looked fine on Lisette's modest feet. She thought they looked well enough, as if she were used to buying shoes every day, but she hesitated about the price, which was four dollars.

The urbane young clerk said, "But, ma'am, they're the latest style, made in Massachusetts. They're from a special shipment brought out for us in the barque, *Maid*."

That ·clinched the matter with Elmer. He had helped bring those shoes around the Horn. They had been waiting in the hold above which he and his bride had exchanged their first words. They were shoes of destiny, and he would not look at anything less. When Lisette had firmly declined to look at dress goods and bonnets, also of the latest style, the clerk asked Elmer, confidentially, if he happened to be interested in a wedding ring. The other stores, he understood, were out of the commodity, but Sylvester's still had some of fine California gold, at a reasonable price.

A ring was the other purchase on Elmer's mental list, and the suggestion was timely. The rings were fine, too, although Lisette had to decide between one that fitted tightly, and one that was too loose. She chose the tighter one, after Elmer had decided against their looking for something more reasonable. The ring was seven dollars. Four and seven made eleven, and eleven from fifteen left two dollars for the minister, and two over for emergencies.

The store was busy, and another clerk sold the larger ring while Elmer was putting the snug one in his pocket, but the urbane clerk treated them as if they were the only customers in the store. Even when they assured him that they did not want to buy anything else, he found a way of serving them further. "You engaged a minister?" he asked in an undertone.

They had not, although that was their next need. "Where can we find one handy?" Elmer asked.

While the clerk hesitated, you could see his agile mind darting about town to see who was most convenient and least busy. "They're having kind of a rush day," he reported, apologetically. Then his mind went out again, a little way, and hit on something. "I'll tell you what, there's a Justice of the Peace across the street and three houses up. He's not likely to be as busy, and he won't keep you as long. If it suits you——"

"That'll be fine." Elmer said.

"The log house on the corner, with a frame lean-to. Better cross here. There's boards laid down to walk on. I wouldn't advise crossing farther up on account of the mud."

"I thank you," Elmer said.

And Lisette said, "Thank you, sir."

"It is a pleasure," the clerk assured them. "Good luck!" They were almost as good as married, after he had provided the ring, and dismissed them with his blessing.

They went out through the store with light hearts, Elmer feeling the band of California gold in his pocket, and Lisette looking down to glimpse the toes of her new shoes. "They're nice." She brushed her skirt to one side so they could both glimpse the sewed boots in their moment of youth and beauty, before they were plunged into the Olympia mud.

Elmer's conscience nudged him when they were on the street. "Is it all right about the Justice of the Peace? I should should have asked you. I'm a Presbyterian. I thought it was all right, but I should have asked you."

"It's lawful, ain't it?"

"Yes."

"Then it's all right," she decided. "Ma was a Catholic; not a very good one, I guess. And Pa drank. I don't know what that makes me. But it's all right if you think so."

He touched her hand in the rain. "You're nice, Lisette." He didn't mean because of her parents, having been brought up to believe that drunkenness and the Catholic Church were forms of wickedness. He liked her because she was honest, and trusted him.

"Anyway," she said, "I reckon it's the man and woman who make a marriage, not the one who says the words over them."

They went to the Justice of the Peace in perfect harmony, and did not have to wait very long. They met one wedding party coming out, and were spectators while the stout Justice performed the service for another couple. While they waited, they had a serious whispered conversation about the chairs in which they were sitting. They were of plain new wood, with low ladder backs and seats of laced rawhide. They were very light and strong and looked well in a log house. "They're made at a factory here in town," Elmer whispered. "They're only two dollars. We'll get some for our house."

"They are nice," Lisette whispered. "We'll get two when we're sure we can afford them."

"There's only one thing you have to be careful about," he whispered, knowingly. "The feet are round and kind of slick. If you lean back too far, the chair goes right out from under you. It isn't safe to lean back any farther than this——"

"Better not," she whispered.

The Justice was saying, "Whom God hath joined—" The chair shot out from under Elmer like a wet pumpkin seed. He made an unseemly crash, with his long legs waving in the air, and Lisette trying to help him up, with her face all dismayed.

"—let no man put asunder."

By the time everything was in order again, the service was over. In a minute more, it was their turn.

The Justice did not embarrass Elmer further by pretending he hadn't noticed the mishap. "You're the fourth who's done that today," he said. "I'll have to post a warning about those chairs; there's a trick to them. It's only safe to lean back just so far——"

Elmer said, ruefully, "I knew that!"

And Lisette explained, "He was trying to show me how far was safe!"

They all laughed, and it was a nice kind of introduction. It was nicer still when the Magistrate found out who Elmer was. "Jarvis is a friend of mine," he said, "I'm proud to say. There's a man so free from snobbery and meanness that talking to him is like a holiday from all the things we aren't proud of. We were talking about him only this afternoon—" He went to the kitchen door and opened it, letting in a sputtering sound and a fine smell of roasting meat. "Ma, come in and be a witness for Jarvis's nephew!"

"In a minute!" a woman's voice answered. "Or I'll come now, if you'll eat burned roast."

The Magistrate came back to them and went on with what he was saying. "We were talking about Jarvis at dinner; laughing about the way he talked the Pikes off Rush's farm. But I suppose you were there, eh?"

Elmer hesitated. Then he said, "Yes." He didn't look at Lisette, but he could feel the flaming of her face reflected in his own. And when he did meet her eyes, during the service, she looked pale and crushed. The ceremony was spoiled for both of them.

When they were on the street again, in the falling dusk and rain, Elmer said, "I suppose we should have gone somewhere else."

Lisette said, huskily, "It don't matter."

"I'm sorry, Lisette."

She said, "It don't matter."

He knew it did matter to her, and he didn't know how to make it not matter. Talking seemed to make it worse. He put his hand in his waistcoat pocket, and had a sinking feeling because something that should have been there was gone. The ring! Then he remembered taking it out, a little while ago, and putting it on Lisette's finger. Of course! "Lisette," he said, "we're married!"

She reached out her hand to him. "I'm your wife."

Their humiliating experience became something magical that changed everything. On one of her fingers he could feel the cold, smooth ring. Their hands were cold in the rain, but while they pressed together they generated a warmth which drove the cold away. "I'm your husband," Elmer said. "I'll take good care of you."

She said, "I'll try to be a good wife." Then she asked, "Do you want to go to the land office now?" Her face looked pale in the gloom and rain—pale and anxious and suddenly dear.

Standing beside her in the mud, Elmer had a confused vision of wild white morning glories and a slender girl in a white party dress. She had recognized him when she was in a crowd of people and was coming forward, eagerly, to meet him. Then she vanished forever, leaving Lisette's anxious, healthy young face before him in the dusk of falling rain. It was a day of gain and loss, and what he had gained was made dearer by what he had lost. It seemed to him he had betrayed Lisette for a wretched five hundred acres, and now it was she and not the land that mattered. Or maybe the land had betrayed him, happily. Anyway, what had started in cold blood had grown warm and come to life.

"Don't you want to go to the land office?" Lisette asked again.

He said, "It don't matter."

"But Elmer," she said, "I thought——"

"It don't matter." He interrupted because he was afraid she might say she thought he had married her to get more land. "We'll go home now, if you like."

Her face was puzzled, but not anxious any more. "Ain't there— Can't you get more land, now that you're married?"

"Oh, if I want to," he said.

"But, don't you want to?"

"I don't care," he said. "It's you I want, Lisette."

Her face was wise and careful as she said, "But I think we need more land!"

"You want me to get it?"

"I want *us* to get it!" she said. "There's two of us, and we have to look ahead. I think we ought to have the land."

"We," and "us" were magic words as Lisette used them. They changed a private shame to the honorable cause of a partnership.

"All right," Elmer said. "We'll go and get our land."

It was a dark night when they were out in the mud of the street again. The fresh air and the rain were reviving, and Elmer asked, "Are you very tired?"

"A little," Lisette said, walking soberly beside him. Then

she said, "It don't matter." After a minute more, she said, "I didn't know fresh air could be so nice."

"It was stuffy in the land office, wasn't it?"

They breathed in the fresh wet darkness, and after a minute they weren't tired any more. They were young and at the beginning of their life, and everything was fine.

Elmer said, "Lisette, there isn't anything more we have to do, except go home!"

She held his arm tighter. "We have each other, and we have our land, and it don't matter if we're tired. We'll get over that."

They did stop in front of a hotel, to look at the sign on the porch which extended over the sidewalk, where planks had been laid down. The porch gave them shelter from the rain, and the sign was something to look at:

HYAS MUCK-A-MUCK AND NO AIRS
EVERYBODY EATS AT THE OLYMPIAN
COME IN AND GET THE WRINKLES
TAKEN OUT OF YOUR BELLY

Elmer had never seen anything like it in Massachusetts. Lisette said it was not like Missouri, either, but she had seen the same kind of sign in Oregon City. So they decided that a new country makes a new kind of advertising.

The sign gave Elmer an idea, and he felt in his pocket to make sure the two dollars were still there. "It's kind of late," he said. "We could have supper here before we went home."

Lisette looked alarmed. "It's awful expensive," she said, "eating in hotels! We mustn't spend your money that way."

"It isn't much," he said. "Aren't you hungry?"

She shook her head. "I ain't hungry a bit." Then she said, "But if you want to eat——"

"No, I'm not hungry," he said. He didn't know whether he was or not, though he hadn't eaten since breakfast. "But it'll be late when we get home."

She said, "We could buy something to eat on the way. That wouldn't be so expensive, and it wouldn't take time, like eating at the hotel."

They stopped at a log house where a widow and her young children baked things to sell. The pies and cakes looked fine, and Elmer thought it would be nice to have a pie for breakfast.

Lisette thought it was a joke and said, "Elmer, pie for breakfast!" as if she had never heard of such a thing. She was willing for them to make the purchase, though. They only gave it up because pie seemed too unhandy to eat on horseback or on foot, and they couldn't think of any good way to carry it home in the rain. A cake would have been nice, but the difficulties were the same.

"We're making a batch of doughnuts," the widow suggested. "They stand up in the rain; the grease kind of waterproofs them. If you like doughnuts——"

They did.

"We'll buy a lot!" Elmer said. "If there're any left, we can have them for breakfast."

Lisette was amused by the strangest things. "Elmer," she said, "doughnuts for breakfast! You'll say 'soup' next!"

Elmer was surprised. "Don't every one have pie or doughnuts for breakfast?"

Lisette looked suprised, too. "Does any one?"

They went out into the rain, eating hot doughnuts.

When Elmer had picked out the right horse from among many in the darkness of Sylvester's shed, they were ready to start home. But even then there was a difficulty. When he help the stirrup for her, she reminded him, "It's your turn. I rode all the way here."

"Your new shoes," he said triumphantly. You'll get blisters if you walk in them!"

"Then I'll take them off." She knelt down in the mud and rain to unlace them. "I should, anyhow, to save them."

He found her arm, in the dark, and pulled her to her feet. "Some of the road is gravel; it would hurt worse than blisters."

"Then I'll have blisters."

"No, you'll ride!" He was still holding her arm, and he kissed her rain-wet face by way of emphasis. Her cheek was cool and smooth. It was nice to kiss, but it didn't help them any on their way home.

"Please, Elmer!" She put her hand on his arm. "We have to share everything!"

He had another idea, an appeal for his own gallantry.

"You have the first turn, Lisette. I'm not going to ride through town with you walking."

"All right," she agreed, "but don't forget we're taking turns. And the one who rides carries the doughnuts. But I'll give you one whenever you want. Do you want one now?"

"I want a kiss," he said.

She said soberly, "I can't deny you anything. But wouldn't you rather have a doughnut before they get cold?"

"Your kisses will get cold too, in this rain."

"No," she said.

He said, "Let's see."

Her lips were cold from the rain; cool and smooth. Then they were warm with some tender, inexhaustible flame. Volcanic fire under snow . . .

"That's enough!" Lisette said in alarm.

With Elmer walking and his bride in the saddle, they passed the last lighted cabin in town and headed northeast. The road was uphill through mud, and it couldn't have been any worse. Before they were half way up the hill, he wanted to stop and catch his breath. But if he suggested that, Lisette would insist it was her turn to walk. And, in the darkness, the mud wasn't fit for man or beast, let alone a woman.

When they got up on higher, level ground, the going was better; there was nothing to contend with but the mud and rain, and walking was like resting in comparison with the long hill. But Lisette stopped almost at once, and dismounted in the mud. "I'm cold," she said, "and I want to walk to get warm. I'm wet through. You take the doughnuts. I've been keeping them under my cloak; they ain't very wet."

When Elmer had planned to have her ride all the way, he'd forgotten how cold and miserable you can be on horseback in the rain. Now he saw there wouldn't be any comfort for either of them until they got home. The best thing was to get there as fast as they could, without losing time in arguments. So he acceped the doughnuts, and swung into the saddle, which was already wet under the pelting rain. "Try holding onto the stirrup leather," he said. "It'll help you along. Tell me as soon as you begin to get tired."

She said, "It's hardly like walking, holding onto the leather."

He could hear her feet in the heavy mud, and knew the walking was bad enough. Riding wasn't comfortable, either. His clothes were wet through in places and his feet were wet, and he couldn't keep the rain from going down his neck. When he kept his head up, it beat into his collar from in front, and when he bent his head, the rain dripped from the brim of his soaked hat and found its way down the back of his neck. Steaming uphill through the mud on foot, he hadn't thought he would ever be cool again. Now, he was surprised to find how quickly he got cold.

From the mud and black rain beside him, Lisette's voice said, "The mud's all soft, Elmer. Couldn't I take off my shoes?"

"No," he said. "There are rocks in places. You're safest with them on."

"They'll get ruined!"

"If they do," he said, "we'll get another pair. Your feet are worth more than shoes!"

"You're nice to me," she said.

"Making you walk in the mud! With any sense, I'd have brought a horse for you."

"No. I wouldn't have liked that!"

He was too cold and wet to think clearly. "Why?"

"It would have seemed like you were too sure of me. If you had, maybe you'd be riding home now with only one of you and two horses!"

He remembered about her walking in new shoes. "Are you getting blisters, Lisette?"

"No, my feet are right comfortable."

Her face was only the dimmest blur beside him in rain that was like the falling of cold ink. Probably she wouldn't tell him even if her feet were blistering. And he was cold and wet all the way through. He stopped the horse and eased himself down into the mud. "I'm too cold to ride any more," he said. He really was.

They found Lisette's carpet bag under the log where they had cached it. They mightn't have found anything if it hadn't been for a glimmer of light in a window of the Sims's cabin. The lighted window meant warmth and shelter, which they wanted almost more than anything else. More than anything else except to get to their own home. So they went on.

Walking was better on the gravel prairie, where there wasn't enough soil to make deep mud. But the road was more exposed to the heavy, driving rain.

They went on, sometimes both walking for warmth, and sometimes taking turns riding. They hardly spoke a word any more. Both of them had been wet through long ago. But even after you are wet through, you can get more and more soaked. They became two half-drowned beings going on, near each other, but separately, through a world of falling water in which they saw nothing. What had started as a kind of adventure became an ordeal to get through, somehow.

Elmer did not think of anything any more except the side road where they were to turn off toward the Inlet. It wasn't much more than a crooked trail through the woods. On a night like this, the opening wouldn't look like anything but a narrow black door in a wall of identical blackness. And that black wall of trees was something you felt rather than saw through the black rain. He hadn't even a hope of seeing where the trail led off through the woods . . . but the half-drowned cayuse should know his way home. All they could do was to give him his head and trust in his horse sense.

When Lisette dismounted into the mud, and it was his turn to ride, she asked, "Are we getting near?" It was the first time she had said anything about the length of their dismal journey.

"We're almost at the trail," he said. "I'm sorry it's such a trip."

"It don't matter," she said. "We're together."

"Are you very tired, Lisette?"

"No," she said. Then she said, "A little. It don't matter." They went on.

All day it had been raining, but only in a way. Comparatively, it had been only a drizzle. Now the rain let go. They heard it coming down through the three-hundred foot trees in a roar that never stopped. It battered down on them with such unloosed savagery that in one minute they felt more wetness than they had known on their whole journey. There was no wind where they were, but the rain was a complete storm in itself, roaring like a hurricane and trying to blast them off the road, which was running with water.

Elmer had been told about the autumn rains, but he was unprepared for such fury. The rain was overwhelming and deafening, and he felt nothing but impotent rage and amazement. Holding onto the stirrup leather, Lisette shouted faintly, "Is this where we turn?"

Turn? For the moment he'd forgotten everything but the rain. Now he sensed the cayuse under him in the act of turning off the road, into the solid black wall of the forest, where he was willing to swear there was no road or path. The forest closed about them, and the cayuse went on, with a more cheerful step. He went on in absolute darkness, without running into anything. The miracle went on and on. Then Elmer stopped and dismounted. "Lisette, it's our road! We're almost home!" From everywhere in the woods about them, there came the sound of falling rain, but its force was broken by the tremendous trees above the narrow road. In that respite, Elmer hugged his companion. "It's our road!"

"It's a nice road," she said. "I was afraid we'd missed it."

"I was, too," he said, "but we made it. Now it's your turn to ride."

She objected, "I just was. You only started."

"It isn't safe for walking," he told her. "There are fallen trees across the road with just notches for wagon wheels. There are boggy places, and the creek may be up——"

"If it ain't safe for me, it ain't for you," Lisette said. "If you walk, I'll walk, too."

He argued with her, but it was no use. She was a difficult bride to get home. And the road was not safe in the dark.

"Can we both ride?" she compromised. "Will he carry double?"

"I think so," Elmer decided, after leaning his weight on the invisible, wet back behind the saddle. The gelding was tired enough to put up with anything, as long as it was on the way home. Elmer located a stump which would serve as a horse block, and had Lisette stand on it while he rode alongside, with the carpet bag balanced in front of him. Wet silk rustled as she adjusted her dress for riding astride, and settled down behind him. The gelding gave a half-hearted snort, but he accepted his double burden and went on through the blackness of falling rain.

Steadying herself with her hands on his hips, Lisette said, "This is nicer than riding alone."

He said, "I'm sorry it's such a bad road, Lisette."

"It's a good road," she said. "It's the best in the world, because it's the way home."

"Hold on tighter," he said. "There're some bad places.".

She locked her arms around his waist and drew closer. "Is that all right?"

"Yes." Then he said, "You're sweet."

"No," her voice said from behind his back, "but you are good to me. I'll try to be a good wife."

"You're the best wife in the world."

"I don't know much about it," she said, "but I can learn." Then she asked, "Are there any doughnuts left?"

"Quite a few." He fumbled for the soggy bag inside his wet coat.

Her arms tightened around him, reassuringly. "I don't want one now. I was thinking we'd have them for breakfast."

"You are sweet," he said. It was the first real chance to visit on their miserable journey. He'd been wondering if he would ever be warm again, and now he could feel the warmth of her body against his back, and a faint circle of warmth about his waist.

She said, unexpectedly, "Elmer, remember that time at the Negro's farm, when you visited our camp?"

"You were nice to me," he said, "and you gave me coffee."

"It was very bad coffee," she said. "It was mostly made of browned peas. I was ashamed it wasn't nicer."

"You were nicer to me than I deserved," he said. "I liked you then."

"I was rude to you," she said. "Part of it was because I hated the great, ugly shoes I was wearing, and the ugly clothes; I wanted to look nice, and I didn't. And I couldn't tell you what I wanted to. Nothing could be what I wanted, and I hated it!"

"Couldn't you tell me now?"

Her arms held him tighter. "I expect I can tell you anything now. I wanted to tell you then that I didn't think it was right for Uncle Dan and his boys to take another's farm, even if he was a Negro. I felt ashamed all the time. And when you told me how wonderful he'd been to people, it made me feel worse; I felt more ashamed, and I wanted to cry. But I couldn't be a traitor to people who'd taken me in and looked after me the best they could. I couldn't do anything but act as if I felt the way they did. I couldn't!"

He balanced the sodden carpet bag with his bridle-arm, and put his free hand over one of hers. "I'd have thought less of you if you had."

"But I did want to tell you!" she gathered his cold fingers into her hand. "And I did want to look nice for you!"

"You did look nice," he insisted. "And it was the first time I really saw your hair. I thought it was beautiful; so blue-black and kind of stormy, like more than hair."

She held his hand tighter, and it began to grow warm. "I'm glad you like what I have a lot of!"

"It was beautiful," he said; "I wanted to touch it." At the time he hadn't known he wanted to touch her hair, but afterward he had dreamed about it.

Lisette said, "You can touch it all you like when it's dry."

He would have liked to touch her hair now, but it was quite impossible, with her close behind him and his hands full. And he had to watch for one more turn in the invisible trail. The cayuse belonged to Uncle Jarvis, and he would certainly head for his own stable, on the wrong side of the Inlet, if Elmer didn't check him where the trail forked.

It was something he worried about beforehand, and when

the time came it was nothing. Before him, the darkness thinned to the leaden, dim gleam of water. On the bay it was black night and rain, but the darkness on the water was light to the darkness of the forest. "Lisette," he said, "there's our bay!"

"It's nice." She said it without too much enthusiasm. Maybe she thought they were having enough water without his establishing their possession to even larger quantities. But after a minute she said, "I can swim good."

The cayuse tried to swing to the left, with his head turned craftily to the right, but Elmer was ready for him, and tightened the rein still more. He gave it up and plunged into unobstructed darkness to the right. And when a gleam of the water appeared again through the trees, it was off to the left. "We're on our own road," Elmer reported. "You're the first woman who ever travelled over it."

"It's a beautiful road!" she held him tighter around the waist. "I'll always love our road because I was the first."

He said, "You are the first in everything."

"You are the first, too," she said.

After a while he thought of the five young men who had proposed to her before he got there. He was a little jealous because it had happened, and sorry because it was his own fault. "I wasn't the first to ask you to marry me."

"The others don't count," she said. "If one of them had, you wouldn't have found me."

"It would have been terrible if one of them had counted!"

"They couldn't!" She sounded positive.

"Why not?"

"Because I was waiting for you," she said.

He felt wildly happy, and unworthy in the same degree. "Lisette, how did you know?"

"I didn't," she said. "But I was hoping you would. I've thought about you ever since that first time on the ship, when you were so nice to me, and I was so rude." She held him tighter while the horse splashed through running water and lunged up a slippery bank on the other side.

"You weren't rude," he insisted. "You were lovely."

"And that time at the Negro's farm," she said. "I wanted to be nice for you, and I wanted you to be there to see me. And nothing was the way I wanted it."

He said, "I wanted to see you afterward, but I was ashamed. You were nice to me, and I was helping put your friends off the place."

She said, "I was ashamed, too, for myself. But both of us had to do what we did."

He remembered the creek they had passed through a while ago. "Lisette, this is our land! We're on our own claim, and we're almost home!"

She tightened her arms around his waist again. "We've got everything," she said. "The rest is how we use it." After a minute she said, "Elmer, if you love me, tell me that you love me!"

Love you! As if she weren't sure, even though it was the first time either had used the word. "Lisette!" he said, like a cry. If only she weren't so far out of reach by being so close behind his back. "Lisette," he said, "isn't there some way I can kiss you when I tell you I love you?"

"You mustn't try!" she said in alarm. "It would be too reckless."

Her cautioning made him reckless. He steadied the carpet bag and doughnuts with his bridle arm, and turned in the saddle enough to put one arm around her.

"Reckless!" she said, like a whisper, and he found her mouth. Her lips were cold with the rain; cool and smooth. Then they were warm with some tender, inexhaustible fire. About them there was the undying storm of the rain coming down through great trees; a roar like the sound of the sea. The roaring deepened and changed, and the rain beat down on them fiercely, but could not quench that tender flame.

The roaring had changed to a fierce drumming overhead, and the cayuse was standing still.

Lisette drew away from him. "Elmer, where are we?"

The rain drummed fiercely overhead, but did not reach them any more. Elmer put out his hand in the dark and touched the miracle of a dry cedar post. In another second he was helping her to the ground. "We're home!" he said triumphantly. "This is the shed and that's the house!"

Against the dim, leaden gleam of water, there was the shape of a roof with a blunt chimney at one end. Their house was waiting for them at the beginning of their life, with warmth and food and shelter.

CHAPTER TEN

THERE IS no such thing as a hasty marriage. It is no more possible than learning hastily to be a good swimmer. To be sure, any one with a few seconds to spare can jump into deep water, but that is only the beginning. If you do not drown, the rest takes a long time. It had even taken time for Elmer to learn that it takes time. At first he did not know what was the matter when their life together was not perfect. He assumed that one of them was at fault. At the time it always seemed to be Lisette. Afterward, as likely as not, he decided the fault was with him. When that had happened often enough, he learned the trick of realizing at the time that he might possibly be wrong. That helped some. It helped still more when he managed to think of Lisette and himself as two inexperienced people on an unfamiliar road.

In the smoke of the damp brush they were burning, Elmer saw many reasons why marriage is a gradual thing. Trees growing in the open are symmetrical, with branches on all sides. Two trees which have grown up close together have the symmetrical shape of a single tree, but that takes a long time and calls for the sacrifice of branches on the side where they are near each other. Lisette and he were two trees which had been transplanted as close together as possible, but they could not be very close together because of conflicting branches. Those branches which would have to die while others developed were habits of acting and thinking which stayed green beyond their season of usefulness. Like Lisette's spells of sullenness which had once protected her from the rough Sims clan. They went on, more faintly, when there was no more use for them and they only interfered with the tenderness which he felt for her and could not always show. And there was her determined modesty which had kept all of her for her husband. Now, going on when there was no more need for it, her modesty kept much of her from him. In bed, at night, he never felt her strong smooth body, without the conviction that it must be beautiful. But he had never had more than a glimpse of odd bits of her. And that was only because their house had one room.

Elmer, too, had habits which had been all to the good when he lived alone, but were not fair to a wife. Like his habit of doing outdoor work by moonlight, or working indoors by firelight, and working so intently that he forgot to go to bed until two in the morning, or until daylight began to glimmer on the Inlet. At such times Lisette worked with him or did things for his comfort and never complained. The only reproach he had was afterward, from his conscience. That was enough, or almost enough, and he tried to keep more reasonable hours. Only there was so much to be done, and when the fever of work was upon him he found it impossible to stop.

Except for small annoyances, Elmer was content with Lisette and with his life. Sometimes at night, after lovemaking, when his mind saw with strange clearness, he understood that their life together was made more rich by what each gave up for the other.

His life was with Lisette, but that did not immediately shrivel up branches which had no place in their life. Even now he was affected oddly by a glimpse of white, seen from the corner of his eye. Once, in the solemn, early morning, it had been a shred of mist, rising from the wet earth and vanishing seaward with noiseless speed. Another time it had been a wisp of steamy smoke from one of the fires. And each time that half-seen glimpse of white had brought up the picture of wild white morning-glories and a girl in a long white party dress coming toward him, eagerly, with a look of recognition, and vanishing. Once at night, tending a log fire in the clearing, he had a vision of a different kind of woman altogether. Partly, the memory was awakened by a Haidah canoe which he had seen that day. The long, foreign-looking craft was slipping through Dana Passage, heading north, while endless strings of wild geese were passing overhead in the other direction. It was the end of the season for both, and while the geese were flying south, the contrary Haidahs were turning north to winter on their arctic island.

Elmer remembered the Haidahs who had attacked the ship in the Strait, and the girl who had stood on a chest in the great canoe and talked to him in Jargon. He had a fair knowledge of the language now, but because he had not understood it then, he could not remember anything she said except "Tillicum," which meant "friend," and which he had mistaken for her name. Elmer remembered her while he was watching the canoe, but at night, by the burning logs in the clearing, he had seen the fire and darkness call her up like the Witch of Endor. He saw her slender body, like smooth polished gold in the light of the long-ago flare, and her exquisite face alive with wicked laughter and the promise of strange delights. . . .

It seemed to Elmer that these visitors to his mind showed something about himself, but he couldn't decide what because they contradicted each other—a young woman who was all mysterious and holy, and a more than half-naked Haidah girl, eager with wickedness. Between those impossible extremes, he had Lisette who was not an angel too good for the earth, and not a shameless bit of savagery. She was a human being of his own race. And though she was quiet, for a woman, and calm and patient, that did not mean she had no spirit. He was beginning to find that out. The earth is calm and patient, too, but you can't take liberties with it; not liberties that do you any good. Lisette was closely related to the sober earth. The mostly sober earth. But, like the earth, she could bloom so richly and profoundly that at moments he was a little afraid of her.

Lisette asked: "Do you think it's time to start another fire?"

He sized up the clearing. "Yes, I should have done it before." While his mind was away, they had been dragging and carrying brush an unnecessary distance.

Near the edge of the stumpy clearing, he began preparing

for another fire. It was not as much a matter of piling up brush to burn as it was of clearing a space around it to keep the fire from spreading too far. The ground was wet underfoot, but there was brush everywhere, and it dried as it burned.

Helping him, Lisette cleared a space around the rhododendrons. Elmer had cut most of them down before they decided to save some for their bloom. At the time, neither of them had much conviction about saving the rhododendrons, but since they had been saved their position had become secure. Their value increased every time one of them looked at the lanky, ten-foot shrubs which would fill out with room to spread. "They look better now, don't they, Elmer?" Lisette was standing back to admire the shrubs whose value she had just increased.

"They look fine," he said. "Just as if they were growing in a garden." They did look much better growing out of the ground instead of through a drift of dead brush.

Lisette said, "Since the night you brought me home, I'd been hoping we could have a garden. And part of it was growing here all the time! We didn't have to do anything to start it; we only had to not do too much." She spoke the wisdom she had learned from the earth. Elmer knew that when she spoke of the night he had brought her home, she was feeling specially nice toward him.

"I won't ever forget the night I brought you home! That storm! Most of the time I could only guess where we were."

"The rain was like people fighting us," Lisette said. "Like a mob we couldn't see, trying to lynch us and drown us. I wanted to hate it, but I was too wet and cold, and I didn't feel important enough for my hating to matter. It all changed in our own house. When we were in—when we were warm and dry and safe, the rain beating on the roof made a lovely sound."

He slipped his arm around her and looked toward their house, with a blue wisp of smoke going up from the chimney and the gray, autumn water beyond it. "It is the loveliest sound in the world," he said. "Rain on the roof at night and a man and woman listening to it."

She asked: "Is it true that the same water gets back into the clouds and falls again in rain?"

"It happens all the time," he assured her. "The same water gets used over and over."

"I'd heard that, but I wasn't sure," Lisette said. "I thought about it that night when I was falling asleep. I was thinking that the same rain was old and new. We were lying there, listening to rain that fell before we were born and rain that will fall a hundred years from now, when we are dead. Only I didn't see why we should ever have to get any older or die when we could reach out and touch the rain that mixes time all up."

"I hadn't thought about it that way," he said. "It makes rain kind of magic, don't it?"

"I think it does," she said. "If it was real magic, you could go out in the rain at night and it wouldn't be any special day or year. You might meet people who lived long ago and people who aren't even born."

Elmer said, "The Nisquallys are afraid to go anywhere at night, even the braves."

"Why?"

"Mary says it is because they believe the kind of magic you were talking about. They believe they might meet men of long ago who lived here before the Indians. They were giants, and at night they come down from Mount Rainier and visit their old hunting grounds," Elmer explained, then added: "You have the same kind of thoughts that Indians have, only yours are nicer. I'm glad you told me, because I'll like the sound of rain better than ever. I'll remember that I'm listening to the past and the future."

"I think about it like that," she said quietly.

He looked at the overcast sky and filled his lungs with damp air, rich with smoke and the perfume of dead leaves. "There'll be rain tonight," he said. "We can listen to it together."

"We'll listen to it together and try to know what it's saying." When that was settled, Lisette suddenly became practical. "This don't burn any brush, Elmer, and it may burn the bread. I'll go and see how it's doing."

They did not talk much after Lisette came back from the house. They respected each other's ideas, and each thought the other a fine worker. So they got along beautifully and did not feel the need of working close together, because they felt so near all the time. Everything was just right. Later on, the rain was certain to begin again, and that night they would lie in each other's arms, listening to the million ancient and unborn voices on the roof. But while the rain held off they would do famous things in the way of clearing, and they would rescue more of their land from the wilderness forever. . . .

Thinking fine thoughts like that, Elmer did not even know when Lisette went back to have another look at the big loaf in the Dutch oven. He only knew she had gone because he heard the house door close.

"*Elmer.*"

He started at the sound of his wife's voice, and turned to see her standing a few yards away. Her face had an alert, anxious look.

"Do you think that's your uncle and aunt?" she asked.

He didn't think it was. They weren't likely to be back from Olympia before evening. And if they did call, they would come directly into the clearing. Maybe it had been the wind. Only there wasn't any wind. "You didn't leave the door open, did you?"

Instead of answering, Lisette pointed toward the house.

A chill raced through his body because his wife looked scared, and she was pointing at something which he could not see because of the smoke. When he stood beside her, it wasn't anything to be afraid of: a face looking out of the window of their cabin. He thought it was the face of a child, though he couldn't be sure. But he was sure the face was frightened. In the distance he heard, or thought he heard, yelling voices. "I'll get my rifle!" He ran in a circle, looking for the stump on which he had left his rifle. Then he remembered he had not brought it out that afternoon. "I'll go and see who it is," he said.

Lisette went with him, carrying the ax which she had found. She didn't say anything until they were near the house, where they had a clear sweep of the Inlet. "There's a canoe coming."

The canoe wasn't more than a mile off, and it looked a hundred feet long. It was driving into the reach with the blurred strokes of many flying paddles. In the canoe there was a jumble of bright colors and brown bodies.

"Haidahs," Elmer said. He opened the door, and was seized by naked brown arms. It was not a formidable attack, but he was nonplussed by the young Indian woman who clung to him, crying *"Tillicum! Boston tillicum!"* and the delicate little face that looked up, pleading, filled his mind with vague confusion. He had seen the face that afternoon, in his daydream, and when it suddenly materialized against his breast he was not sure whether he was asleep or awake. This time her face was alive with fear instead of youthful wickedness, but he recognized her, and she was real. He could feel her, panting and trembling in his arms while she pleaded in tumbling Jargon. She was begging him to save her from the many *cultus man* who wanted to take her back to the Land of Darkness.

"What is it, Elmer? What is she saying?" Lisette had barred the door and was standing there with his rifle.

"Those Haidahs are after her," Elmer explained. He didn't have to tell her which ones; they could hear the thin, rolling yell of voices, coming nearer. "She wants us to save her. We've got to hide her, somewhere!"

"Tell her to go into the woods; they're sure to find her here!"

Elmer saw that was true. He explained to the girl, but she clung to him like a frightened child, insisting he must go with her. His arguing only increased her panic and tightened the grip of her determined arms about his waist. He felt gallant and warm with pity for the exquisite, hunted thing that had taken shelter in his arms. But it was embarrassing and not at all useful. He looked at his wife's pale, quiet face and met her questioning eyes. "She won't go without us. She's scared to death."

Lisette did not answer.

He looked past her, about the bare, neat room. "We have to do something!" Only there wasn't any place where the girl could be hidden: no cellar or attic or closet; nothing except the lockers under the berth, and even her lithe body would never fit in one of them. Suddenly the berth gave him an idea. "Lisette, we can hide her in the mattress! Come on!" He untangled himself from the slender brown arms. *"Hyak!"* He could hear the fierce throb of paddles as an undertone to the yelling voices of the pursuers.

The mattress was a mass of dry ferns, covered with a blanket which was tucked under on all sides. They pulled the ferns away from near the wall, and the girl crept into the narrow space and lay on the bare boards. She was very quiet now and ready to do anything they suggested.

"We'll have to cover her pretty well with ferns." Elmer was already packing them around her.

"She can stand it," Lisette agreed.

Elmer wasn't sure whether she meant the girl could endure it, or whether it was intended as a criticism of her costume. She was naked except for a short skirt of woven bark or grass, and moccasins. Elmer thought she was beautiful, and covering her with the dry ferns was like packing away some precious heathen idol. He had another thought, and took off one of her moccasins. She could not have known why, and there was no time to explain, but her face looked up at him, out of the drift of sere ferns, with smiling trust.

"I think we can cover her with the blanket now," Elmer said.

Lisette helped draw the blanket over her and tuck it in place again. With a little smoothing and patting of the bed, the effect was fine. He could hardly believe any one was there. But his wife allowed him little time for admiration. She was already spreading the second blanket, and he helped her with it.

"I hope she don't smother," he said.

"She won't," Lisette said. "She's more likely to sneeze, but we can't help that if she can't." Elmer had never seen her so pale before. With its color gone, her face looked very clear and firm, like marble, but she was capable and kept her head. When they were through with the blanket, she asked, "What do you aim to do with the moccasin?"

"Throw it out in the clearing," he said, "back of the house. They'll think she's gone into the woods."

When he came back and stood beside her, the enormous canoe was running straight in for the beach, with Indians standing up in the canoe and on the thwarts. Seen that way, head on, the high prow was like a rushing black pyramid, and above the black there rose a still higher, many-colored human pyramid. It was grand, in its way, like some picture of reckless, barbaric adventure.

Lisette's voice asked in awe, "What kind of Indians did you say they are?"

"Haidahs, from up near Alaska." Most of the paddlers had stopped, but the great canoe carried weigh on it for a surprisingly long time. It glided in swiftly, like a clipper, with a big, glassy ripple of a bow wave.

Lisette's voice spoke again, quietly. "Is that girl the same kind of Indian?"

"Yes," he said. Above the sharp cutwater of the oncoming canoe he made out, crouched, a carved black figure. Again he marvelled that these hard-bitten northern savages had achieved the lines of the clipper ship, complete even to the unnecessary figurehead.

"If they're after her," Lisette's voice said, "they aren't likely to harm us, are they?"

"I don't think so," he said. "They're likely to steal anything that's lying around, but you'll never see them do it."

"Why not?"

"I don't know. At Steilacoom they steal the buttons off the soldiers' uniforms while they're talking to them, and none of them has ever been caught at it."

Lisette said, "If they take anything of ours, I'll know it!"

He hardly heard her. The black, pyramidal bow of the canoe lifted as it took the beach. In the same instant the human pyramid above toppled forward like a wave, and the beach was swarming with men.

"Elmer, look at them! You ain't going to try to keep them out, are you?"

"It wouldn't be the least use," he said. "All we can do is not make them mad."

"I'll try to hide things," Lisette said. But there wasn't time.

A few seconds after the canoe landed the Haidahs were coming up over the bank as if they were springing out of the ground. They were larger than most Americans, and larger than other Indians Elmer had seen; with their demonlike agility they gave the feeling of an invasion from another world. The air was swarming with their eager voices and they were knocking on the door with what sounded like a war club.

Elmer raised the latch and stood in the half-opened door. He wasn't afraid now because he couldn't afford to be. *"Klahowya!"* he said. *"Icta mika tickey?"* ("What do you want?")

On this more peaceful expedition there were no bird or animal helmets or wooden armor in sight among the Haidahs. But there were the familiar conical straw hats above the almost-oriental faces, and that same look of reckless pirates who forever feel the forward swing of their lives and find it galling to stand still and use words instead of action.

"Icta mika tickey?" Elmer asked again.

A man with thin, drooping moustaches and angry eyes glared at him while he toyed with a canoe-shaped club. *"Tickey nesika kloochman!"*

"Kloochman?" The boy's surprise was almost genuine. In the excitement he had nine-tenths forgotten the girl hidden in the mattress behind him.

"Nesika kloochman! Cumtux?"

The voice was dangerously arrogant, and Elmer thought it advisable to *cumtux.* *"Tenas kloochman?"* He indicated the approximate height of the girl. When the Haidahs agreed the *kloochman* was about that size, he told them, with suitable gestures, that she had crossed the clearing and run into the woods.

Most of the Indians scattered about the clearing at a fast trot, but those nearest the door pushed forward. Elmer was trying to block the doorway, without actually using force to keep them out. They did not use much force to get in, but they were quick and very strong. He felt a rapid series of elastic blows as they drove past him into the cabin.

When the Indians were inside, they paid no more attention to the boy and his wife. There were seven of them and they went about, picking things up and putting them down with clear-cut gestures. While they looked, they talked in light and rapid Haidah guttural, of which Elmer did not know a word. He hung onto his rifle and stood beside Lisette; there didn't seem to be anything else to do. And he didn't think the Haidahs suspected that the fugitive was concealed a few feet from them. The room looked so bare and neat that even to one who knew better it seemed improbable.

Lisette touched his hand. The color had come back into her face and she did not look afraid any more, only thoughtful. "It's safe to be poor," she said. "We ain't got much they could covet."

"I don't think they'll stay long," Elmer said. By the sound of their voices, he thought the Indians were almost convinced that the girl wasn't inside. One of them had already prodded the mattress a few times with a short spear, without conviction or result. After a minute more, they seemed to settle on the lockers under the berth as the last remaining possibility. Two of them pulled out the lockers and convinced themselves that the girl was not there. One of the searchers was an older man whom Elmer remembered from the attack on the ship. Under his conical straw hat he had a smooth, good-natured moon-face with flat eyes and a thin drooping gray moustache which gave him the look of a Chinese mandarin. He pulled out a locker, slid it back in place, and pulled it out again, admiringly. Then he looked up at Elmer, smiling, *"Klosh! Hiyu klosh!"* congratulating him on the ingenious contraption.

Elmer warmed at the praise of his handiwork and admitted it was *tenas klosh.* He was not so well pleased when the genial Haidah began examining the contents of the locker. Lisette's sewed boots took his fancy, and he held them up for the others to see. The boots, too, it seemed, were *hiyu klosh.*

"Do you think he'll try to take them, Elmer?" Lisette's face was darkening with subdued anger.

"I don't think so." But he noticed that the sewed boots were put down on the floor, and not back in the locker.

Next, a petticoat was gravely examined and commented on, after which it was laid aside on the earth floor.

"I wish they'd let my things alone!" Lisette's face was still darkening, and it gave Elmer the feeling of a coming storm.

"We have to be patient." They were completely at the mercy of these northern rovers, and losing clothes was not as bad as losing their lives.

Now the fat Haidah was holding up a pair of Lisette's muslin drawers. He made a short speech about them, and called attention to the ruffles. His voice was grave, while its tone made the garment sound like something very special.

"They'd better let my things alone!" Lisette's voice said.

The speech about the drawers was in a proper and judicial tone, but it was welcomed with ribald, appreciative cheers which made the cabin ring like the fo'c'sle of a ship. Elmer wanted to comfort his wife by explaining that all seamen are like that. But, with his own sea-chest in the corner, he was on delicate ground.

Putting the muslin garment on the floor, the moon-faced Indian took up a black ball which was Lisette's best stockings. He could make nothing of the ball until he discovered that it could be unrolled, then he realized it was something else ingenious and *hiyu klosh*. He rolled the stockings back into a ball to learn how it was done, then unrolled them again. . . .

Lisette was standing at Elmer's side, and then she was no longer there. He saw her, suddenly, among the Indians by the berth. Her black eyes were blazing and her voice crackled. "Get out of here! Take your *kloochman* and go home!" She ripped the blankets off the berth, scattering dry ferns. "Take her, and get out of here! *Klatawa!*"

Elmer stood in a daze, looking at a scene which did not seem in the least real because it was something he had not expected and could not understand. He saw the dainty fugitive hauled out of the berth, with her face red from half-suffocation and bits of fern sticking to her. He saw Lisette put the last of her rescued belongings into the locker, and push it shut. "*Klatawa!*"

Instead of the Haidahs going out, more came in. One of them was holding up a moccasin and calling something with obvious triumph.

Answering him, the moon-faced humorist hoisted the girl

into view with one arm, and the man with the moccasin sub-
sided under a blast of laughter. Without knowing any of their
language, you could see the shape of the joke. The newcomer
said, "Look, I found her moccasin!" And the old rogue said,
"Look, I found where it belongs!"

Lisette was not interested in the joke, or in anything except
getting the Indians out of the cabin. She hurried about trying
to drive them from the cabin and saying, *"Klatawa!"* It was
one of the few words of Jargon she knew, and she used it like
a flail. Some of the Indians gave her ugly looks, and one of
them seemed to be suggesting something unpleasant, but the
genial one who looked like a mandarin forbade it. Apparently,
Lisette was excused because she was a woman, and because she
had delivered the fugitive into their hands. And the Haidahs
had the look of going. One or two of them had already gone
out and were calling back the searchers with a long-drawn
"H-o-o, h-o-o!" The others were drifting toward the door with
the subdued captive, who looked at neither her unsuccessful
rescuer nor her betrayer. The invasion was about over, Elmer
decided. Then his foreboding of trouble came back in the form
of Lisette, who was white with anger.

"They've stolen the bread," she told him, "right out of the
oven! And it was such a nice loaf!"

"It don't matter," he said.

"It does matter! Tell them to give it back!"

He could not think of the Jargon word for "bread," and he
was not trying to remember. "Let them keep it," he advised,
"or they'll take the oven, too."

Lisette did not see things that way. She darted about among
the Indians, inspecting those who were not naked to the clout.

He followed, to stop his wife before she stirred up the hornets' nest. For a moment he lost sight of her. Then he heard
a shout, and saw her in combat with an Indian whom she had
pushed against the wall. She was holding his arms under the
red blanket in which he was wrapped, forcing them down while
he tried to raise them. Suddenly the Haidah's face twisted
and he gave a cry of pain. Lisette released him and stooped to
pick up the loaf which had fallen from under the red blanket.

As she stooped, Elmer lunged forward, with his rifle raised to ward off the blow of a canoe-shaped club which was poised over her head. But the blow did not fall. The moon-faced Haidah had caught the club with one hand while he pointed with the other to the man who had felt the hot bread on the wrong side of his belly. He was rocking with laughter and shouted something which the others repeated. The unsuccessful thief had won a nickname that would certainly outlast his blisters.

It was a dangerous triumph for Lisette, but she did not seem to notice the club, or anything else except the recaptured loaf which she carried back to the oven. She had won her point, but Elmer was sweating for the chance she had taken, and he had the extra discomfort of a splinter which had got in his shirt and was sticking him. He tried to brush it away, and cut his thumb on the razor-edge of a spear that was touching him between the ribs. When he became aware of it, the obsidian reminder was removed.

"Tatoosh-kloochman!" the old Haidah pointed at Lisette.

"Hiyu skookum tatoosh-kloochman!"

Elmer agreed that his wife was a brave eagle-woman.

"Spose mika swap?" He pointed at the subdued captive. *"Cumtux?"*

The boy shook his head. *"Halo swap."*

"Mika tickey chickamun?" He unfastened the pouch at his belt and offered two eight-cornered slugs of gold as an extra inducement.

Elmer shook his head again. *"Halo swap!"* He was not tempted. Only, when the door was barred after the last invader, it occurred to him that it would have served Lisette right if he had swapped her for the girl she had betrayed—and thrown her precious loaf of bread into the bargain. He stood at the window and watched the Haidahs disappearing over the bank in a drizzle of rain, and reappearing on the beach. In the grayness, the waiting canoe stirred restlessly on the incoming tide, and he had a last glimpse of the captive, with one of the men twisting her arm. He did not want to see any more, and he turned away from the window, with a sigh.

Lisette was sitting on the edge of the disordered berth, as if her legs had suddenly grown too weak to support her. His own legs did not feel too strong, and he sat near her. He had a growing desire to scold her, but she looked upset already, and he did not want to make her cry. So he only said, "They're gone."

"I'm glad," she said. "I'm scared!"

"You didn't look it when they were here."

She accepted it as approval. "Did I help any?"

He bit his lip. He wouldn't scold her, but his curiosity demanded some satisfaction. "You were fine," he said, "but I was wondering why you turned the girl over to them like that, and then risked your life for a loaf of bread."

"If I hadn't, they'd have stole everything we own. We need the bread for supper. We didn't need the girl."

"No," he said, "I suppose we needed the bread more."

It was a kind of relief when Lisette noticed the ax had been stolen. She had brought it into the house when they saw the girl, and now it was gone. The theft was an excuse for him to go out and see if they had stolen anything else.

They hadn't taken very much: the paddles from the dugout and some salmon from the smokehouse and the drawknife from the shed. The ax and drawknife were the only things which couldn't be replaced without money, and he could get them on credit at Sylvester's. Probably the Haidahs had taken everything they wanted, anyway, and the sacrifice of the fugitive had been as useless as it was cold-blooded.

When he had checked up on everything, Elmer turned his attention to the neglected fires in the clearing. He nursed them, like the fires of resentment, in the growing dusk and drizzle of rain until Lisette called him to supper.

She had put the house to rights and made up the berth so neatly that you would not think the Haidah girl had ever been concealed there. Or you might think the neatness was a deception, and that she was still there. Both of them felt her presence, though they did not mention her while they tried to eat, and talked of other things.

Afterward, Lisette washed the dishes, while Elmer sat on

the bench by the fire, with the butcher knife and a split-cedar board, making a paddle for the canoe. It was the first step toward replacing what the Haidahs had taken. It was good repairing the damage of the day. And the warm firelight thawed them a little and made them more friendly; they could at least be friendly about some things. Outside, the rain was increasing and its sound became audible on the roof. That helped, in a way, but it also had a kind of mockery. Earlier, they had planned to listen together to the rain and try to learn what it was saying. Now, when the night had come, they could not even say what they wanted to, and they could not quite understand each other.

When Lisette had finished with the dishes and put a pot under the eaves to catch water for washing, she came back to the fire and sat on the bench near him. She even offered to help with the paddle making, but that was impossible because of the missing tools. Elmer felt a little sorry, knowing she wanted to do her part in repairing the damage. She did help, in a way, picking up the shavings he cut and throwing them among the burning logs. But that was not enough for her, and there were other kinds of damage which she wanted to repair. Suddenly she brought their quarrel into the open.

"Elmer, you won't say it, but you think I did wrong to let them take that girl!"

"It isn't what I would have done," he said.

She threw another shaving into the fire, and watched it flame and blacken. "With the house full of savages, like that, you don't think what you're going to do. You just do it."

He said, "I thought we agreed to protect the girl."

"We kind of did, without talking about it. There wasn't any time to think. And afterward you told me they were the same kind of Indians."

"Does that make any difference?"

She thought it did. "That made it a family quarrel, and we don't know who was right or wrong."

"She wouldn't have taken that chance for no reason," Elmer insisted. "Probably she was a slave."

Lisette did not think much of that. "Even if she was, Americans ought to free their own slaves before they bother with the Indians'."

"But we'd made an agreement with her," Elmer said. "We'd promised to protect her, and then we didn't."

"You think I did wrong!" She met his eyes, steadily, with her face pale under the blackness of her heavy hair, and her eyes had a look which made her seem taller than she was. "Elmer, I don't say that what I did was right! I don't know whether it was right or wrong. Only I did what I thought was best." There was an uncomplicated nobility about her wrongness.

"But we agreed to protect her, and we didn't!" Elmer had said that before, but its meaning had been lost on her. Her passion was in justifying herself. When she talked about the Haidah girl, she talked cold facts. There was no feeling of human warmth or gallantry. She had not even commented on the girl's strange, oriental beauty.

Lisette said, "We were going to save her if we could. Then I knew we couldn't without losing everything we had. You saw them putting out my clothes to take along."

He said, "I didn't think you valued your clothes so much that you would——"

"It wasn't because they were my clothes!" she cried. "It was because you would have had to buy me new ones. I wasn't thinking about me; I was thinking about us!"

Elmer had been upset because her conscience did not seem to bother her for what she had done. Now his conscience was like a splinter in his shirt—or the point of a Haidah spear. Maybe he had thought more about the girl than about "us." He felt the need to justify himself. "Even if it had cost us something, wasn't the girl's life worth more than a few clothes?"

That was the very substance of their disagreement, and with both of them looking at the same substance they saw different things.

"Why?" Lisette had a look of honest blankness. "We need our things, to live, and we don't need the girl for anything. She was nothing to us."

"No." He went on dubbing the edge of the paddle which he had roughed out of the cedar board. He wasn't going to say any more. She saw things her way, practically and in cold blood. Her conscience did not trouble her because she could not see that she had done wrong. There was no use arguing with her.

Lisette was not willing to let the subject drop, and she felt that he had answered her question too briefly. "She wasn't anything to us, was she?"

"No," he said, carving at the soft, reddish cedar.

Again she seemed to think his answer too brief. "Elmer, was she some one you knew?"

He said she wasn't, which was more true than not. He hadn't really known the girl. She was mostly an idea of something which had been out of his reach until it was too late. Something savage and shameless and gentle and complicated which a modest and practical young woman like Lisette could not understand. The girl was the symbol of something he wanted from life. Even if he had never seen her, the need would have been there: the need of an antidote to his straight-laced upbringing.

Lisette seemed almost satisfied with his assurance. She was picking up his shavings again, and throwing them into the fire. The occupation didn't have anything to do with making the house neat—any more than you toss pebbles into the sea with the idea of tidying up the beach. It was nice to see the shavings blossom into clear flame, and the gentle roar of rain on the roof-shakes was comforting. But still the two did not understand each other. Lisette was trying to understand. "If the girl didn't mean anything to us, I don't see why she should make us quarrel. You'd think there'd been a witch in the house!"

There had been, in a way, but Elmer did not want to say so, or argue any more.

"They were all of the same tribe," Lisette said. "I think it was right for them to take her home."

That soothing statement rubbed Elmer the wrong way, terribly, and it put his resentment into words. "Don't you think she was different?" he demanded. "Didn't you think she was finer than the others?"

His wife looked honestly blank. "I didn't notice anything special about her. I thought she was like the others, except for being a female." She looked at him, wonderingly. "Did you notice anything special about her?"

Chagrined to the core, he said, "I thought I did."

She continued to look puzzled. "I don't remember anything except that she was very stupid to hang onto you, like a monkey, when she could have run into the woods and got away."

He bit his lip and frowned into the fire. That was a piece of bad judgment which he could not defend.

Lisette followed up her advantage. "What did you think was special about her?"

He retreated to the only undebatable ground in sight. "Didn't you think she was pretty?"

"*That* girl?"

"Yes," he said.

Lisette looked wondering. "That naked little Indian hussy?"

"I can't help what you call her," he said. "I thought she was beautiful."

Her eyes grew sullen. "I know what I'd think of myself if any one saw me like that!"

"Sure," he agreed. "I know what you think!" They had been over the same ground before, though less bitterly. "You think about a flannel nightgown from your ears to the floor. But I was talking about beauty."

Lisette got up, angrily. "I ain't a savage," she reminded him. "A woman has to be decent!"

"Sure," he said. "Go ahead and be decent, but don't get mad because a Haidah girl happens to be beautiful."

She said bitterly, "Ma Sims was right; men are all alike!"

He answered with a shrug. "I suppose they are, in some ways."

She said, "That's the way I was thinking about." When he did not answer, she said, "If I ain't beautiful enough for you, why didn't you trade me for that little hussy? They wanted to trade, didn't they?"

"Yes."

"Why didn't you? You'd have got what you wanted!"

He said curtly, "Don't be a fool!"

After she was gone, he concentrated on the paddle, thinning and smoothing the edges of the blade with extra care. When you haven't been quite just to some one, you have to make it up to some one else, or to the work you're doing.

He heard her open a locker to get her nightgown, and after a while he heard her brushing her hair. Go ahead, he thought, get ready for bed. Climb into your flannel nightgown in a hurry. I won't look. Modesty's your right. I won't interfere with it. Only don't get mad if I prefer the looks of a Haidah girl in a little bark skirt. . . .

Instead of going to bed, as Elmer had predicted, she came back to the fire and sat on the cougar skin before the hearth. She did not say anything at first, and he did not say anything. It seemed too natural to be new. It was more like something brought back by the primeval rain which roared in the darkness outside. Some other time, carving a canoe paddle, he must have heard that rain while his companion crouched by the fire, with her hair like a torrent of darkness over her naked shoulders and back.

Lisette was the first to speak. "The fire feels good," she said.

"And you look good," he said. She wasn't like the slim Haidah girl, but she was more of a woman. Her richly curving body had such a look of womanliness and enduring strength and tenderness. She was perfect in her different way. "You're beautiful!" he said.

"No." She shook her head, stirring the black torrent of hair which seemed like more than hair. "No," she said. But she blushed and looked pleased, and that made her more beautiful.

"You are!" he said with conviction.

She said, "I ain't as beautiful as that girl."

He was taken all aback to discover that she believed it after all. Wonderingly, he said, "But you said she was just a shameless little hussy!"

She looked down at herself, and blushed again. Meeting his eyes, she said, "I expect I am, too." Then she said, "But I ain't as beautiful as she was."

"You're more beautiful," he insisted. "You really are."

"No," she said, but she looked pleased. "I'm sorry I let them take her." Then she added, "But I'd do it again if I thought it was best for us!"

He did not answer because he was fumbling with the discovery that the same thing has different meanings in different settings. Half an hour ago he was convinced that he could never quite forgive Lisette for what he saw as the cold-blooded sacrifice of another. It was something he couldn't forgive a civilized woman. The setting had changed to one less civilized and he was secretly proud of the directness with which she had hewn to the line. There was something behind the old Haidah's offer to trade, with a hundred dollars in gold thrown in.

Part of the conversation came back to him. He said, "Do you know what the Haidah chief called you?"

She shook her head again, stirring the profound darkness of her hair.

"I like to see you do that," he said.

"Why?" she asked.

"Because your hair looks so much like a piece of the night brought in. When you move it I expect to see stars in it."

She looked at him, happily. "It's certainly black enough!" Then she said, "Her hair wasn't any nicer than mine, was it?"

"Nicer? It wouldn't have made one strand of yours!"

She was content with that, and asked, "What did the chief call me?"

"He said you were a *tatoosh-kloochman*."

"What does *tatoosh* mean?"

"It means 'eagle.' You're my eagle-woman."

"Is it something good?"

"It's the best," he said. "An eagle-woman is fierce and brave, and she helps her husband fight——"

She reached up and took his hand. "I ain't so brave. But if being ready to fight for you helps, I'm certainly your eagle-woman!"

He put down his work and sat beside her on the cougar skin, in the secure glow of the fire. "You are lovely," he said, playing with the enchanting blackness of her hair.

"Am I a shameless hussy?" she asked.

"No," he said, kissing her. Then he saw she was disappointed, and took back his unwanted gallantry. "You are my shameless hussy!"

She looked content.

CHAPTER ELEVEN

CHRISTMAS of 1854 was a good Christmas, only Governor Stevens spoiled it a little. Lisette said so when she was cutting Elmer's hair. "I don't see why he had to pick Christmas Day." She snipped her disapproval and Elmer ducked.

"If the Governor makes a good treaty," he said, "it'll be a Christmas present for everybody."

"The treaty'll be all right, but couldn't he let us have one real holiday?"

Elmer said, "He's been away for a year. Now he's going to do everything in a month. I don't suppose it would make any difference to him whether it was Christmas or Sunday or his own wedding day." Then he said, "Remember that isn't the Governor's ear."

Snipping, she said, "If it was, it'd hear plenty! I'll try to remember it was Governor Stevens and not you who took Uncle Jarvis away on Christmas Day. Why do you keep turning your head?"

"So I can look at our tree." Their Christmas tree was standing on the table, and while they owned fir trees up to three hundred feet tall, the one they had selected was a very little tree. That was because they had only a little colored paper and tinfoil for decorations. But it was their first Christmas tree and it looked fine.

"If you turn all of you," Lisette said, "you can look without having to turn your head. It's nice, ain't it? Isn't it?" She was learning to say "isn't," when she remembered. And she remembered oftener when she had her silk dress on, as she did now. After they had admired the tree together, she went back to her haircutting and her grievance. "If you're taking the Governor's part, I'd like you to tell me why he couldn't wait until next week."

"Next week he'll be away, making a treaty with the Chehalis Indians."

"What about the week after?"

"He'll be east of the mountains, making treaties with the Cayuses and Nez Perces and Klickitats and Snakes——"

Lisette interrupted him. "I can see that'll be a busy week, but what about the one after?"

"He'll be in the Blackfeet country, making treaties with the Rocky Mountain tribes."

He felt Lisette's counting fingers on his head. "That's only three weeks. Couldn't we wait that long for a treaty?"

"After that," Elmer said, "he'll probably be riding hell-for-leather to Washington to tell the Great White Father about all the treaties he's made."

Lisette's voice did not sound gay any more. "Can he make treaties that fast, and make good ones?"

"Even if he could, Indians don't like to be rushed this way." Then he said, "I'm glad the Nisquallys are our neighbors."

"Why, Elmer?"

"Leschi foresaw this. He has his people used to the idea, and he has his reservation planned. He knows just what to ask for. Maybe it won't be as clear sailing for tribes that haven't looked ahead."

"Drat the Governor!" Lisette sounded vexed with herself as well as with him. "It's Christmas Day, Elmer, and we've talked nothing but politics! That's *his* fault, but we won't let him spoil everything. I'll go with you tomorrow and see them sign his treaty, but not another word about it today!"

"You're right," he said. "How's my Christmas haircut?"

She combed his stubborn hair and looked at him earnestly. "It ain't, it's not a very good haircut, but it makes you look nicer. You look handsome."

"I'd better," he said, "going out with any one as beautiful as you!" Lisette was wearing the black silk dress she had inherited on her mother's death on the plains. It had a very full skirt and puffed sleeves, and the low neck gave a daring glimpse of her flawless white bosom. But it wasn't only the dress which made her look like a fine lady. There was her heavy blue-black hair which stirred wonder even in some one who saw it every day. It was parted, accurately, in the center and swept back, dipping low over her ears, to the heavy knot at the nape of her neck. Her face had too much strength and seriousness to be pretty, but it was a strength which could change to tenderness. And the excitement of being dressed up and complimented lightened her seriousness and gave her eyes a look which made her beautiful.

She told him, happily, "You say such things!"

"Such things as what?"

She hesitated, then said, "Such things as I like to hear!"

He drew her toward the bench and brushed his face against her dress. "You're lovely," he said, listening to the silk, "and you have a fine dress." After a minute, he said, "If I never saw the world again, I think the rustle of silk is one of the sounds I'd always remember."

She swished her skirt, thoughtfully. "It is exciting, isn't it?"

"One of the most exciting sounds there is," he said. "It makes me think of my Aunt Caroline's house in Fairhaven on special evenings. There'd be lots of people, beautifully dressed, and spermaceti candles burning everywhere with a nice smell and reflected in the polished floors and furniture. There'd be music, too. Maybe dancing. When I was small I thought the rustle of silk dresses was the real, secret music. It seemed like the voices of all the fine things, whispering that things would always be exciting, and every one would always be rich and happy."

Lisette took a deep breath, and the silk dress rustled against his cheek. "It must have been very grand," she said.

He looked at the earth floor of their cabin. "That's the way it seemed to me when I was little. Aunt Caroline was very strict, and I guess some of the people were pretty stuffy. Do you know who was the grandest one ever there?"

"Who, Elmer?"

"Uncle Jarvis," he said.

She said loyally, "I wouldn't trade him for all the others!"

Talking of Uncle Jarvis reminded them of the inconsiderate Governor who had borrowed him on Christmas Day. Their family celebration could only be the scraps of the day which the Governor left. But they were not going to talk about that any more.

Elmer asked, "Is my Christmas haircut about done?"

She disengaged herself from his arms and walked around the bench, with the scissors in one hand and the comb in the other. It made him feel like a tree being trimmed. "Almost," she decided, coming back to him. "Just a little off here." Snipping, she said, "There's something about cutting hair— Barbers are supposed to be awful talkative, aren't they?"

"I think so," he said. "I don't know. I've never been to one. At home, Mother did all the haircutting, and on board ship Old Tom was our barber. And before we were married Uncle used to hack off some of my hair when he thought I was getting to look too much like Daniel Boone."

She said, "I wouldn't have known how much you needed one if you hadn't put on your best clothes."

"It was the clothes, then. I told you my hair was all right. If I'd dressed like an Indian, my hair wouldn't have been long enough."

"Not quite long enough to braid." She took the towel from around his shoulders, and shook it in the fireplace. "Now you look civilized; you look fine."

"I'd better, going out with a beautiful lady." The broadcloth suit had been made for his brother Charles who slept somewhere in the China Sea, where he would never need it. Like Lisette's dress, it was enjoying a kind of immortality. It was a little tight, and the coat sleeves did not go all the way with Elmer's long arms, but it was a fine suit and its tightness was a reminder that he was dressed up.

Lisette said, "I'll have to look at my Christmas present and see who this woman is you're talking about!"

He stood behind her while she looked into the new mirror on the wall. Elmer had made it by framing a piece of glass and a thin board, with black cloth stretched between the glass and wood. It was a mirror in which one saw darkly, as the Bible says. In it, Lisette was reflected like a girl who keeps the bloom of youth in the twilight of an old daguerreotype. The mirror had the accursed trick of making every reflection look wistful, and a happy face most wistful of all.

Elmer did not feel right about the dark mirror, but they had been doing without any, and his wife thought it a fine present. And he had the comfort of looking from her dark reflection to herself, like turning from a picture of old times to the warm and living time itself.

"I don't see any one beautiful," Lisette said, "but I'm certainly happy. Shall we go over now?"

He said, "I think we might as well. Mary could probably do with some company."

"And some help." She tied her bonnet before the new mirror. "It must be vexing, trying to get a big dinner without knowing what time it's for."

"I don't think he'll be very late," Elmer said.

The cabin across the Inlet had only two rooms, but when you came from a one-room cabin it seemed like a big house. And it was full of good smells and holiday preparations.

Mary was dressed for the holiday, too. She wore a new dress of red calico, with an Indian beaded belt, and many strings of blue and white Hudson's Bay beads around her neck. Apparently, she had even thought of putting shoes on her bare feet. She met them at the door with a new pair in her hand, but she did not actually put them on. A minute of *"Klahowyas"* and "Merry Christmases" and compliments on her dress encouraged the rebellion of her feet. She put the shoes under the bunk, took a clean plate from on top of it, and pattered about in search of others. "S'pose we *muck-a-muck* now, h'm?"

The echo of Uncle Jarvis was warming, but it was also a reminder that his canoe hadn't even come in sight around the point.

"S'pose we wait for Uncle?" Elmer suggested.

"I think we should," Lisette said. "He may not be here for hours."

Mary saw no difficulty in that. "We can *muck-a-muck* while we wait for him."

"Then he would have to eat alone."

"*Wake*," Mary said. "We will *muck-a-muck* with him."

Lisette looked alarmed, and Elmer explained, "But, Mary, we couldn't go on eating that long!"

"*Wake cumtux.*" She pointed at the food, which was everywhere. "We have *hyas muck-a-muck!*"

They laughed, and the boy patted his middle. "*Hyas muck-a-muck, tenas aquatine!*"

"Merry Christmas is a *potlatch*. You *muck-a-muck* all day, h'm?"

"*Wake*," Elmer said with regret.

That was because Bostons *muck-a-muck* too *hyak*, Mary decided. She tried to tell Lisette how fast Elmer used to eat when he was building his house. In pantomime, she showed him paddling swiftly across the Inlet, with a preoccupied face that was very funny. Arriving at the dinner table in his canoe, he took one hand from the paddle and reached out for food, which he carried to his mouth. Then he put his hand back on the still-moving paddle, and turned toward his own shore, without having missed a stroke.

It was a good pantomime, and Lisette said her husband looked just like that when he was working seriously. "Any one would know you were his aunt," she told Mary. "You can look just like him!"

Mary was pleased and patted her nephew's arm. "He is a fine man," she said, "and some day he will *memaloose* himself by eating too *hyak*."

When Elmer reported the canoe, it was past the middle of the afternoon. The Inlet was gray with rain, and rain clouds were ghosting past the big fir trees on the other shore. Uncle Jarvis had rounded the point and was heading straight for the house.

Lisette came over to the window and assured herself that it was Uncle Jarvis. Her face was rosy from the fire, and she brought good cooking smells with her and made the boy hungry again.

"It'll take him about twenty minutes," he said. "Will dinner be ready?"

She gave him a despairing look. "It ain't that kind of dinner! The venison was done hours ago, and lots of other things. But the grouse are still roasting, and the winter salmon broiling. And the sticks of clams and other things aren't even started. A *potlatch* dinner seems to be like a brook: It's here, and it's gone and it's still on the way. You don't know whether you should stop where you are, or run after it, or go to meet it!"

"You wouldn't be so confused," he said, "if we'd kept up with the dinner, eating it."

"Maybe not," she said, "but I'd have been worse than confused!"

When Uncle Jarvis came in, he put his arms around the three of them, and kissed the women roundly. "Merry Christmas!" he said, "and Happy Days!" His unfamiliar frock coat was wet and cold from the rain and his eyes looked tired, but he was so big and welcoming that Christmas seemed to start all over again. "It there anything to eat?" he asked. "I've had nothing but words today."

Mary looked pleased and thought there was *tenas muck-a-muck.*

"*Cult-a-mana!* I still have chores to do! You can help me, Elmer. Get your coat, or you'll drown."

Elmer put on his oilskin coat and went with him though he couldn't think what chores needed to be done at that hour.

In the hard winter rain, his uncle said, "When I was building here, Captain Crosby talked me out of an 'L'. He said there wasn't enough cold and snow to need it. There's not, but next time I'd build a covered bridge, h'm?"

When they got to the barn, Uncle Jarvis didn't pretend any more about chores. He looked grim and said, "Well, the fat's in the fire!"

Elmer stared at a Mexican saddle hanging on the wall and heard the rain beating harshly on the shakes outside. "How do you mean?"

"*That damned treaty!*" he roared.

The boy was bewildered because he'd never had any real doubt that the treaty would be all right. "Is it very bad?"

His uncle said, "It sounded bad enough for me to refuse to witness it. I'll go with you tomorrow to be in at the kill, but only as an unpopular spectator, h'm?"

The boy floundered in his mind and looked for straws of hope. "Is all of it bad?"

"Some of it's quite reasonable. The Squaxons are getting their island for a reservation. That means they'll have what they had before, except for a little company."

"What about the others?" The big man hadn't said anything about the Nisquallys.

"Fair to bad, Elmer. Some very bad!"

"What about the Nisquallys?"

"The worst of all!"

The boy sat on the plough beam because his legs were suddenly trembling. His claim wasn't three miles from the Nisqually camp, and there mustn't be any trouble. He and Lisette had so much to do. "But why?"

"They're allowed one section of land. That's about two acres for each Indian. Generous, h'm?"

Elmer stared at the trampled straw on the floor, while the rain clattered harshly on the shake roof. "One section. That isn't a tenth of what they're using now!"

"It isn't any of it," his uncle said grimly.

"How do you mean?"

"I mean it don't include any of the land they occupy. They have to abandon all their houses and herds and everything else they can't carry with them."

The boy's mind refused to believe what it was hearing. "I don't understand," he said. "Where is the reservation going to be?"

"On the bluff above McAllister Creek, about two miles inland."

He tried to locate the place in his mind. "There's nothing there!"

"Nothing but fir woods and gravel. Not even a stream."

"It must be a mistake!"

Tramping about on the littered earth floor, his uncle said grimly, "It is a terrible mistake!"

"It don't make sense!" Elmer insisted.

"It could make sense in a way."

"In what way, Uncle?"

"It sounds as if the Governor had said, 'Some of you Nisquallys are canoe Indians. All right, I'll put you on a gravel bluff where you'll never see the water. You depend on salmon for food. All right, I'll put you in a place without streams, where no salmon will ever come inland to spawn. The rest of you are horse Indians. All right, I'll put you in a fir wilderness so thick that no pony could ever get through. You have herds on the big prairie. All right, I'll take the prairie from you and put you in a place that hasn't forage for a goat. You want to learn agriculture. All right, I'll put you in a hell of fir woods and gravel that a generation couldn't clear and only a madman would try to cultivate!'" The big man glared at his nephew, without seeing him. "It makes sense if Governor Stevens is that kind of man, h'm? It hangs together if he wants the Nisquallys to chose between death by starvation and death in war."

"It can't be that!" Elmer insisted. "They've never made any trouble, and every one trusts them. The Governor couldn't have anything against them! He can't know what he's doing——"

"As I heard it," Uncle Jarvis said, "he asked the opinion of one man. He showed the treaty to Colonel Shaw and asked if the Indians would sign it. The Colonel said, 'Sure, they're trusting people. I could get them to sign their death warrant.' And the Governor said, 'Get them to sign this.'"

The boy felt crushed under the weight of something too monstrous to believe and impossible to understand. "Hasn't any one told him——"

"Some people don't like to be told, h'm? I got as far as telling him my conscience wouldn't let me witness such a treaty. He said, 'I don't need you,' and turned on his military heel."

"But why?" Elmer sat on the plough in the cold barn, staring at a saddle on its peg and hearing the rain, like shot, on the roof-shakes overhead. Then, among the jumble of ruins in his mind, he saw the shape and extent of what had been destroyed. "But Leschi wants peace. He had his reservation planned, and he was learning to farm so he could teach his people. The Governor was supposed to want peace, and to have the Indians go on a reservation and learn farming. When they both want the same thing, couldn't they have fixed things up?"

Tramping about, Uncle Jarvis said, "It wasn't any question of 'they.' Governor Stevens don't consult people; he tells them!"

Elmer said, "The Indians don't have to sign, do they?"

"No, but most of them will."

"The Nisquallys won't!"

"Quiemuth will."

"He's not important."

"He's chief of the tribe."

It was news to the boy. "Since when?" he asked.

"Since Stevens appointed him. As Superintendent of Indian Affairs he's selected chiefs to look out for the interests of the different tribes. And, as Governor, he's dealing with them."

It didn't sound fair. "The Indians should be allowed to decide who their chiefs are!"

"That would only make confusion," his uncle said. "Their chiefs might not be willing to sign the treaty, h'm?"

"The Nisquallys would certainly have chosen Leschi," Elmer said.

"I'd say the Governor recognized that when he chose the lesser brother. That puts it in the family, like something near the truth. He made Leschi one of the sub-chiefs."

"Does that give him any power?"

Uncle Jarvis shrugged his great, square shoulders. "Enough so he's not ignored, and not enough so he can have any effect on the treaty. If he signs it, and there's trouble afterward, the Governor can say, 'This treaty was signed by your most trusted and powerful citizen. It is a pity your confidence was misplaced.' If he refuses to sign, the Governor can say, 'He was only a sub-chief, with no real power.'"

It was cold in the barn, and there was no comfort in the harsh rattle of rain on the shakes, or in what Uncle Jarvis was saying. Elmer shivered and got up from his hard seat on the plough beam. "It don't sound good, does it?"

"It's a bad business, and I can't see the end of it." Then his look changed, and he clapped his nephew roughly on the shoulder. "God damn it, boy, I didn't want to spoil your magnificent young appetite! I wasn't going to give any of you a peek at the Governor's Christmas present to a happy country. I made up my mind to that, and then I found I was so mad that if I didn't tell some one I'd tell every one. You're the sacrificial lamb. We'll go in now and give our women a good Christmas, h'm? Eat, drink and be merry, and tomorrow we'll die in our burning cabins, or in some lousy ambush in the woods."

That was not a cheerful closing note, but its effect on Elmer was cheering. It put him on his mettle and cleared his mind. The nameless dread had been brought out into the light and defined in words. That made it a hard fact to be dealt with, not a shadow to avoid.

They had a fine Christmas. Uncle Jarvis had never been in quite as good spirits or as gallant to the women. He had bought a gallon jug of whiskey for the occasion, and he poured it out almost like water. Mary was not offered any because whiskey has a bad effect on Indians, and Lisette would not take any because her father had taken too much. But Uncle Jarvis drank recklessly, without getting drunk. It only made him more gallant to the women, and better company. Elmer gave up his too-ambitious resolve to take drink for drink with his uncle, but he set a record for himself. And he thought it the best whiskey he had ever tasted, with the best effect. It made the bonds of love and friendship as visible as the layers of tobacco smoke which hovered and shifted and wove patterns above the table. And it joined the four of them in one warm, human glow. That glow was only made more living by the cold rain outside the window and by a procession of rain clouds that swept by the opposite shore, sometimes revealing and sometimes covering the three-hundred-foot trees with their misty skirts.

The women did not drink, and they did not seem to need it. Lisette's face was changing all the time from delicate to deeper pink and her black eyes flashed in answer to Uncle Jarvis's compliments. He had become interested in her mother's maiden name, which was Lannes. The name was famous in France, he said, even before Marshal Lannes distinguished himself with Napoleon. And some of the family had come to New Orleans. By a series of magnificent guesses, he established Lisette's relationship to the family and with the aid of a few more drinks he traced her looks to a famous beauty by that name. Lisette resembled her in a certain portrait, he insisted, even to the French cut of her gown. . . .

A woman can be important to a party because of what she says, or because of what is said to her. Mary did not get so many compliments, and she was not raised to a mysterious importance which made her change while the others looked at her, until the whole atmosphere was touched with glamor. But Mary did her part by telling stories of her people while dusk closed down outside and the world became a black night of rain. Uncle Jarvis had carried in logs as if they were feathers, and built up the biggest fire the hearth had ever seen. The women were afraid the cabin would catch fire, but the big man seemed to think that the house had had a few drinks and could stand it. And Elmer, who had also had more drinks than one, backed him up. So they had a magnificent fire which kept them well back from the hearth. They sat on deer- and bear- and cougar-skin rugs, while Mary told stories of her people. Elmer had heard some of them before, without thinking much of them. But now he saw they were fine, important stories. And there was one famous Nisqually story which he had heard of but never heard. That was the story of the Wild Woman.

Maybe it was by accident, and maybe it was because Mary was a woman, but she told the story of her famous woman ancestor who was a foreigner to the extent that she was not a Nisqually. The telling of the story was complicated because part of it was in Chinook Jargon, with sentences of English. And finer points were explained in Nisqually, which Uncle Jarvis translated to the others. Put together, it was like this:

I will tell you a story about *ancuttie* people and the first white men who came here.

There was a great tribe living at the mouth of a river near the place where Old Town is built. There were a thousand people in the tribe. They were not Nisquallys or Puyallups or any other tribe we have today. No one remembers their name, because they were all *memaloose* long ago. All except one who lost the power of speech. When she learned to speak again, it was in another tongue. So the name and language of her people is forgotten.

These people were canoe Indians. They lived on clams and fish and berries. When the salmon tribe visited their river in the fall, they caught and smoked what they needed. And they shot arrows to kill birds and deer.

One morning in summer, they looked across the water at something they had never seen before. It was a great canoe with wings. Really, it was only a *tenas shipo,* but it seemed great to them. The ship came into the mouth of their river and stopped. There were white men on the little ship, and they were the first the Indians had ever seen. Some of them had yellow hair and blue eyes. And they had beards, and they wore hard moccasins up to their knees, and belts outside their clothes. These men told the Indians, in signs, that they had come from the north, where it was cold, many "sleeps" away. They must have been from the country you call "Alaska," and Indians call the "Land of Blue Ice and the Home of the Thunderbird."

There was no Jargon in those times, but the white men showed the Indians furs, and made signs that that was what they wanted. The Indians had only what they needed, but the men told them to get many furs. They would come back another year and buy them. Soon they went away in their little ship.

There was one bad thing. On the little ship some of the

men were sick, with sores all over them. And the Indians who went on the ship said it had a bad smell. But they did not know what it was, and they thought white men smelled like that.

After the ship was gone, the Indians got the sickness. First it was only a few, and then there were many hundreds sick. They did not know about smallpox. They only knew that fevers should be cooled in water. When they were burning with the fever, they went to the beach and lay in the salt water. They never got up again, and when the tide went away from them the beach was covered with *memalooses*.

Soon there was only one Indian left. She was maybe fourteen years old. All the others were *memaloose*. This girl saw that the land of her people was not good any more. If she stayed, she would be *memaloose*. She had seen that any one who touched the sick or anything they touched got the sickness. She was afraid to take anything with her. But she took fire, which is clean. She made a tinder from the inside bark of cedar and put it in a split stick and lit it from the last fire of her people.

The girl went away in the morning, with the fire-stick in her hand. She was like the first girl, when the Thunderbird had just made the world. She did not know any people except her own, who were all *memalooses,* and she was alone.

She went far away from the salt water and found a cave in the hills. There she made a fire with her tinder, and lived alone. . . .

Many years after, there was a young Nisqually chief. He was a horse Indian and a great hunter, like Leschi. One day he was hunting with some of his braves. They went into the hills, farther than they had ever gone before. They were in a different country, but the chief was not afraid.

While they were hunting, a woman jumped out of the bushes and ran away. She was all naked, and she ran as fast as any deer.

The braves said, "A *pelton kloochman!*"

The young chief said, "Catch her!"

They spread out like a net and went after her. She ran and

ran over the hills like a deer that is never tired. After a while they caught up with her and made a circle around her. She tried to fight them with a stone knife, but there were too many of them. They lassoed her and took the knife. It was just a piece of flint, like men would have used when the world was new. The woman was *hiyu skookum,* and she was very brown and naked. Her hair was as thick as Lisette's, and it was so long that it touched the ground. When the Nisquallys tried to talk to her she did not *cumtux.* She only made animal sounds.

The Nisquallys did not know if she was *pelton,* or a savage from some tribe they did not know.

When she saw the Nisquallys did not mean to hurt her, she did not fight them any more. She led them to her cave, where she had kept her fire burning all those years. The Nisquallys knew she was not *pelton* because of her fine cave. She had the skins of animals she had killed for a bed. She had arrows with sharp flints on them, and a bow with some of her hair braided for a string. She had much smoked salmon, and berries which had been smoked and dried in the sun, and there was a deer hanging in the cave. The woman had everything she needed, only she did not have any people.

So the young chief said they would take her to the land of the Nisquallys. It was not good for her to live there alone. They told her, in signs, that they were going to take her with them, and after a while she understood. She did not want to go at first; then she was willing. Maybe she began to remember her own people, who were *memaloose.* Before she would go with them, she made a tinder of cedar bark and put fire in it. She put her tinder in a split stick to carry to the land of the strangers. She thought she had the only fire in the world.

The Nisquallys took her home. They taught her to wear clothes, and to speak. At first it was like teaching a child, but she was not *pelton.* She was wise and brave, and she learned to speak good Nisqually. And she told them what she remembered about her people. The Indians called her "the Wild Woman," because of the way they found her. The young chief married her, and she gave him eight *tenas men.* Many

Nisquallys are the children of her grandchildren. I am one of them, and Leschi is one. That is what makes him wise and brave and a great hunter. We say when a *tenas man* is born, the *tamanous* of an ancestor comes to live in him. He may be like his mother's father, or one of his father's people. It depends on the *tamanous* that lives again in him.

Leschi thinks like a wise Boston. He likes the Bostons' religion and thinks every one should follow it. Particularly the Bostons. He is a wise man who thinks much. But sometimes he is restless and can't stay on the flats or the prairie any more. Then he goes away to the mountains to hunt. When he is restless like that, it is the *tamanous* of the Wild Woman. She wants to go back to her hills and be free again.

When they asked her, Mary did not think the Wild Woman was very free in her civilized life, with eight children. And she did not think the chief took her hunting. That was for men, while women picked berries and dug *camas* and *kalse*.

But the Wild Woman was a good wife, and she was the most famous of all Nisqually women. She had the greatest number of children, and she was always strong and healthy. Her seed helped make the tribe strong.

Uncle Jarvis must have heard the story many times, but he was full of questions about it, and some of Mary's answers made him roar with laughter. He said, "But I don't see what made the Wild Woman so strong and healthy! And what made her hair grow down to the ground, h'm?"

Mary was sitting on a deer-skin rug, with her bare feet toward the fire, and her braided hair coming down in two straight lines to her hands in her red calico lap. Her homely face looked wise in the firelight, and nicely amused because her husband did not understand what should be clear to any one. Patiently, she explained: "That was because she led a healthy life. She lived outdoors and let the sun shine on her body. She ate healthy food and drank pure water. She lived with nature. That made her *hiyu skookum*.

They all laughed at that, and Uncle Jarvis laughed until his eyes filled with tears. Wiping them, he said, "I think the

story's true, most of it. That's what makes it so God damned
funny! You'd think it had been written by some wistful Indian
Rousseau!" He went back to reasoning with Mary. "So you
think the Wild Woman practically went to the city to live
when she joined up with the Nisquallys?"

"It was like that," Mary agreed.

"You think the old-time Indians didn't live with nature,
h'm?"

"It was better than now," she admitted, "but the Nisquallys
have always been too civilized."

"Didn't they live outdoors, like the Wild Woman?"

"Not as much," she insisted. "They have always built plank
houses."

"But the Wild Woman had a cave, h'm?"

"That was for her food and fire. Maybe she slept there
when it rained, but she lived outdoors in the fresh air and
sun."

"Don't the sun shine on other Indians?"

"Not enough," Mary said. "They always wore too many
clothes. Blankets now. It used to be skins."

"You said the Wild Woman was strong and her hair grew
down to the ground because she ate healthy food."

"That was part of it."

"Didn't the Nisquallys eat healthy food?"

"It was not the same," Mary said. "They have always eaten
too much cooked food."

The big man looked fierce because he could not get the
best of her. "If your Wild Woman ate her food raw, what
was she doing with that fire in the cave?"

Elmer and his wife looked at each other, laughing. It was
getting to be a kind of game, and every one knew it.

Mary said, "She had to smoke the salmon and berries so
they would keep. And some food has to be cooked——"

"Ha!" Uncle Jarvis looked triumphant, and poured more
whiskey in his glass. "Your Wild Woman was a humbug!
Everything she ate was smoked or roasted. She slept indoors
and ate the same food as other Indians. She breathed the
same air and drank the same water. If she was any stronger

than the others, it was because she started that way. She didn't get smallpox because she was tough to start with, h'm? She practically wasted her time in those hills."

"*Wake.*" Mary was shaking her head and smiling at the fire. She wasn't convinced by a word of it.

"As for her getting more sun," he said, "I'll bet she was covered with clothes. D'ye hear me? Covered with clothes!"

"*Halo.*" She was still smiling and unconvinced. "She had nothing——"

"When they saw her. Of course! She was a woman, and a good showman, h'm? She knew how to attract Nisqually braves. D'ye think they'd have chased her if she'd been dressed like all the other *kloochmen?*"

"*Wake.*" The Indian woman smiled and shook her head and would not be convinced by anything he said.

"As for other Indians not getting enough sun," Uncle Jarvis said, "what about the papooses I see running about Nisqually, h'm?"

"That is because of the Wild Woman," Mary said. "It was that way when I was *tenas.* The Wild Woman is our ancestor. When we are *tenas* she tells our hearts that the Thunderbird has just made the world, and we are free. She tells us to run naked in the sun and rain, and to eat raw food. When we are a little older, people who are still older teach us to wear clothes and have civilized ways. Their voices are the voices of the old Nisqually people speaking to the Wild Woman when they brought her home. Our story is like her story. Only we change too soon, and we learn not to hear the voice of her *tamanous* any more. Leschi is a great man because he still hears the voice that spoke to him when he was a child."

They watched the fire for a while, and then Uncle Jarvis sighed. "Maybe all of us have the Wild Woman for an ancestor, h'm?"

"*Wake.*" Mary lit her pipe, which had gone out. "She became a Nisqually. She is my ancestor. She could not be yours."

He looked exasperated. "I can't get any satisfaction out of her! She was a humbug, and that is all nonsense about her healthy life."

"*Wake.*"

"Would I get big and strong if I ran around the hills like a *pelton man?* Would the women chase me, h'm?"

When the young couple left, they were still arguing about it.

The rain had almost stopped, but it was a black night on the Inlet, and black on their own shore. Their fire had gone out and the house was cold, but their little Christmas tree looked beautiful and mysterious in the light of a grease lamp.

Elmer had drunk too much, but he was still feeling fine. "It was a good Christmas, wasn't it?"

"The nicest I ever had," Lisette told him. "Coming home is nice, too. Our little tree was waiting for us." She fixed a bit of tinfoil as if it were a ribbon on a child's hair. "Did something go wrong about the treaty, Elmer?"

He had drunk a lot of whiskey, trying to forget the treaty. He had forgotten it and felt fine. Now he didn't feel so fine. He only felt as if he had drunk too much. "I think it was only preliminaries today."

She said: "You don't have to tell me anything, unless you want to. I made you promise not to talk about it."

"I don't think they did much today."

"I suppose not." Then she asked, "Is it very bad?"

"We didn't talk about it. Why should you think it was bad?"

"I just knew," she said. "It ain't very bad, is it?"

"No. Everything's going to be fine. Shall we go to bed?"

"All right. If you'll unhook my dress. You aren't going to be sick, are you?"

"No," he said. "I feel good. I'll feel fine, holding you."

"All right," she said. "I want you to hold me tight."

CHAPTER TWELVE

THE TREATY ground was on a bend of Medicine Creek. Looking north, one saw the creek going away between the rich bottom land and the foot of the high bluff, which it separated. Half a mile from the tide flats, Medicine Creek joined the Shonadaub and for their brief stretch together they prospered as a sizable river. Had they been married earlier, they might have done great things. As it was a ship could sail half a mile inland at high tide, though only a canoe could go farther. The two-masted schooner, *R. B. Potter,* was now lying at that head of navigation, with her gray sails furled in the rain. Governor Stevens had chartered the schooner to take his party to the various treaty points on the Sound, with gifts for the Indians.

To the north and east of the treaty ground was the Nisqually council ground. The creeks harbored the canoes of the fish Indians. That was the council ground as it had been for centuries. There the braves who found the Wild Woman had brought their captive home. There, nine years ago, Leschi had brought the first American settlers.

Elmer pointed out to Lisette the two great hollow cedar stumps in which the McAllister family had lived while the Kentuckian built his house, with the help of the Indians; also the two-story log house and orchard and prosperous fields between the two creeks. The thousand-acre farm in the heart of their council ground was the Indians' gift of welcome to the first family of settlers. It was the first American footprint in the land of the Nisquallys.

The second footprint was this treaty ground of today.

The third footprint was being surveyed on top of the hundred-and-fifty-foot bluff, close to the west. There a mile-square patch of sterile wilderness was to be the Nisquallys' home tomorrow.

On three sides, the treaty ground was defined by the loop of Medicine Creek, and on the fourth by the steep bluff. It was a few wooded acres which rose like an island from the lower bottom land. The underbrush and some of the fallen trees had been cleared away, making a rough park. Except for the rain, it was something like a park on a holiday, and something like a fair. The woods were full of people, walking slowly and talking in groups, or standing close under the big trees for shelter. Most of them were Indians, with their heads protected by their drawn-up blankets, or by identical new straw hats such as farmers wear in the hayfield. By way of holiday music, there was the occasional buzzing whine of a jew's-harp, played by an Indian boy under a tree. Sometimes there was a duet or trio of them. There were signs of refreshments, too. The grounds were dotted with identical empty molasses jugs. Occasionally there was a discarded straw hat, or a jew's-harp edged with a film of rust after one night in the rain.

Once they passed an old Indian, sitting on a log with a molasses jug beside him. His blanket had slipped down from his gray head, which was wet from the rain, and his withered face stared at the wet, hacked salal before him. He looked so woebegone that he might have been funny in his grief which seemed to have something to do with the molasses jug. But they did not know whether he had taken too much of the sticky stuff, or was regretting the sale of his birthright for a quart of blackstrap.

The straw hats and jew's-harps and jugs of molasses were the presents which had been given out the day before to put the Indians in good humor for signing the treaty. They had not been too successful. Word had been sent everywhere of the fine presents the Indians would receive when they came to the treaty. When the presents were given out they were not very much. Many of the Indians had refused the things, or given them to the children.

They were fine presents for children, and when the three articles were used together they made a good showing. Under one tree there were three boys wearing straw hats and playing jew's-harps and eating blackstrap all at the same time. Two of the boys were Indians, with broad faces and narrow black eyes, and the third was a fine-looking white boy of eleven or twelve. They were sitting on the ground about a molasses jug with a big splinter of wood sticking out of the uncorked neck. The white boy was the orchestra leader, and he was trying to get the others to play in unison.

"We're going to play 'Home, Sweet Home,'" he said. *"Cumtux?"*

"Wake nika cumtux," the first Indian boy said.

"It goes like this:" The white boy put his jew's-harp between his teeth and beat the metal tongue with a molasses-stained finger. While he played something like a bumblebee's version of "Home, Sweet Home," the second Indian boy took the stick out of the molasses jug, leaned back until his straw hat fell off, and let the blackstrap drip into his open mouth.

"That's the way it goes," the white boy said. "I'll have a taste of that molasses, and then we'll go to work." He leaned his head back until his straw hat fell off, and let the black molasses drip into his mouth. While the molasses dripped, water from the sheltering fir tree dripped on the white boy, and on the Indian boys who fingered the jew's-harps between their teeth, trying to make them play "Home, Sweet Home." The boys did not mind the dripping rain, or the wet ground on which they were sitting. And if they did not understand each other's language, they understood each other and were having a fine time.

"Now we'll go to work." The American boy put the stick back in the jug, returned his straw hat to his dark head, and wiped the jew's-harp on his sleeve. "Are you ready?"

They were not ready because the first Indian boy had taken the stick out of the blackstrap and was letting it drip into his mouth.

"We have to get together on this," the white boy said. "I got work to do. Pretty soon I have to sign that treaty." It had an important sound, but the others did not understand English, and they were already engaged in the only part of treaty making which they understood. The white boy did not seem to remember for very long. By the time the well-licked splinter of wood was returned to the jug, he had a new idea. And when the spectators moved on, the members of the orchestra were dripping blackstrap on the tongues of their instruments in the hope of improving their tone.

Lisette asked, "What do you suppose he meant about signing the treaty—the one who looked like a white boy?"

"He is a white boy," Uncle Jarvis said. "That's Governor Stevens's son. I'd take it that he's to witness the chiefs' marks on the treaty, h'm?"

Elmer wondered if the boy was taking Uncle Jarvis's place, but he did not want to ask. It was the first time the big man had spoken since they reached the treaty ground, and he was only silent in a bad mood. So Elmer compromised by looking back at the distinguished boy—and bumped into some one coming from the other direction.

"Cult-a-mana!"

"Pardon me!" Elmer said.

The Indian was already going away among the trees: a supple-waisted young brave in checked shirt and leather leggings, with a blanket over his arm and the smell of a wet horse about him.

Their collision had been nothing, and the impatient oath was nothing, but the boy smarted with hurt surprise. It was his first discourtesy from an Indian of the Territory. He had always felt as safe among them as if he had been on the street at home. The shock of collision was nothing to the shock of realizing that Indians could be unfriendly.

Ahead, the crowds were thicker, with an occasional settler or blue-uniformed soldier among the blanketed Indians. Army tents and campfires were in an open space under the trees. The fires looked honest and good on a wet December morning, and wood smoke sharpened the stimulating smell of hot coffee.

Just ahead of them, Indians and white men were clustering

around a man who was addressing them in a big, soft voice
that had a familiar twang.

Uncle Jarvis looked over the heads of the little crowd. "It's
'Old Cush,'" he said. "Wouldn't you know that voice was
from Maine?"

They worked their way around the circle until they found a
break where they were able to see the best story-teller in
Washington Territory. Every one who heard him agreed he
was better than Joe Miller's Joke Book, and Indians who did
not know a word of English listened to him with profound
attention and delight.

Cushman was a stocky man with bright blue eyes and a
great red beard. He was saying in his soft northern voice:
"Boys, God outdid himself that morning! Just before we
got to the fa'm where our friend was going to preach, He
sent a sma't shower of rain. The rest of us was prepared for
it, but I cal'alated the preacher was wet through, and I was
ready to lend him my hunting knife so he could get out of his
delightful buckskin undergarments before they squeezed him
out . . ."

As he went on, Old Cush was no longer telling the story; he
had become the minister, preaching a sermon from the grip
of wet buckskin underwear that was closing him in its terrible
vise. He was almost killing them with laughter by not being
funny. He was mortified, preaching a serious sermon and
fighting with the imaginary buckskin underwear as modestly
as possible. Every gesture was a triumph because he tried to
make it casual, and tried to conceal it from the ladies of the
congregation.

The boy's aching ribs were jostled by the elbow of some one
pushing his way into the circle. He turned and saw a large,
dirty hand laid on his wife's shoulder.

"*Liza.*"

Looking up, Elmer saw the black-bearded face of one of
the Sims boys. He hadn't seen any of them since the trouble
on Rush's farm. He had almost managed to forget them, and
he resented this one showing up in time to spoil Cushman's

sermon-dance. The act was spoiled, because he did not feel like laughing any more; he felt uneasy.

Lisette looked uneasy, too, and she murmured without enthusiasm, "How do you do, Joshua?"

He looked over her head. "If you ask me, yonder preacher's having fits!"

The crowd was closing in in front of them, while Old Cush's voice boomed solemnly from somewhere out of sight. It sounded as if the circulation had gone from his legs and he was preaching from the ground. It must be very funny, but the fun was spoiled.

They moved away from the roaring circle, with Lisette asking dutifully after the Sims tribe.

"Aunt Bess told us you was married," Joshua said. "This your man?" When they were introduced, he looked harder at Elmer, with a start of unpleasant surprise. "Ain't you—?" Then he saw Uncle Jarvis, who had followed them. "Liza, is he one of your kin, too?" Apparently, Lisette's foster parents had not told anything that might bring trouble. Their loyalty gave this meeting an awkward hitch.

"How's your father, Joshua; the old fighting eagle?" Uncle Jarvis did not seem to feel anything awkward about the present or the past, and he was holding out his hand.

"Paw's well enough," the young giant admitted, grudgingly.

"That's good. Tell him I was asking for him. You came alone, h'm?"

"I got an interest in this treaty," Joshua explained. "I'm going to get me a farm outen it."

"How'll you do that?" Lisette asked.

He said, "You'll see, when they clear the varmint outen that bottom land!"

Elmer felt low. He knew in a general way that the Nisquallys would lose their land, and that white settlers would move in after a while. But he hadn't thought of people waiting like buzzards, before the treaty was even signed or ratified.

Lisette put it into words. "You know about waiting for dead men's shoes, Josh. The treaty ain't signed yet."

"It'll be fixed up before noon." Then he became affable. "They got a joke about it. The new reservation's kind of held up for a while."

When the others did not say anything, Uncle Jarvis asked, obligingly, "How's that, h'm?"

"The Governor can't figure no way of getting his men up on the bluff to survey it!" He laughed, and the boy hated him. At their other meeting he had been almost sorry for the outnumbered Pikes who made him think of big, stupid animals in a trap. This time there was no trap. Joshua had the law and the government on his side with a vengeance. It was a triumph over everything Uncle Jarvis believed in; a bigger triumph than if they had driven Rush from his farm. Joshua mightn't know that, but the treaty was giving him an advantage over people of another color. It gave him confidence and brought out something brutal which did not have to hide any more.

"That's a good joke," Uncle Jarvis said. "A damned fine joke! D'ye think the Indians will see how funny it is?"

Joshua showed his long yellow teeth through his beard. "That's being fixed up, too," he said.

"It is, h'm?"

"Mike Simmonds was out our way last week. He said the Governor says we got to get up a militia, in case of varmint trouble."

When the big Pike youth was gone, the three were relieved but not very cheerful, and they didn't find much to say. Uncle Jarvis saw Jim McAllister in the crowd, and went to talk to him. Elmer and his young wife wandered away and stood in the shelter of a big fir tree. It was not raining much, but it was a wet, chilly morning, and there wasn't anything happening to make them feel warm or encouraged.

Elmer took out his clasp-knife and whittled at the fluted bark of the tree which sheltered them. The bark was rough and gray outside, and smooth and brown inside. Lisette watched as if his work were important and would mean something when it was done. But he was only slicing at the bark because it was better than doing nothing, and she was watching him because she hadn't anything else to do. After a minute, she said quietly, "I hate Josh!"

Elmer did not like him, either.

"One of these days his meanness is going to get him into bad trouble."

He was not so sure, carving an "L" on the bark which he had smoothed. "Do you think so?"

She looked about to make sure no one was near. "On the Sweetwater, near Devil's Gate, he killed an Indian out of meanness."

The boy was not surprised.

"I don't suppose there was any law against it," she said, "and the Indian was stealing something out of the wagon. But he didn't have to kill him. Josh shot him out of meanness, and because he'd got that navy revolver at Fort Laramie. He wanted to try it on somebody."

Carving an "E" on the smooth, grainless bark, he said, "I remember looking into that revolver."

"He got into trouble at home," she said, "killing a nigger on a river boat. He got out of that because he was going west. That time he had a new bowie knife."

Elmer stopped in his carving and looked at her. "I hope I don't meet him when he has a new toy!"

She smiled faintly with her lips, but her eyes were grave. "He's childish that way," she said, "but he's cold and mean. There's something in him that likes to kill."

Carving, he said wisely, "I suppose wanting to kill people is childish. Boys always play at killing."

"I guess it is childish," she said, "but it don't make it any safer." Then she noticed what he was doing. "That's nice, Elmer. Some time we'll come back to see if it's still here."

It was one pleasant thing to remember about the place: this big fir on the treaty ground. Deep in the warm brown bark he had cut their initials, surrounded by a heart.

The treaty making began at nine o'clock, though it seemed almost noon to people who had been up since before daybreak. Every one gathered in front of the Governor's open tent, where there were chairs behind an unpainted kitchen table with neatly arranged papers and pens and ink. In front of the tent, there were camp stools for the white settlers who were witnesses to the treaty. Just back of them, the Indians had gathered in the half-hearted rain, with Mike Simmonds coaxing them into a semicircle, according to their tribes. Colonel Simmonds had already escorted the three objectors to camp stools. His gallantry was displayed by sweeping bows, with his broad felt hat in his hand—and by a readiness to forget the treason or any other crime of a lady's escort.

Lisette thought the Colonel's gallantry was too extravagant to mean anything, but Uncle Jarvis saw it otherwise. "Remember," he said, "when Mike got here there were only three white women living in a territory as big as all New England and New York. That made women so precious in his sight that he's never been able to devaluate them, h'm?"

When he was not in gallant action, the Colonel had a lost Babe-in-the-Woods look about him, and he had a soft, wheedling voice and a colicky smile on his baby face. He did not look like anything suited to the frontier, but he was known as the "Daniel Boone of the Territory," and he had great influence with the Indians. Just now he was marshalling the nine tribes into a semicircle, joking with them and wheedling in half a dozen primeval languages and dialects.

The nine tribes were difficult to understand, even when you saw them. There were about a thousand Indians at the treaty. Nine hundred of those were Nisquallys and Puyallups, who had been lumped together with the same government-selected chiefs representing them. Most of the remaining hundred were Squaxons, while the remaining tens were divided into six tribes, each with its separate representatives. Some of the tribes looked like one small family, with the decrepit father dignified as a chief. The forlorn groups had names like "Steh-Chass," "T'Peeksin" and "Squiaitl." Tribal names no one ever heard of before, nor ever heard of afterward.

It seemed a friendly act to recognize the last shadows of peoples as separate tribes before they were poured together into one reservation. But that made it more difficult to understand why the important Nisquallys and Puyallups were treated as one tribe. They had different needs and were being placed on separate reservations, but the same chiefs decided matters for both. It was one of the mysteries of the Medicine Creek Treaty which was never satisfactorily explained.

The buzz of the gathering changed and sank as three men took their places behind the table in the open tent. Colonel Simmonds, sweeping the rainy air with his hat, led the crowd in giving three cheers for Governor Stevens, and the treaty making was ready to begin.

"He looks like a child!" Lisette whispered.

The Governor hardly came to the shoulders of the military men who flanked him. In size, he was like a frail, half-grown boy with a too-large head, but the resemblance did not go any farther. He was roughly dressed in a red flannel shirt and dark frock coat, with trousers tucked into the tops of his high boots, "California style." Under his wide black felt hat, his face was swarthy, with a small but thick black beard. Walking, he staggered a little, and standing he swayed as if from fatigue. But looking at his massive head you almost forgot his frail stature, and in his face you glimpsed the devils of determination that drove his body beyond its natural limits.

Governor Stevens cleared his throat and spoke in a distinct, resolute voice:

"*This is a great day for you and for us, a day of peace and friendship between you and the whites for all time to come.*" The Governor paused, glancing toward his left, and Colonel Shaw, in blue uniform and silver buttons, translated into Chinook Jargon. The Colonel was a red-headed young man in his early twenties, with a seriousness that was as far beyond his years as his military title.

When the sentence had been mangled into that three-hundred-word language, a swelling babel of sounds rose from the semicircle around the camp stools and tent. From nine different places the Jargon was transmuted into singing noises, clacking and sputterings and chest tones that were like the bumping of heavy rocks. After the others had finished, one voice went on for half a minute more, singing and grunting and making sharp clattering noises, like a machine that did not know when to stop. That was the bowed chief of a tribe that was not much more than the shadow of a shadow. He stood in the falling rain, holding his blanket like an old woman's shawl, while he translated the few words of Jargon for his three followers. By the time he finished, every one had turned to look, and Colonel Simmonds was patting the old man's back. It put the company in good humor to note that the littlest tribe had the biggest language.

The Governor went on:

"You are about to be paid for your lands, and the Great Father has sent me today to treat with you concerning the payment."

The grave-faced Colonel Shaw turned it into Jargon, and the Indian interpreters changed the Jargon into strange noises. They stopped, except for the one old voice that clattered on.

Uncle Jarvis whispered, "You'd think, by God, he was improvising on a theme!"

There were many pauses for translation, but put together the Governor's speech went like this:

"The Great Father lives far off. He has many children. Some of those children came here when he knew but little about them, or of the Indians, and he sent me here to inquire about these things. We went through this country this last year, learned your numbers and saw your wants. We felt much for you, and went to the Great Father to tell him what we had seen."

During the translating pause, a settler with tobacco-stained brown whiskers and sharp blue eyes turned and said hoarsely, "I thought he went to the Great Father because Jeff Davis was trying to stop his railroad job!"

Uncle Jarvis rumbled, "Anyway, he stopped Davis, h'm?"

Elmer knew his uncle did not like the Governor, but it did not seem to give him any pain to credit the little man with besting the Secretary of War and saving the railroad survey.

Governor Stevens went on: *"The Great Father felt for his children. He pitied them and he sent me here today to express those feelings, and to make a treaty for your benefit."*

The youthful Colonel translated it rapidly into Jargon, and the Indian translators responded in strange dialects that died away until only the one old voice grunted and clattered on in its clumsy vehicle of speech. When that stopped, it was the Governor's cue to continue. He opened his mouth, but the silence was disturbed by a confusion in the Nisqually ranks, and some one called *"Wake nika cumtux, six!"*

The Governor looked impatiently from the massed Nisquallys to his interpreter.

"They missed part of it," Shaw explained. "Will you read that last line again, your Honor?"

The swarthy face darkened with anger or impatience, but the little Governor repeated the sentence carefully and distinctly: *"He pitied them and he sent me here today to express those feelings and to make a treaty for your benefit."*

It was repeated in Jargon and Nisqually, and when the Nisqually translation ended, the translator for the shadow of a tribe was singing and grunting and clacking away again. Amused settlers turned to look, and Colonel Simmonds ran in entertaining panic to quiet the wordy old man.

The Governor's speech went on: *"The Great Father has many white children who came here, some to build mills, some to make farms, and some to fish; and the Great Father wants you to learn to farm, and your children to go to a good school; and he now wants me to make a bargain with you, in which you will sell your lands, and in return we will provide all these things. You will have certain lands set apart for your homes, and receive yearly payments of blankets, axes, etc. All this is written down in this paper* [holding up the treaty] *which will be read to you. If it is good, you will sign it, and I will send it to the Great Father. I think he will be pleased with it and say it is good, but if not, if he wishes it different, he will say so and send it back; and then, if you agree to it, it is a fixed bargain and payments will be made."*

"I will now read the treaty." The little Governor put his speech aside, and took the sheaf of papers which his interpreter handed him. He swayed uncertainly as he cleared his throat, but there was nothing uncertain about his swarthy face, with its look of driving determination, or about his voice. He read carefully and you could see him trying to make every word distinct.

The treaty had thirteen articles. They were not very long, but the double translating took a long time. Even then it did not satisfy every one. During one pause, the settler with the tobacco-stained whiskers turned and said hoarsely, "It's not the same thing when it gets into Siwash!"

Uncle Jarvis rumbled softly, "Shaw's doing his best, but the Jargon ties his hands, h'm?"

The boy remembered that his uncle understood at least one of the Indian languages. "What does it sound like in Nisqually?" he whispered.

"Going through Jargon," the big man said, "it's like getting a bouquet through a knothole. It's a hard pull, and when it's through about all you know is that some one sent you flowers."

When the final article had been read and translated into Jargon and the Jargon translated into the Indian languages, the little Governor put the treaty carefully on the table and addressed the Indians:

"The paper has been read to you. Is it good? If it is good, we will sign it; but if you dislike any point, say so now. After signing, we have some goods to give you, and next summer we will give you some more; and after that you must wait until the paper comes back from the Great Father. The goods we will give you when you have signed this paper are not in payment for your lands; they are merely a friendly present."

Governor Stevens sat down and listened to his own speech going on in its multiple translations. Apparently, he found it too long, because he consulted his watch and looked displeased. Then he rearranged the pens and ink on the table, as if they should already be in use according to schedule.

With all the translating, it had been a long time since the Indians were invited to say so if they disliked any point of the treaty. No pause had been allowed for that, and since then all the talk had been about the presents they would receive when they signed the treaty. It did not look as if there would be any objections.

The last translator stopped and turned from the three members of his tribe. Holding his blanket at his withered throat, like an old woman's shawl, he quavered: *"Hyas Tyee!"*

There was going to be an objection, after all. The settlers half-turned on their camp-stools while the chief of the dim tribe addressed the Governor in Chinook, and Colonel Shaw translated into English.

"One time," the old man said, "when my people were a great people, my father's father was taken from this land by the evil Haidahs. They took him and other slaves to paddle their canoe. The Haidahs took them north, through the *skookum-chucks* and over the great *salt chuck* to the Island of the Haidahs. There they sold them to Thlingets. The Thlingets took them farther north to their land. . . . "

While the translating was going on, Elmer felt his uncle nudge him. "I suspect the old bastard of a filibuster!"

"It's a good story, anyway!" Elmer smiled at his uncle and Lisette, who smiled back at him. They were close together and friendly, like children whispering in school.

The old chief went on with his story, in an earnest, quavering voice. "While they were in the land of the Thlingets, a great evil happened. The sun got sick. It tried every day to lift its head in the sky. Every day it was weaker. The sun's head fell back and did not try to lift any more. It was *memaloose,* and that place became the Land of Eternal Darkness. My father's father was there when it happened.

"The other slaves saw it happen. After that it was always night. They were afraid to live in that land of darkness by the icy *salt chuck.* They stole a canoe and started for their own land. All of them died of the cold except my father's father. He found a Boston ship that caught whales. The Bostons cared for him, and the ship sailed out of the Land of Eternal Darkness. One morning he saw Tatoosh Island. He told the Bostons his people lived on the long *chuck* that held the island in its mouth. They could only *cumtux* a little. They put him in a canoe that came to the ship. It was a Makah canoe. He was a slave of the Makahs for many years before he got away. Then he found our people. . . . "

It was a good story, but it did not seem to have anything to do with the treaty. The swarthy little Governor looked at his watch again and whispered impatiently to Colonel Shaw. It did not look as if they would let the story go on much longer. But the old chief quavered on and came, surprisingly, to the point.

"My father's father was a good man. He only told what was true. Every one who heard believed him. Since then we have always called the land of the Thlingets the Land of Eternal Darkness. We know that the sun of that land lifts its head no more.

"*Hyas Tyee,* that paper says when the Great Father wishes he will take us from Klahshemin to a new place. We have heard it will be north on the *salt chuck.*

"*Hyas Tyee,* hear an old man! Do not send us to the Land of Eternal Darkness! My little people would die beside the icy *salt chuck* when no sun ever shines!" He finished, sobbing, while he leaned on his staff and held his blanket about him like a shawl. The three tribesmen wept with their chief. And the forlorn little group, bowed in the rain, looked like pilgrims already on their way to the Land of Eternal Darkness.

When the appeal had been translated, the Governor did not look impatient any more, and he spoke kindly through the interpreter. "Tell him," he said, "that the paper only says the Great Father *might* move the Indians from their new reservations, if the interests of the Territory require it. That is not likely to happen if the Indians conduct themselves well, and I am sure they will. Tell him that if they are moved, it will be to fine reservations which they will like. I will see to that. And tell him what he has heard is only evil talk. It is impossible because the Great Father does not own the Land of Darkness and could not take Indians there."

Elmer saw tears in his wife's dark eyes, and he could not help feeling touched by the plea of the forlorn tribe. So he whispered manfully, "Where d'ye suppose the old fellow got that notion?"

His uncle only gave him an odd, warning look, but the owner of the tobacco-stained whiskers turned around. "I've heard the same evil talk from one of the Governor's party," he whispered hoarsely. "He said if the Indians were found to be in people's way, they might all be dumped on the Alaska coast."

The old chief's appeal did not seem so childish now. He was looking out for his people to the last.

"*Hyas Tyee!*"

"Slugia," Uncle Jarvis whispered, "Leschi's nephew. A bad actor even if he's speaking in a good cause." This time it was a young, defiant voice from the Nisqually ranks. Turning, Elmer recognized the horseman who had bumped into him earlier and cursed him. Now the supple young brave was addressing the Governor with the same insolent air.

"*Hyas Tyee,*" he said. "We do not like your gifts. Colonel Simmonds said this would be a *potlatch,* with fine gifts. At *potlatches,* Indians give good presents. Rich Indians fight each other by giving away horses and slaves and blankets. When one gives much, the other must give more. They give until one rich man has nothing. Then he gives away the blanket he is wearing. He is a poor man, but he is honored.

"You tell us the Great Father is a rich man. He has not made himself poor by giving us blackstrap and toys. He is not honored by his gifts. I have spoken."

The Governor's face turned almost as dark as his beard while the interpreter spoke to him in an undertone. He seemed on the point of some furious outburst. But when he spoke it was in a controlled voice, and he weighed his words. "Tell him Bostons think less of the price of a gift than of the friendly spirit in which it is made. Tell him we have better gifts for the Indians when the treaty is signed. Tell him we did not have as much time as we wished to select gifts. We will tell the Great Father, and he will send better ones for next summer, and the Indains will know he is generous."

When that had been translated, Governor Stevens looked resolutely about the semicircle of Indians. "Are you ready?" he asked. "If so, we will sign the paper."

Shaw translated the question into Jargon, and the Jargon was translated into the Indian languages. There were some uneasy mutters of consultation in the semicircle, but most of the Indians were looking toward the Nisqually ranks. There some fierce, half-suppressed argument was going on, but no objection was immediately voiced.

"I will sign the paper first," the Governor said. With the members of his party standing at attention he sat at the table, dipped a pen in the ink and wrote his name, impressively.

Colonel Shaw looked at what the Governor had written, nodding his head as if to say it was a very good signature indeed. Then he looked up and called, "Quiemuth, Chief of the Nisquallys!"

The agile Colonel Simmonds had already reached the Nisqually ranks, and he made himself a kind of guard of honor for the chief as he walked to the table.

Quiemuth was a solidly built man of middle-age, more stolid than his half-brother Leschi, with less fire, but he walked with dignity and looked like a chief. With Simmonds walking beside him, murmuring in his soft, wheedling voice, he strode up to the table. Colonel Shaw handed him a ready-dipped pen. He took it in his fist, like a stick, and crossed an "X" near the interpreter's fingertip on the treaty.

The Governor stood up and shook hands with him. "Let's give three cheers for Quiemuth!"

Simmonds led the cheering in which some of the Indians joined with shouts of "Aye Iah!" Then he accompanied the chief back to the semicircle, patting him proudly on the back.

"Snohodumset, sub-chief of the Nisquallys and Puyallups!"

The Daniel Boone of the Territory accompanied the gray-haired Indian to the treaty table, talking encouragingly and patting his shoulder. The old sub-chief looked doubtful all the way, but he took the pen and made a mark after his name on the treaty.

The swarthy little Governor stood up and shook hands with him. "Three cheers for Snohodumset!"

"Hurrah! Hurrah! Hurrah!"

"Aye Iah!"

The cheers rose and were echoed back, harshly, from the great fir trees on the treaty ground. Then old Snohodumset was led back to where Nisquallys stood in the December rain and heard their doom.

"Leschi, sub-chief of the Nisquallys and Puyallups!"

To Elmer, the name was always like a great cry. And by the gathering silence you would think it had some special meaning for every one there; some meaning of hope or fear. In the silence you became aware of the still treaty ground in the falling rain, and the great fir trees on a strange planet whirling through space. Under those mysterious trees, people clustered together to decide how things should be. And they tried to decide what was right or profitable by the color of each other's face. But none of them knew what was right or what would be profitable. And they did not know what they were doing or how it would end. The planet, whirling its great firs through space, remained as unknown and strange as any other planet that hung in the sky at night. It was stranger, when you saw it close, because it was so much more complicated than one bright star. One spot under the great trees became a thousand people. And of that thousand not one really knew what was in the heart of another, or what they were doing or how it would end. . . .

Leschi and Colonel Simmonds reached the treaty table. Half way, the Colonel had stopped his wheedling murmur and his patting of Leschi's shoulder. Perhaps the silence made it too conspicuous, or the response was wrong.

"He's homely, isn't he?" Lisette whispered. Then she decided, "I like him!"

Looking at Leschi, you did not think about his race or yours. He was like a wise and homely friend you had always known and would trust in everything. He was standing beside the unpainted wooden table, and Colonel Shaw was holding out the ready-dipped pen.

Leschi's arms were folded under his tawny Hudson's Bay blanket. He did not seem to notice the pen. In the stillness you could hear the falling rain. Then Leschi spoke in Jargon. "I will not put my name on that paper. My people need land they can plough, and prairie land for their herds. They need the creek for their canoes. I have told Governor Stevens these things. Even if my heart had changed, the need of my people has not changed——"

The three men at the table were beginning to stir, like hornets in a disturbed nest, and the interpreter dipped the dry pen in the ink. "Put your mark here," he said. "Don't talk!"

Leschi ignored the pen and went on speaking in deep-voiced Jargon, while the men at the table consulted, with their eyes on him. "I want the Nisqually people to live in peace," Leschi said. "I want them to learn to farm. I have told Governor Stevens these things. . . . "

At the mention of his name, the Governor said angrily, "Tell him to sign! Tell him the treaty cannot be changed!"

When it had been repeated in Jargon, Leschi went on firmly, "Governor Stevens said he wants us to learn to farm. He gives us farmers' hats, but he does not give us farms!"

The buzz at the council table was echoed in the ranks of Indians, some one shouted, *"Aie Iah! Leschi!"*

The Governor was on his feet, with his face darker than that of the Nisqually who towered above him. "Tell him to be quiet! Tell him to sign or go away!"

Colonel Simmonds was beside Leschi again, with a colicky smile on his baby face, while he talked soothingly in Nisqually. When that brought no result, he started to pat the chief's arm. His hand touched once, and then it was flung aside as Leschi whirled on him so swiftly that he blurred.

"Klatawa!"

Simmonds recoiled, with a singed look, from the great explosion of a word.

Leschi turned back to the angry little Governor, and looked down at him with blazing eyes. "We ask for farms, so we can live, and you give us gravel for a burial ground! *We ask for bread, and you give us a stone!*"

"Aie Iah, Leschi!" The name had become a great cry in more than the boy's imagination.

"Right in his teeth!" Uncle Jarvis muttered. The Indians were buzzing in arguments, with some of them shouting, *"Aie, Iah!"* The settlers were turning on their camp stools, consulting or looking about uneasily. Jim McAllister was on his feet, looking from Leschi, to whom he owed his farm

and wealth and a thousand kindnesses, to the Governor to
whom he owed his allegiance as a citizen. He looked ir-
resolutely from one to the other. Then he sat down, heavily.

At the treaty table they were trying to shout Leschi down.
The furious little Governor was shouting, "Tell him he is a
Klickitat! Tell him he has nothing to do with this treaty!"
And Shaw repeated it in Jargon.

In answer, the Nisqually drew a folded paper from inside
his blanket. The others quieted as he held it up. "If I am a
Klickitat," he said mildly, "why did Governor Stevens give
me this paper which makes me a little chief of the Nisquallys? That was yesterday. Today I am a Klickitat with
no business here. But if I had put a mark on that paper,
Governor Stevens would not remember my Klickitat mother.
I would be a great Nisqually today. Governor Stevens made
me a little chief so I would do my people a big wrong. This
is my answer:" He held up the folded paper so every one
could see, and tore it into long strips which he dropped on
the muddy ground.

"*Aie Iah!*"

"Go away!" the treaty-makers were shouting. "We don't
want you here! You have no business here!"

Leschi raised his powerful voice. "I am going, but hear
one thing: Burn that paper or it will burn you! That evil
paper means war!"

CHAPTER THIRTEEN

*H*AYING in Paradise.

Their scythes hung in a tree beside the creek, near the spot where they had eaten lunch. Their rifles leaned against the trunk of another tree, and the two bucks they had killed hung from branches, with their slender legs extended in the attitude of flight from death.

It was a warm summer afternoon, but there was pleasant shade along the creek, and the water made a cool, laughing sound among the trees. In the sunshine, the wild hay had a piercing sweetness you never tired of because it seemed always on the point of going away. When the oxen moved on to the next shock, the clean wagon wheels rolled among bluebells which the scythes had missed. The sweetness of the wild hay was mixed up with the sound of meadow larks that were singing madly everywhere. The boys had heard the meadow larks every minute of the day, but when one sang near the wagon they listened by silent agreement. There was some trick about the last note of the song which always escaped them; something bright and twinkling which they saw rather than heard; a kind of vanishing spark, struck in bright sunshine, where they would not expect to see it at all.

Beyond the mown patch where they worked, the big prairie opened away, a sea of waving grass with little islands of scrub oaks and Christmas-tree firs. On one of the islands, in the shade of the trees, were dimmed calico and buckskin and darker shapes and one pale horse that stood out against the shadows of the grove. Indian ponies playing at shipwreck on a pleasant island in the sea of plenty. Farther away, a herd of eighty or a hundred animals grazed, shoulder deep in waving grass. They looked like tame cattle until some of them moved with slow, high leaps and flashes of white, proving they were deer. Still farther away twinkled the white flashes of another herd. Beyond the grassy sea and island groves, Mount Rainier loomed in the sky to the southeast, like the enormous white headland of another world.

Elmer pitched the hay up on the wagon to Paul Porter, who built the load. Paul was fine to work with. He knew the importance of listening to a meadow lark when one sang near the wagon, and from the white shadow of the mountain in the sky to the flowers under the clean wheels of the wagon, no sight or sound or perfume was wasted on him. Sometimes he said this was like making hay in a dream. But he did not dream about his work. He built a tough, well-bound load for the four miles of bad road that lay beyond the Nisqually prairie.

Paul was shorter than Elmer, but he was strong. Even on hot days he did not bother to wear a hat, and his brown hair was bleached and his face tanned until they were about the same color. That day at Rush's farm, a year ago, Elmer had been greeted by the sunburned faces of Paul and his brother, Bob. They had made fine plans about hunting together, but nothing had come of it because work interfered. Now, work had brought them together.

That was because of the simple and complicated way things happen. In the battle at Rush's farm, no one could have foreseen the organizing of a timber camp, but that was one of the things which had come out of it. In the ranks of the settlers there was Uncle Jarvis who had fine timber at the water's edge, and the leisurely idea of logging sometime, as a man from Maine should. There was Elmer who soon acquired timber land, and who wanted to get ahead. And there were the brothers from New Jersey; fine, steady workers, in need of cash, with several yoke of good oxen in the family.

Everything necessary to the project was there, except the feminine spark to set it off. And that was not far away. It was at their backs, concealed by a wagon-cover, in which loopholes had been cut. Lisette was there, beside Maw Sims and her squirrel rifle, with a large-bore derringer in her trembling hands. She did not like what was going on, and she was not going to use the pistol, because Elmer was among the enemy. Though she told him afterward she had been tempted to use it for the very reason that he was there—with no thought of her.

It would be wrong to suggest that Lisette held a pistol while she encouraged the men to start a timber camp. Women have their own and better means of doing things. Lisette did it almost humbly. They were in debt at Sylvester's for their winter supplies. There was no hope of their raising a crop which would more than feed themselves another year. And no matter how much they raised and hunted and went without, there were always things they had to buy. Other people had timber camps, and they paid wages as high as four dollars a day. That showed there was money in it. And when land is logged-off it is half cleared and fit for pasture. Elmer and Uncle Jarvis had talked about logging, and spring was a good time to begin. More than ever, Elmer saw that being married makes a difference without really changing a man. A wife does not change her husband's good intentions; she only makes him carry them out.

Lisette knew nothing about logging, and left the details to the men. Probably she had not considered that doing almost anything leads to something quite different: working on salt water leads you to the prairie, and the decision to cut timber leads you to cut hay. She left the details to the men. And one of the details was the work oxen, which had to be well fed. So, at odd times, Paul and Elmer cut hay on the big prairie. And because men as well as beasts have to be fed, they did some hunting, which they had planned to do, long ago. Only, when they planned it as play, nothing came of it. And when they went to work it happened, inevitably.

On top of the well-built load, Paul received the last fork of hay from a shock, and stood in the afternon sun, against the blue sky, listening to a meadow lark. Elmer stood among the flowers, listening, with his eyes on the singer. The trees along the creek were sending cool shadows out toward the loaded wagon, and the brown-and-buff bird was poised on a bush between the tides of sunlight and the shadow, singing deliriously of summer on the Nisqually plain. The song went up and up, recklessly, to the last note, which they saw rather than heard, like a vanishing spark, or a star glimpsed in the day-time sky. . . . The boys went on listening to what was no longer there except in the memory of their young ears. Then they caught another familiar sound. This one was the gross kind which you feel rather than hear. It was a monotonous, insistent beat, like the pounding of a great leaden heart. It came from miles away, but at that distance it had the feeling of blows which would crush them if they came too close.

Smiling gravely, the sunburned Paul looked down from the load. "Well, Elmer, I reckon that's about all she'll take!"

"Looks like enough to me!" Elmer worked around the wagon with his fork, trimming the load of loose wisps of hay. After a minute he called up, "All right, Paul!"

Paul cracked the long whip and shouted. The oxen leaned against the yoke and the wheels turned with a leisurely rumble. Sometimes Elmer was beside the wagon and sometimes he lagged behind, gathering bluebells for Lisette. But he made a point of being at their camping place in time to get in front of the white-faced oxen, with his arms out to stop them. Otherwise, they might have continued their deliberate way home, with Paul protesting from above.

They boosted and hauled the two bucks to the top of the load. Elmer handed up the rifles and climbed aboard by way of the wagon tongue, with a fistful of flowers. The hay was soft and it smelled good, and there was a fine view from up there.

In some ways the view was too good; they saw too much. Off to the right there were the toy shapes of long-horned Spanish cattle beyond an endless zigzag rail fence, with two posts crossed in an "X" at each new hitch of the fence. That was one of the fields of the Puget Sound Agricultural Company, which was the Hudson's Bay Company turned farmer. Back along the creek and ahead was a thin scattering of cabins, newly built or building. Those were the cabins of squatters who were waiting to file on the land when the Hudson's Bay Company's title was extinguished.

It was only from the ground, looking toward Mount Rainier, that they saw the Nisqually plain as it had been from the beginning of time, and would not be again. But it was pleasant, swaying home in the shade of late afternoon, in the sound of the creek and madly singing meadow larks that kept faith with a lovely world which was drawing to its close. The boys were bringing home fragments of that world: a load of wild hay and two dead deer and a handful of flowers, things cut off from life so recently that they still kept their bloom and sweetness. Even the faces of the bucks on the hay had the gentle, princely look of living deer.

Watching over them from the sky, the enormous mountain loomed whiter as the plain darkened with lengthening shadows of island groves. Over the plain, from far away, came the throbbing of the dull drum. And still the meadow larks sang of Mount Rainier and the glory of summer on the Nisqually plain.

Paul cracked his long whip and said, "I wouldn't mind being buried here, where the meadow larks would sing on my gravestone all day long."

When you're young and single, like Paul, you sometimes like to talk about your own death. But it's different when you have a wife waiting for you at home. Then there isn't much satisfaction in it. You're too much tied up with life. So Elmer said, "You can get more out of the place when you're alive."

Paul turned to give his friend an amused look, and his tanned face and deep blue eyes were almost as beautiful as the place where he was asking to be buried. "Yankee!" he said.

Elmer laughed. "Are people from New Jersey so very different?"

"I don't know," Paul said. "They're not Yankees, anyway. They're just people who do the best they can."

"They sound very much like Yankees!"

Paul said, "They don't bargain with life. They don't try to put no saddle and bridle on it."

"Yankees don't either," Elmer said, "not really. Or if they do, they only get thrown." What they were saying was mostly nonsense. People are much alike everywhere, and all different. And he knew, or thought he knew, what his friend meant. He wasn't really thinking about death; he was thinking about being a part of nature. When a place is beautiful enough, the ideas of life and death get mixed up. They seemed part of the same thing here, under the mountain as old as Ararat, with wild herds drifting in the sunshine, the creek laughing among the trees and meadow larks singing deliriously from every bush as the wagon lumbered home with the spoils of the prairie. And from the Nisqually camp, far across the prairie, there came the dull, insistent throbbing of the drum.

The boys seldom mentioned it now. During the summer they had grown used to that leaden sound, heavy with hate. There wasn't anything they could do about it, and they had to go on living. There was no one who could do anything about it, except Governor Stevens. And he was away in the Blackfeet country, making more treaties.

The Governor had not been near his capital for half a year, but news came back of his exploits. The latest was the boast that he had extinguished the Indians' claim to an area bigger than New England. He had done it in a few months for a cash outlay of a few thousand dollars. That was the kind of news that came over the mountains as the little Governor went from triumph to triumph.

There also came over the mountains parties of Klickitats, dissatisfied with one of the Governor's lightning treaties. The Klickitats came every summer to visit and race horses with their Nisqually allies. But this summer there were more of them, and they were better armed and brought fewer women with them. Some prophets expected them to attack the settlers, and others thought they would attack only if the Nisquallys did. Opinion was split on what the Nisquallys would do. There was most agreement on the belief that the tribes would make war or stay at peace depending on Leschi's decision, and opinion split again on that. The most hopeful sign was the fact that Leschi was taking no part in tribal affairs. He had withdrawn to his farm on the prairie and was laying out his fields for fall ploughing. Meanwhile, in the Nisqually camp, the people he had planned to lead the ways of peace had gone back to war dances and war paint, and the initiation of young men into the brotherhood of the braves.

Reading about a war in history, it seems very clear and simple. Being in what may be the beginning of one, it is not simple. It is sad and complicated. And after a while, when the first excitement has passed, no one wants to talk about it any more.

One of the complications was Leschi. He had not signed the treaty, and he had said it would mean war. But he took no part in warlike preparations. The Indians who had signed the treaty were bitterest about it, and most warlike in their talk. Even there the complication did not end. Settlers who had not been at the treaty believed Leschi had signed. The Governor's friends who had been there told people who had not that Leschi had stepped up to the table and signed without protest, like all the others. In proof, there was a mark after Leschi's name on the treaty. The treaty was witnessed by some of the settlers and members of the Governor's party, including the Governor's twelve-year-old son who had sat under a tree with the Indian boys, eating blackstrap and playing a jew's-harp.

One more wave in the sea of complications was the fact that nothing was being done about moving the Indians to their reservations. The treaty had been ratified months before, but with the Governor and the Superintendent of Indian Affairs away in the same person, there was no one to put it into effect. It had been rushed through in such haste that Christmas had been trampled under muddy work-day boots. And after that there had been seven months of awkward pause while the Governor travelled farther and farther away, setting new records for speed in treaty-making, and new records for obtaining the maximum of land at minimum cost to the government. While that was going on, the Medicine Creek Treaty remained something technical on paper. Nothing had been changed except for bad feeling and war dances and war paint among people who had never raised their hands against the white race.

Those who believed the Indians would not fight took comfort in Jim McAllister, whose farm was in the heart of the Nisqually camp. The Kentuckian and his wife and large family lived their usual life in the midst of councils and war dances. Rather than expecting trouble, McAllister had completed a sawmill on the creek and was building a new and pretentious frame house. It was not even going to be fortified like the old log one which the Nisquallys had helped him build, and which the Haidahs had besieged in the early days.

When the possibility of trouble was mentioned, McAllister would say, "I ought to know the Nisquallys better than any one else. I've lived with them ten years and never had anything but kindness from them. They're so gentle I could drive the whole tribe before me, like sheep." The opinion that the Indians could be driven like sheep was so reassuring that McAllister was encouraged to repeat it whenever he was in town or with other settlers. He repeated it so often that if he had had any doubts about it in the beginning, he had none now.

People like Uncle Jarvis said Jim McAllister was talking about what the Nisquallys were by nature. But if they were driven too far, only God knew what they might be.

That and a great deal more was behind the ominous drum which the boys hardly ever mentioned now. They did not talk about it because it was nothing they could help any more than the coming of winter. And life was as full and pleasant as this summer, with no room for war or politics. The sound of trouble to come was almost shut out by their adjustable young hearts.

After a while, the road led through woods which were decorated with wisps of hay from other trips. In that green twilight the boys no longer thought about the drum because they did not hear it.

When they came out of the woods into the open of the timber camp, Elmer felt like a man who had helped found a city or a civilization. Three yoke of red-and-white oxen stood near the landing, to which they had hauled the last length of piling for the day. Paul's brother, Bob, and Uncle Jarvis and

Nisqually Jim were rolling the log onto the skids that sloped down to the beach which was covered by high tide. Their different-colored backs bent and straightened together and the slender log rumbled down the skids. Dark water turned dim white, and big ripples went widening through the twilight. Inside the floating fence of the boom, the logs were like fine cattle in a pasture. That dark oblong mass was a herd of choice piles for the San Francisco docks, rafted together and ready for loading. Farther away, a well-known barque, with a white woman for a figurehead, rode at anchor. She was not big or important in the world of ships, but lying in the narrow Inlet, where nothing larger than a brig had ever come, she looked like a great ship and the most important thing in the world.

Elmer tried to bring something matter-of-fact from the center of his expanding pride. "It's the *Maid*," he told Paul. "I thought Captain Wallace would be in this week."

"It's your old ship, isn't it?"

"That's her." It was his old ship, with a new meaning. As a common sailor, he had helped bring her to the Northwest coast. Now, as a partner in a timber camp, he was providing her with a cargo. He was getting on in this magic new world, where everything was possible.

There had never been as fine an evening in as fine a world. The mountain which had watched over the Nisqually plain was watching over the calm Inlet from above the forest on the other shore. The mountain was blue-veined with shadows and flushed with pink and gold from a distant sunset on the Pacific. Here, sunset was over long ago, but the twilight of northern summer lingered like another season of the day. With no light seeming to come from anywhere, everything was softly visible, as if objects stored their own light during the day and used it when the sun was gone. The magic twilight seemed to make sounds gentler and smells more rich. That world of flat light and darkness without shadows was alive with the smell of salt water and wild hay and the pitchy incense of fresh-cut fir, and it was pleasant with the sound of voices: Bob swearing softly at the oxen as he drove them away to the fenced field for the night. Uncle Jarvis and the Indian boy discussing some detail of logging in the Nisqually language. The strange, musical chatter of two Sandwich Islanders in the *Maid's* gig, waiting an oar's length offshore. On the shore above them, a big-shouldered man in a frock coat and tall hat, talking with two women. Captain and Mrs. Wallace and Elmer's own wife. The voices of the present and the past mingling in the twilight.

Elmer slid from the high load and greeted them, unmindful of the hayseeds which covered his front.

Mrs. Wallace laughed, "You're still a farm boy, Elmer!" Maybe with just an edge of reproach.

Shaking hands strongly, Captain Wallace said, "We could use that hay on board. I know by the smell that it's better than the chaffy stuff they sell us in San Francisco."

Lisette said, "You're late, Elmer. I was beginning to won-der——"

He was looking confusedly at the baby in Mrs. Wallace's arms. "I didn't know you had a baby!"

"Born in April," the captain said. "We're raising him to be a first mate."

Mrs. Wallace said, "We had a house in San Francisco, but now he's old enough to travel."

The captain said, "He's got his sea-legs before he's learned to walk!"

Elmer had already been told it was a boy; he couldn't ask which it was. So he said the other thing. "He's nice-looking, isn't he?" He didn't know about babies, but he was going to learn. What he would have liked to say was that Lisette was going to have a baby. But a woman decides when to tell such things. It wasn't really noticeable and if Lisette hadn't already told Mrs. Wallace, she probably wouldn't. Women tell each other everything in the first half hour, or they don't at all. So he looked at the baby in the mother's arms and said, "He's nice looking, isn't he?"

"He's very good." Mrs. Wallace smiled down at the baby, who was wriggling now, but not crying. "He's a fine boy." In the twilight her clear face was smiling and mysterious and not quite real; like the figurehead of the *Maid*. With a kind of guilty start the boy remembered the Haidah arrowhead which was buried between the breasts of her image. It was superstition and it was nothing. More than a year had passed without her or the ship being stricken. Nothing had happened other than a fine boy. The omen sank down in his mind, discredited by time. Mrs. Wallace was looking at him and saying, "You're invited to have supper on board, Elmer, if the timber camp can spare you. Lisette thought you could manage it."

"I thank you," Elmer said. "I'd like to."

"We tried to get Jarvis and Mary, too," the captain said. "But they can't leave the hands to feed themselves."

Uncle Jarvis was still talking to the Indian boy, explaining something to him in Nisqually.

The captain raised his voice, "Jarvis, sure you can't come with us?"

"Not this time, Cap'n!" Jarvis came over to them with the young Nisqually. "But you can help us with an astronomical matter, h'm? You've had dealings with the sun. Jim believes that in the land of the rising sun and the land of the setting sun, otherwise the east and west, the solar body comes much closer to the earth, grazes it in fact." He demonstrated with his long, pitch-spotted hands, speaking as gravely as if he believed there might be something in the idea. "You're a seafaring man, and you've been around the world. Have you noticed anything of the kind, h'm?"

Captain Wallace laughed. "I've never noticed it grazing the trucks!" he said. "Ninety-two million miles is close enough. Sometimes, around the Line, it's too damned close!"

The big man nodded gravely, and translated into Nisqually. When the boy did not sound convinced, he said, "Will you demonstrate it, h'm? Why the sun seems closer to the earth morning and afternoon?"

By then Captain Wallace must have realized that Jarvis was trying to enlighten the boy and not make fun of him. He gave a good demonstration, rotating one clenched fist around the other to represent the earth and sun, and explaining the movement of light on the earth's surface.

Nisqually Jim listened gravely, though he understood only simple English, and he watched the captain's face even more than his demonstrating hands. The captain had made a mistake in joking about the subject at the beginning, and now he had to prove his own sincerity as well as his point.

Jim was a square-built boy of about twenty, with a broad, homely face and intelligent eyes. He wore a hickory shirt and Kentucky jeans and moccasins, like Uncle Jarvis whom he admired as a white *tyee*. He was a good worker who fitted in well with the logging crew and could be trusted in every way. But, without his job he would certainly be dressed in a breechclout and face paint, with eagle feathers in his hair. And he would be occupying himself with war dances which are less profitable than logging and have a dubious future. The only important difference between Jim and the other Nisqually young men was that Uncle Jarvis paid him eighty-five dollars a month and board, and otherwise treated him the same as every one else. Which Elmer thought showed the civilizing influence of a good job.

When Uncle Jarvis had conferred with the boy in Nisqually, he reported to the captain: "Jim thanks you for explaining. He says you may be right, and he'll think it over. But there's something he would like you to think over, as a stranger. He's lived hereabouts all his life, and he's noticed that this is the place where the sun reaches its highest point in the sky. I've noticed something of the kind myself. Think it over, h'm?"

"All right," the captain said. "And I'll have the longboat here to catch the morning tide with those piles." You could see he was anxious to be on board. He very likely thought Jarvis had spent too much time, his own and the captain's, on something unimportant. But Uncle Jarvis was always like that. And his nephew wasn't sure that he considered any one important or unimportant. That was his weakness or his strength. Whichever it was, that was Jarvis, and there wasn't any use trying to change him.

CHAPTER FOURTEEN

——

D INNER on board was a great luxury after the roughness of life ashore, and it was a double luxury to the boy who had eaten so many meals in the fo'c'sle. The cabin was panelled with Florida mahogany, and nicely lighted by the swinging lamp over the big table. They sat in comfortable armchairs and ate off china in the company of linen and silverware. It was a good dinner of soup and sea trout and roast beef with fresh vegetables. Young John and the baby had been fed and put to sleep, and the five at the cabin table were served by a Sandwich Islander who waited on them nicely and moved silently between the table and pantry on bare brown feet. Elmer wondered what had become of their steward from Fairhaven, but as the first deserter from the ship he had no right to ask questions.

The five of them at table were Captain and Mrs. Wallace, Elmer and Lisette and the first mate, Mr. Lang. He was a cheerful, dissipated-looking young man who talked easily and gave the ship a worldly air which was as foreign to her as a rake escorting a virtuous girl. You couldn't help contrasting him with Mr. Holbrook, who was unaccountably absent, and who had been a fine officer and a serious sort of man. Styles and times had changed, and the change had forced its way to the captain's own table in the dashing shape of an officer he would not have engaged at home.

The talk was about San Francisco and clipper ships. Elmer was deluged with shining names: *Golden Eagle, Golden City,* and *Golden West.* Shining names, and names boastful of speed: *Hurricane, Tornado, Flying Cloud, Sweepstakes* and *Winged Racer.* Even the gentle and thrifty Mrs. Wallace had felt the

222

influence of the racecourse between San Francisco and the East. "The world is mad for speed," she told Elmer, "but it does make lovely ships! Before you give up the sea for good, you must visit San Francisco. You must see the clippers racing up to the pilot ground from China and around the Horn. I've never seen anything so triumphal!"

It seemed to Elmer that he had already given up the sea for good, with a wife and home and a timber camp. He didn't know whether she was only being polite, or hinting that he should make another voyage in the *Maid*. But he was flattered by her wanting him to see something beautiful which she had seen. At the same time, without looking at Lisette and without her having said anything, he knew that she did not like Mrs. Wallace.

The captain had laid down his knife and was stroking his soft brown beard. "I used to think ocean races were only in a manner of speaking," he said. "But the clippers really do race. It's amazing what close contests they make of it over a course of fifteen thousand miles; really amazing. The *Red Rover* and *Seaman's Bride* and *Winged Racer* sailed from New York in January, on the twenty-first and second and third, I believe. The *Bride* and *Racer* came through the Golden Gate on the twenty-fourth of May, on the same tide. And the *Rover* turned up the next morning."

"Some of the races are closer than that, Ma'am," the mate confided to Lisette. "They tell a story about Bert Palmer, one of Cap'n Nat's brothers, who has the *Celestial*. He came out of patchy fog on the 'Frisco pilot grounds, fanning along with stuns'ls and ringtail. Nearly ran the pilot schooner down. While they were lowering away and he was taking in his light canvas, he bawls through the megaphone: *"What time did the 'Stingray' get in?"*

"She's not in!" the schooner captain says through his megaphone. *"Is she overdue?"*

"Yes!" Cap'n Bert tells him. *"She left th' Hook six hours ahead of me!"*

Just then one of the pilots points out a big clipper ramping out of the fog astern. *"There she is now!"*

"My God," Cap'n Bert says, all relieved, *"I was afraid something had happened to her!"*

"It was really as close as that," Captain Wallace admitted. "And it's all the more remarkable when you consider that they left New York in the unfavorable season. It was a fight all the way, and the best they could do was a hundred and twenty-nine days."

"Flying Cloud has done it in eighty-nine," the mate explained to Lisette. "That's the best, so far."

"These races are like a war," Mrs. Wallace said. "Some one wins a fine victory, but unless you happen to see the battlefield you don't stop to think about the cost in human life and effort."

"In blown-out sails and lost spars, too," the captain said. "I can imagine what my partners would say if I had to rerig the *Maid* every voyage or two."

Mrs. Wallace gave him a secure smile. "We'll leave the clipper ships for others, won't we, John?"

He said, rapping the table lightly with his big fist, "I've never lost a man or a spar. I'm not going to begin now."

"It's a short life, but a merry one," the mate assured Lisette, "cracking on till the spars begin to buckle." He looked as if he had a merry life behind him, and a short one ahead. Judging by his expression, he was wondering why any one with the captain's regard for men and spars should go to sea. That problem and the domestic bliss about the table seemed too much for him. He finished his coffee hastily, and excused himself.

When the mate was gone, Captain Wallace stroked his beard, and smiled. "Mr. Lang is a good officer," he said by way of apology. "He's only a fire-eater in conversation, for the benefit of the ladies."

"It was mostly for your benefit," Mrs. Wallace told Lisette. "If you had given him any encouragement, he would have dismasted and rerigged himself in a hurricane."

"He's really an excellent officer." Captain Wallace took two long cigars from his pocket and gave Elmer one. "Shall we smoke on deck—for the benefit of the ladies?"

When they reached the poop, it was not quite dark. Some of the summer dusk still lingered, caught in the mirror of the Inlet, and in the southeast sky Mount Rainier was bathed in gleaming twilight. The tide was going out, silently, and the *Maid* had swung so that her bowsprit pointed straight inland to where the still, dim water narrowed between the walls of forest and ended in darkness. She looked like a ship that had sailed to the end of the earth and let her anchors go in the last dark reach.

"Well, Elmer, what are you going to do?" The captain's voice loomed through Elmer's comfortable thoughts like the stem of a colliding ship appearing in a fo'c'sle where men have been pleasantly asleep.

Startled, Elmer asked, "About what, Captain?"

"Don't you calculate you're in for some trouble here?" The voice was significant and grim.

"You mean the Indians?"

"That's what I mean." The captain stopped at a pinrail and tidied a carelessly coiled halliard. "Working through Nisqually Reach this morning, I couldn't help hearing the war drums."

Elmer said, "We can hear them from the prairie, too. They've been going for a month."

"And Nisqually isn't the only place." Captain Wallace dusted his hands and frock coat. "This voyage, we've been hearing war drums ever since we got into the Strait."

"The Nisquallys have been at it for a month," Elmer said. "Most people don't expect them to fight."

They stood at the rail, smoking and looking toward the black wall of the shore. Everything was so still that when the captain brushed the ash from his cigar you could hear its brief little hiss in the water below. "Nothing's being done to pacify these Indians, is there?"

"Mason, the Lieutenant Governor, has asked the old settlers to use their influence with the Indians—tell them everything will be all right."

"Is that all that's being done?"

"I think so," Elmer said.

The captain snorted. "The settlers could do as much good telling each other that everything will be all right."

"There's no one here with authority to do anything," Elmer explained. "The Governor hasn't been here since last winter. He's somewhere in the Blackfeet country, making treaties."

"Don't you think he's about a thousand miles too far away," the captain suggested, "with war dances going on in the front yard of his own capitol?"

"The Indians here never have attacked the whites," Elmer said. "Most people don't think they will now."

"What about these Klickitats?" the captain asked. "Aren't they a more warlike breed?"

"I think so," the boy said. "But they've been coming over here every summer since I don't know when. They have a regular trail that crosses north of Mount Rainier. There may be more of them than usual this year, but they haven't made any trouble."

Captain Wallace said quietly, "They have, on their own side of the mountains."

Elmer had not heard of any trouble. "When was that?"

"Recently, I judge. They'd just heard about it yesterday at Steilacoom. I don't know all the details, but it seems men had been leaving somewhere-or-other all summer for the mines at Prosser. Now it's discovered that they never arrived at the mines or anywhere else."

"It don't sound good, does it?"

"Not to me," the captain said.

"Are they doing anything about it?" Elmer asked. "Trying to punish the Indians, or anything?"

"Nothing so far as I heard," the captain said. "Nothing beyond discouraging men from going to the mines. I don't know the lay of the land, but as I understand it, there are a handful of soldiers at Fort Walla Walla, in a region with ten thousand Indian warriors. Trying to punish them would be courting trouble."

"I should think so!"

"On the other hand," the captain said, "things like that can't go on. It's too good an example to other Indians who are already beating the war drum. Not that I think your neighbors need much encouragement."

Elmer scowled at the darkening shore: a wall of black forest, and at its base an oblong of dim silver-gray that was the roof of his cabin. A few miles beyond, the forest was cut by the Nisqually valley. In that valley, men were painting their faces and doing war dances, and the drums were going night and day. Some people said there would be war, and some said there wouldn't. Captain Wallace, who was an outsider, was trying to show him there couldn't be anything else. In his own mind, Elmer was trying to distinguish between what was likely to happen, and what he wanted. Maybe, if he were an outsider, he would be as certain of war as the captain. But he was tied up with the country, with his house and clearing and the timber camp which promised fine profits. He couldn't really believe there would be a war because he had no time for one, and it would inconvenience him if it happened. Maybe all the other settlers who said the Indians wouldn't fight decided things the same way. It was like belonging to a political party, where you have to support things which you can't defend. "So you think we're in for trouble," he said at last.

Captain Wallace said grimly, "I believe it enough to clear out of here when I'm through loading!"

The boy was shocked. "You aren't coming back?"

"Not until things are settled." When Elmer did not answer, he went on: "I have to think about the safety of my family and my ship. I don't intend to be caught here when this territory goes up in flames. Even if it were safe afloat it could hardly be profitable. No one is likely to get out timber cargoes at such a time."

"What do you calculate to do?" Elmer asked.

The captain said, "Go back to Fairhaven."

The news affected Elmer strangely. If he stayed on this deck, in this ship, he would find himself at home again. It would be as simple as that. The Northwest coast would be a dream: a dream of Mount Rainier and summer on the Nisqually plain, and the still reaches and immense forests of the Sound. The little barque was in this place, but she was not of this place.

She was a fragment of the world of his boyhood which had
come into a distant dream. He had only to keep hold of her
and he would find himself at home again. It was what he had
planned to do at the beginning. He could see it would be beautiful and comforting, like going back to the security of his
mother's arms. But even if he were single and free to go, that
would have its implication of failure. It would be admitting
that he had no security in himself. He blew an idle jet of cigar
smoke toward the night shore. "So you're going home."

"It seems the prudent thing to do," the captain said.

"Timber carrying is profitable, isn't it?"

"It has been," the captain said. "It will boom when this
trouble is settled."

"And you're giving it up?"

"While it's unprofitable and dangerous, yes."

Elmer was beginning to glimpse the shape of things. "Then
you're coming back?"

The captain hesitated, a big, shadowy figure, with his arms
on the rail, looking down at the dark water. "A master has
to look ahead, Elmer. He has to calculate how things are going
to be, and make his plans. I expect things here to have blazed
up and quieted down again by the time I get back."

"Then you are coming back!"

"Possibly with a larger ship," the captain said, "one better
suited to the trade. I'm going to take that up with my partners and see what we can manage."

"We'll have plenty of timber for you," Elmer said. In his
mind, he was already enlarging their crew and extending the
logging works to his own timber, and after that putting up a
steam sawmill. . . .

"There's a depression at home," the captain said. "New
ships are selling for twenty-five per cent off, and good sea-
worthy vessels are going for much less. If my partners see it
as I do, we should be able to manage something quite handsome. We might even keep this one in the trade, along with
something more burdensome."

It sounded like good business, playing a war on one side of
the continent against a depression on the other. Elmer saw

that Captain Wallace would go far. And he and Uncle Jarvis
would go far, with the *Maid* and a bigger ship to be counted
on for regular cargoes. "We'll have plenty of timber for you,"
he said.

"That's for the future," the captain said. "What are you
going to do in the meantime, Elmer?"

It seemed to the boy that his life was already full, without
thinking up anything more to do. "Sit tight," he answered,
"and get along as best we can."

Captain Wallace asked disapprovingly, "Sit tight on top
of a volcano?"

"It doesn't seem like that when you're used to it."

"Quite so," the captain said, "and that's a dangerous way
to feel. It makes you blind to what a stranger can see in five
minutes."

Elmer said, "I guess you don't think much about dangers
that are part of your life."

"Quite so. That is the way most people get killed."

He was probably right, the boy thought, but that didn't
change the fact. You don't think much about dangers when
you are used to them. And it takes more than some one's talking
to get you unused to them. There were even dangers in going to
sea, but the captain would not think much of that because he
was used to them.

"When we were talking at dinner," Captain Wallace reminded him, "I said I wouldn't have anything to do with clipper ships and record runs. I said that I'd never lost a man or
a spar," he hit the rail with his knuckles, like knocking at the
door of the future, "and I didn't intend to begin."

"Yes, I remember."

"I meant that," the captain said. "For almost every fast
run made by a clipper ship, there's at least one empty grave in
some New England burying ground, and a stone paid for out of
hard savings. On the stone there's the name of the ship from
which the boy was lost, and the name of her master. Some
masters whom I meet in San Francisco have their names on
a score of tombstones, linked until Judgment Day with the
men they lost."

"I know," Elmer said. He knew very well, though Captain Wallace seemed to have forgotten, that his brother Charles had been claimed by a following Pacific sea as the *Stag Hound* was running her westing down.

"Often it's not their fault," the captain went on. "No master loses men deliberately. Blame it on speed, whoever is to blame for that. But I'll not have my name posted in a score of burying grounds. To a man with a conscience, that would be like dying twenty times, with as many reckonings to meet on Judgment Day."

Elmer listened, wondering. It was the first time he had seen inside the captain's mind, and it was not as much like a counting house as he expected. It was more like some austere New England parlor, with trophies of the sea, where conscience kept its watch over sailors. . . .

"I don't coddle my men," the captain said, "but I never forget their lives are in my care. And life is sacred, though there's little enough else that's sacred about a sailor."

The captain became more personal. "I didn't coddle you, Elmer, when you were a green hand, fresh from your father's farm. But I didn't gamble with your life, either. I made Mr. Holbrook answerable for your welfare, and I saw to it that you weren't sent higher than the tops'l yard until you were sure of your footing."

"I remember," Elmer said, "and I thank you, Captain Wallace." At the time, the footrope of a topsail yard had seemed cruelly high and insecure, but, looking back, he could see that he had been broken in very gently. It hurt his conscience to remember that he had been the first to desert the *Maid*.

"I would have looked out for you in any case," the captain went on, "but your mother entrusted you to my care. I promised to bring you home safely, God willing."

The boy stirred uneasily and shifted his weight as he looked down at the dark, ebbing tide. The captain's talk made him think of Sundays on board in good weather, when all hands were mustered aft for church services. Gathered on the quarterdeck, every one had a kind of equality, but the solemn tone of the service did not encourage the sailors to feel like officers.

Rather, it made the officers seem like humble foremast hands in the presence of God, whom the captain interpreted. Now, sharing the quarterdeck with the captain, Elmer felt the same kind of uneasy humility. "I'm very grateful," he said.

The captain went on without acknowledging the boy's gratitude. "Ordinarily, I would feel that my responsibility ended when you left me; when you cast your lot with Jarvis——"

"You did your best for me," Elmer said. "I'm very grateful. Mother understands, and she's used to the idea of my staying out here——"

"For all that," Captain Wallace decided, "I was responsible for bringing you here. I would feel some responsibility if you were wiped out by an Indian massacre."

"You can't be responsible for what the Indians do!" The boy was embarrassed to realize how far the captain's conscience went. "I'll manage to look out for myself."

The captain went on grimly, "I haven't noticed any of you here considering your safety. And you have a wife to think about."

"We've talked things over," Elmer said. "Lisette thinks we're safe enough here."

"Do you?"

"I don't know." Then he said, "I don't see any immediate danger."

"And after that?"

"I don't know." It was true he didn't see any immediate danger. It was also true that things couldn't go on as they were, indefinitely. After a while he asked, "What do you think we should do?" Since Captain Wallace was so discouraging about things as they were, he should have something better to suggest. While Elmer was waiting for an answer, the quiet summer night was disturbed by the cry of a cougar from the shore on his claim. It couldn't have been less than a third of a mile away, but the sudden tortured scream stabbed through the darkness and made the captain start.

"What the devil was that?"

"Only a cougar," Elmer said.

"Humph!"

"It's over on my place."

"You sound as if you were proud of it!"

"They're everywhere," he said. "You get used to them."

"How can you tell the difference between that and the cry of a woman being murdered?"

"Why, does it sound like that?"

"The one I heard sounded just like that."

"You get used to them," Elmer said.

"It takes me back to a side street in Buenos Aires, where a woman was being knifed by her lover."

"It'll scream again in a minute."

"That's a comfort," the captain said. He went back to their interrupted conversation. "You asked me what I thought you should do."

"Yes."

"Why not come back with us in the *Maid?* I could find a berth for you."

"What about Lisette?"

The captain considered, lighting his cigar which had gone out. "It wouldn't do to make a change for her safety and then leave her out of the plans, would it?"

"Hardly," Elmer said.

"Hasn't she a family or some safe place where she could stay while you're away? It probably wouldn't be more than a year."

A year's separation would seem like a small matter in Fairhaven or New Bedford, where wives sometimes waited five years or longer for the whalers to come home. But this blackwalled reach of water was not Bedford Harbor. Captain Wallace could not recommend a separation from personal experience, and Elmer had no wish to try one. "I'm afraid it wouldn't do," he said. "Lisette hasn't any family, and we like to be together."

"You could find a place for her in San Francisco," the captain suggested. "It's quite a city now, twenty-five thousand people. Mrs. Wallace found it comfortable."

"Lisette would never agree to that. I wouldn't like it, either."

"There could be less pleasant separations," the captain reminded him.

"We like to be together," Elmer said. "We'll make out all right."

The captain sighed. "I am not anxious to separate a man and woman who are devoted to each other. But it seems sad and foolish when people refuse to leave a sinking ship."

"We'll make out all right," the boy said. "We'll be careful."

The captain did not find the reassurance worth answering. "Suppose we took your wife along?"

Elmer was staggered. "You mean—you would do that, Captain?" He grew dizzy with the thought of such a swift success. Two years after he left home, penniless and uncertain of himself, coming back with his wife for a visit. Coming back to bring out a bigger ship for the timber enterprise. He had promised himself that some day, when he was prosperous, he would take Lisette on a sea voyage. He would go home as a man of some importance and have his revenge on the poverty of his boyhood. But he hadn't dreamed of it happening so swiftly and without warning. And even though he had an uneasy feeling of some hollowness about the plan, he could not see anything wrong with it. "You would do that?" he asked, wonderingly.

"It's only a thought," the captain said. "I would have to talk it over with Mrs. Wallace. But I think we might manage something. Your wife would be a help to her, and the women would be company to each other."

"I don't know how to thank you," Elmer said. "I don't know—. I'll have to talk it over with Lisette." Each of them had to talk it over with his wife. Meanwhile their wives were talking things over in the cabin. Probably they had got farther along than the men. "I don't know," Elmer said. He wanted time to think it over on his own account. Two bells were struck forward and echoed precisely from the shore, with a tone as familiar as the church bells at home.

"I might even have a second mate's berth for you," the captain said. "You are short on sea experience, but you have more education than most men, and I presume you are willing to learn."

"Yes," the boy said. It was an honor he had never thought

of for himself, and his "yes" sounded unappreciative. He had already been offered so much that he was numb to more. It only added to the confusion of what he had to think over.

The stub of the captain's cigar hissed in the dark water alongside. Beyond the shadow of the barque, the Inlet was like a dim polished mirror, reflecting stars, and the gray amphibian beach was coming out between the water and the land. "Shall we go back to the ladies?"

The end of Elmer's cigar followed the captain's. But his mind hesitated. "I ought to look in at the fo'c'sle," he said.

"Of course." The captain went forward with him, stopping once to put a bucket in its rack. "You won't find many of your old friends," he said. "Enough of them have gone away to doubtful adventures."

The boy couldn't say anything since he too had gone away to what the captain considered a doubtful adventure.

"You don't have to consider the fo'c'sle too seriously," the captain said. "I think we can find a berth for you aft."

"You're very kind," Elmer said. "I'll think it over."

The captain stopped near the black foremast shrouds which were like a section of some great web in which stars had been caught. "Come back to the cabin when you have paid your call," he said.

Elmer opened the well-remembered door and stepped over the high coaming into the fo'c'sle. He had the sensation of having blundered into the wrong place.

In the light of the lantern, the brown faces of Sandwich Islanders looked at him from the berth which had been his and from Harry's berth above it, and from Cal's berth forward, and Charlie's. On the starboard side, two more were crouched on Stirling's old berth, playing a game of cards, and there were still others. The fo'c'sle was as clean as ever and the short brown men looked like sailors. They looked friendly, too, and one of them said "Helloa." But the fo'c'sle seemed a strange place. The New England faces were gone, and Elmer had the feeling of having blundered into a Sandwich Island boarding house. There wasn't anything to stay for.

To complete the formality, he looked around the door at the remaining berths on the starboard side. Like a ghost of the past, he saw Old Tom, the whaleman, sitting in his lower berth, knitting a sock. Like an old woman, except for the bulge of a quid in one cheek and his strip of white beard from ear to ear. "Tom!" he said.

"I'll be God damned if it isn't the boy Elmer!" Sam Cutler's long, homely face was looking down from the berth above.

Elmer blinked, half expecting to see familiar faces appear from everywhere.

"It's all right," Sam assured him, "we're not ghosts." He let his lanky, underwear-clad body down from the high berth and shook hands. "We're the ones who were too old to get away."

Tom moved up a bench for the visitor, and gave his breeches a hitch. "We get along." He shared his bunk with Sam, and the returned sailor sat on the bench, dazed by change. "Where are the others?" he asked.

Sam shook his head reproachfully. "And you the first to leave us!"

"Zeke is still here." Tom opened his silver tobacco box and took out a well-bitten twist of pigtail. "He's on anchor watch."

"You know how much company he is," Sam said.

"But where is every one else?"

"Scattered and gone," Sam told him, "like you."

"Cal and Charlie cleared out in San Francisco," Tom said.

"They were going to try their luck at the diggings," Sam explained. "That was last fall. We haven't seen hide nor hair of them since."

"Stirling left to go logging."

"He's foreman of a timber camp at Port Townsend, making good money." Sam chuckled, wryly. "The Old Man won't take any cargo there, being as Jack left him in the lurch."

"You have a new second mate?"

"We have our old one back," Tom said.

"Jones?"

"Yes. I calculated he was through for good that time he

ran us aground in the Strait, but he bounced back to his old berth when Jack went ashore. The Old Man can't pick and choose out here."

"Hopkins is working in Yesler's mill at Seattle."

"We have a new first mate, too," Sam recalled.

"I saw him," Elmer said.

"Hopkins has a claim on Lake Union," Tom said, "back in the woods from Seattle, on fresh water. And him a sailor!"

"We got our new mate off the beach at 'Frisco," Sam said. "He'd broken down there. I can't think why, unless it was too many drinks and women."

"Mr. Holbrook left us two trips ago," Tom said. "I don't know where he went."

The old sailors were like the survivors of a hurricane, taking pride in the damage done by the storm, but to the boy each missing landmark was a new and lonely pang. He had changed, to be sure, but he hadn't foreseen that everything else would change. It hadn't occurred to him that when he tried to go back to the security of the past it would be scattered and gone.

Afterward, when he was alone on the starlit deck, he thought of what his uncle had said the year before when he was leaving the ship at Steilacoom—about America reaching her destiny and going ashore. It looked that way, all right, with the *Maid* left to sailors who were too old to start over in a new world, and to mates who had failed in one way or another. That didn't affect his going back to help bring out a bigger ship for the timber trade. If he went back. The prospect did not seem so attractive after he had seen the nakedness of the ship. With his enthusiasm cooling, he began to see flaws in the plan.

When he went back to the cabin, he was struck by the feeling that the women hadn't got very far with their talk, whatever it had been. Nothing more was said about the plan until he and Lisette were on their own shore, and he had pulled the dugout up on the beach.

Standing beside him, she said quietly, "The captain and his wife would like to take you back with them."

"Both of us," he said.

"They'd take me if they had to."

"They want us both to go."

"They think we're going to have trouble here," she said.

He looked at the broadside silhouette of the *Maid*, riding on the starlit tide. "That don't mean we will. Skippers have to be cautious."

"They think we're going to have bad trouble."

"Shall we go with them, Lisette?"

"I wouldn't want the baby to be born at sea."

"No," he agreed. Though it could happen under worse conditions; during an Indian attack, for example. "We may have trouble here."

"I know that," she said. "I'm not a child."

He stared at the comforting silhouette of the barque, with her anchor light like a star against the blackness of the land. "You'd be safe there, anyway," he said. "It might save a lot of trouble."

"I suppose so."

"Should we go, Lisette?"

"Do you really want to?"

"I think you should decide it."

"I don't want to go," she said. "I wouldn't, even if I knew trouble was coming."

He felt relieved, though it didn't solve the problem of safety.

"This is our country," she said. "If we left it while there was trouble and then came back, it wouldn't be as much ours as it was before."

"Like summer people," he said.

"Who are they, Elmer?"

"We have them at home," he said. "People who spend the summer in the country, and go back to town as soon as the nice weather is over. Some of them do it all their lives but they never really belong."

"We're not summer people," she said. "We're here to stay."

CHAPTER FIFTEEN

WHEN the timber camp closed down because of the Indians, the Indian boy was the only one who stayed. Really, it was because of the white settlers who were nervous about the Indians. They were beginning to keep together as much as possible, and in some places two or more families slept in one house while the men took turns standing guard. Things were going like that around the middle of September when Levi Porter rode over from Scatter Creek and took his boys and oxen home. It was then too late in too precarious a year to think of finding more oxen and more hands.

Elmer told himself it was the kind of catch he might have expected. He should have foreseen that when he was finally on his way to prosperity everything would be upset by people balking on their way to starvation. Even those who defended the Governor's harsh bargaining were making a disagreeable discovery. By taking everything away from the Indians, the treaty had given them a desperate kind of advantage: they had nothing to lose by making trouble.

So far the Medicine Creek Treaty Indians hadn't done anything, but there was trouble east of the mountains, where so many men had disappeared on their way to the mines at Prosser. An Indian Agent who had gone to investigate vanished after the vanished miners. Now a company of regulars from Fort Steilacoom and two companies of volunteers were on their way over the mountains to punish the Indians.

In a darkening and uneasy world Nisqually Jim alone kept faith with the silent timber camp by living there in his summer hut of poles and mats. He no longer drew wages, but he worked for Jarvis and Elmer by turns and ate with whichever one he happened to be helping. Elmer did not pretend to understand the arrangement. Maybe Jim was living on the pleasant memory of the wages which he had buried somewhere under a tree. Maybe it was a kind of adoption. Elmer did not know. He asked Jim about it that morning when they were taking salmon out of the little creek. "Why do you work for me," he asked, "when I can't pay you?"

Jim's broad brown face widened slightly with a grin, while his eyes kept their usual look of alert melancholy. "You don't pay me, you can't fire me," he said. "I can work easy. What-the-hell?"

They weren't working hard, if they were working at all. They had been taking salmon out of the creek a little above where it crossed the trail, but there were so many salmon and it was so easy to lift them out of the shallow water with their pitchforks that they had lost interest. So they worked up along the creek, exploring. They had nothing more definite or useful in mind than to settle a friendly dispute. Jim had told about a boy who walked across a creek on the backs of salmon, without getting his moccasins wet. Elmer said it was impossible. He was sure it could not be done, and the Nisqually boy was just as sure it could. So they had started up the creek with the idea of finding a place where the salmon were packed solidly. It was an idle kind of errand and a good excuse for exploring the creek.

In the same spirit of idleness, Elmer was trying to find out why Jim had attached himself to the non-working timber partnership. "I don't expect you to work for me when you don't get paid," he said.

"Sometime you work hard and get no *chickamun*," Jim reminded him. "You get no *chickamun* for your garden or the salmon."

"Then I work for *muck-a-muck*."

Above the noise of salmon fighting their way up the narrow stream, Jim said, "I work for *muck-a-muck*, too. What-the-hell? I *muck-a-muck* with you. Sometime *Tyee* Jarvis and you sell timber for *chickamun*. Then you give me *chickamun*. Sometime you work for *muck-a-muck*. Me same."

Elmer said, "I see."

The young Nisqually looked doubtful. "Spose I *klatawa?*"

"I'd rather you stayed, Jim."

"All right," Jim said. "What-the-hell?" They went on up the creek.

It was the second fall Elmer had seen the salmon run in the little creek, but it was as much of a wonder as ever. Ordinarily the stream was about eight feet wide and a couple of inches deep at the riffles. Nothing lived in it but minnows; it wasn't big enough for anything else. At home, nature would have let it go at that. But out here salmon were asked to do the impossible, like an army sent to its death by some wrong-headed general. Thousands of full-grown salmon, heavy with eggs or milt, were crowded into the narrow and shallow stream where they were defenseless against men, and against bears who fattened on them in the fall. It would have been altogether impossible for them to get upstream at most seasons of the year, but that was provided for, after a fashion. Just at spawning time the autumn rains swelled the creek enough to provide a kind of lubrication. What had been impossible became just possible. The salmon went upstream, sometimes with their backs out of water; sometimes everything but their bellies out of water as they wiggled across riffles. Sometimes all of them out of water as they jumped up waterfalls or over fallen trees. They went on like that, fasting and without pause, until their obscure orders were carried out. Then they came drifting downstream, with their color gone and their fins and tails like frayed rope, battered and bleached and dead or dying. You could almost say they were no longer salmon after they left the salt water for the creek. They became a force of nature: something that did not eat or rest or think of its own safety until its force was spent, and then it was finished. Up and down the creek there was a constant threshing sound of salmon driving upstream with the cold-blooded passion of nature. Salmon on their way to die for love, if you could call that love: the female dropping her eggs in some cold pool, roiled with autumn rains, and the male coming along after she was gone and leaving his milt. Both of them drifting downstream,

but separately, exhausted and dying as they drifted. There
didn't seem to be much in it for the salmon: ordeal and death
in a creek of raw, new-fallen rain.

There was no rain now, but it had been raining earlier.
The creek air was raw and Elmer's clothes were half wet from
the bushes along the bank. That was the catch about the salmon run. It happened in wet places in rainy autumn weather.
In some ways it was more interesting to talk about than to see.
A disturbed branch showered cold water down his neck and
cooled his enthusiasm a few more degrees. He remembered
promising Lisette that he wouldn't be gone very long. It was
about time to turn back.

In the water at his feet he saw a small, trim salmon, darker
than the others, with a gamey look. It was only a red salmon
and not as good as the silvers, no better for smoking than the
dog salmon. But it looked more desirable because it was different. He raised his pitchfork for a try at it, but it shot away
upstream like a dark arrow, passing a hundred others before he
lost sight of it. The little beauty seemed to have the strength
to reach the spawning ground and come back that afternoon
without being tired. But in one way or another it too would
manage to be dead by the time it reached salt water, because
that was the fate of salmon. Strength and quickness made no
difference.

Jim had stopped and was pointing. When Elmer came up to
him he said, "I told you." He was pointing at a riffle which
was packed with salmon working their way across: silver
and red and dog salmon, making a close, wet pattern of gray
and red and dull gold, blur-spotted with water from threshing
tails. On the bank there was a mess of bones and a half-eaten
silver salmon where a bear had gorged himself.

"See? I told you." Jim pointed at the creek, paved with
smooth, many-colored backs. *"Hyas* salmon, *halo chuck!* Easy
to walk on."

"No," Elmer said. Though it almost looked as if you could
walk across on them.

"It's easy," Jim told him. "What-the-hell? You try."

Elmer laughed and shook his head. He wasn't going to demonstrate when he had argued all along that it was impossible. "You try."

"*Wake,*" Jim said. "It's easy. I know; don't have to try. You think not. You try and learn."

Elmer was laughing at him. "I'm not going to get wet learning what I know already. You try it."

It might have been fun if it had been summer, but it was not summer, and the raw autumn creek took away their courage for pranks. Neither of them wanted to try it himself. They even gave up urging each other to try, and agreed it was time to go back.

Then, perversely, Jim decided to make the attempt. "You watch," he said.

"All right, but you'll get wet."

"*Wake.*" Jim stuck his pitchfork in the wet ground and measured the creek with his eye. It was only about twelve feet wide at the riffle, and he crouched on the bank for a springing start. With luck, he might get across by only touching once in midstream.

In case he made it, Elmer got ready to say it didn't count because that was jumping across and not walking on the backs of the salmon.

"You watch," Jim said.

"You'll get wet."

"*Wake.*" Jim leaped more than halfway across the salmon-choked riffle, with the look of touching once, lightly, and going on. But he touched on slippery footing which threw him off balance in the twinkling of an eye. The creek resounded with the sudden plungings of salmon going away to make room for him to sit down. Without taking time to get up, he called, "I slipped!" Just as if he had been prepared to say that in case he didn't make it.

"I saw you slip!" Elmer teetered on the bank, with the muscles along his ribs aching from laughter. "You slipped, all right!"

"What-the-hell?" Jim said deprecatingly, sitting in the creek. To cover his defeat, he threw himself on a stranded salmon and got one hand through its gills. He stood, holding up his threshing consolation prize. "I make it, but I stopped for this!"

"I saw you change your mind!" Elmer said.

Jim's grin went out as if something had changed inside him, and his eyes went listening and intent.

"What is it?" Elmer couldn't hear anything except the noises of the salmon and the creek, but the change in the young Nisqually's face chilled him with anxiety.

Jim let his prize slip back into the water. "You hear something?"

Elmer shook his head, but he wasn't going to waste any time in getting home.

"I ask Mama if she hear something." Jim waded out of the creek and crouched down, with one side of his face against the wet earth. After a few seconds he got up. "Horses." With a gesture he indicated the trail to the cabin. "Horses going *hyak.*"

Elmer had already started down the creek. Lisette was at home, alone and unprotected. He had known in his mind that the times weren't safe, but the knowledge hadn't spread into his body. It hadn't got through him that he was living in a dangerous world. All of him knew it now.

He got his rifle from where he had left it in the hollow cedar stump, and went on, looking at the priming as he ran. The muddy trail was cut deeply with the unshod hoof-prints of ponies travelling fast in single file.

"Six horses," the Nisqually said, running beside him in wet clothes with a pitchfork in his hand.

No good asking what kind when every one rode unshod horses. And whatever color the riders might be there were probably Indians mixed up in it. Elmer cursed the obscuring woods. It wasn't more than two hundred yards to the house, and he couldn't see a trace of it, let alone what was going on. He flew on over the mud, with his lungs raw and hurting and hot sweat inside his clothes. In the wet mud ahead there was something black and smooth and dry.

"Thunderbird," Jim grunted.

Elmer was using all his breath and did not answer, but he had seen the eagle feather as he passed over it. "I'll never leave her alone again," he promised himself, "never!" He couldn't understand how he had done it this time. It was all his fault, but back of that it was Lisette's, too. They could have gone to safety in the *Maid*. But they had been brave and stupid, and stayed. It was no kind of world to be in when a few hoof-prints and a feather could distort it into horror.

They burst into the clearing, and Elmer had the feeling of falling into a vacuum because everything was so orderly and unalarmed. Unhurried smoke was going up from the fireplace, where Lisette would be cooking dinner, and the barebacked ponies were waiting quietly near the door, with one Indian on a buckskin holding the bridle thongs.

"Spose we walk," Jim panted, "like men not afraid."

Elmer thought it was a good idea. He changed to a fast walk, panting and blowing the air from his sore lungs out of his mouth. Now he could see that the Indian horse-holder had black stripes painted across his red-brown face. From close up it looked like tiger skin, and his body was oiled and slippery-looking.

Other Indians were coming out of the open doorway. One of them had black spots on his face, like some pestilence. Elmer counted four Indians coming out, then he saw Lisette standing in the doorway and he knew everything was all right. She had a wooden spoon in one hand and looked as if she had been cooking while she talked to her visitors. Elmer wasn't afraid any more, and he caught his breath enough to say "Hello" to the Indians and "What do you want?" *"Klahowya? Icta mika tickey?"*

"We came to talk," one of them answered in English. They didn't look hostile, except the young brave whose black-spotted face looked as if some plague had broken out. He glared at Elmer with active dislike, hate and maybe scorn. Elmer had seen him before, though he couldn't remember where, and he had never had any quarrel with an Indian.

"I'm sorry I was out," Elmer said. "We were spearing salmon."

Jim added something in Nisqually, and called attention to his wet clothes.

"I have words from Leschi," the spokesman said, "for *Tyee* Jarvis and you. Open your ears."

"All right," Elmer said.

"Will you tell *Tyee* Jarvis, *hyak?*"

"I'll tell him *hyak.*"

"Open your ears. Leschi says tell all people the Nisquallys don't want trouble. They will not make it first. If there is trouble, the Nisquallys only fight those who fight them. The Nisquallys love peace. All who live in peace are their friends. Stay on your farms; you will be safe there. If there is trouble, while the Nisquallys are away fighting they are the friends of Bostons who stay on their farms. When trouble is over, they will come back to their own farms and live with you in peace. They will be your friends who will not have to go away to trouble any more." The spokesman talked slowly and earnestly. Elmer would have known who the message was from even if he had not been told.

"I'll tell Uncle Jarvis right away," Elmer promised. The message made him feel fine and at ease while he stood among the Indians who were going on the warpath. "Leschi is a good man."

The Indian looked at him searchingly. "He is a good man," he said. While they talked the other Nisquallys had taken their ponies from the horse-holder and mounted. The one with black spots on his face sat on his calico pony, close to Elmer, with his rifle held upright, looking at him venomously. *"Cultus Bostons!"* He spat on the wet ground at Elmer's feet.

"Good-by!" the spokesman said. He vaulted onto the back of his pony and the Indians were gone like a flock of birds swooping away across the clearing. Soft earth muffled the drumming of hooves and the forest swallowed the riders.

Elmer went over to his wife and put his arm around her. "Are you all right?"

"I'm fine," she said. "Let's go inside before Jim catches his death."

"I jump in the *chuck* to catch a fine salmon for you," Jim said as they went in.

That was not the way Elmer remembered it, but the ingenious Nisqually had done more than that for Lisette, so he did not contradict him.

"I'm glad you came back when you did," Lisette said. She was beginning to be afraid. She and Elmer sat on the bench while Jim stood on the hearth with the rear of his steaming jeans turned to the bright fire.

Elmer held his wife's hand, tightly. "I shouldn't have left you alone," he said. "I won't leave you again."

"I'm a little scared now," Lisette said, "but it seemed all right then. The one who talked to you was nice; he told me not to be afraid."

"I'm glad of that," Elmer said.

"We talked about babies."

"Babies?"

"Yes," she said. "He told me his wife was going to have one soon. He asked me if I was sick in the morning. It seemed personal, but when I told him I wasn't he said that was fine. He talked to me nicely all the time when he wasn't arguing with the others."

"What were they arguing about?"

"I don't know," she said. "That was in their own language. Most of it was with the one who had black spots on his face. He acted mean."

"I saw that, all right," Elmer said. He asked Jim who it was.

Jim said it was Slugia, Stahi's *tenas man*. Stahi was Leschi's half brother. Elmer remembered bumping into him at the treaty ground, but in the excitement and with Slugia's face painted he hadn't recognized him.

"Slugia is a *cultus Siwash*," Jim said, drying his jeans at the fire. "He hates Bostons. He hates Leschi because he has Boston *tillicums*."

"The Nisquallys must have heard something was happening," Elmer said. "That message was from Leschi, all right."

"They acted like something was up."

"We'll give Uncle Jarvis the message, anyway."

"Do you boys want to eat first?" Lisette asked. "I've started dinner." Pregnancy had given her a kind of calm bloom and with it the conviction that there was no hurry about things.

Like babies, they would happen when their time came. Nature working in her had taught her some of its secrets.

But Elmer could not take events so calmly. "I think we should go now," he said. "I promised to."

Lisette was agreeable, even though she did not see the need for hurry. "All right, I'll move the kettles off the fire."

Elmer did it for her, with Jim moving his half-dry jeans out of the way.

"You must have fallen in good," Lisette told him.

"*Wake,*" Jim said. "I walk across the *chuck* on salmon. No get my moccasins wet."

"That's right," Elmer said. "He landed with his feet in the air."

"Landed where?"

"On his stern in the creek." Elmer demonstrated, using the bench to represent the creek.

"*Wake!*" Jim insisted it hadn't been that way at all. "I walk dry. Then I pick a fine salmon for you. That makes a hole in the bridge and I fall in. *Cult-a-mana!*"

"That's true," Elmer said. "The part about his falling in."

"You boys have a fine time," Lisette said, with her voice nice and warm. She was only eighteen, but she smiled at them as tenderly as if she were their mother who wanted them to go on having good times for always.

CHAPTER SIXTEEN

UNCLE JARVIS met them on the beach in front of his house and helped Lisette out. "You had callers, h'm?"

"We had callers, all right," Elmer said.

"I didn't see them until they were going away." Jarvis looked anxious, but he didn't say or ask anything to make the visit seem more alarming than it had been.

"They had a message for you from Leschi," Elmer said.

He wasn't surprised. "Come up to the house and tell me about it. You're staying for dinner."

When the men were by themselves Uncle Jarvis said, "Leschi sent a message, h'm?"

The boy told him what it was, repeating the words as nearly as he could remember them.

"'Going away to trouble,' h'm," Uncle Jarvis said. "It was a kind of farewell."

"Something like that." They were walking along the edge of the damp October land, toward the deserted timber camp. Farewell to summer. Farewell to profits from getting out timber. Farewell to sleeping safely at night. Farewell to a lot of other things if trouble came.

"D'ye know what happened, Elmer?"

"They didn't say, and I was too excited to ask."

Uncle Jarvis talked about it to Jim in Nisqually, but he didn't know either.

Elmer said, "I don't understand why they came to my place, when the message was mostly for you. It's the same distance, and your road is better."

"Maybe they felt safer on your lonely trail, h'm?"

Elmer hadn't thought of that. "Do you suppose any one is after them?"

They stopped at the log dump and sat on the length of piling which lay at the top of the skids. It had been abandoned there, like a lost soul, when the camp shut down. It had been killed as a tree, and it hadn't been brought to life as useful timber. Probably it would rot where it was——

"Slugia was one of your callers, h'm?"

"He was the only one who seemed dangerous," Elmer said. "If he'd had his way I guess they would have killed us."

"He hates Americans," Uncle Jarvis agreed, "with ample cause. Still, I don't approve of him. That much hatred turns a boy rancid. And no race deserves mass condemnation—not even our own."

Jim did not find the conversation interesting. He had picked up a broken cant-hook, also abandoned, and was going through the motions of launching the log on which the others were sitting down the skids. Jarvis noticed him and smiled. "The old war-horse," he said. "You can't keep Jim from logging!"

The Nisqually heard him and paused, with a grin on his broad face and his eyes sad. "Logger!" he said, pounding his chest. "What-the-hell?"

Like an echo from Jim's pounded chest, the pounding of hooves swelled from the forest.

"Your callers are coming here," Jarvis said.

The horsemen burst into the clearing at a hard gallop. This time there were about a dozen of them, and they were not Indians. They were bearded white men, riding big American horses and carrying rifles.

Uncle Jarvis and Elmer got up and stepped over to the road. The horsemen looked noble and determined, but there was no point in their thundering up to the house and scaring the women out of their wits.

Drawn up short, the horses slid in the mud and reared up as their riders dismounted, rifles in hand.

"What the devil is this, h'm? An army?" Jarvis did not sound impressed.

"Puget Sound Volunteers," one of the men said, dismounting from his powerful bay horse. Elmer recognized him as Charlie Eaton, from Chambers Prairie, near Olympia. Among the others there was Jim McAllister and his son, George, and Milt Wallace.

"Be you volunteers for anything in particular," Uncle Jarvis asked, "or just on general principles?"

Eaton's serious, bearded face looked from Nisqually Jim, with the broken cant-hook in his hands, to his questioner. "Send that boy away, and I'll tell you."

"I'll be damned if I will," Jarvis said independently.

"It's serious," Eaton said.

Jarvis decided to compromise. "I'll tell Jim, and he can suit himself." He spoke to the boy in Nisqually, explaining the situation.

"What-the-hell?" Jim said, indifferently. He threw down the old cant-hook and walked away.

When the boy was out of hearing, Eaton said, "Saddle up and come with us, Jarvis. Orders of the acting Governor. Bring your rifle."

Uncle Jarvis looked surprised, but in no hurry to obey. "Mason told me only last Friday that he had no authority to act while the Governor was away."

"He has to act in an emergency," Eaton said. "Come on, Jarvis; you've sulked in your tent long enough. We need you."

The big man said, "Before I gallop around the country like a cadet school, I want to know why."

"We're going after Leschi and Quiemuth."

"What crime have they committed?"

"They haven't done anything yet," Eaton said. "But Mason's decided things can't go on the way they have been. Too many people think it's war or peace depending on what Leschi decides to do."

"Has he tried promising the Nisquallys land they can live on?"

"You know an acting Governor hasn't power to do that."

"But he can send an armed posse to arrest men who haven't done anything, h'm?"

"He has to protect the settlers," Eaton said.

"What are you going to do with Leschi and Quiemuth when you catch them?" Uncle Jarvis asked. "Shoot them?"

Eaton accepted it as a joke. "Mason is going to keep them in Olympia until things have quieted down. They'll be given food and lodgings and allowed to have their families with them. Quiemuth agreed to that in case there was trouble, and he's the chief; you know that."

"Stevens gave him a piece of paper that said so, but Leschi is chief. You know that when you say it's war or peace depending on what he decides."

"I haven't time to argue about it," Eaton said. "But Quiemuth is certainly under his power. So we're going to get them both."

"Yes, going like a cavalry attack!"

"There's more than that to it," Eaton explained. "Yesterday Mason sent us to invite them to Olympia. But the news leaked, somehow. When we got to Leschi's farm, the birds had flown. Leschi had started his fall ploughing. According to the Indians who would talk, Leschi was holding the plough while Quiemuth drove the horses. If we'd been a little earlier we'd have got them both. They'd only gone about a hundred feet when they heard we were coming. The plough was still in the crooked furrow, but Leschi and Quiemuth had lit out for the Puyallup with their families and a party of braves. Leschi hadn't even taken the time to get his horses in from the prairie; he'd just lit out with what was at hand. We're getting more volunteers to go after them."

Uncle Jarvis said bitterly, "I suppose all that proves that Leschi was prepared to go on the warpath, h'm?"

"No," Eaton said. "It looked to me as if he wasn't going to fight. But nobody feels easy while he is at large. Mason thought——"

"The fat's in the fire now, by God! You've found out that Leschi's intentions were peaceful—by driving him to war!"

"Maybe it was a mistake," Eaton said, "but Mason did what he thought was best."

"Mason's a fine boy," Uncle Jarvis said, "and he's been left with a lapful of wrongs and no authority to right them. But what about you men, h'm? Are you going to carry out another of Mason's blunders? Are you going to get a war started in earnest?"

"We're going to get Leschi and Quiemuth," one of the volunteers said, "that's what!"

Uncle Jarvis looked at him sharply. "You're going to get shot, Connell, that's what!" He said it with such harsh conviction that Connell started and changed color. "No!" he said, like a man protesting a sentence of death.

"If Mason hasn't the authority to prevent a war, by God, he hasn't the authority to start one!" The big man's voice dropped from a roar to gentle persuasion. "Let's forget about arresting innocent people and think about doing something to keep the peace. Governor Stevens should be back soon. The last I heard he was about through making treaties——"

"He won't be back for months," Eaton said. "Mason's just heard from him. He's on the other side of the Rockies, in Nebraska Territory——"

"Good God! What's he doing there? Making more treaties?"

Eaton was embarrassed because the sarcastic suggestion was the case. "When he got through making treaties in this Territory, he offered to help bring the eastern Blackfeet into line——"

Uncle Jarvis exploded: "Good God and good Jesus defend us from our Governor! He makes a hell out of our peaceful Territory and then abandons us, to conquer new worlds!" He towered above the captain of volunteers, with his hands clenched and his eyes all on fire. "Haven't we guts enough to save ourselves from this ambitious little Governor who sheperds other people's Indians while the war drums beat in his own capital?"

"Mason's in charge," Eaton said. "And we're carrying out his orders."

"I'll come with you," Uncle Jarvis said, "if you'll come with me and talk to Mason. You can tell him I stopped you at the point of a gun. I'll do it, too, by God! You're not going to plunge us into war!"

"Now, Jarvis," McAllister said good-naturedly, "I can't see where you get all this talk about war, war! I know the Nis-

quallys better than any other man in this Territory, and I
know they won't fight. They've never attacked white men, and
they won't now."

"That was true. And nothing has changed since except that
they've been forced to choose between starvation and war. Now
you're forcing war on them! D'ye think that any creatures, no
matter how small and outnumbered, won't fight against the
dogs before they die?"

"The Nisquallys won't fight," McAllister said. "They're so
gentle I could drive the whole tribe before me, like sheep."

"That was true," Jarvis said, "and nothing's changed except that they've been changed to wolves. You'll drive them
just so far and then, by God, they'll turn on you and tear you
to pieces!"

"You don't know them the way I do." The grizzled pioneer
felt in his pockets and took out a plug of tobacco and offered
it to Jarvis.

"I thank you." He returned the diminished plug. "I don't
know anything about the kind of Indians you're talking about;
they're not human!"

McAllister worried off a piece of the plug. "If I thought
there was going to be any trouble, do you reckon I would be
leaving my lady and little girls in the middle of the Nisqually
camp with only a boy of twelve to protect them?"

"Good Christ!" Jarvis looked at him, blankly. "You're doing that?"

The Kentuckian nodded.

"I don't understand you," Jarvis said. "Those lovely little
girls— In your place, I wouldn't leave a pet bird there and
expect to find more than two scattered feathers."

"You cain't scare me, Jarvis!"

"Nothing can scare you," Jarvis agreed. "I don't understand you, Jim! Don't anything go on in your mind? Your
life's tied up with Leschi. Since the day he met you, as an emigrant, on the Cowlitz River, you've prospered through his
help. D'ye think it's a fair return to arrest him for fear he
might object to seeing his people stripped of everything?"

"Don't shame me, Jarvis!" McAllister said hotly. "If I've

ever wronged any man, Indian or white, you can shoot me down like a steer! Leschi was my first friend in this Territory. I've never had a better one, and I aim to be his friend as long as I live. I didn't write the Medicine Crick Treaty. I don't like it and it wa'nt right——"

"You don't think it's right, but you'll help throw Leschi into jail because he don't think it's right!"

"Nobody's going to be thrown into jail," McAllister said. "We're going to take Leschi and Quiemuth to Olympia where they'll be safe and well treated. I'm going because Leschi is my friend and I don't want to see him in no trouble. I'll tell him going to Olympia is the only safe thing he can do. It would be suicide for the Nisquallys to think of fighting!"

"And suicide for them not to!" Uncle Jarvis said. "I'd think, by God, after they've made you prosperous you could do better than point out to them that the rope is less painful than the knife!"

"Don't shame me," McAllister said. "You know, Jarvis, that if there's anything I can do to help the Nisquallys I'll do it!"

Jarvis said bitterly, "You could have helped that Christmas Day, when we found out the kind of a treaty Stevens had written! You could have joined me in refusing to have anything to do with it. If there had been enough of us, it might have been a different treaty, h'm?"

"There's some things a white man cain't do, even if he'd like to," McAllister said. "He cain't side with Indians, against the government."

Jarvis said, "I see. You're going to drag your innocent friend to jail because you are a white man, and there are different colors of justice!"

"You cain't talk to me like that!" McAllister said. "I'm going because I aim to talk to Leschi. I aim to show him that going to Olympia is the best thing he can do. God knows I'm ashamed it is the best."

Eaton turned from tightening the girth of his saddle. "Jarvis, we haven't any time to waste. Are you coming with us, or aren't you?"

"I'm coming with you, and you're coming with me to talk
to Mason!"

"Don't be a fool," Eaton said. "We're not going to ride
back five miles on any such errand."

"You'd go back if it was a hundred yards, h'm?"

"Maybe. But it isn't a hundred yards; it's five miles."

"It's a hell of an economy to start a war because you won't
take the trouble to go back five miles! It's only five miles now.
By tomorrow it'll be a thousand, and you'll never be able to
go back."

Eaton put the reins over the neck of his big bay horse with
the white blaze on his forehead. "We haven't any more time
to waste, and there isn't going to be any war."

"I heard from Leschi this morning," Jarvis said.

"The hell you did?" Eaton withdrew his foot from the stirrup as he was about to mount. "Why didn't you say so before?"

"He made it very clear that there will be war if you force
it on the Nisquallys."

"What did he say, Jarvis?"

"He said the Nisquallys want to live in peace, and if there
was trouble they wouldn't be the ones to start it. They will
fight whoever fights them, and be the friends of every one who
stays on his own claim and minds his own business."

Eaton was not impressed. "He said that, eh?"

"Yes. And I think it's what you could call new evidence,"
Uncle Jarvis said. "It's plenty of reason for you to go back
with me and talk to Mason. I received the message, and I'll
take the responsibility."

"That's nothing new," McAllister insisted. "Leschi told
me about the same thing the last time I saw him. He wanted
me to stay neutral if there was any trouble. I told him there
was nothing to stay neutral about, and there wouldn't be any
trouble."

"It isn't really anything new," Eaton agreed.

"I'd never heard it just that way," Connell said. "It wouldn't
do any harm if we talked to Mason again———"

"We can't waste any more time," Eaton said. "Mount up, men!" Horses trampled and leather creaked as the volunteers swung into their saddles. The captain looked down from his big horse with displeasure and grudging respect. "Since you're not coming with me, Jarvis, I'm going to get out of here, by God, before you take any of my men away from me!"

"I'd like to take them all and you, too. Give up this suicide's picnic and come to Olympia with me, h'm?"

Eaton said, "I have my orders."

"There won't be any trouble," McAllister said.

"Not for you," Jarvis said. "Your troubles will be over by tomorrow. But we'll be left with your bastard war!"

"There won't be any war," McAllister said.

The volunteers wheeled and galloped away through the timber camp. Uncle Jarvis looked after them and sighed.

"Do you think they'll get killed?" Elmer asked.

"I said that hoping they wouldn't. Sometimes you can prolong a man's life by predicting his death, h'm? Probably they'll learn caution on the way."

"The Indians must have known the volunteers were coming here," Elmer said. "That could be why they came to my place."

"There may still be time to do something." Jarvis turned toward the house, walking with long strides. "I'm going to Olympia to have another talk with Mason. Not that he isn't tired of listening to me, but the message from Leschi will pay my way in, h'm?"

Elmer was six feet tall, but he felt like a schoolboy, trotting beside his uncle to keep up with him. "Do you want me to go with you?"

"I want you to stay here," Jarvis said. "I don't know when I'll be back, but I want you and Lisette to sleep here nights until we know what's happening."

Elmer was relieved, but he also felt a little disappointed in his relief. "Don't you believe what Leschi said about our being safe if we stayed on our farms?"

"Safe from his warriors, yes." He was walking more slowly. "But we'll have to keep our eyes open for the ones who are too lazy or cowardly to go on the warpath, h'm?"

"I don't quite see why," the boy said.

"Because the rules of civilized warfare have never yet been observed by the patriots who stay at home," his uncle said.

"I hadn't thought of that," Elmer said.

"The war with Mexico didn't mean much at home, I suppose?"

"There was news about it in the paper, but we hardly ever bought a paper."

His uncle looked down at him with a wistful grin. "I wish we could take care of this one by not buying the *Pioneer & Democrat!*"

CHAPTER SEVENTEEN

*T*HAT MORNING Elmer visited his claim alone. Lisette wanted to go with him, but he persuaded her not to. Nothing had happened since the volunteers went to arrest Leschi and Quiemuth. But Mason had rented a blockhouse from the Hudson's Bay Company and urged the settlers to move in. The blockhouse was a cattle barn at the edge of the prairie, surrounded by a stockade. It was a place to keep in mind, but Mason's urging seemed premature and only a few families had gone. But talk of a blockhouse encouraged prudence, and Elmer felt freer when his wife was on the safe side of the Inlet, with Uncle Jarvis and Nisqually Jim and Mary.

Feeling free made him remember a little how it felt when he was alone on the land at the beginning of his life. It made him remember what he had sometimes noticed before, that this world is many different kinds of worlds. One kind is when you are with some one you love, and then you try to tame the world and make something of it. Another kind is when you explore it alone. Then you are closer to nature and the beginning of things. You travel faster and see more and have less to show for your adventure.

He had told Lisette that he was going to the creek for salmon to salt down for winter, and he took a pitchfork with him, and the new wheelbarrow, but maybe that was only to fool part of himself. He also took a hatchet, which has nothing to do with getting salmon, but is useful in trail blazing.

When he reached the creek, he hid the wheelbarrow and fork in the brush and started up the creek, with his rifle in his

258

hand and the hatchet in his belt. He was wearing his sea boots and walked in the creek when that was easier than going through brush on the land. The salmon run had slackened and if he had ever been in danger of having to walk on the slippery backs of salmon, he wasn't now. The only ones that didn't get out of his way were the dead and dying ones drifting downstream or stranded along the edge of the creek.

Everything in nature is afraid of one thing or another, and Elmer was afraid of the Nisquallys. That was why he was following the creek east toward their encampment. He was exploring the land of fear that lay between his shore and the Nisqually valley. He had been fascinated by the idea for the past two days. Ever since he and Jim had come back to their salmon gathering which had been interrupted by the message from Leschi. That day he had heard the war drums clearly and decided that the sound followed the creek. By doing the same thing, he should be able to get close to what he feared.

So he went on up the creek, toward the oppressive, fascinating throbbing of drums. He already thought their sound was louder. Even if that were not so, they were going faster today, as if moving toward some crisis. Their excitement urged him on. So far as he knew, the creek had never been explored and no one knew its length or source. That alone would have been reason enough for exploring it in better times. Now he wasn't giving it much more than a blow of the eye in passing. He was using it mostly for a road. And as a road it was doing well. So far as he could judge it had been flowing in a northwesterly direction, which was all to the good. It had taken him through a tangled northern jungle of great cedars and alder and hemlock and salmon berry brush and devil's club, savage with needle-thorns. It was rich land, and it was his, but without the creek his progress through it might have been a mile an hour—if he didn't get lost, which he certainly would.

The creek was a good road only by comparison with the jungle through which it cut. In places the brush along its banks met solidly in midstream, and there were many windfall logs which made the going awkward for anything but salmon. One fallen fir, ten feet through, had a passive genius for obstruction. It made such a low bridge that he could not pass under it without getting down on his belly in the water, like a salmon, and its top side was so high that he could not get over it without getting up onto the bank and tunnelling through the brush which had closed over the log.

It was a cool, cloudy day, but Elmer was hot with sweat as he went on without pausing. He knew, or thought he knew, that he was travelling as fast as if he were walking in the open; he was young and tough and the obstacles only took more out of him without having much effect on his speed. Half consciously, he was keeping pace with the nearer, excited pounding of drums.

The creek was narrowing, and it seemed to him he must have about reached the head of navigation for salmon, but they had no sense of the fitness of things. They were still fighting upstream with him, while the dead and dying were drifting back, their pilgrimage accomplished. To show how little he knew about what salmon recognize as the head of navigation, there was a branch stream coming in from the right. It was not much more than a shallow ditch, three feet wide, leading off into the woods, but it was full of salmon, churning inland, with their battered backs exposed. The bank was littered with bones and partly eaten salmon, but still others were turning into that death-trap, as if they were weary of the sea and anxious to go as far inland as possible before they died. Elmer watched for a minute, panting and blowing, his heart pounding with the drums ahead. Watching, he saw that some of the salmon passed the entrance to the ditch of rain water as if it did not exist and went on up the creek. Others turned into the ditch without hesitation, as if their sailing orders called for that turn. Salmon were a mystery and nature did impossible things with them.

Following the creek, he had climbed gradually from the bottom land into the upland, where the woods were more open and the going was better because there were fewer windfall trees across the stream. His progress improved with the going, and the storm of drums sounded as if it were coming from around the next bend of the creek, though more likely it was two miles away.

So far there had not been a sign that any human being had ever passed that way. The Nisquallys might visit his claim by salt water, or by way of the road, as they had done before, but he did not think there was much chance of their bursting out of the woods to the east of his clearing, as he had seen them do in dreams. The land of fear had been discredited by daylight exploration.

Farther on he traced the creek to its source in swampy ground. Part of his mind told him he had gone far enough. He had explored the creek and travelled most of the way across the little peninsula, with a growing feeling of security in that direction. He had made good time and would be able to get back to his claim before they began to worry about him on the other side of the Inlet.

But he went on through the swamp, keeping out of the worst of it by walking on logs that were hull-down in the mud, and jumping from one log to another. He got into the mud only a few times and it was not very deep. It was an upland swamp that did not amount to much. In a few minutes he found himself on the other side, on solid ground and in fairly open woods, with the drums going like mad just ahead.

He knew that the drums might be much farther away than they sounded, and if the valley was not in sight from the next rise of ground he would certainly turn back. But the cautious part of his mind which decided that also encouraged him to put blaze marks on trees as he went along. It did not trust the other parts of his mind very far.

The Nisqually valley was not in sight from the higher ground ahead, but the storm of drums seemed louder. Twice he thought he heard the faint *crack* of a rifle, but he was not sure. Listening, he did not hear any more, but he made out something new in the storm of sound: a dim, swelling overtone, like the crying of wind in icy rigging heard through the thunder of seas in Cape Horn weather.

He pushed on, steering by the sound and leaving bold blaze marks on trees every fifty feet or less. With all the noise ahead he was not afraid of any one hearing the sound of his hatchet.

The country he was passing through was all fir trees and stunted salal. The roots of the firs were mostly on top of the ground because they had not been able to penetrate the hard gravel. The roots were more like limbs than roots and they had the same kind of bark from living in the open. They went out everywhere like octopus arms, and between them there was stunted salal and in some places a kind of dry, dwarfed grass, as fine as the hair on a man's chest and about as long, but not as abundant. All the fir roots and stunted growth together were not enough to cover the naked gravel underneath. The quality of the soil and the absence of any sign of water made Elmer think he was getting into the land which had been set aside for the Nisqually reservation.

For a long time he seemed to be almost on top of the storm of noise, so close that all his efforts did not bring him any closer. Then the thickets ahead stood out clearly against a wall of gray pervading light, as if he had come to the end of the earth, with nothing but sky or sea beyond the jumping-off place. The furious storm of drumming and yelling suddenly swelled louder as if it were boiling in a great cauldron at his feet. He crept through the last thicket, to the end of the earth, and lay there, looking over the brink of hell.

He was looking down on two creeks that met and formed a short broad river which flowed along the base of the bluff to tide flats and salt water. On one of the creeks there was a small sawmill, with a pyramid of yellow sawdust against one side, and a pile of yellow lumber and a heap of brown-and-yellow slabs in the mill yard. Between the creeks was a prosperous farm, with a half-ploughed field: one half of it rich black earth and the other half still green with the mild, damp autumn. In another field of autumn green horses and cattle were lying asleep, though it was strange that they should all be asleep at such an hour, with wild pandemonium filling the valley.

Elmer had followed the storm of noise to its source. Below him and not a hundred yards away, naked Indians with oiled bodies and feathers in their hair were milling around a big log house. Just beyond it was a big new frame house which seemed to be deserted or not yet occupied. There was a fenced yard around the log house, and the yard was filled with Indians, at least five hundred of them, Elmer thought. He could not see the drummers, but the drums were going like mad and Indians were waving rifles and knives, and pairs of them were pretending to hit each other over the head with clubs. Near the side of the house they were waiting in line for something, disappearing into the milling crowd and reappearing after a minute, waving hatchets or knives and pretending to scalp each other. When the crowd thinned for a moment, Elmer saw that they had a grindstone in front of the window.

At first he had the feeling of looking down at happenings on a strange planet. It was a minute before he connected it with his own world. Even then it did not seem real. His eyes told him that those were the long-suffering Nisquallys, and the furious human storm was beating around Jim McAllister's house. But his mind did not want to believe what his eyes saw.

He looked away and saw familiar landmarks, like the faces of friends mocking him with their indifference in a nightmare. To the north he saw Nisqually Head and the flat, placid waters of the Reach carrying a branched tree trunk on some idiot's errand. Beyond he saw the gray-green ragged bulk of Anderson Island; beyond that the gray and ragged silhouette of McNeil's Island, and far off in the grayness the flat shadow of Fox Island. Nearer and to the east he saw Ketron Island, like a ship loaded with fir trees standing in toward Nisqually Reach. Beyond Ketron he saw the flat sails of a brig becalmed off Steilacoom, with the trancelike indifference of a ship in a picture.

In the valley below him he saw the Nisqually River hurrying to the sea, and the two creeks that became one creek, wider than the river. There was something confusing about that because the two became one and they also remained two. The cattle and horses in the fields were still strangely asleep. Then he saw that all of them were lying on their sides in the same attitude, with their legs stiffened out in death. There was a little flock of sheep, too, huddled in a fence corner where they had been shot down. They were all still except one that was dragging itself along the ground with torturing slowness to join the flock in death. Every living thing had been killed by the Nisquallys who could be driven like a flock of sheep.

Some one had once said that: he could drive the whole Nisqually tribe before him, like a flock of sheep. Jim McAllister had said that long ago, three days ago, riding away with the volunteers to take Leschi and Quiemuth to Olympia as hostages. He had said also that he was leaving his wife and children at home, in the middle of the Nisqually camp, with his twelve-year-old son to look after them. This was how they were faring! Inside that house, bedevilled by hundreds of frenzied Indians, was a woman and her eight children: five little girls and three boys, the oldest of them twelve.

Tardily Elmer realized that he should do something to save the besieged family.

He thought of going to the blockhouse on Muck Creek, but he only knew in a general way where it was, and he could not even look for it without going through the valley, which was impossible. There was the fort at Steilacoom, a dozen miles away across the valley. Without a canoe or a horse he couldn't hope to get there in time. And he had his own wife to think about. Probably the wisest course would be to spread the alarm at home. For all he knew, Uncle Jarvis's house was also under siege, or would be before the day was out.

Elmer decided to get back to the Inlet without wasting time, but curiosity held him a minute longer. Something was happening in the mob about the log house. Two Indians were dragging a dark object up to the house, while others waved hatchets and knives in a yelling storm of approval. Whatever they were dragging seemed to be heavy. Elmer wondered if it was a cannon, but when he got a glimpse, it turned out to be an unwilling brown dog. He lingered, wondering what a dog could have to do with the siege of the house.

While he watched, the mob drew back from the house in a semicircle. In the open space they left under a window two men held the dog down on the ground. A third held a sharpened stake against its side, and a fourth swung a wooden maul, nailing the dog to the earth. The boy heard two blows of the maul, like shots, and then he did not hear anything but the terrible yelping of the crucified dog, going on and on.

He jumped up, forgetting where he was, and scratching his ears and neck against the bushes of the thicket. More than anything else, he wanted to stop the awful yelping that stabbed his hearing countlessly and without one instant's pause. If he could not stop it he only wanted to get away. There was relief in hearing the Indians yelling again; it drowned out the noise of the sacrifice. They were pouring out of the yard like a flood of dark water, and some of them had already reached the barn gate. The gateway was high and framed with heavy cedar poles, like the frame of a gallows. The gate was partly open and a horseman was trying to get through. He was hatless and red-headed, riding a powerful bay horse with a blazed face, covered with sweat and foam. It looked like the horse on which Charlie Eaton had galloped away with the volunteers to arrest Leschi and Quiemuth. But the red-headed youth was not Charlie Eaton. As he stood up in his stirrups, arguing with the Indians who blocked his way, Elmer recognized him as George McAllister who had been among the volunteers with his father. Where were the volunteers? And where was Eaton, and where was Jim McAllister? It was strange that the boy should have come back alone on the captain's horse to face a mob of raging Indians.

But there was no sign of the other volunteers, nothing but the dead horses and cattle and sheep lying in the fields. Only the boy at the open barn gate, standing up in his stirrups and arguing passionately with the mob that blocked his way. It was George McAllister, but something had happened to his face. The lower half of it was darkly streaked and the shape of his mouth was wrong. His upper teeth showed all the time in a kind of grin and his mouth moved clumsily when he talked. He was trying to force and argue his way to the house, but the arguing did not do any good and his exhausted horse was stuck in the mob as solidly as if it were set in stone. He looked like a boy in a picture, painted in the act of trying to force his way through a pack of Indians. As long as the picture lasted he would never advance one inch or give up trying.

Then Elmer saw a man in a faded hickory shirt threading and pushing his way through the packed crowd between the house and the barn gate. He thought it was a white man until he noticed the black, braided hair. Then he decided it was one of the McAllisters' Nisqually servants. The Indians did not actually stop the man, but they were packed solidly and would not open a way for him. He was working through the mass of them as slowly as a swimmer forcing his way against a powerful current, and probably with as much effort. As Elmer watched, he saw the faded hickory shirt darkening with its owner's sweat and oil from the naked bodies which continuously blocked his way.

It took the man minutes to reach the barn gate and the boy on the stalled horse, but they met at last and exchanged a few words. Then they began the journey to the house. When they were separated one of them had been barely able to get through the crowd and the other had been stopped completely. But when they were together, with the Indian leading the horse by the bridle, they were able to make their way slowly through the mob which kept up a low, sullen roar that was like thunder to the lightning yelps of the dog writhing on the stake by the house.

Their journey was almost done when they reached the gate to the yard. There the packed Indians inside stopped them like a wall of stone. The young Nisqually tried to smash his way through, bodily, but was bounced back from the yelling human wall. The white boy dismounted and they tried pushing their way through together, but it was no use.

But the two had gone that far and they would not give up. The Indian boy climbed on the fence as if he meant to leap on the ready knives on the other side. Instead, he stood on the square top of the gate post and made a speech. Seen full length, he looked much like Nisqually Jim or any other young Indian. By his gestures, he was threatening and arguing and pleading by turns. Because the mob was never really still, Elmer caught only one word of the speech, *"Leschi."* But he was able to understand part of what was going on. After each threat or plea the speaker asked the crowd something. Each time there was an ugly roar of refusal, and afterward he had trouble making them listen to him.

Finally the Indian's speech seemed to turn to himself and he struck his breast as if offering himself as a guarantee of something. This time, instead of asking the mob to let him through, he seemed to tell them that he was going through. Then he climbed down from the gate post, and he and the white boy started confidently toward the house, with the big blaze-faced horse following. Two Indians seized the bridle and the horse tried to rear, but was too tired. He stood still while the boys went on without him. But they went on, with the mob giving way a little to let them pass and closing in behind them.

Elmer watched until they were out of sight behind the house, pushing their way toward the door. From the top of the bluff it was like looking down at a map and he did not lose sight of them until they were close beside the house. He did not have any doubt that they got in. The crowd was flowing back around the house like a returning brown tide, and the siege went on. Maybe it was enlivened by the fact that the Indians had another victim in the house. They were yelling triumphantly, fencing with clubs and pretending to scalp each other. Some of them were beginning to hack at the logs of the wall with their sharpened hatchets.

Elmer did not want to see any more. He started back through the woods with wilder yells sounding in his ears, and fear in his heart.

CHAPTER EIGHTEEN

W HEN ELMER got back to the Inlet his house hadn't been burned down, and everything looked all right across the water. Lisette and Nisqually Jim were on the other shore, watching for his return. He shouted and waved, and Lisette waved her handkerchief. He would have started across directly, but the big dugout was on his beach and he knew his uncle must be somewhere about, looking for him.

His shout was answered from north of the clearing and after a minute his uncle came out of the woods with his rifle. "Hello," he called, "where the devil were you?"

Elmer ran toward him, through the stumpy clearing. "The McAllisters," he called. "They're attacking them!"

"They've all been killed!" his uncle answered.

On his way back to the creek the boy had been lost once, but he had not thought he was away long enough for anything to happen. He was bewildered by the speed with which news travelled.

"That isn't all," Uncle Jarvis said when they met. "The Duwamishes have massacred the settlers on White River. All of them except three children who are missing. They found the body of one woman and her baby in the bottom of a well."

"Christ!" Elmer said. He was sick with horror and the effort of racing home, too late.

"What about the volunteers?" Elmer asked. "They didn't arrest Leschi?"

His uncle said grimly, "It didn't turn out to be an arresting matter! Jim McAllister and Connell were killed from an ambush, and the others are probably wiped out by now."

Elmer didn't really know Connell, but every one knew McAllister. He had believed to the last that there wouldn't be any trouble. It didn't seem real that he should be the first to die. "I liked McAllister."

"We should go back," Jarvis said. "Is there anything you want at the house?"

The boy looked at himself. His clothes were snagged and muddy and wet with creek water and sweat. "I'd like to change my clothes," he said.

On the way to the house they talked about Jim McAllister. "He tried to be loyal to both sides," Uncle Jarvis said. "That's what killed him and started the war. Not but what it would have started anyway."

"What happened?"

"As I heard it," Uncle Jarvis said, "the volunteers got to Van Ogle's farm, on the Puyallup, late in the afternoon. They'd heard that Leschi and Quiemuth's Nisquallys and the Puyallup warriors were camped a little farther up the river. Eaton decided to camp where he was. He knew by then that he'd never take Leschi and Quiemuth except by force, and he was going to send for help. That was the prudent thing to do, h'm?, if there is any prudent way of starting a war.

"But there was Jim McAllister and his conscience. He told us he was going because he was Leschi's friend, h'm? He was going to persuade him, as a friend, to come to Olympia because that was the best thing he could do."

"I remember," Elmer said. "He said he was ashamed it was the best."

"It was poor enough, h'm? But at Van Ogle's farm McAllister found himself part of a military expedition that was going to take Leschi by force, dead or alive. There wasn't much friendship in that. McAllister told us he couldn't side with Indians against the government, even though he thought the government was wrong. But when it came to a test neither could he attack his best friend, h'm? His conflicting loyalties wouldn't let him steer to the left of the reef or to the right, so he took the middle course.

"Jim told Eaton that he would ride on, alone, and find Leschi and talk with him. Eaton said it would be suicide, and it was against orders. But Jim wasn't used to taking orders, and he had made up his mind. It was getting dusk then, and he told the others there wasn't much time left and he had to do what he thought was best. When they saw he couldn't be changed, Connell decided to go with him.

"Because it was a peaceful mission, they left their rifles behind and took only their revolvers. McAllister's Indian farm hand, Clipwalen, went with them, though he told Jim he was going to his death. And they had Stahi to guide them——"

"Stahi?" Elmer said. "Slugia's father?" They had reached the house and he stopped in amazement, with the latchstring in his fingers. "They trusted him?"

Uncle Jarvis said as they went in, "I don't know. Clipwalen warned him that Stahi would lead him into an ambush. But Stahi knew where the Indians were camped, and that was where Jim wanted to go."

Pulling off his wet clothes, Elmer said, "I wouldn't even trust him to lead me into an enemy camp!" He knew nothing about Stahi, but had formed a bad opinion of him because of Slugia.

"Stahi led them toward the enemy camp, all right," the big man said. "He was going that way himself to join the Nisquallys, and he probably didn't object to leading a few volunteers into a trap. They went a mile or so, and the Indians opened up on them from an ambush. Stahi immediately joined the enemy, and the others headed back for camp. McAllister had been hit twice, but he said it didn't amount to anything. He was saying that when another ambush opened up on them, and he fell off his horse. Connell was shot through the body, and Clipwalen had five bullet holes through his clothes. He took to the woods and called to Connell to do the same thing, but Connell galloped back on the trail and was riddled from a third ambush. The Indians had three along the way, and the first two had lain low. McAllister's party was cut off and surrounded before they knew anything was wrong.

"Clipwalen was the only one who came back alive. He headed for Nisqually, spreading the alarm as he went. As I heard it, he got back in time to be wiped out with Mrs. McAllister and the children."

Putting on a dry shirt, Elmer said, "George got back, too. I saw him get through the mob, as far as the house. An Indian boy came out and helped him get through."

"You saw them, h'm?" Uncle Jarvis looked puzzled and interested. He had had so much news of his own that it hadn't occurred to him that Elmer might have something worth telling. "How long ago was that?"

"Two or three hours ago," the boy said, putting on his coat. "I don't think it was more than three."

"D'ye suppose the family was alive then?"

Elmer said, "The Indians hadn't broken in. They acted as if there were people in the house, and they were trying to scare them to death."

"We'd better report that," Uncle Jarvis said. "When people are excited a rumor becomes a fact before night, h'm?"

When they were going, Elmer looked back at the cabin which had been his home. Now it was like some half familiar place. It was not the house but he who had changed. He had been undone by something outside himself. In a way, he and Lisette had lost their home because the Nisquallys were losing theirs. It was as catching as smallpox, only the men who had made the Medicine Creek Treaty hadn't foreseen that. They had thought they could wish a plague on part of the community and leave the rest healthy. God damn their treaty and all the disaster it had made!

In his heart he blamed the Indians more. Going to the beach with his uncle, he could see and hear again the nightmare of horror at McAllisters' farm. And he knew what the White River massacre had been like. Only there every family had been wiped out, and there had been a dead woman with a baby in her arms at the bottom of a well. Lisette was expecting her baby within a month. It wasn't a fit world for women and children and it wouldn't be while Indians like that were at large. It was no good to think about having a home or about living until the business was settled. With their feet sounding harshly on the gravel of the beach, he asked, "How much does Lisette know?"

Uncle Jarvis picked up the anchor, with his rifle tucked under one arm, and coiled the painter neatly as he walked toward the canoe. "She knows in a general way what has happened. It's no use distressing her with details, h'm?"

"I should think not!" They put their rifles in the canoe which made a harsh, protesting roar as they ran it down the gravel slope into the water. "I'm going to take her to the blockhouse," Elmer said.

His uncle did not say anything.

"Don't you think I should?"

"I don't know," his uncle said. "Really, I don't know." He stood there, pondering, with his feet in the water and a bight of the anchor line in his hand. "I'd hate to advise you, and have it turn out wrong, h'm?"

"She'll be safe there, anyway."

"I suppose so, but she'll be damned uncomfortable. The place is nothing but a stock barn. If people crowd in there like cattle it won't be much of a life."

Elmer said, "But it isn't safe here."

Uncle Jarvis did not say anything to that.

"Do you think we would be safe?"

"I could answer that like an oracle, but afterward it might turn out that I was wrong."

They got into the big dugout and started across the Inlet. The boy was in the bow, where he could see his wife and Nisqually Jim waiting on the shore. Through the plunging sound of paddles, he heard his uncle's voice from aft. "If it weren't for the baby, I'd advise you to stay with me and ride out the storm here. It'd be more comfortable, and it might be just as safe."

"What about the Indians?" Elmer asked with some bitterness.

His uncle's voice said, "That's why I'm not advising you, under the circumstances. Qualchin is supposed to have crossed the mountains with three hundred warriors to join the Klickitats who are here. There's always the off chance that they might forget Leschi's promise to respect settlers who mind their own business."

Elmer asked with more bitterness: "What about Leschi's own Nisquallys?"

"I wouldn't have any worries about them."

"You would," Elmer said, "if you'd seen the mob at McAllister's house!"

His uncle said, "Jim McAllister was asked to remain neutral, and he went with the others to arrest Leschi. The mob took it out on his family. You or I wouldn't whip one dog for what another had done. A dog wouldn't either. But mobs are neither men nor dogs."

The mention of dogs made Elmer feel ill. "It was horrible!"

"I don't doubt that," his uncle said. "And it is horrible that good-natured people like the Nisquallys have been driven mad."

Elmer agreed with that in part of his mind, but it did not change his feeling. It seemed to him that things had got to where it only confused matters to remember the Indians' side of the story. The only way you could put things to rights would be to forget what had led up to the trouble, and punish the Indians for the terrible things they had done. After what he had seen and heard he could never trust Lisette to the mercy of Indians. "I'm going to take Lisette to the blockhouse today," he said. Tomorrow might be too late, and deciding to go in time lightened his heart.

"Before I do anything else," his uncle said, "I'll go and see if help can be sent to McAllister's family. It looks to me as if they were alive hours after they were killed by a rumor."

"Shall I go with you?"

"You've been away from your wife enough," Uncle Jarvis said. "And you'll want to be getting your things together for the blockhouse, h'm?"

The canoe was gliding in toward the mud and green seaweed of the beach, and a big flounder sailed away through the shallow water. Beyond the band of mud and seaweed, the beach was clean gray gravel. Lisette and Nisqually Jim were walking across the gravel to meet the canoe. Lisette was rather big with child, but she looked fine and reassuring.

When the canoe was pulled up on the beach, he gave her his arm and walked with her, slowly, while Uncle Jarvis and the Indian boy hurried on ahead. "I didn't mean to be gone so long," he told her.

"I wondered what was keeping you," she said, "but I wasn't really afraid. I knew you would get back all right."

"You are a brave wife."

"I'm not brave," she said, "but I don't worry any more." Pregnancy was becoming to her, with a calm, mysterious bloom. It made her saner than any one else and less troubled. She was on the side of nature which went calmly about its duties on the earth. While destruction was taking place, the streams would flow and the earth would be nourished. Fruit and grain would grow and babies would be born, and war would be trampled down by the unhurried march of life. Sometimes Elmer was pleasantly in awe of his wife who shared the work and the mysterious calm of nature. She was wiser than he and saw much farther. But there was also danger in that, because she could not quite see the war which was here and now. And she was so defenseless and unafraid. It was his duty to see that she was defended. "You are brave," he said, "and I'm going to take care of you."

Walking close beside him, she said fondly, "I know you will!" But when he looked at her she was smiling with a kind of absent tenderness, thinking of more important things.

"I'm going to take you to the blockhouse," he said, with his feet sounding loud and harsh on the gravel of the beach.

"No, Elmer." She answered as if she had half heard him, at the edge of her mind, suggesting some unwise trifle.

"We have to go," he said. "We're going today, Lisette."

She stopped and looked at him, puzzled, with the smile fading from her lips and eyes. "Why do we have to go?"

"You know there's been trouble with the Indians," he said.

"None of you tell me much." Then she said, "They've killed some people, haven't they?"

"Yes." He and Lisette stopped at the upper edge of the beach and sat on a gray granite boulder, looking across the water to their cabin.

"But they're not attacking the settlers," Lisette said. "Not the ones who aren't fighting them."

"They did up on the White River," he told her. "They attacked everybody." From the shore above, he heard the drumming of hooves dying away through the timber camp as Uncle Jarvis rode for help for the McAllisters.

"Those were Duwamishes," Lisette said. "The Nisquallys aren't attacking settlers who stay on their farms. They won't bother us if we stay here."

"They're attacking the McAllisters," Elmer said.

"Is that where you were this morning?"

"Yes," he said.

She put her hand on his and pressed his fingers. "You shouldn't have done that, Elmer. It was dangerous."

"I saw them from the bluff," he said. "It was like looking from another world. I was never in any danger and I couldn't do anything for them. But I'm glad I went. Uncle may be able to get help in time."

"Then I'm glad you went. But you can't blame the Nisquallys for being mad when Mr. McAllister went to arrest Leschi. That was fighting them."

"I suppose it was, but McAllister didn't see it that way."

"If we stay here, like Leschi said, they won't bother us."

Elmer said firmly, "We can't do that!"

"Why not?"

If she had seen what he had seen she wouldn't be arguing about it. He had to make her see the danger without frightening her. "It wouldn't be safe," he said. "When the Indians are worked up you can't tell what might happen."

"Uncle don't think they'd attack us," she said.

He told her grimly, "Uncle can't be sure of that, and neither can anybody else. If something went wrong, it would be too late to get to the blockhouse. I'm not going to take chances with your life."

"It isn't much of a chance," she argued. "I want to take it, Elmer. I want to stay here. I want us to go on with our fall work." She was as gently obstinate as nature opening flowers in the path of a forest fire. "We can't live without taking risks. I don't want to go away from here, Elmer!"

"You want to stay here, in danger, when we'd be safe at the blockhouse?"

"Of course," she said. "That's what I've been telling you."
He asked, wondering, "But why?"

"Because we belong here," she said. "If death did come to us, it would find us where we belong, doing what we want to do. That wouldn't be a bad thing. We would be living all the time we were alive, and we would be together. That's the best people can ask for, when they can't live forever."

He kissed her and said, "At the blockhouse we'll be living, too."

"No," she said. "Keeping from getting killed isn't the same as living. We'd be like things in a warehouse. When we got out it wouldn't be the same. Our lives would be kind of dusty and rat-eaten."

He didn't want to go to the blockhouse, either. They were going because of her, and it wasn't fair for her to make it so difficult. "But we have to go!"

"We don't have to do anything we don't want," she said gently. "If you're thinking of me and the baby, I'm safest here because I'm happy. You know I've been happy, and I've been so well. I haven't worried——"

"You've been grand," he said.

"That was because I was happy," she said. "It won't be the same, with a crowd of people in a cattle barn——"

"Please, Lisette!" He was desolate and uneasy. If she made up her mind that it wouldn't be the same at the blockhouse, it would not be the same. He leaned his rifle against the cold stone on which they were sitting and put his arms around her. "I know more about what's going on than you, and I've seen what can happen. We're going to the blockhouse because I'm not going to have anything like that happen to you. We have to go!"

"When?" she asked, and he knew that she had given in.

"Today," he said, kissing her. "It's the only safe thing to do. I don't think we'll have to stay very long. Uncle said he'll take us in the wagon when he gets back."

"Then we should be getting ready," she said quietly.

He had won a victory, but he was uneasy. There was no springiness in her voice now, and her look of peaceful and

mysterious bloom was gone. Maybe it would come back, but
now she was only quiet and obedient and a little anxious.
"Please, Lisette," he said, "we won't stay any longer than we
have to!

She had drawn away from his arms, but held his hand
tightly. "Elmer, do you think we can come home before the
baby is born?"

"We might," he said. But it didn't seem likely.

"I wouldn't want our baby to be born in a cattle barn, among
a crowd of people!"

"We'll come home as soon as it's safe," he said. "And you'll
be brave, won't you, dear?"

She smiled a little, trying to be as brave as he was asking
her to be. But the smile made her tears overflow. She bowed
her head against his breast and sobbed, clinging to him as if
they were about to be separated by some sentence of death.

He tried to comfort her, when he wanted comforting himself. That day at Rush's farm, long ago, Leschi had said that
land without peace was a dream. Elmer felt the weight of that
now. His own land had become a dream, mocking him silently
from the other side of the Inlet, which was gray with the leaden
waters of autumn. Through the gray and green peace of the
landscape there looked the nightmare face of things. Leschi,
whom he admired, was tangled with evil. Jim McAllister, who
had said there would be no war, was lying dead in the woods.
And only a few miles away a woman and eight little children
were besieged by a raging mob of Indians—if they weren't
already hacked to pieces. It was no time to sit and argue, or cry.

"Lisette," he said, "we have to get ready. The blockhouse
will be safe, anyway, even if it is a cattle barn!"

She sat up and dried her eyes, and he took up his rifle and
helped her to her feet. She had got some comfort from crying,
and even smiled a little. "If we can't get home in time," she
said, "I'll remember that the mother of God wasn't too proud
for a stable."

CHAPTER NINETEEN

MARY was crying bitterly when they left for the blockhouse in the rain. She kissed Lisette half a dozen times at least and held Elmer's hand in both of hers. She couldn't say much because she was crying all the time as if she never expected to see them again. She was all broken up because her people and her husband's people had started killing each other. Her nicely braided hair was getting wet while she kept the army wagon waiting, and tears and drops of rain were rolling down her cheeks. Crying made her look old and homely, and Elmer was very sorry for her. He also felt guilty, remembering she had always been as kind to him as his own mother, and had never spared herself in doing things for his comfort. He had accepted it all without doing anything special to show that he was grateful. He had never stopped to think how grateful he was until now, when he and Lisette were in the wagon, going away, and Mary was crying so hard there wasn't much chance to say anything. At the last minute he leaned out and kissed her on the cheek, awkwardly. "It's all right, Aunt Mary," he said. "We'll be back soon."

Uncle Jarvis said, "Let us know if you need anything," and "take care of Lisette!"

The driver cracked his whip and swore at the mules, and they rattled away through the yard and the deserted timber camp in the rain. The two soldiers sat on the wagon seat, with their rifles between their knees and their light blue overcoats getting dark in the rain. Elmer and Lisette sat in the wagon box, where they would be safer if they were fired on. Elmer

278

had his hand on his rifle, but it did not show because he was holding it under the tarpaulin to keep the priming dry. He felt very much a civilian and a refugee, huddled in the wagon box with his wife, among their possessions. Lisette had a shawl over her head and she held it at her throat with one hand while she braced herself with the other against the hard jolting of the wagon. Her face was pale and in the frame of the shawl it looked like the face of a Madonna.

Elmer had expected to drive his uncle's wagon to the block-house in fine style, not to go like a piece of household goods. But the government had taken a hand. Mason was anxious to get all the settlers to safety, and wagons were being sent even for families who did not want to leave their farms. Elmer thought that in the confusion too much was being done and not enough. His uncle hadn't got much satisfaction about help for Mrs. McAllister and her children. Through some mistaken rumor they had been officially dead since the day before, and it required time and red tape to make them a living issue. On top of that, there were only three squads of soldiers attached to the blockhouse. The sergeant had orders to use his men in guarding the blockhouse and bringing in settlers who were within reach. They were not to engage in outside hostilities. A messenger had gone to Fort Steilacoom with Elmer's story, third hand, and even to him it seemed to get vaguer and less convincing as it went away into the distance.

The driver was in a hurry to get them to the blockhouse. Sometimes he kept the mules at a trot, and sometimes at a gallop. The wagon banged over notched logs and tree roots and whizzed through mud. Once the bearded soldier beside the driver turned his head and called, "Hang on, ma'am!" Lisette held on, with Elmer helping her, while the wagon dipped into a hollow, churned through the swollen creek and bounced up on the other bank, with the mules slipping and bounding on the muddy track.

When the mules had quieted to a trot and the wagon was doing only its normal amount of swaying and jolting, Elmer squeezed Lisette's arm. "Are you making out all right?" he asked.

She smiled faintly and nodded.

He didn't know anything about such things, but he hoped the rough, jolting ride wouldn't be bad for a woman who was eight months gone with child.

Once they stopped to listen, but there was nothing to hear except the sound of rain falling quietly in the woods. The driver stung the mules with his cracking whip and they rushed away again through the wet gray-green twilight. The boy and his wife held hands, and sometimes they smiled at each other, faintly. The two soldiers sat on the wagon seat in their wet blue overcoats, with their rifles between their knees and their high, flat-topped caps swaying jauntily with the motion of their vehicle. The ride did not encourage talking. Lisette's look of calm bloom was gone; she was tired and quiet. And the soldiers spoke only occasional words to each other. Elmer was interested in their Hall rifles, which loaded at the breach instead of the muzzle. The rifles sounded like a fine invention and Elmer would have liked to see how they worked. But he could see very little of them while they were being held between the soldiers' knees. And he could hardly ask to see one of them, like a toy, when they might be needed any moment for defense. He got just a glimpse of the lock of a rifle where it came below the seat, with its butt resting on the floor of the wagon bed.

In the woods there had been nothing to suggest war, but when the wagon was out on the prairie and going more quietly they could hear the swift dull thumping of drums from the Nisqually camp. Lisette had not been on the prairie since early summer, and she asked what the sound was. She only said "Oh," silently, but her eyes looked puzzled. Maybe she was wondering why they were going toward the sound of war drums for safety.

The mules shied at something and swerved off to the left so suddenly that they nearly upset the wagon, and Lisette's head struck Elmer a hard crack on the cheek bone. It hurt wildly and filled him with futile rage. They loved each other and neither would have willingly hurt the other. But, striking him that way, Lisette's head was a hard, impersonal weapon which hurt as much as a war club. And instead of the satisfac-

tion of being able to strike back he had to worry about the
weapon that had hurt him and hope it had not been hurt in the
process.

Looking back, he saw that the mules had shied at a dead ox.
Then the wagon passed another which was lying near the road.
Farther away there was a red-and-white colt, with its long legs
sticking out stiffly. It looked like a painted toy which had fallen
over and could be set on its feet again. Elmer felt sorry for it
while he touched his cheek bone, tenderly, and felt sorry for
himself and for Lisette. His pain would stop after a while and
the bump on Lisette's head would go down, but the world was
over for the gaily-painted little colt which had never understood what the war was about. It had not known that it was
on disputed ground and it had played on the prairie in all innocence, thinking the land belonged to God or perhaps to its
mother who was lying a little way off.

Ahead, Elmer saw the prairie littered with dead horses and
cattle. That was the paradise where he and Paul had cut wild
hay during the summer. Now the prairie was gray in the falling rain. The meadow larks were gone and the flowers were
gone and the herds cut down as by a frost. And Mount Rainier
was gone behind the rain clouds and mist. The rain would be
falling on the mountain as snow, but you could not even see
where it was.

They went on past numberless horses and cattle lying dead
in the rain: the wealth of settlers wiped out in the twinkling
of an eye. And once, off to the south, rifles cracked with
vicious sharpness and they saw men on horseback riding around
a small herd, firing into the massed animals. While they
watched, the herd broke away and streamed across the prairie:
calico and buckskin and darker ponies. A man on a white horse
and another on a bay kept pace with them, firing revolvers. In
the wake of the stampede three ponies were down, kicking, and
as Elmer stared in dismay two more fell. One of them, a bright
sorrel, rose again on its forelegs and tried to follow, but something was wrong with its hind legs which did not move. It sat
there, pawing the ground with its forefeet, screaming terribly.

The two horsemen were still pursuing the herd, firing, and another pony had fallen.

Lisette was crying, and she reached up and touched one of the soldiers on the arm. "Stop them!" she cried. "Stop them before they kill everything! Please——"

The bearded soldier looked around, embarrassed. "I'd like to, ma'am," he said above the clattering of the wagon, "but we're not allowed to shoot settlers!" Then, in case it was not clear to her, he explained, "They're getting even with the Indians for killing their stock!"

Lisette did not say anything; she only bowed her head and cried at the senseless slaughter. Elmer put his arm around her and tried to comfort her. He hoped that she would continue to look down; there wasn't anything in the landscape that was pleasant or restful to look at. "We'll soon be there," he said, "and you can rest." He thought if he went on talking to her and not noticing anything beyond the wagon she would not notice either. But almost immediately he was aware that the driver was pointing at something and the other soldier was following with his eyes.

Off to the north the prairie ended against a ragged wall of fir timber. Between the timber and the wagon track a man was racing on foot: a bareheaded, bearded man in a checked shirt and blue jeans. He was running desperately, and the motion of his arms and legs suggested that it was a race for life. He was not going very fast, but looking at him it was plain that was as fast as he could go. When he glanced back over his shoulder, with his arms and legs working up and down, the shape of fear which pursued him became almost real. Any moment, Elmer thought, mounted savages would flash out from behind some point of timber, overtake him and cut him down. At first the man did not even seem to see the army wagon, but he veered gradually toward the wagon track. The driver slowed the mules to an easy trot and the man drew alongside.

"It's that Bill fellow," the driver said.

The other said, "I wonder what's happened to his horse?"

The wagon stopped and the mules and the four people in the

wagon waited in the rain as the runner came up, tottering with exhaustion.

"What's up?" the driver said.

In answer, Bill put one foot on the brake-block, stumblingly, pulled himself up and rolled into the wagon. "Drive on!" he panted. His forehead was pale and thickly dewed with drops of sweat and his chest heaved as he panted through his open mouth and sent to leeward the aroma of sweat and whiskey. Looking at the rescued man and prompted by the smell of alcohol, Elmer recognized him as the Bill who had been so drunk during the trouble at Rush's farm. He seemed sober enough now; sober with fright and exhaustion.

As the wagon rattled on, the bearded soldier turned and asked, "What happened, Bill?"

"I was ambushed," Bill said, "so help me!"

Lisette reached under the tarpaulin and pulled out a blanket. "Put this around you," she said, "before you catch your death!" She was happier with some one to care for, and she did not even notice when the wagon passed close to a wounded dun-colored ox which looked as if it had been dying for a long time.

"It was all my wife's fault," Bill began his story. "We were safe at the blockhouse, and she found she'd forgotten the coffee grinder. That was yesterday, and she was set on having it. I talked her out of it then, but today I had to go back for it." He looked with appealing eyes. "What do you think of a woman who values a coffee grinder more'n her husband?"

Out of loyalty to her sex Lisette only murmured soothingly, but the bearded soldier asked, "Did she need it bad?"

"She ground coffee with it," Bill said, "and wheat for porridge. I told her it would be my death but she said, 'Never mind your death; get the grinder!' And she gave me a list of other little things she wanted from the cabin." His voice was bitter with the memory. "I went because what else can you do when a woman's like that? The house hadn't been broke into by the savages or anything, and the coffee grinder was there on the wall. I picked up what she wanted and started back through the woods. 'Dolly has fool's luck,' I said to myself. 'She'll get her grinder and her husband, too, when she don't deserve either.'

"I was saying that to myself when rifles blazed out all around. My horse was shot from under me, hit by a dozen bullets, and one took off my hat. As my horse fell dead, I hit the ground running, with bullets whistling around my head and the savages after me, hollering and yelling. I turned around once and fired; killed a big fellow with a war club and feathers in his hair. Then I dropped my rifle, seeing I wouldn't have time to load again and I couldn't afford the weight. Jesus, how I ran with bullets whistling past my ears! Luckily I wasn't hit, though one bullet went through my shirt." He slipped the blanket from his shoulders and held out the side of his checked shirt, under his arm. There was no bullet hole. "It was the other side," Bill said. He held out the fullness of his shirt under the other arm, and there was no hole there, either. "Must have been my other shirt," he muttered obscurely, and drew the blanket about his shoulders.

"What did you do then?" Lisette asked, helpfully.

Bill's eyes were fixed and mournful and he asked with vague sorrow, "What had I just done?"

Lisette reminded him, "You were running, with bullets whistling past you."

"I ran some more," Bill said. "I ran like hell and after a while I was out on the prairie and saw the wagon."

"It was a mercy we were here," Lisette said.

Bill was not cheered. "That's what comes of Dolly sending me for the coffee grinder," he said. "I lost it and I lost my rifle and my horse, and I nearly lost my life."

"That was a good horse you lost," the bearded soldier put in.

"It was the prettiest horse I ever saw." Bill looked ready to cry. "And the best trained." He turned his bereaved face to Lisette. "It was a buckskin with a silver mane and tail. Prettiest horse you ever saw, and it followed me like a dog."

Lisette said, "I'm sorry he got killed."

Elmer added his sympathies, and he was grateful because Bill's sorrows had lightened their own and drawn Lisette's attention from the desolation of the prairie. Now there were no more cattle or horses lying along the way, and the blockhouse loomed up ahead in the rain: a big building of split cedar behind a stockade of sharpened logs. He pressed Lisette's hand. "We're just about there, dear."

"It looks good," she said.

"It's safe, anyway." The blockhouse looked fine and safe, but when Lisette had been so opposed to going, he wanted her to discover the advantages of the place and do the praising.

As they came up, a door of close-set sharpened poles opened for them and the mules trotted into the enclosure. A soldier in a wet blue overcoat, with a rifle in one hand, closed the gate behind them. Inside was a big muddy barnyard with wagons lined up near the stockade, and two unharnessed mules standing in the rain, eating hay out of a wagon. The stock barn was even bigger than it looked from outside, and along one end there was a high lean-to shed, open on the sides like the porch of a house. On the gravelled ground under the shed men were gathered around a small fire, and the rain from the eaves fell into overflowing water pails.

The driver backed his wagon up to an open door of the barn and in another minute Elmer and Lisette were inside, with their belongings following in willing arms. Guided by a young army sergeant, they passed a row of partly curtained booths and stopped at a horse stall. There was hay on the floor and in the manger. The stall was separated from the one on the left by a patchwork quilt which had been hung up for a curtain, and on the right there were unoccupied stalls. The place smelled faintly of the stable and wild hay, and behind the patchwork curtain pots were being rattled.

"This stall and the next one are yours," the sergeant said. "Luckily there aren't a dozen of you; we're allotting two stalls to each family, big or small. If you have any spare bedding you can put it up for curtains. You can get food at the commissary store and if you need any help we'll do what we can for you. I hope you'll be comfortable, ma'am."

"I thank you," Lisette said, "we'll be all right."

"We'll make out fine," Elmer said. When the sergeant left they were alone among the clean smells of horses and cattle and wild hay. There was the even roar of rain on the roof, and voices of children playing in the hay on the other side of the partition. Lisette sat on the edge of the manger and took the wet shawl from her head and hung it over the edge of the manger. She was big with child and she looked pale and tired but very sweet. Elmer kissed her and asked, "Are you very tired?"

"I'm all right," she said, taking his hand. "I'll rest a minute and then we'll put things away."

"You rest," he said, "and I'll look after things."

They were still talking when a woman came from behind the patchwork curtain, briskly, with a hammer in her hand. "Let me help settle you," she said. "You're new to this hotel for horses. Have you a spare blanket to nail up here?" She was a fair, thin woman of about thirty, with a decisive look about her clear-cut face. "I'm Dolly Slocum," she said. "I live behind that quilt."

They introduced themselves, and Lisette decided on the yellow blanket for a curtain. "It's not much privacy," Dolly said, "but at least you don't see all the empty stalls. Now, young man, if you'll give me a hand——"

"It's kind of you to help," Lisette said, with tired warmth in her voice.

"It's the one comfort of this place," Dolly said, "having neighbors close enough so you can give them a hand. Anyway, I had the hammer and nails out. I was going to put up the coffee grinder, but my husband isn't back with it."

Elmer and Lisette exchanged doubtful looks. Her husband was back, but not with the coffee grinder, and he must have his own reasons for staying outside.

While Elmer nailed the blanket to the partition frame, Dolly pulled more hay from the manger and spread it evenly on the floor of the farther stall. She said, "This is as far as I can put you from Bill who snores like a grampus. If a better snorer moves in on the other side, you can always move your bed." She took a blanket from Lisette's hands. "Keep setting, and tell me what you want. You look tuckered out."

"What can I do to help?" Another woman appeared with a round-faced, dark-haired little boy clutching her calico skirt in one determined fist. She decided to help arrange the larder.

"We put our food in the manger," she said. "That keeps it from underfoot." To the little boy, she said, "Now, Buck, if you'll let me, I'll show the lady how we do it." She was stowing things neatly in the emptied manger when another woman came to see if she could help.

Elmer was grateful to be among friends and he knew Lisette would be well looked after, but the stall was getting rather full of helping women and children and he was only in the way. He ducked into the farther stall which was quite taken up with Dolly and the fine bed she was making. She gave him a pleasant-sour look of understanding and made a shooing motion, telling him to run along and leave housekeeping to women.

He left to join the men in the open shed. It was late afternoon and raining hard, and the fire looked good, though it was colder out there than in the unheated barn. The men were sitting around a small fire, where lead was melting in a crucible. "Have a chair, boy," one of them said, indicating the woodpile with his pipe. Elmer drew up a chunk of wood and joined the circle. He did not know any of the men very well, but none of them was a stranger except the soldier who was standing near the fire with the look of pausing only long enough to get warm.

Pouring liquid metal into a bullet mould, a rangy settler remarked, "What I don't understand is why there was only one ambush. The 'Squallys like to plant two or three on a trail."

"Maybe they was Klickitats," some one said.

The bullet-maker put the crucible back in the fire. "We'd be in a bad way if they started operating here."

A thin-faced little man said, "Anyway, it was a miracle that Bill's life was preserved; truly a miracle!"

Bill said earnestly, "It was positively the biggest miracle I've ever been in. I hope Dolly thinks so, too." But his face was sad and he did not seem to have much hope; not enough, anyway, to face his wife.

"Even if they weren't Klickitats," some one said, "they soon will be. If we don't get out and fight them, they'll come here and fight us!"

The bullet-maker said, "I'm going to join the first company

of volunteers that comes along." He turned to Elmer, "How about you, boy? You look like a soldier."

"I expect I will," Elmer said. His voice was not very loud, but he had decided during the day that there could be no peace or safety until the Indians were defeated.

"Good boy! We'll knock hell out of the 'Squallys and get back in time for our spring planting."

A horse whinnied somewhere, and the sentry was unbarring the stockade gate.

"Here's more company!" The soldier left the fire and walked to the end of the shed, pulling his neck farther into his collar in preparation for the plunge into the pouring rain.

The heavy gate swung open and a horse dashed into the enclosure, the stirrups of the empty saddle dangling with dreadful jauntiness. The sentry closed the gate, significantly, after the riderless horse. There was no one else to come in. You could almost see the shape of death in the empty saddle.

At the end of the shed, the soldier who was about to go out into the rain turned and called, "Mr. Slocum, here's your horse!"

It was a buckskin with a silver mane and tail, and when it stopped in the shelter of the shed, Elmer saw the coffee grinder tied on behind the saddle. Bill was staring, owl-solemn, while the others crowded around the wet and steaming horse.

"Is he hurt bad?" The tall bullet-maker peered over the heads of the others. "Where was he hit?"

"Not a scratch on him!"

They looked at Bill, whose face was as blank as theirs. They heard the urgent guffaws of the soldier as he went away in the rain to tell his comrades. Then they suddenly realized it was funny and began to laugh. And while he held his aching sides, Elmer knew dimly that he was laughing so hard because of that glimpse of death in the empty saddle. You don't often get the chance to laugh down death, and when you do have a triumph like that you make the most of it, even at the risk of a rupture which might kill you bye and bye.

"You got a good hoss, Bill," the bullet-maker said. "He even picked up the rifle you threw away after you shot that Indian!"

The little man with the goatee said, "You lied to us, Bill. You said when they shot your horse you ran."

Bill sounded hurt. "I ran like hell," he muttered.

"Look how hot he is." The little man touched the buckskin's steaming shoulder. "He's galloped all the way, but you beat him by an hour. You must have flown!"

Their laughter changed to apologetic silence and a woman's voice said, "Bill!" Dolly was there with a gray shawl over her head and a chilly glint in her eyes. "Bill," she said, "you knew I was waiting for that grinder, and you stand out here telling stories!"

Some one said, "He told us a good one, ma'am!"

Bill was untying the saddle thongs from the grinder and the little man was helping as urgently as if he had been at fault. "I'd have brought it sooner," Bill mumbled, "but I had to wait for my horse."

His wife accepted the coffee grinder in the midst of unaccountable laughter. "You men!" she said.

The open shed was one of the good features of the blockhouse. Between outdoors and indoors, it was a common meeting place where settlers gathered to talk; a soldier on duty could stand there a minute beside a fire, in sight of the stockade gate, and a woman could run out from the barn without taking more than a few steps in the rain. And there was a kind of perfection about the shed as a public kitchen. The roof sheltered the cooking fires and the open sides allowed the smoke to escape. In case of fire there were the overflowing buckets under the eaves. When it was not raining the shelter was unnecessary and fires were made in the open.

Supper was like a picnic to which Elmer and his wife had been invited. Lisette was allowed to contribute food, but that was all. Dolly insisted it was as easy to heat a roast as a slice, and two quarts of coffee were as easy to make as one. She seemed glad to have a family about her, and she devoted herself to Lisette. You could see it was not just because Lisette was tired and needed help. Mostly it was because Lisette was going to have a baby which Dolly thought was a wonderful thing.

They sat on blocks of wood or pieces of board, with their plates on other blocks of wood or on their knees. The open shed was draughty and once in a while a gust of wind blew in cold rain, but the fire suggested warmth, and hot food and coffee tasted good. Instead of lamenting the good cabins they had left, the settlers recalled fierce rainstorms on the Platte River and thirst in the desert mountains by the Snake River. Compared with those hardships life in a cattle barn was luxury.

While they were eating, the sentry opened the gate and armed horsemen poured into the stockade. There were about twenty of them, but they suggested an army, splashing through the rainy dusk in a dark double column, with the failing light gleaming on wet rifle barrels. The exiles in the cattle shed got up and gave them a cheer as they rode in, and some one asked, "What company is that?"

"Stark's Mounted Volunteers!" the horsemen answered, like a battle cry.

Elmer and Bill and some of the other men went out to meet them. The leader of the volunteers was Adam Stark who had commanded Elmer's column in the battle at Rush's farm. Behind him came the gaudy Albert and Paul Porter and his brother Bob, friends with whom Elmer had ridden in the cause of what was right. Familiar voices called, "Hi, Elmer! Hi, Bill!" When the column halted Paul leaned down and gripped Elmer's hand. "Are you with us?" he asked.

"I'm with you!" Elmer said. He had already found that he couldn't live in a cattle barn while others fought for peace and their homes.

The volunteers only stayed until the sergeant had directed them to the other end of the barn where there were another cattle shed and stalls reserved for horses and soldiers. When they splashed away through the muddy barnyard, Elmer's heart rode with them, though he and Bill went back to the fire and their wives.

The women could not have heard anything that was said out there in the rain, but they seemed to know how things were.

Lisette held Elmer's hand, close, as if she had not expected him to come back at all. And Dolly said, "You men going to join the volunteers?"

Bill said mournfully, "Guess I might as well."

Elmer said, "We've all got to help, if we want to go back to our homes."

Dolly said, "God knows you're no use round here!" Lisette's hand tightened in warm protest, but Dolly went on, looking at Elmer, "There's nothing like doing something useful. I can look after your wife better without any men under my feet."

Lisette looked at Elmer with a sharp intake of breath, and her hand protested that she did not want him to go. But he knew what he had to do, and he did not give her time to object. "I know you'll take good care of her," he said. "I don't know how to thank you."

"Forget it, man!" There was a frank and friendly light in Dolly's thin, strong face and gray eyes. "Sometime you may be able to do me a good turn."

CHAPTER TWENTY

THE RAIN had let up when Stark's Volunteers left the blockhouse in the early morning. There were forty of them now, and Elmer and Bill rode behind the Porter brothers; Bill on his buckskin with the silver mane and tail, and Elmer on a red-and-white calico pony. He had fancied that color of pony when he was a boy at home, dreaming of being an Indian fighter on the Western plains, and when it came to choosing a mount for hunting Indians he had picked out a calico from among the captured stock. He felt a certain pride in the fact that the pony had belonged to Leschi. And his conscience troubled him at moments. He had with him a proof that Leschi had not planned for war and had to leave his herds behind him on the prairie when he was driven from his plough.

But war is war, and thoughts like that did not come very often. Also, Adam said most of their trouble would be with the Klickitats who had crossed the mountains, looking for trouble. They had joined with the Duwamishes in the White River massacre, and he didn't think they were likely to spare women and children elsewhere. Looked at the right way, it was a war to protect women and children from the Klickitat invasion. Under those circumstances, a man had no choice but to fight. Elmer had seen the logic of that when he allowed himself to be sworn in for six months.

So when the sentry opened the stockade gate, Elmer rode out to the Indian war on a calico pony as he had dreamed of doing long ago. He was realizing a boyhood ambition, only something was a little wrong. The man who rode the gaily-painted pony was not the boy who dreamed of doing it. He regretted the opportunity and was going only because it was his duty. It was a bleak duty, with the salt of Lisette's tears still on his lips and her dear, lost face troubling the eyes of his mind. She had been fine and brave all along, but the rough ride to the blockhouse had upset her and she had a restless night. Once in the morning she complained of cramps and he was afraid she was going to be sick. At the last minute she had broken down and begged him to stay. That was impossible, and since he had to go, he wanted to go quickly. The baby wasn't expected for a month, and Adam had promised him leave for the event. With luck, the war might even be over and he would not have to go away again. . . .

From the blockhouse Stark's Volunteers rode northeast in the early morning that was wet underfoot and gray overhead. Their orders were to go to Van Ogle's farm on the Puyallup where other volunteer companies were gathering for an attack on the Indians' stronghold in the swamps. The Dutchman's farm had already been a battleground. It was there that Eaton's Volunteers had camped on their way to arrest Leschi, and a mile or so away Jim McAllister and Connell had died in an ambush. Eaton and his men had been besieged in the cabin the same night. And George McAllister, with his upper lip shot away, had slipped through the Indians' lines for help, and escaped on the captain's horse. The Indians had gone back to the swamps before daybreak, taking the rest of the volunteers' horses with them, and Eaton's men had retreated south on foot.

So far as Adam knew, that was the history of the fighting to date. He had explained to Elmer, reluctantly, why help had not been immediately sent to the McAllister family. Captain Maloney was on his way across the mountains with nearly all the troops from Fort Steilacoom. An express rider had been sent after him with word that war had broken out at home, but until he returned the skeleton force that was left could not do more than guard the fort and the blockhouse. Six hundred Nisquallys were staying in their home camp in the valley without doing any more damage than killing or stealing cattle, and it was best to let sleeping dogs lie.

Riding out with the volunteers, Elmer looked toward the wet, dark wall of the forest that separated the prairie from the

Nisqually valley, and his heart misgave him. Down there was a force of Indians so big that there weren't enough troops west of the mountains to invade their camp. All the troops were on their way to fight Indians beyond the mountains, where there were no real settlements. And all the volunteer companies were on their way north to fight Indians gathered in a distant swamp. Maybe he would have been equally brave and much more useful if he had stayed at the blockhouse, as Lisette had begged him to do.

They halted a mile from the blockhouse, and at the head of their column Adam Stark was looking intently to the north. Far away, a yoke of oxen hitched to a wagon had come out from behind a point of timber and was creeping across the plain toward the blockhouse. A horseman rode close on each side of the team as if the oxen were something precious which needed to be guarded. Then walking figures straggled out of the timber, following the wagon. At first the volunteers could make nothing of it: the horsemen guarding the oxen so tenderly, and leaving women to get along as best they could on foot. While they watched, the oxen suddenly bolted at a clumsy gallop, with the horsemen galloping close beside them and the women running after the wagon but falling farther behind.

"They're being attacked!" Paul said.

From the head of the column Stark shouted, "Follow me!" They raced across the wet prairie like a cavalry charge. The steady thunder of hooves was like the roll of drums and the rush of wind was music in Elmer's ears. His piebald pony kept pace with Bill's silver-maned buckskin, smoothly and without effort, as if he could run forever and only regretted the slowness of the horses ahead of him. And once he went over the carcass of an ox with the lightness of a swallow.

Their charge was fine and thrilling, only it did not last long enough. Before they had gone half a mile, Adam slowed the column to an easy gallop. A mile or more ahead, the ox-wagon had stopped altogether, while the two women and a boy walked slowly to overtake it. The emergency, whatever it was, seemed to have passed.

Galloping beside Elmer and looking solemnly at the priming

of his rifle, Bill said, "It beats me who could be coming in from the valley!"

Until then, Elmer had been too excited to think where the party was coming from. Of course, they were coming from the direction of the Nisqually valley! And there could be only one family there—if it was still alive. "Bill, it might be the McAllisters!"

Bill said, "They were all killed two days ago!"

Again it was rumor triumphing over fact. Elmer hoped if it turned out to be the McAllisters, people would believe they had been alive all along. But it was beyond imagination to think, that a boy of seventeen and an Indian boy not much older could snatch a woman and eight little children from as many hundred Indians.

From up ahead some one called: "They're sending a wagon for them!"

A wagon with two soldiers on the seat was drawing away from the distant blockhouse, with the mules at a gallop. The volunteers quickened their pace to be first at the rescue.

"Why do they run that way?" Bill asked. The oxen had bolted again, at a clumsy gallop, with the horsemen riding close alongside.

From behind them some one shouted with hoarse discovery: "Them oxen are wild! Looks like their first time under the yoke!"

This time the oxen hardly ran a hundred yards before they stopped short in their tracks. The horseman on the near side was riding a big bay that looked familiar. Finally it turned its head enough to show the white blaze on its forehead. "Eaton's horse!" Elmer shouted. "That's George McAllister!" He was terribly excited and as happy as if he had fallen into a gold mine.

In a minute more even Bill admitted it was the McAllisters, and helped out with the cheer that ran along the galloping column. There was George McAllister on the tall bay horse, sticking close to the near side of the ox team. The man on the other side was not the Nisqually boy, but a grim-faced young settler, Joe Buntin, who was married to the oldest McAllister girl. The oxen were swaying on their feet and lolling out their foam-covered, dripping tongues. They looked ready to fall, but the young men were taking no chances; they held firmly to ropes about the beasts' horns.

The volunteers drew up silently beside the grim little procession. The young men did not look as if they wanted to talk, but George said, hoarsely, "We've had a hell of a time!" He formed the words with difficulty because most of his upper lip had been shot away. He didn't have to explain why they had taken such pains to control the wild oxen. A logging chain was stretched across the wagon bed, and to the chain there clung five girls with red and blond pigtails, and two little boys. The oldest of them couldn't have been more than ten. They had scratched faces and torn clothes and bleeding elbows and blood on their clenched hands, but they sat in the wagon like little wild things keeping still while death is hunting for them through the woods.

Paul and Elmer rode up close beside the wagon and asked the children how they were. The littlest boy made a choking sound, with tears overflowing his blue eyes and his lips drawn in and pressed together between his teeth. An older sister, sitting beside him, saw what was the matter and spoke to him kindly:

"It's all right," she said, "you can cry now."

The little boy began to sob, with two of his younger sisters keeping him company. The ten-year-old who had given them permission had a deep scratch across her forehead, and a piece of the twig that had made it was still tangled in her red hair, but she was capable and polite and she remembered to answer the question which Elmer had forgotten. "We're all right, I thank you," she said. "But we got bounced around every time the oxen ran away. When we were in the woods, the branches scratched us."

"We saw a bear," one of the younger girls said. "We thought it was an Indian."

"It was walking on its hind legs," the older girl explained.

"You're Sarah, aren't you?" Elmer asked.

The redhead nodded. Elmer had seen her in Olympia with

her parents, but in the first excitement she had been just one of a wagon full of nameless red- and fair-haired children.

He asked, "how did you get away?"

She explained, "Sister and Joe came to the house yesterday. The Indians let them through because there would be more of us to kill. That's what they thought. Last night Joe and Brother went out and found two wild steers the Indians hadn't killed. They tied them near an old cattle road where there was a wagon for hauling wood——"

Paul asked, "Didn't the Indians stop them?"

"There weren't many around," Sarah told him. "They're afraid of the dark and most of them were in their own houses. And Clipwalen said they could kill him if any of us got away, but he was helping us. In the morning there were hundreds of Indians in the yard, but we walked right through them."

"They didn't try to stop you?" Elmer asked.

"They wanted us out of the house so they could take everything," the child said. "As soon as we were out they started taking things. We went across the creek and along the road. They didn't follow us because they all wanted their share of our things, and they had men waiting along the road to kill us. But we went through the woods to the old road that was all brush and logs and got into the wagon. When Joe and Brother untied the oxen they ran away with us. The wagon nearly tipped over lots of times and we got bounced around and hit by brush. But we'd been told to hang onto this chain and not make any noise, so we didn't say anything."

"You're brave children," Paul said.

Sarah looked at him curiously. "We aren't brave," she said, "but we didn't want to get killed, so we kept quiet."

"I got a tooth knocked out," one of the others said. She opened her mouth to show them where it had been. "It was loose, anyway."

"What are they doing with Mother?" Sarah asked suddenly.

The army wagon had stopped beside the other and two of the volunteers were lifting Mrs. McAllister in.

"She's fainted," Paul said.

Elmer said, "She'll be all right in a minute."

The girl still looked anxious. "Mother don't often faint," she said, making no allowance for the occasion.

"Bring the children over!" Adam called.

"You're going to ride the rest of the way in an army wagon," Elmer said as he and Paul dismounted. He reached up his arms to Sarah, who was nearest. "You're first."

"I'll hand the little ones out," she said, but she only sat where she was, looking at her hands.

"I can't let go," she said wonderingly. She had been gripping the chain so long and with such determination that her hands were locked around it and would not come away. Elmer had to pry her stiffened hands open before he could lift her down.

She said, politely, "I thank you." And when Paul wanted to carry her to the other wagon, she told him, "I can walk." But when she tried, her cramped and bruised legs would not work. They folded under her and she sat down on the wet ground with a look of grave surprise. She had to be carried, after all.

Paul and Elmer scrambled into the wagon to help the others, and they all needed help. Not one of them was able to let go the chain of his own accord. Gently breaking the grip of little hands, Elmer was awed by the strength and wisdom of young human things. This nestful had known that their lives depended on keeping quiet and hanging on. Even the bruised and scratched three-year-old had not cried until he was given permission, and his grip on the chain would have lasted after death.

The volunteers made the most of it and accompanied the wagons to within a quarter of a mile of the blockhouse, though the soldiers pointed out that there was no need for it. By then the two wagons were surrounded by armed settlers who had ridden out from the blockhouse. The volunteers shouted good-bys and swung off to the east, toward the upper crossing of the Nisqually River. But they kept looking back until they saw the big stockade gate open, like a door in a wall, and they saw the army wagon roll in, flanked by horsemen and people on foot.

Behind the army wagon, the empty ox wagon moved at an even pace until it too disappeared into the stockade, and the big gate closed. In one journey the wild steers had become well-broken oxen. But what a journey, and at what a cost of blood and sweat!

They talked about the rescue for the rest of the morning, and often afterward. Having talked to different members of the party, they learned more by talking it over. Elmer and Paul agreed that little Sarah had given the clearest account of any one. Maybe that was because she had seen their journey as a natural happening. But Sarah had not remembered everything. According to Bob, who had talked to the married sister, the Nisqually boy, Clipwalen, had come with them as far as the prairie. He had only turned back when he saw they were safe, with the volunteers riding to meet them.

Bill said, "It still beats me how they got away! Everybody thought they were dead." He said it mournfully as if he still did not believe what he had seen to the contrary.

"There were friendly Indians with them in the house," Bob said, "and plenty of guns. They knew it would be bad for every one if the women and children were killed. Mrs. Buntin said they'd never have escaped without their help."

By talking it over, the volunteers learned better what had happened, and the rescue colored their morning. It also changed their plans a little because they stopped at Fort Steilacoom. Adam wanted to report that the McAllisters no longer needed help.

They travelled north all morning without seeing anything but the road and the gravel prairie, dotted with islands of fir trees, and deserted homesteads. The whole troop rode up to the first cabin, half-expecting to find massacred women and children. But the place was swept clean, deserted and very still in the rain that was beginning to fall. After that, when they saw a cabin, four or half a dozen of them would gallop away to investigate. They dismounted in many dooryards and peered through windows into empty rooms and heard the rain falling on lonely roofs. But they never found any one, living or dead.

That morning the volunteers saw the country, but they saw it piecemeal: on the way to Steilacoom, the land and cabins and barns which could not be moved; at the fort, everything that could move or be moved. They had only a glimpse of the fort itself which was almost smothered under the community, like a lone soldier overwhelmed by a thousand women rushing to him for protection.

For the last quarter of a mile they rode slowly through a tangled herd of horses and cattle, with sheep and pigs under their feet. The herd was guarded by dispirited horsemen who were soaking wet in the steady rain. The volunteers rode through the tangle of livestock, over ground that was like a barnyard, and they were appalled. It seemed incredible that any one could have expected hundreds of cattle and horses and sheep and pigs to be sheltered in the little stockade around the very small fort. But more likely, each settler had thought of saving his own animals, and when all their thoughts and all their animals rushed to one place the result was madness.

When they got up close, it was worse. Outside the stockade there was a jungle of wagons loaded with furniture and household goods and every kind of gear. In one wagon Elmer saw a piano and a plough, with the rain falling on them. In another there were a four-poster bed and a rocking chair and sacks of grain. A roan colt had bitten a hole in one of the sacks and was foundering himself on the grain while escaped chickens clustered under his forefeet, gobbling what he dropped. Among the goods and under the wagons there were crates of chickens and ducks and young pigs making the sounds of a great, unhappy farmyard. Scolding women and crying children were rooting among their wet possessions in the wagons, and once Elmer saw an angry-faced man beating a boy for some obscure reason. He thought of the quiet cattle barn on the Nisqually plain and thanked God he had taken Lisette there. Having no stock of his own to lose he was almost grateful to the Nisquallys for killing the cattle down his way and saving this kind of sickening confusion. And he was grateful that most of the settlers had been drawn to Fort Steilacoom because of its secure sound.

A road had been left through the jungle of wagons and at the end of it they came to the stockade gate. The gate was closed and guarded by a very wet sentry, with a bayonet fixed to his Hall rifle. On each side of the gate unloaded furniture and trunks and crates of poultry were piled against the stockade, like things cast up by the sea.

When Stark's Volunteers rode up to the gate the sentry made no move to open it for them, but he talked civilly to Adam. He opened the gate a crack and spoke to some one inside, then closed it again.

"They might at least let us inside," Bill grumbled to Elmer.

Bob turned on his horse to say, "You'd think, by God, we were Indians!" They were all cold and wet and discouraged by the dreadful tangle and uproar about them, and they felt ill used at being kept outside. When they saw Adam dismount they followed his example and drew as close about him as they could, stretching their stiff legs and threshing their arms for warmth. Some one called, "How about getting in, Captain?"

Adam seemed sorry to disappoint them. "Orders of the commanding officer!" Then he said, "I guess there ain't room for us in the stockade."

"There really isn't, sir." The sentry turned to stop a woman who was carrying a teakwood writing desk. "Sorry," he said, "you can't take that in."

The woman had a thin, refined face and she looked ready to cry. "It belonged to my husband," she said. "He brought it home from India when——"

"Only food and clothes, ma'am."

"But, please," the woman faltered. Then she saw it was no use and went away in the rain with the little writing desk in her arms.

"It's like that all day," the sentry told Adam. "Sorry, ma'am." He barred the way of a girl with a rocking chair.

"But Ma wants it——"

"Only food and clothes," the sentry said.

The gate opened a little and a lieutenant came out and shook hands with Adam. "Sorry I can't ask you in," he said, "but there isn't a place under cover where we wouldn't be stepping on beds and people. And the stockade is a madhouse. At least it's quiet here." Maybe it seemed quiet to him. He looked very young and haggard, and one of his worries had followed him: a big red-faced woman with spectacles and a small nose. She caught his arm and said, "I *will* have my ducks inside! I *won't* have them out where they'll be scalped by Indians!"

"*Madam,*" the lieutenant said, and went on listening to Adam's account of the rescue.

The woman looked angrily at the lieutenant, but she did not interrupt again. She went prowling among the crates of poultry, muttering darkly, "I *will* have my ducks inside!"

"Lieutenant Nugen!" A woman with a sharp, freckled face under a wet sunbonnet came up, dragging a whimpering boy by the hand. "Lieutenant, isn't it true your soldiers shoot bad little boys?"

"*Madam!*" The lieutenant spoke wearily and without rancor, but something in his patient look said he would dearly love to shoot all the little boys and all the little girls in the Territory, and most of all their parents, beginning with their mothers. But he only said "Madam," reprovingly, and he went on listening to Adam's report. When it was finished, he said, "That's good. There wasn't one man I could spare to help them. I'm glad the McAllisters are safe." But you could see that with so many women and children on his hands he could take no personal joy in hearing that more had been raised from the dead. While he was saying, politely, he was glad, another woman came out of the stockade and interrupted him. She was a pretty young woman with bright chestnut hair and blue eyes, and it was a miracle to see her so clean and charmingly dressed in that hell of filth and confusion.

"Lieutenant," she put a gentle hand on his uniformed arm. "I'm only a woman——"

"Madam," he said reprovingly.

But she went on, like a song, "I'm only a woman, but I want to help! It breaks my heart——"

"*Madam,*" the lieutenant said. "I am busy."

She lingered until Albert sidled toward her from the volunteers, preening the wet orange silk handkerchief about his neck.

Then she flounced through the stockade gate which the sentry opened for her, willingly.

The lieutenant was saying to Adam, "It's not my place to advise you. The volunteers are under Mason's orders."

Adam was disappointed, but he tried again. "As a military man, would you advise us to attack tonight?"

The lieutenant was getting wet out there in the rain, and he looked very young and haggard, and his eyes were bloodshot. "I am not advising you, Captain." He sighed. "If I were, I would advise you to let the Indians alone."

The volunteers stared at him and then at each other, and Adam looked dismayed. "But, Lieutenant! Why——"

"We get some information," the lieutenant said. "I have a Nisqually deserter in the fort now. He says it was Leschi who stopped the massacre before it got to the Puyallup River. The Klickitats and Duwamishes had planned to kill every one as far south as Olympia. They are wild because Leschi blocked them, and he is disgusted with them for killing the women and children on White River. His own nephew, Slugia, and some of the other Nisquallys were in favor of the massacre, and their camp is split wide open. They're fighting among themselves. If they're let alone the whole alliance will break up. Then we can suppress the tribes one at a time. If they're attacked now, they'll patch things up and fight together because they have to."

"I see," Adam said. "Thank you, Lieutenant." Then he said, "But Mason's orders were to push north——"

"Certainly," the lieutenant said. "You are under Mason's orders, not mine. I'm not advising you."

There didn't seem to be anything else to say, so the volunteers swung into their wet saddles and said good-by.

"Good-by," the lieutenant said, "and good luck!" But he did not look as if he expected any one to have good luck. When they looked back, riding through the wet hell of livestock and furniture and wagons, they saw him still outside the stockade gate, surrounded by clamoring women. He looked like a very tired and patient stag at bay among female hunters.

CHAPTER TWENTY-ONE

ADAM had said they would meet other volunteer companies on Vaughn's Prairie and attack at once. It sounded fine and clear-cut, but when they got to Vaughn's Prairie in the afternoon they didn't see any volunteer companies. They didn't explore the whole prairie, which had islands of timber and brush scattered over it, the heavily timbered river bottom to the east and heavy timber and swamps to the north. Professional soldiers know how to explore a place like that without being killed by an invisible enemy, but they were only volunteers. Adam looked over the field in a pour of icy rain, and decided to fall back and wait for reinforcements.

They fell back to the crossing of the Puyallup River, and in the shallow water they clubbed enough salmon for their supper. Adam thought it was a good piece of strategy which would help save the army rations in their saddle bags. But he saw other military aspects in the salmon run and decided there was no hope of starving the Indians out. Their stronghold was looped by the Puyallup River and White River and Green River, and through those rivers nature was delivering thousands of tons of salmon to the Indians' iniquitous door. The war did not seem very real to the boys killing salmon with clubs. They were cold and wet and very hungry, and they could not feel bad about the Indians getting salmon since they were going to have plenty for themselves.

They got all the salmon they could use, and fell back along the Military Road to the first deserted homestead. But it was not deserted; Smallwood's Volunteers were there, waiting for reinforcements. There were sixty men in the company and the house and shed were very full of them. Stark's Volunteers fell back to the next farm. The rain was their real enemy and it followed them with its cold scourge all the way to shelter.

At the farm it was fine. The windows and doors of the cabin were boarded up and Adam would not let them break in. But there was a big shed which they took over and called "Headquarters." It had started to be a barn, but wasn't finished; just a shake-and-pole roof and one sheltering wall held up by big cedar posts set in an earth floor. Firewood was stored there and shakes for finishing the sides of the barn; also some corn in a slatted crib.

The horses had to be left out in the rain on a picket line, but they got some comfort out of huddling close together and eating corn.

In the shed each squad had its own fire. Bob Porter was the corporal of Elmer's squad. While his men were cleaning salmon and drying their clothes, he went out to have a look around. Captain Stark had already warned them against foraging and reminded them that they were there to protect property and not use it up. He had only yielded, reluctantly, to using some of the corn because their horses would not understand going hungry when there was food in sight.

Bob was not gone long, but he came back with a watering can, which was all right to borrow and just the thing for boiling their salmon. But when he put the can on the fire there were clean-washed potatoes in the water.

That was a good night. The boys were full of boiled salmon and potatoes and coffee; their clothes were almost dry, and Bob showed them how to make camp for sleeping. He drove four stakes in a square about the fire and had them tie their unfolded saddle blankets between the stakes. When the blankets were stretched out and their outer ends weighted down, they had four lean-to tents facing each other around the fire. There was a big square opening for the smoke to go out, and the low sloping tents reflected the heat like Dutch ovens. With a small fire and one blanket each the squad was reasonably warm while others with two blankets each coughed and piled more wood on the fires and complained of being cold. Bob said he got the idea from the Indians.

Full of food and warm in their Dutch-oven tents, the tired squad dropped off to sleep, not very much disturbed by the restlessness of other less comfortable squads. The only thing which disturbed Elmer was Bill who shared the same section of tent with him. As Dolly had said, Bill snored like a grampus, and it seemed to be Elmer's fate in war, whether at the blockhouse or in the field, to listen to Bill's earth-shaking noises. Even that did not keep him awake long. Through Bill's snores he heard the calm sound of rain on the roof which he thought was the happiest of all meetings of nature and man-made things. He thought of Lisette and the blockhouse, and of Dolly who was so clear and hard and so heartless and compassionate. He thought about her because they had changed jobs. He lay near Bill and listened to him snore, and she slept beside Lisette. The only comfort he got out of it was knowing that Lisette would be well cared for.

The next day was much more military. After breakfast the volunteers saddled up and rode over to the next farm where they found Smallwood and his men saddling up in the barnyard and declaring they were ready to put in a good day's work killing Indians. When they were ready, both companies advanced along the Military Road, an army riding out in the morning. The boys looked at each other and agreed with their eyes that this was something like, and they looked forward and back with invincible pride at the long double column of horsemen and the alert rifles pricking the low-hanging gray sky.

Their army crossed the Puyallup River and advanced onto Vaughn's Prairie. There they halted while the two captains withdrew a little from their commands, dismounted on the wet prairie and held a council of war. They looked fine: Adam in the prime of life, well-built and healthy and bearded, and Smallwood lean and tough-looking, with a long, graying moustache and sharp black eyes in a pale hawk face.

The main body of Indians was supposed to be camped on Connell's Prairie which was on the other side of the heavily timbered swamp through which the Military Road passed. The Indians held the swamp and had ambushes along the road. The road was the only way through the swamp which was a mile-deep jungle of standing and fallen timber, brush and deep bogs that would be filled with water after the very recent rains. The captains' problem was how to get their commands through the ambushed swamp without their being killed. While they talked, Elmer's mind wrestled with the problem. He was glad the decision was left to wiser heads because he did not see how the thing could be done.

The captains talked a long time, and while they talked the rain began to fall again. First it was scattering drops, like spies testing the volunteers' dry clothes. Then, liking the taste, they called their friends who came down by the million in a steady, hissing roar. That was the last day of October, 1855, and the rain was very cold and wet. You could see it hastening the decision of the two commanders. They agreed on some plan, swung into their saddles, smartly, and returned to their waiting columns. Elmer could hear his own heart pounding as he watched Adam ride up, with his bearded face inscrutable.

Adam drew up, facing his column, and cleared his throat. "Well, boys, we've decided to fall back to headquarters and wait for reinforcements." Then, with something like apology, he added, "There's no use getting soaked."

They fell back to headquarters, wet through, but with the rain moderating south of the river. Bob got permission to take half his squad and scout the immediate neighborhood for Indians.

At first Adam frowned and said, "It ain't necessary. We've fallen back enough to be safe from attack."

Standing very straight before his captain, Bob said, "I know that, sir. But there's all those deserted houses. One prowling Indian could damage a lot of property."

Protecting property was a strong point with Adam. "All right," he said. "I wish you had a hammer and nails. Some of those cabins were boarded up in a hurry; they ain't so secure."

Bob said modestly, "I've found some nails, captain, and I'll take an ax along."

"I'll trust you to do a good job," Adam said.

"Thank you, Captain." Then Bob had another thought. "This floor is kind of hard to sleep on. Coming up, I noticed a straw stack outside a barn where they'd been threshing. Think it would be all right if we brought a little to sleep on?"

Adam frowned again. "It don't look good, Bob, carrying stuff away. But straw—. Hell, we need something to sleep on! Bring me some, too."

They did not find any prowling Indians or damaged property, but they did pretty well. Paul found fourteen eggs which would certainly have gone bad if they had been left in the settler's hen house until the end of the war. Bill found turnips and carrots in a garden, and Elmer got two smallish chickens which could be explained as grouse when they were plucked. He had never stolen chickens before, but war is war, and riding in the rain gave the boys the appetites of young wolves. They all did pretty well, but Bob had the real instinct for such things. He found a firkin of butter in a shed and a two-quart measure for carrying his tribute away. Where the others had found nothing, he cut down a side of bacon and a ham from the fragrant darkness of a smokehouse. Following the captain's orders, he nailed a heavy bar of wood across the door of the now empty building.

Late in the afternoon they rode back to headquarters with bulging saddlebags and borrowed sacks stuffed with straw. Each one had a sack balanced on the croup of his horse and steadied with saddle thongs, and another balanced on the horn of the saddle. Paul's chin rested on the sack in front of him and he had the bridle reins over the sack. He said it felt like driving a hay wagon. None of them looked very military, Elmer thought. But it was not a specially military war. If soldiers want to keep alive they have to learn to make use of their surroundings. Under their corporal's guidance they were learning fast.

Afterward they wondered if their straw hadn't come near being the death of them. At first glimpse the man they met could hardly have seen more of them than their heads above the sacks. With Bill's buckskin horse and Elmer's calico he probably mistook them for Indians who had been plundering the houses which they were actually protecting.

The horseman came along the road, but they did not see anything until he was almost on top of them. Elmer only remembered a grove of fir trees obscuring a bend in the road, and a rise of ground. Then a slight, hatless man seemed to leap out of the ground with infinite speed, with a foaming black horse under him. He made a swift, ducking motion and straightened up. Then he was flying past them, with the bridle reins in his teeth and a Navy revolver in each hand. Through flying mud and gravel, the boys saw the leather case drawn out behind his back by the wind as he diminished down the road.

Bill said, "Jesus!" with his eyes very big.

"Dispatch rider," Bob said. "We'd better get back, in case something's going on."

At headquarters there was exciting news, good and bad. Maloney's regulars and Hays's Volunteers were marching on the Indian stronghold from the north. The express rider had overtaken them in the snow at the foot of Naches Pass, and they had turned back at once. They would reach Connell's Prairie in about two days, when operations against the Indians would begin.

Part of Maloney's staff was at Smallwood's headquarters, and two more of the party and the army surgeon's horse were lying dead in the swamp between the two prairies.

Six of Captain Maloney's staff had started back with the express rider, and they rode head-over-heels into the war camp at the edge of the prairie. Clearly the Indians hadn't expected any one to approach from the north. They had no sentries or ambushes posted in that direction, and the party suddenly found itself among squaws and papooses and painted warriors who were at least as surprised as the soldiers. The Indians made no show of fighting and they seemed as eager to be rid of the intruders as they were to go.

When they were clear of the camp and in the woods, they drove the spurs into their horses and bolted south. In their flight they thundered down on the ambushes waiting for the volunteers to come from the opposite direction. Surprised from the rear, the first ambush had only time to fire a few wild shots. The second wounded a soldier and the third, with more warning, killed Maloney's aide-de-camp, Moses, and a soldier named Miles. The Irish surgeon, Burns, had his horse shot dead under him, but made his way out of the woods on foot.

Talking it over, the boys decided the hero of the day was the express rider, Billy Tidd, who had overtaken the troops in the mountains, and turned back at once with dispatches for the fort. He had been riding for three days without sleep, and twice he had gone through the Indians' war camp and the ambushed swamp without getting more than a few bullet-holes through his clothes.

One man in their squad, a teamster named Harland, knew Tidd personally. He said that in private life Billy Tidd was a carpenter at Steilacoom. He had a fat wife and three little girls, and was hardly ever seen on horseback, probably because he did not own a horse. He was a good carpenter, and he sometimes made coffins, though he did not like to, and only did it to oblige somebody or because he needed the money. He did not make much money because he was timid about asking what he should for his work. Even then he was not always paid.

The volunteers stayed at headquarters two more days, but now they had something definite to go on. During the day they kept scouts posted on Vaughn's Prairie, and in camp they polished their rifles, overhauled their equipment and groomed their wet horses. They also washed their shirts and undershirts because Adam had heard somewhere that a dirty shirt made a wound worse. It was inconvenient because they were called out on a false alarm while their shirts were still wet. Some of the men grumbled over rations, which were running low. But Bob's squad did not grumble. At first Adam said they could not take their straw beds with them because it would look unmilitary. After a while he said it would be all right if they weren't going into battle immediately.

The troops from the north arrived on November second, and the war began to move. It had moved before the volunteers got the news. Albert was the one who brought it, galloping at the head of his scouts. "Maloney and Hays have come!"

he shouted, reining up at the headquarters shed. "They have two hundred and fifty troops on the prairie! They've got the whole damn place, swamp and all! The Indians cleared out without firing a shot!"

The volunteers cheered. It was a bigger and swifter victory than they had dreamed of. There's nothing like regular troops in a war.

Albert went on, "The soldiers are looking for the men who were killed in the swamp. They've pack horses to bring the bodies out."

"What are Captain Maloney's orders?" Adam asked.

"We're to report to him on Connell's Prairie." Albert squeezed water from the wet orange silk about his neck. "He said we're to advance when we're ready."

"Pack up, men!" Adam ordered. "We're advancing in fifteen minutes!"

The volunteers tumbled over each other, cheering, to obey. The war was really on and they knew there wouldn't be any more falling back. Only Bob was thoughtful, and he took advantage of the excitement to break up some shakes and put them in the sacks which the others were stuffing with straw. "We can find Indians any time," he said, "but dry kindling'll be scarcer'n hell on the prairie."

Elmer thought their corporal had no soul for the thrill of war and he resented taking part in the advance with a disfiguring sack of kindling and straw balanced on the croup of his pony. When they galloped he had to steady the sack with one hand to keep it from bouncing too hard, and he cursed it many times. Later he wished they had brought the shed.

The volunteers rode into the savage woods where the rains had turned the swamp to knee-deep water and mud. Once they paused beside a pack horse and a group of mud-smeared soldiers with strained faces. The soldiers had the blanket-wrapped body of a man who had been lying in the swamp for many days and were loading it on the pack horse. A sergeant said it was McAllister's body, found beside a fallen tree, carefully covered over with green branches.

The volunteers splashed on through the swamp and came out

into the open on Connell's Prairie. There were soldiers in wet blue and volunteers in ordinary clothes and saddle horses and pack horses on the prairie, and smudges of blue-gray smoke where men were building fires on the soaked ground in the rain. And there were men in the edge of the woods, cutting fuel and cursing the brush which showered them with icy water at every move.

When Adam had gone in search of the commanding officer, the volunteers dismounted and stood close beside their horses for warmth. Elmer had expected, somehow, that the rain would stop when the United States regulars appeared in the field. If anything, it was heavier, and it had a cold, determined sting. But their squad had a good corporal. Bob was less pessimistic than usual, when you might have expected him to be more so. He talked to his men and said they would get along, somehow, if there was any getting along for any one. And he told them to watch the regulars carefully. They did not have any tents, either, and by watching them the squad could learn how soldiers manage for warmth when they camp in the open in the rain.

But the boys did not learn very much that way. When Elmer asked a squad of troopers how they managed, their replies were hardly fit to repeat. The troopers were huddled round a smoky fire which went out under a deluge of rain while Elmer watched. He was disappointed to observe that regular troops get as wet as any one else, and that most of the troopers had bad colds. About all he learned was that the encampment already had a name. It was Camp Misery.

The regulars did not have much to contribute, but that only made Bob more determined. He led and drove his squad between the swampy woods and the bit of rain-scourged prairie which was their camp. In the woods they cut poles and pried great slabs of loose bark from a windfall fir. The bark was several inches thick and water-soaked. It took four of them to carry each big slab, and they sweated and steamed in the rain on the way to camp. But they cooled off on the way back. In the woods every bush and branch was loaded with ice water, ready to shower down at a touch.

On those trips Elmer noticed that there were different degrees of being wet through. You can work hard enough to keep almost warm in a steady rain. But the warmth of your body cannot keep up with wet woods that constantly dump water on you. With each new deluge more of your strength and warmth and courage flows out of you and it is something like bleeding to death.

The squad only went on with the dismal work because Bob planned everything for them and did more work than any one else. Whenever they wanted to quit he threatened to resign as corporal. Demoralized by cold and the woods that drained the life out of them, they hated his blue eyes and his grim young face, but they did not want to loose him. When it came to turning their materials into shelter, they did not need any urging. Before dark they had shelter: a gable roof of bark slabs supported by a ridgepole set in forked stakes. The shelter was not high enough to stand in, but there was room for eight men to sleep close together, around a small fire. There was a hole in the roof for the smoke to go out, and they had enough bark left to cover the wet ground.

For the last two hours they had worked as silently as animals. They were almost silent, spreading their wet blankets on damp straw. When that was done they sank down in luxury with sighs of exhaustion and watched Bob start a fire with shakes intended for a settler's shed. There was room for only a small fire, but that meant less wood to carry. And their low, sloping roof reflected heat and gave more warmth than the huge bonfires which some of the soldiers had managed in the rain.

With shelter and something like warmth they began to be men once more. Their voices came back to them and they talked of how they would improve their house another day. Bob took up the problem of food. "There's army rations in the pack train," he said, "and we'll have some. But I only feel right when we have a leetle extry. We'll send a detail to the river tomorrow for salmon. I'll work a scouting expedition. I bet there's plenty of stuff at the White River settlement that was wiped out."

"Bob, you wouldn't do that!" Paul looked shocked. "It wouldn't be right!"

"We have to eat," his brother said. "The settlers up that way are all dead. They can't use the stuff."

Shelter and warmth were making them human again and bringing back the luxury of ideas about right and wrong. And pride came back to them when a bearded trooper thrust his head and shoulders into their shelter. "A palace," he said wonderingly. "A palace, by God! I'm going to join the volunteers and live in comfort!" He was the first of many to admire their shelter. Because he was the first they were flattered and invited him in to get warm. "I wish to Christ I could," he said earnestly, "but I'm carrying a message. When it's delivered, I'll come back and live with you, by God!"

Elmer thought the trooper was too flattering, but he changed his mind. He stuck his head out of the leaking bark shelter, and it was like the Elect looking down on the damned in hell. Dusk was falling and in the icy November rain horses on picket lines huddled together, with their heads down and tails toward the wind. But the horses did not look as miserable as the hundreds of wet men huddled around smoking campfires or staggering up with more fuel that could never warm the soaking prairie and the wild autumn night. Some parties were already making hasty copies of "The Mansion" and working on lean-to shelters of fir boughs or bark. But they had started too late to manage more than wretched little shelters, and they did not have the hard genius of Bob Porter to direct and drive them on.

The squad was more flattered when their captain looked in and said, "I might have known it was your squad! You have it comfortable in here." He found it so comfortable that he came in and paid them a visit. He did not ask about the ham the boys were frying, or the foraged potatoes roasting in the fire. "You know how to get along," he said, looking at their fine house. "Tomorrow I'll advise the others to build shelters like this. That is, if this is going to be our base of operations." He became more military as his clothes dried a little and he warmed up. "Maloney's scouts have found the Indians," he

told them. "They're holding the right bank of the White River.
The troops will attack in the morning."

The boys had forgotten all about Indians. On this battlefield
which Leschi had chosen it took all their thought to keep alive
and avoid pneumonia. A human enemy seemed quite super-
fluous. The squad did not say anything for a minute, trying
to get their minds adjusted to what they were there for. Then
Bob asked, anxiously, "Are we going to advance, Captain?"

Adam said, "I don't exactly know. Maloney is going to engage them with part of his force, some regulars and Hays's
Volunteers. I asked him to try and work us in on the fighting."

They all said, "Good!" Bob said, "You've got the fighting
spirit, Captain!"

"It ain't that," Adam told him modestly. "I'm no fighting
man; I'm a farmer. I figure that if we crush the Indians in a
hurry I can get back to my fall ploughing."

CHAPTER TWENTY-TWO

THE SQUAD was improving the shelter when the war party rode out of camp to battle with the Indians: fifty very wet regulars under Lieutenant Slaughter and fifty very wet volunteers under Captain Gilmore Hays. Slaughter was a serious-faced young officer with a moustache, and he was riding a gray horse that had a cough. Hays was a fine-looking settler with a broad forehead and clear eyes and a rugged beard. He sat with quiet dignity on his wet roan horse, and except for his frock coat he looked as much a soldier as the army man. Adam was there, too, riding beside Captain Hays. The boys waved to him as he went by and Paul said: "If our captain had a uniform, he'd look like a general."

Adam did not belong with the expedition. He was going as an observer, and if the battle developed that way he had permission to bring up his company as a reserve force. He was thoughtful of his men and wanted them to get all the experience they could in the field. Big Harland said they were there to fight, and he was seconded by every one except the corporal and Bill. Their corporal observed that it was raining only moderately, and a fine opportunity to cut firewood and make their shelter more comfortable. Bill did not have any quarrel with any one, white or red, except possibly his wife, who had shooed him off to war.

The other squads were coming to life, numbly, around their fires, drinking coffee and trying to dry blankets and clothes before the fires in the rain. A few were carrying bark and dragging brush for shelters. They looked as if they had already been in battle and were recovering from defeat.

The war party had not been gone half an hour when there

was a faint burst of rifle fire from the east. It was answered by a cheer from wet men. The troops had met and engaged the enemy.

They were testing the girths of their saddles when Albert galloped into camp, with his orange scarf flying. "Come on!" he shouted. "We're going! They've started fighting!"

The volunteers clustered about him. "Are we going into action?"

"Not exactly," Albert panted. "They're fighting at long range—across the river! Slaughter has men—posted on the bluff—counting the Indians they kill! Slaughter says—we can help count!"

It was very serious and exciting at the time. Bob was the only one who laughed. "Come on, boys," he said. "It sounds like the right job for us!"

They rode out of camp to the northeast, where the open prairie became clogged with low brush. The falling rain did not amount to much, but the brush was loaded with cold rain which had already fallen and in a minute they were wet from the waist down.

As the volunteers drew nearer the river, the rifle fire sounded more ominous. Elmer was not sure it was as much of a joke as Bob pretended. And Bill, riding gloomily beside him, unburdened his heart. "You saw my wife," he said hoarsely. "Dolly's a fine woman; she's smart, too. Why d'ye think she treats me that way? It ain't because I drink. I only drink because she treats me that way. She's crazy about children and she puts all the blame on me because she don't have a baby. That ain't right when it's probably her fault. Why does she go blaming me, Elmer?"

Elmer was sorry for his companion and would have liked to help him, but he could not think clearly, going into battle for the first time.

The sound of rifle fire was louder and through it they could hear the cold roaring of the river. Ahead the land ended in tree-tops against the wet gray sky. Against the tree-tops and the sky half a dozen soldiers and two volunteers stood at the edge of the land, with excited backs. Two of the soldiers were looking through field glasses and the crackle of rifle fire swelled up from the valley. It was very military and exciting, and Elmer scented the sharp smell of powder smoke.

They were picketing their horses when Adam came to greet them. "They've killed nine Indians already!" he said. "Our forces haven't lost a man!" He was as excited as a boy. "The army sharpshooters are knocking hell out of them!" He led them to the edge of the bluff where they could look down into the valley of the White River, where the battle was going on.

The valley was a wild-looking place. The bluff fell away steeply for six hundred feet, and at the bottom the river was a mad white torrent, raging among sand bars and boulders. The cold, plunging roar of water came up to them with the sound of rifle fire. Trees clung to the side of the bluff and among them you could see parts of a narrow trail which descended from the high ground to the river bottom. On each side of the river were driftwood and bleached logs which looked as if they had been hurled out in disgrace because they were too slow for the maniac torrent. Far below, on their side, the volunteers saw men with rifles lying behind logs and boulders, firing at puffs of smoke among logs and driftwood and boulders on the other side of the river. Puffs of blue powder smoke blossomed and turned gray in the rain and faded. Elmer wondered how the troops knew that they had killed nine Indians, neither more nor less.

Adam explained the battle to them. "You'll see how it works," he said. "There won't be any firing for a while, and then an Indian will stick up his head from the brush or behind a log. The sharpshooters will fire at him, and then the Indian sharpshooters will fire at their puffs of smoke. Then more of our troops will fire at their puffs of smoke, and more of them will fire at more of our puffs of smoke. And then—" The details became confusing. "And then," Adam said with dignity, "firing becomes general."

As the firing was dying away, he said, "If you watch closely, you'll see an Indian stick up his head and get plugged."

They watched for several minutes and nothing happened.

The firing had ceased and the valley was silent except for the cold roar of the river.

Adam said with apology, "Maybe they've found it too hot. —*There!*"

A hat lifted cautiously behind a log. Half a dozen rifles cracked from their side of the river. The hat jerked and toppled out of sight.

"A hit!"

"They've got him!"

"That makes ten, at least!" Adam said.

"*Ten!*" a soldier called, with field-glasses poised.

On the other side of the river puffs of smoke blossomed from the brush and logs in answer to the crackle of musketry from the opposing drift. In Elmer's mind there wasn't any doubt that he had seen an Indian killed. It had happened just as Adam predicted.

When the fire became general there was a great deal of noise, but it was monotonous after a while because no Indians showed themselves. There was nothing to see but sudden wisps of smoke from across the river. The rain was getting heavier and as the volunteers got wetter their enthusiasm for the battle sank.

They were nearly discouraged when Adam came back with exciting news. "You're going to see something now," he said. "Hear those axes?"

The sound of chopping rose from the brush at the foot of the bluff.

"They're going to force a crossing of the river," Adam said. "See that sand bar in the middle? It's only about fifty yards. The water looks shallow on the other side. They're going to drop that big fir tree across for a bridge. When the tree falls, Slaughter's men will rush the Indians. Hays's company will follow, and if the battle develops right we'll follow Hays and go into action on the other side."

After that the boys paid more attention to the ring of axes than to the noise of firing. They kept their eyes on the big fir tree whose top was three hundred feet below them. There was a fascination in looking at it and thinking that in a little while they might be racing along its trunk, with the White River foaming under their feet and bullets whistling around them . . .

Elmer's daydream of danger and glory was interrupted by Paul's voice.

"They've quit chopping," he said.

Big Harland said, "The shooting drowns it out." But the fire on their side of the river was slackening, and the double ring of axes had ceased.

A soldier came out of the brush at the foot of the slope, and shouted up through his cupped hands: *"Doctor Burns!"*

"Coming, Lieutenant!" One of the observers snatched a black case from the wet bushes and ran along the edge of the bluff.

"Hurry!"

The boys looked at each other, and Paul's face was pale. "They've got some one!" he said.

Below, they saw the army surgeon's wide hat and medical case hurrying on the slippery trail along the edge of the bluff. While they watched, the sound of a single ax began again. It was a brave sound, answered by the sharp crack of rifles from the other side of the river, then drowned out by the musketry from the near side. When the noise of firing died away, the lonely ax was silent.

The boys looked at each other, unhappily, in the falling rain. They were not cheered when the firing began again and the observers called out that the sixteenth Indian had been killed. They watched the big fir tree for a long time, but there was no more sound of chopping. Presently a small procession passed below them on the trail along the face of the bluff: the surgeon led a wet black horse with a bowed trooper in the saddle. Behind him a soldier led a horse with another trooper. He was laid across the saddle, with arms hanging down on one side and legs on the other. His arms and legs swung limply as the horse walked and wet bushes at the edge of the trail clawed at his dangling head.

The troops killed fourteen more Indians, which made thirty

altogether. It was a kind of victory, but the boys could not enjoy it in the November rain which was beginning to be whitened by sleet. They were disappointed because the tree felling had turned out badly, and they did not have anything to do.

They made several trips to the patch of brush near the observers to see if the wounded trooper needed anything. He was lying under an extra overcoat, with his hands pressed against the right side of his breast. The blood from his nostrils and mouth was bright and mixed with foam, and he did a great deal of choking. They asked if he wanted anything, but he shook his head. The boys were a little afraid of him at first, but he lay there patiently, and when he was not choking his eyes were friendly. Paul stroked his forehead, tenderly. The wounded trooper belonged a little to their squad. He had been the first to admire their shelter, looking in with his big bearded face. He had said, "I'm coming back to live with you, by God!" He did not look as if he would live with any one very long.

The other trooper looked more comfortable, lying a little way off, with a neat bullet-hole above one eye. He had been covered over, but Bob decided the wounded trooper needed the overcoat. His comrade did not mind. His beardless young face met the sleet and rain without flinching.

Around the middle of the afternoon the firing dwindled on both sides of the river as the rain thickened with sleet. Troopers and volunteers began coming up the slippery trail along the face of the bluff, sodden with rain and brush-water and shaking with cold. It looked as if the Indians were withdrawing, but it was too late in the day to force a crossing of the river, and it was not worth staying to fire at sharpshooters who did not show themselves. So they fell back to Camp Misery with their dead and wounded.

That was the Battle of White River.

The Battle of Green River was fought next day. Stark's Volunteers were not selected for the expedition and Adam did not ask to accompany it. He talked it over with his men and explained it was better strategy to stay in camp. "We'll do what we can about shelter," he said, "and save our strength, so we'll be in better shape to fight when our turn comes."

He did not have to apologize. The volunteers had a war of their own in camp, fighting the wet and cold. When the sleet let up a while Bob took his three scouts back to the Puyallup River for salmon. They went as far as Smallwood's deserted headquarters to see that the property had been left in good order. It was very neat, considering. But their corporal found a keg of potatoes which had been overlooked, and they rode back with bulging saddlebags.

At dusk, in driving sleet, they saw Slaughter's regulars and Hays's Volunteers return, half-frozen and exhausted, bringing their wounded with them. About all they learned was that the expedition had found the White River battlefield deserted. They had forded the wild river and climbed the slippery Indian trail up the bluff on the far side, and tracked the Indians through the wet jungle to Green River. It took plenty of strength and courage and endurance just to reach the battlefield. When they got there it was like the Battle of White River over again. Only the Green River was a wilder river in a deeper canyon. They arrived in the afternoon, wet to the skin and chilled to the marrow and lashed by sleet. All they saw of the Indians was the smoke of their rifles from cover on the far shore. It was then too late in the day to attempt a crossing, and after exchanging fire with the invisible enemy, the commanders decided there was nothing to gain by staying.

The volunteers in the bark "palace" were congratulating themselves on having made better use of *their* day when Adam's fatherly face looked into their shelter. "Well, boys," he said, "we're going into action tomorrow." He sat by their fire, on Bob's saddle, and explained, "Captain Maloney has chosen our company to go with the regulars. Some of Hays's men are wounded, and they need a rest. It's our turn."

The volunteers said they were glad.

More apologetically, he said, "It's hard to dry things in this weather, but it would be a good idea for you to wash your shirts. Just in case you get hit, you know."

They agreed it was a good idea, without intending to follow

the suggestion. Pneumonia threatened every one in Camp Misery, but bullets got only a few.

"I'm going to Maloney's shelter now," Adam said. "Lieutenant Slaughter will join us there, and we're going to work out the strategy." He looked as military as a man can look going out of a bark shelter on his hands and knees.

Elmer could not sleep for a long time. He was haunted by thoughts of floundering through wet jungles and along the face of slippery bluffs, and fording wild white rivers. Outside he could hear the sleet pattering on their shelter. Probably some of the others were thinking or dreaming the same nightmare. They stirred restlessly in their damp blankets and coughed more than usual. Bill's eyes were closed but he did not snore for a long time. When Elmer was almost asleep, he was disturbed by some one getting up on the other side of the fire. It was tow-headed Miller, who was usually so quiet. He was quiet now, taking off his shirt and holding it out in the rain on the end of a ramrod. Elmer heard him sigh as he wrung the water out of it.

Morning was more cheerful. The sleet had stopped and only rain fell. While they were saddling up, Bob talked with Albert, and came back to his squad smiling. "We're not going to Green River," he announced.

They looked at him, staggered by relief. Not going?

"We're going to look for Indians on South Prairie."

"I'll be damned," Harland said. "But the Indians are at Green River!"

"Never mind," Bob said. "Mount up, now, and keep your saddles dry!"

When the two forces were across the Puyallup River, they divided. Lieutenant Slaughter and his company took the trail to South Prairie and Stark's Volunteers went around by way of Finnell's Prairie. One prairie opened into the other and there were no jungles to get through and no treacherous trails along the face of bluffs and no raging rivers to cross. Except for the rain it was a fine place to look for Indians. Sometimes Adam led his company at a gallop, like a cavalry charge. That was fun, even though every one was very wet by then. With

Leschi's calico pony bounding smoothly under him, Elmer got back some of the good feeling of war. It was a little like his boyhood dreams of fighting Indians on the plains. No one with judgment would ever dream of fighting them in wet woods. They saw no sign of Indians on Finnell's Prairie, but the lack did not spoil the fine feeling of war; it let Elmer enjoy it in something like comfort.

The volunteers' gallop was not just for fun. As part of their strategy Lieutenant Slaughter and Adam had compared their watches and arranged to descend on South Prairie at the same moment from opposite directions. In the event of any Indians being there, they would be trapped between the two forces.

Adam timed their attack splendidly. When they came within sight of the meeting place, he halted his company behind a point of timber which partly separated the two prairies. He sat for a minute on his wet bay horse, with his opened watch in his hand. Then he closed his watch and put it away inside his two coats. *"Gallop!"*

Following him at a hard gallop, they swept around the point of timber and out onto South Prairie. It was empty except for occasional clumps of brush and a house and shed which looked very deserted in the November rain. While they were still galloping, troopers in wet blue rode out from the other side of the island of timber, a quarter of a mile away. The strategy had gone like clockwork, and the two forces met on the prairie between the timber and the abandoned house.

Saluting, Adam said, "No Indians on Finnell's Prairie, sir!"

The lieutenant smiled and returned the salute, easily. "We didn't see any either, Captain." Then he said, "We'll send a squad to look at the house."

Ahead of Elmer, Bob raised his hand, like a boy in school, volunteering for the assignment. But Lieutenant Slaughter sent a squad of his own men. They galloped in the rain, and were back in ten minutes.

"Windows and doors boarded up, sir," the corporal reported. "Everything is in order."

There didn't seem to be anything to stay for. The army officer and the volunteer captain conferred a few minutes, while the horses snatched mouthfuls of wet gray bunch grass. Then they started back to Camp Misery by the way which the regulars had come.

Riding beside Elmer, Bill said, "When it comes to fighting, I want to do it on the prairie every time!"

"Me, too," Elmer agreed. They were passing within seventy-five yards of the island of timber: big fir trees rising out of luxuriant brush, and the brush rising out of a thick growth of Oregon grape and salal. Every twig and leaf of that jungle was heavy with ice water. Elmer was soaked through, but he shivered at the thought of plunging into that cold vampire jungle which bleeds the warmth and courage out of you with the touch of every leaf.

While he looked and shivered, fire flashed at the edge of the wet woods; fire out of smoke. There were four explosions, dull and heavy and close together. Some one cried out sharply, then everything was mixed up. Troopers were turning in their saddles and firing as they galloped away. Ahead, a volunteer leaned crazily toward the woods. He leaned so far that his horse galloped from under him and he rolled on the wet prairie. The air was blue and stinging with powder smoke. The volunteers behind were firing, and Elmer's pony jammed against Bob's. Paul had stopped, too, and was sliding out of his saddle. Volunteers were galloping by, and one of them scraped Elmer's hat with the muzzle of his raised rifle. He ducked as the rifle exploded, and hot powder stung his neck. Bob had the wounded volunteer in his arms and was staggering under the weight of a man bigger than himself. Elmer helped him, catching the man under the arms. "You take his feet!"

"Put him on my horse," Bob said.

Paul was holding the horses, and the three of them were alone in the smoke and rain with the wounded man. The man was heavy and he kicked rapidly as they tried to boost him across the saddle of Bob's horse. The horse snorted and shied away from the burden. While they were trying again, troopers in single file swept by between them and the woods into which they were firing. One of Elmer's hands was warm and wet under the volunteer's arms.

"All right, I'll take him!" Albert had galloped back to help. Without dismounting, he helped them drape the man, belly down, across the pommel of his saddle. "Let's get out of here!" He galloped away.

By then Elmer had had time to be afraid. He leaped into the saddle and raced after Albert, with the Porter brothers on his heels. The eyes of his mind had a shocking picture of the three of them bunched together and struggling with the wounded man within easy range of the woods. He thought they had been there a long time and managed very clumsily, and it was a wonder they had not all been killed. But he did not remember hearing any bullets.

Their company had stopped ahead where the prairie widened so they were out of range from the woods, and some of them had dismounted. Perham, of Harvey's squad, was sitting on the wet ground, with his coats off, and Adam was helping with his blood-soaked shirt. The wound was in his back, below the shoulder blade. It looked bad, but Lieutenant Slaughter found the bullet in the muscles, a few inches from where it had gone in. It was a trifling wound, made by a spent bullet. The bullet had lost its force going through the body of Jack Edgar who had been riding beside Perham. Edgar was the man Elmer had helped pick up, and he was dead when Albert brought him in.

Three of the troopers had been hit. A corporal had his left arm broken. One private had a bullet hole through his shoulder, and another, shot through the lower jaw, was spitting out blood and pieces of broken teeth.

Adam bandaged Perham's wound, and Slaughter did what he could for his wounded men. Then they lashed Edgar's body across his saddle, and started back to Camp Misery in the steady rain.

That was the battle of South Prairie. Stark's Volunteers had had their baptism of fire, if you can call one bullet a baptism. The bullet had killed one of their men and wounded another. And each of the three bullets fired at the regulars had found its mark. That was the oddest part of the battle. Nearly every one agreed the Indians had fired only four shots. There had been four puffs of smoke from the woods and four banging sounds. After that they heard nothing more from the Indians, and they saw nothing of them at any time.

When they talked it over, back at camp, Bob thought there had been only four scouts in the island of timber. They had blazed away at the troops when they got a good chance, and withdrawn into the fortress of the jungle. The explanation seemed as reasonable as it was discouraging.

The next day the only battle fought was against a driving storm of sleet in camp. In the evening, Adam looked into their chilly shelter, with wet snowflakes melting in his beard. "Well, boys, I have news for you!"

Their groans were audible, but Adam went on, "Get your stuff ready to march in the morning. Captain Maloney has decided to fall back to Fort Steilacoom."

The squad cheered as their captain's splashing footsteps went away to the next shelter, and Bob looked carefree as he set their empty coffee pail outside. "When it's full," he said, "I'm going to wash my shirt!"

"But why?" Paul asked. "Nobody's going to shoot you now!"

"I ain't washing my shirt for Indians," the corporal said. "They can shoot me as I am, or let me alone. I saw a girl at the fort . . ."

They were all excited and carefree, and Elmer thought happily that in two more days he would see Lisette. He would be there when the baby was born, as Adam had promised. He felt kindly toward every one, and he thought their captain was the best military man in camp.

CHAPTER TWENTY-THREE

THE CAMPAIGN against the Indians had been a failure, but the retreat was fine. The weather improved steadily while they travelled southeast through country free of Indians. And the Military Road was less lonely. Here and there they saw chimney smoke, and sometimes a settler at his interrupted fall ploughing. A few days of the terrible crush at the fort had been enough for the bolder ones. They preferred the risk of a few Indians to the certainty of being smothered by too many of their own kind.

For those who had wives at the blockhouse, it was a perfect retreat. Instead of having to ask for leave, all the volunteer companies were sent to the blockhouse which had become Camp Montgomery in their absence. Though it was a mystery where two hundred and forty volunteers were going to sleep.

But when they came through the belt of timber on the Nisqually plain, they cheered and knew that the war was going to be a success. Beyond Muck Creek, the cattle barn and stockade were only part of what they saw. There was a tall pole with the stars and stripes hanging still against the clearing western sky. In front of the stockade, flanking a wide parade ground, were double rows of army tents. On the parade ground a company of men in settlers' clothes marched proudly with rifles.

All that slowed their approach to Camp Montgomery was the wagon that had been sent with them from the fort. One of the bodies under the tarpaulin was Jim McAllister's. Stark's Volunteers, who had helped rescue his family, were escorting his body home. Though there did not seem much kindness in presenting the family with the body of a man dead two weeks. The other body was Jack Edgar's. His Indian wife was waiting for him at the blockhouse.

So the volunteers approached at a stately pace. At the edge of the parade ground, the camp commander met them on horseback. He was Colonel Shaw who had been the interpreter at the Medicine Creek Treaty and said he could get the Indians to sign their own death warrant. He was young for a colonel, being twenty-two or three, but he had a serious face and red hair, and he was a friend of Governor Stevens. His orders to Adam were definite. "Instruct your men to uncover their heads as they go in," he said. "Precede the wagon with half your command, and have the other half follow. Leave the wagon close to the stockade with two men to guard it, and instruct the teamster to unhitch. Then lead your command out, and I will assign your quarters." The hit-or-miss days were over and things were done in a military way.

As Stark's Volunteers crossed the parade ground, the drilling company was doing "Squads left wheel," and "Company halt," and "Present arms," and other manœuvers which the volunteers had had no time to learn because they were soldiering. The recruits looked hungry for news, but they stood in ranks, manfully, to show that they too were soldiers doing their duty. When the funeral escort passed, the drill-master marched them away in the opposite direction, barking, *"Left foot, right foot! Left foot, right foot!"*

The stockade gate opened a little for a woman with two water pails. But instead of going on to the creek, the woman flourished her pails excitedly and darted back to spread the news. When the volunteer sentry swung the gate wide, and the company rode in with uncovered heads, women and children and outnumbered men swept about them in an eager wave. Elmer stood in his stirrups looking for Lisette, but he could not see her. Instead he saw pale Mrs. McAllister, standing between her married daughter and her oldest son, with his bullet-torn face, and he saw the red and blond heads of the younger children about them. A young Indian woman with her hand at her throat was swaying on tiptoe while she looked along the column and called anxiously, *"Jack! Jack!"* Under the tarpaulin in the wagon, Jack Edgar did not hear her.

"Dolly!" Bill called.

Elmer dismounted as he saw Dolly coming toward them. She was pushing her way through the crowd with an excited look on her sharp, clear face, and Elmer knew the baby had come. "Dolly," he called, "Dolly, how is Lisette?" Near them, a woman's voice was crying, "Where is he? Jack! *Jack!*"

"Hi, Dolly!" Bill said as his wife reached them, panting.

Dolly hardly noticed him. She caught Elmer by the wrist. "Lisette's all right," she said quickly. "She's all right, Elmer! I made her promise not to get into the crowd, but she's all right."

He knew something was wrong. "Has the baby——"

Her fingers were hurting his wrist, and she said fiercely, "You mustn't think about it! You can have plenty more!"

It had never occurred to him that the baby might die. They had counted on it as certainly as the coming of spring. And Lisette had been so well and proud. "Then it's dead."

"You can have plenty more!" Dolly was still holding his wrist, fiercely. "You mustn't think about it! You mustn't let her think about it, Elmer! It don't matter because she's all right and you can have plenty more. We thought she was going to die, but she's all right."

"Where is she, Dolly?" He wasn't thinking of the baby any more. Dolly was right that it didn't matter. Lisette was all that mattered, and she had come near dying. He left his horse in the stalled column and pushed his way through the crowd.

Lisette had promised to wait outside the crowd, but Elmer met her trying to get through. He saw her eyes looking at him and her lips getting ready to call to him. She looked very dear and familiar and changed. Her mass of black hair seemed so much thicker because her face had thinned. She was thinner than he had ever seen her before; thinner, with no look of buoyancy. But she was dearer to him than ever, and holding her in his arms was like a miracle.

She clung to him tightly for a minute while the noise of the stockade rolled about them, dimly, and a woman's scream stabbed like lightning through the cloud of other noises. Lisette said, against his shoulder, "Elmer, the baby——"

"I know," he said, "Dolly told me. But I have you, Lisette." Feeling her trembling against him, he asked, "You are better, aren't you?"

"I'm all right," she said. "Only I'm not good for much. Everything used to be so easy, Elmer! Now I'm tired doing nothing. Dolly doesn't let me do anything. I expect I wouldn't have lived without her."

"I'm very grateful to her," Elmer said. "We'll make it up to her, Lisette."

"Dolly says not to think about the baby because we'll have more. But she feels as bad about it as I do, Elmer. She's never had one of her own, and this was going to be a little bit hers."

He said, "Let's go where we can sit down. You shouldn't be on your feet so much, dear."

Holding his hand tight as they were going into the barn, she said, "You never saw him!"

After the autumn sunshine in the stockade, the barn seemed almost dark, and it smelled dimly of horses and cattle and wild hay. In that strange half-darkness, going past curtained stalls, he thought: No, I never saw him. That's the way it happened. He was the little one who got lost in the shuffle of war. He came and went away again while I was somewhere else. I never saw him. But I'll always remember him because I wanted to see him so much.

His eyes got used to the dim light, and when they reached their compartment, he saw how nicely everything was arranged. In one stall there was a bed made of deep straw; a bed with a feather pillow in place of a saddle. Lisette's clothes were hung on nails in the partition. In the other stall, housekeeping things were neatly arranged, with clean hay on the floor and a bench, and a skillet and pots hanging on the partition. Seventy feet overhead was the magnificent, beamed roof of the barn. After a bark shelter where you had to go on your hands and knees, the roof looked as high as heaven and the stalls elegant.

They sat on the bench, with their hands married, and Lisette said, "I'd been so well, Elmer! I didn't think I was going to be any trouble, and we were going to have a fine baby. But everything went wrong. They even had to get a doctor. He said it was a month too soon; that's what made everything go wrong."

He asked, "A month, Lisette?"

"Yes. It started the day you left; I was afraid something was happening, but I wasn't sure. The ride here in the wagon was too much, the doctor said. Dolly was with me all the time, and the other women did everything they could. Mr. Shelton brought Doctor Tolmie from the Hudson's Bay fort. Everybody did so much, Elmer. They were so kind!" She gave a shuddering sigh, and he felt her hot tears fall on his hand. Afer a minute, she said, "He was born the morning after you left, and he looked so sweet. He looked so sweet, Elmer! They wrapped him up warm and laid him in the manger. That was like a dream. I thought maybe I was dead, and I was afraid when I heard them say they would put him in the manger. But they hadn't any other place for him. Everybody said he looked so sweet, but he didn't live. All the life he had was part of that day, and it was raining hard all the time."

"You mustn't think about it, dear." He caressed her shoulder, trying to comfort her, while she sobbed against him. "That's the way it happened. We'll have another when this trouble is over."

With her face muffled against his breast, she said, "He looked so sweet, Elmer; he looked as if he wanted to stay. But we had so little to offer him: a cattle barn with a crowd of people, and rain and war going on outside. It wasn't a good time for a baby."

He said, "We didn't know."

"We buried him outside the stockade," she said, "on the prairie. One of the men made a coffin, and Dolly lined it. The men dug the grave in a nice place and put a fence around it, but it was raining when we buried him. We waited a long time, but it never stopped, and we buried him in the rain."

"That's the way it happened," he said, soothing her. "You mustn't think about it, Lisette."

She said, "I try not to; not too much."

After that day Lisette did not talk so much about the baby. Elmer saw her growing stronger as the days passed and she spoke of it less frequently. In his mind he related the two things, and he never referred to their loss. But he felt what he could not afford to show.

He felt it that daybreak, when he was on sentry duty outside the stockade. What he felt wasn't sharp grief, but it was all through him and about him. He and the morning and his lost son were together and part of the same thing. He had the feeling of understanding a little how things were, and he wanted to share what he felt and maybe excuse himself for what he had not known.

So he walked over to the burying ground which was a little way from the stockade gate. The grass was white with frost and there was furry white frost on the rough boards of the little fence. It was like white fur trimming on the winter clothes of children who are fortunate. Outside the fence there were the mounds of raw gravel where Jim McAllister and Jack Edgar were newly buried. But Elmer did not look at their graves. He stood close beside the little fence and leaned on the barrel of his rifle, with its iron butt-plate on the frosty grass.

"My son," he said, "I'll stand guard beside you for a while. I suppose you don't need me, but I wasn't able to do anything for you when you were alive. So I'll stand guard beside you now. I didn't expect it to be this way. I was making a cradle for you, and I never thought you would do guard duty with me in the cold. If you had lived, I wouldn't be talking to you this way, and we would have kept you warm and safe. Only, my son, we do not always know what is safety. The one thing I tried to do for you turned out badly. I brought your mother to the blockhouse because of you; I thought you would both be safe there. But you weren't safe, and now you are outside the stockade. If I had not brought your mother here, you wouldn't be born yet. You would be safe, and you would have been born at the right time, and had a life. Your mother did not want to go to the blockhouse; she was afraid something would happen. Because I made her go, you were lost in the shuffle. I know that and she knows it, but I don't think she will ever say that to me." The solemn murmur of his voice had a lonely sound, and the frosty air stung his nostrils when he stopped with a sigh. But still he hadn't said what he wanted to say. He tried going on. "You were our first," he said, "and we loved you. I am standing guard beside you because it is the best I can do, and it isn't so lonely for me. It is early in the morning, with white frost over everything, and the sun just coming up over the plain, like fire. We are alone out here, while your mother is asleep in the blockhouse. You don't need me, my son, but I had to talk to you. It don't sound fair that I did nothing for you, and then come to you for comfort. But that's the way it is."

Elmer still hadn't said what he wanted to say, but he couldn't go on. He leaned over the fence, without touching its white, fragile bloom of frost. "Good-by, my son." He thought that wasn't the way to talk to a baby, but this was the first and he hadn't much experience. He tried again and said more softly, "Good-by, little one." Then he took up his rifle and went back to the stockade gate, through the frost that was over everything.

From the gate he saw his footprints going and coming across the frosty grass. In the light of the rising sun the white trimmed fence was edged with clear fire, and up in the southeast he saw Mount Rainier coming out in the sky. For weeks it had been blotted out while the wet autumn rolled over it, but now it was like some vast white island rising from the sea. The rain which had scourged Camp Misery had fallen on the mountain as snow, and it was muffled in new white. . . .

Elmer caught up his rifle before he really heard the sound of hoof-beats. Then he relaxed as the familiar figure rode into sight from around the south end of the stockade. He knew his uncle hadn't approved of his joining the volunteers, but he still didn't see what else he could have done, and he was ready to meet displeasure and argue the point if he had to.

But Uncle Jarvis looked quietly pleased to see him, and did not say anything about his enlistment. He dismounted and took the boy's hand and looked down at him as steadfastly as the mountain in the sky, and more comfortingly. "I'm sorry about the baby," he said. "I had counted on it."

"We counted on it, too, Uncle."

"Lisette is getting on well, h'm?"

Elmer said. "I couldn't expect her to do any better."

"I've never had a son of my own that I know of." He sighed. "I'm not sorry for you, boy. You'll have more." He grinned, faintly, with his eyes sad. "Sounds like that crazy Slocum woman, Dolly, who's been devoting herself to Lisette, h'm?"

"She still is," Elmer said, "though there's less need for it now."

"I'm like her," his uncle said. "I say, enviously, 'You'll have more,' and inside I'm not sorry for any one but myself."

Elmer didn't know what to say to that. It hadn't occurred to him to think up comfort for his uncle. He'd expected it to be the other way round and he was unprepared.

"Dolly Slocum's right," Jarvis said. "Divine madness, h'm? You fight against being cheated out of immortality." Then he said, "I'd have seen Lisette oftener, but I'm not popular here."

"It was good of you to come," Elmer said. He was very glad to see his uncle.

"I have business this time," Jarvis said. "I've some vegetables and fresh meat for Lisette, and I wanted to make sure everything was all right at your camp."

"I thank you, Uncle." Then he said, "It's always quiet here."

"No savages about? You weren't attacked during the night, h'm?"

Elmer thought his uncle was making fun of him. "We chased the Indians across Green River," he said, repeating the volunteers' boast.

"That's odd," Jarvis said. "Last night I had a visit from Leschi and some of his braves."

"*Leschi!*" The boy was stunned by the news.

"They couldn't have passed far from this camp," his uncle said. "I thought you might have seen them."

"We must tell Colonel Shaw!" Elmer said. "How many were there? Where did they go?"

"You don't have to be excited," Uncle Jarvis said. "They were on a peace mission. Leschi wanted me to take terms to Mason. I'll do it, and be damned, h'm?"

Elmer asked, "But how did they get down here without being seen?" It sounded impossible.

"They were seen, all right," his uncle grinned. "Leschi told me they'd captured all the settlers along the road to keep them from spreading the alarm. He said they were taking care not to hurt any one, and they were going to turn them all loose on the way back."

"I've got to tell Colonel Shaw!" Elmer said. He saw it as a desperate business. God knows what had happend, with the Indians holding the Military Road all night. "I've got to call him!"

"Of course," the big man said. "I want to talk to him myself." But still he seemed in no hurry. "Before we wake the dogs of war I want you to think about something more important. This isn't much of a life for Lisette, living in a stable. And you don't love a place where you've suffered too much. I want you to think about letting her come home to Mary and me. She'll be at least as safe as here, and we can give her some kind of life."

Elmer could not think clearly, but it was already on his conscience that he should not have brought her to the blockhouse in the first place. "I'll let her go if she wants to," he said.

CHAPTER TWENTY-FOUR

NOTHING came of the peace terms which Uncle Jarvis presented to the acting Governor. The Indians asked only for land they could live on and Mason was a reasonable young man, but he could not do anything about it. As acting Governor he could make mistakes of his own, but he had no authority to right mistakes made by his absent superior. He could only try to punish the Indians for going to war. But they were hard Indians to punish, and the first expeditions against them had not been a success. Because the new expedition had to be better prepared, it did not start north until late in November. Lieutenant Slaughter went with his regulars and Hays's and Wallace's Volunteers who had been drilling at Camp Montgomery.

Stark's men saw the expedition off in an icy rain that roared down through the dark November morning, and they said that some people have all the luck. But they did not say which people. Elmer always remembered Lieutenant Slaughter as he saw him then muffled in his dark blue overcoat and wide campaign hat. His face was smooth and boyish, and his moustache did not make him look any older. He had led every attack on the Indians, and now he was going away to attack once more; back to Camp Misery and the wild country beyond, with the Indians encouraged by victories, and winter setting in. He looked sad and patient, giving orders quietly and leading his troops away in that morning of black rain.

More volunteers arrived after Hays's and Wallace's companies left, and camp was a stirring place. Companies drilled on the parade ground and bugles blew and riders galloped, and the American flag kept watch in the sky on the rare occasions when it was not raining or snowing.

Stark's Mounted Volunteers was a real company now, with sixty men. It had started with forty, and Smallwood's Volunteers with sixty. When Captain Smallwood was taken home in a wagon, agonized by rheumatic fever, the two companies were combined. Out of the original hundred, sixty men answered the roll call. Some of the missing forty were dead or wounded and the rest were crippled by rheumatism and rheumatic fever.

The survivors of the two companies had tents facing the parade ground. Elmer's squad had the best one. It had a wooden floor, which was not regulation, but a great comfort. Bob had brought the lumber from the mill at Chambers Creek in a volunteer wagon. It was never clear who, if anyone, paid for the lumber, and how he managed about the wagon. As nearly as Elmer could make out, Bob had commandeered the wagon on the grounds that there was lumber to be brought from the mill, and he got the lumber from the mill on the grounds that the wagon was there for it. The New Jersey corporal was ingenious and confident and looked after his men with tough-minded devotion. As a result, his squad was the only one which had come, unbroken, through the hell of water and sleet at Camp Misery.

The men in Bob Porter's squad were proud of their corporal, and looked upon themselves as something special. All of them bought high laced boots into which they tucked their jeans, "California style," and red flannel shirts. It made a kind of uniform, and they swaggered in places; but not on their company street. Nixon's Volunteers were on the other side of the street. Captain Nixon was a big man who looked as if he was covered with hard fat. His face was hard and fat and red, and he had small hands and feet. No one knew much about him except that he had come up from Oregon in answer to one of the later calls for volunteers, and had raised a company. Like himself, most of his followers were Pikes. One of them was Joshua Sims, and when he and Elmer met they sometimes spoke, but only out of politeness. Joshua asked where "Liza" was, and Elmer said she was at Steilacoom, which seemed safer than telling where she was. Soldiering was making him tougher, but he did not feel easy in the company of a murderer, and he was not sure that the Sims tribe had forgiven him for their defeat at Rush's farm.

Joshua was the biggest man in Nixon's company, but there were other big men. They were sometimes drunk and often quarrelsome, and at night they gambled in their tents by the light of candles stuck in whiskey bottles. "Taps" did not signify anything to them, and often they kept Stark's Volunteers awake until almost daylight. When Adam spoke to their captain about it, he did not get much satisfaction. Nixon admitted his men were rough, but they had hearts of gold. When men are risking their lives for their country, it is natural they should want their fun.

Sometimes in the evening Elmer's squad talked about the expedition against the Indians and wondered how it was making out. The hopeful ones predicted a victory which would end the war. Bob offered to bet that Slaughter and his mixed command would be forced to retreat even if they never met the Indians. The weather was bad enough on the plain, and it must be hell in the forests of the river country, at the foot of the mountains.

Both predictions were wrong. There was no news of victory from the north, and Lieutenant Slaughter never came back. When they heard of him again, he was dead in a surprise attack on his camp near White River. The survivors of his force were trying to fight their way out to the north, and a company of regulars from the fort were on their way to rescue Wallace's Volunteers who were cut off and surrounded at their camp on the Puyallup.

Those were gloomy days, but everything turned out better than seemed possible. The rescue party brought back most of the volunteers, and the survivors of Slaughter's main command came back to Steilacoom by steamer. Under Lieutenant Cowan they had cut their way out to the north and reached Seattle.

More than seemed possible had been saved out of the disaster, but the punishment of the Indians was farther away than ever. The next move was up to the acting Governor and the military, and it was hard to see what they could do.

But Mason made a fine move. Adam brought the news one evening when the squad was warming its hands round a charcoal stove which Bob had rigged. "Well, boys, I shouldn't be surprised if we'd be on the march soon." He sounded cheerful, but there was no enthusiasm from the squad.

"You mean there's going to be another campaign in the river country?" Bob asked. His face was dark with the stubble of a beard he was growing and a streak of charcoal across his forehead, and he looked and sounded grim.

"Not this time, boys," Adam said, filling his pipe, "Mason has decided to use the armed forces to protect the settlements. The families who moved back haven't been attacked. Mason told the Legislature today that with protection more settlers can go back and look after their property."

"Leschi wanted the settlers to stay on their farms," Elmer remembered. "He promised not to bother them."

"Leschi's our enemy." Adam looked displeased for a minute. "But Mason's right; we can't let everything go to hell. I'd like to be looking after my own place right now."

Bob wanted to get the thing straight in his mind, "Then nobody's going to attack the Indians, Captain?"

Adam hesitated, "Not for the present. Captain Maloney and his staff have decided it's impossible to fight the Indians in winter in the region of the Puyallup and Green and White rivers. Mason agrees with them."

Bob said, "Since the Indians won't fight anywhere else, that's kind of definite."

Adam did not like the corporal's summing up, but he only said, "Anyway, we know where we're at. And Governor Stevens should be back soon."

Miller, who was usually so quiet, looked excited. "Maybe there won't be any more fighting! Maybe the Governor'll make peace with the Indians, and we can all go home!"

Adam frowned, doubtfully. "The Indians have to be punished for the massacre, and one thing and another. But God knows we all want to get back to our farms."

West of the mountains there was no fighting during the rest of December and January. No military expeditions crossed the Puyallup to punish the Indians in the river country, but south of the river the volunteers were active. They went on scouting expeditions and patrolled the Military Road, helped move settlers back to their farms and gave them protection after they were there. It was the return of peace which every one hoped would last, and there was good hope for it lasting. None of the returned settlers was attacked, and none of the soldiers or volunteers was fired on. The Nisquallys who had stayed at their camp in the valley had given up their arms and were being moved to an emergency reservation on Fox Island. They were put in charge of an agent named Swan who treated them so well that the ones who ran away came back of their own accord and brought their families with them.

Fox Island was in sight of Steilacoom, and when the volunteers paused at the fort on their way north Elmer admired the peaceful island across the water. It was steep-sided and high, like a land that had risen above trouble. Columns of blue smoke were going up from the edge of the still green timber, and Indians were digging clams on the beach and fishing from small dugouts near the high shore. It was a magic island where peace was made out of war.

The only Indian killed during that time was a Hudson's Bay Indian, who was not in the war. He was working with a French Canadian on company property when a party of volunteers came along the road. The woodcutters had paused in their work to watch the volunteers pass. While they were passing, one of the volunteers raised his rifle and shot the Indian through the belly. Then the party galloped away.

Plenty of blood boiled when they heard about it at Camp Montgomery. Adam said it was murder, even though it was an Indian who had been killed, and he said the murderer would be hung if he was caught. Even Captain Nixon, of the Pike company, said that such things should be punished. But half a dozen companies and details of companies had been out that day. Colonel Shaw was still investigating when Captain Stark went on patrol with the original half of his company.

It was not an exciting or dangerous expedition, but Elmer knew it was the kind of warfare of which his mother would approve. She had to know, sooner or later, that he was in an

Indian war, and he was afraid it might be over before he got any credit for it at home. He wrote:

"This is a quiet afternoon in camp. We are bivwacked on the Johnson place south of the Pualup River. In some ways it is like home because this was the headquarters of our Volunteer Company in November when we were waiting for reenforcements before the Battles of the White River and Green River and South Prairie. In some other ways our camp is not like home. It is just a big open shed and we are camped inside. Outside the shed it is snowing hard. It is not like the snow at home, it is very wet and such big flakes, as big as white rose petals. It is pretty to look at but we do not care for it much because it soon turns to rain when the flakes get that way. Then everything is slush and rain and wet mist. It don't get really cold here, but it feels colder than at home because of so much wetness.

"Captain Stark has a touch of the rumatism from sleeping in damp places and some of our men have bad coughs, but I keep healthy and all our squad is fine. Our corporal, Robert Porter, gets most of the credit for that. He is a genius at making our camp comfortable and finding food where there don't seem to be any. We have army rations but he isn't satisfied except when we have what he calls 'a leetle extry.'

"We are protecting the settlements now and haven't seen an indian this expedition. Most of the settlers are back on their farms, some with their families, and things look better already. Many think the war is over. I hope so. Lisette is staying with Uncle Jarvis and his indian wife who have been so good to both of us. But 'there's no place like home' and there is so much we want to do.

"We have been in the field almost two weeks but expect to go back to Camp Montgomery soon, when another Company comes up to relieve us. A squad of Wallace's men were up here yesterday. They came with the Preston family who are moving back from the Fort. The Military Road is well travelled. I dont think Leschi, the Nisqually chief, will capture it for any more raids!

"I'll mail this letter when we get back to Steilacoom. There aren't any post offices or anything up here.
"Your Loving Son, .
"Elmer Hale"

"Post Scriptum   Camp Montgomery, 7th Jan.

"While we were gone Leschi and some of his braves were down this way. They came in war canoes and captured the Reservation on Fox Island. There was a lot of excitement because the Reservation is in sight of Steilacoom. Nearly everybody was on the bluff, watching. They could see the big canoes and men on the beach, and with glasses they could see Leschi. A man who had a telescope charged four bits a look and made a lot of money. But some of it was on credit.

"Some men wanted to go in boats and canoes and whatever they could find and attack, but it was too dangerous. Capt. Keyes borrowed the Hudson's Bay steamer, *Beaver,* but she had to be brought from the landing at the mouth of the Nisqually. By then it was too late to attack and she lay at the dock all night.

"She sailed in the morning loaded with Regulars and Wallace's Volunteers who had marched over from Camp. Everybody turned out to watch, even the Minister. It was Sunday, but he did not say anything about services. The tide is very swift past the Island and there is no steamer landing. They probably would have lost the steamer if they tried to beach her. Leschi had only about forty men on the Island and the steamer was almost sinking with Soldiers and Volunteers. But they had only one small gig that would carry about five men, counting the rowers. The indians could have shot them as fast as they were landed, and there wouldn't have been any one to row back for the next lot.

"The crowd at Steilacoom was wild with excitement and a boy fell off the bluff and broke his arm. Some people paid a dollar a look through the telescope and they saw indian sharpshooters behind logs and rocks on the beach and up in the trees on the Island. Maybe. All I ever saw of an indian sharpshooter was a puff of smoke. Anyway, those who were lucky saw Jack Swan, the indian Agent, come down to the beach and wave to the steamer. Two sailors rowed ashore and brought him off. The crowd at Steilacoom cheered because the story had got around that Swan was killed the day before when Leschi's men took the Island.

"The gig took Swan ashore again and left him there, and the *Beaver* headed back for Steilacoom. It looked crazy, but it turned out all right. Leschi had captured the Island because he'd heard about Swan and wanted to talk to him. He said if other Bostons had treated the indians as well in peace as Swan did in war, there wouldn't be any trouble. So Swan went on board to tell them that he was busy talking peace and that Leschi was peaceful. He made them take him back because he had given his word.

"That was an exciting Sunday for these parts. 'Leschi's Navy' left that afternoon, and Swan visited the Fort on his way to Olympia to report. Leschi had invited him to come up to his stronghold in the River Country and talk peace with all the indians. Swan will go if Mason approves. He trusts the indians as they trust him.

"So maybe the raid has brought peace nearer. I don't know. Mason can't really promise anything, but Gov. Stevens is expected back any day, and we shall see."

Elmer had not mailed his letter at Steilacoom because he wanted to add news of the raid on Fox Island. Before sending it he had opportunity to write another piece of news; but he mailed the letter as it was.

Three companies had been drilling in battalion formation on the muddy parade ground, where the last patches of snow were disappearing magically under a Chinook wind, blowing soft and warm from the south. They were being dismissed when Colonel Shaw rode up and called them to attention again. The Colonel's face was pale and grave. Everything went still except for the rough muttering of Nixon's men, who were never really quiet.

Three men on horseback were crossing the parade ground.

One of them was a big, dignified man in old-fashioned clothes. Elmer could not see the others clearly. A whisper ran along the company front like a wind through a row of trees:

"They've come for the murderer!"

Elmer remembered about the Indian woodcutter who had been shot through the belly, and he recognized the man in old-fashioned clothes as Doctor Tolmie, the Hudson's Bay factor. One of the other men had a star on his coat. The third was short and dark.

Elmer's conscience was clear. He had not killed any Indians, even in war. But he felt nervous as the factor and the sheriff and the French Canadian moved slowly along the company front. It seemed to him he was looking very guilty, but the Canadian's dark, liquid eyes rested on him only a moment and passed on. He was suddenly light and weak with relief, and he looked gratefully at the solemn, thickly bearded face and kindly eyes of the factor. He had seen Doctor Tolmie only a few times, at a distance, but he remembered that the doctor had come to the blockhouse at night and probably saved Lisette's life. There was talk about the Hudson's Bay Company being the enemy of American settlers. But Elmer had never heard anything but good about the big Scotch factor. Undoubtedly the Hudson's Bay Company was opposed to the American settlement of territory it claimed. But it was also true that Doctor Tolmie had sent wagon loads of beef to the invaders when they were starving. He had doctored them when they were sick, and he was a man.

So Elmer looked at the big factor with respect and gratitude. He was relieved when the examination of the company was completed without any one being accused. Adam looked grateful, and instead of telling Albert to dismiss the company, he said warmly, "Thank you, boys. You can go to your quarters now."

They broke ranks, but they did not go to their quarters. There was too much fascination in watching the man-hunt. The Hudson's Bay men and the sheriff were passing slowly along the line of Nixon's Volunteers. The Pikes were keeping up a contemptuous muttering, while their big, red-faced commander stood by, negligently, without calling them to attention. They were his rough men with hearts of gold, and he was never hard on them.

The dismissed volunteers crowded as close as they could to watch, and Elmer could hear his own heart thumping above the mutter of Nixon's men. He saw the French Canadian stop to look at one squad, excitedly, and crane his neck for a better view of the rear rank. Then he indicated the squad with a gesture as he turned to the factor and the sheriff. "These men I saw! They were with the murderer!"

Nixon's men answered with contemptuous snarls and a few of them spat at the French Canadian as he rode on a few steps. "These too!" He pointed with both arms, indicating two squads. "From there to there." He wiped his face on the sleeve of his coat, as if some one had spat in it, and pointed at a man. "And there is the murderer!"

Looking over craning heads Elmer saw it was his distant relative by marriage and adoption, Joshua Sims. Joshua was quaking as if he would fall, and his face was white and sweating above his black beard, and his eyes were wild with fear. Elmer pitied him, but he also knew it was a good thing that he should finally have to pay for one of his senseless murders.

The snarls and mutters of the Pike company had sunk to a faint, dangerous hum, and everything else was still as death on the parade ground. Then Doctor Tolmie asked distinctly, "Jules, are you certain he is the one?"

Before God," the accuser said, "he is the one!"

"Touch him with your hand."

He rode a step closer and reached out his hand toward Joshua's shoulder. "He is the——"

Crack! It sounded like a shot, but it was only the barrel of a rifle clubbing the outstretched arm. Then everything changed. Elmer saw the French Canadian wheel away from the Pike company, with his face twisted and one arm hanging limp, and he saw the men break ranks and lunge forward. He saw them driving the sheriff and the factor back, with cocked rifles pointed in their faces, and he saw them kicking at the legs and belly of the factor's horse. He saw them point rifles at Colonel

Shaw and drive him back when he tried to interfere. But nothing he saw was as alarming as what he heard: the hoarse, snarling yell of the mob. It was terrifying. Something had changed which could not be changed back again. Some wolfish thing had broken loose in the world. In that deep yell the beast declared its freedom, and its hatred for civilized things which had kept it a prisoner.

The Pikes had cowed every one who tried to interfere with them, but their hatred was for the Hudson's Bay factor. He was still facing them and trying to speak, and they were threatening him and shouting him down. "Get out, you British bastard!" "Get out, you old son-of-a-bitch!" "Get off our parade ground or we'll shoot you off!"

The only one who was not cowed was Captain Nixon. He stood by, with his frock coat unbuttoned and his thumbs hooked in his belt, and now and then he called reprovingly, "Boys, boys!" as if they were spoiled children of whom he was rather proud. Elmer hated him, but there wasn't much else he could do.

The doctor and the French Canadian with the damaged arm were howled and stoned off the parade ground. The sheriff went with them.

When they were gone, Nixon's company marched back, cheering for their victory, with the men in the first squad carrying Joshua Sims. It made Elmer feel sick. He had expected to see Joshua elevated on a gallows, not on the shoulders of his fellow men. Joshua was still pale from fright, but he was showing his yellow teeth through his beard in a smile, and holding his rifle conspicuously, and he looked tremendous and evil against the sky. Captain Nixon was leading the parade, his hard, swollen face shining. He was waving his hat while he shouted hoarsely for the other companies to join in three cheers for Joshua Sims. He and his men were drunk with victory and the tramp of their feet was terrifying to the boy who saw what was on the march in a once orderly world.

CHAPTER TWENTY-FIVE

*I*N THE timber it was terribly still except for the crunching of hooves as they broke the crust of the snow. The men in the squad did not talk much and when they did their voices sounded apologetic. Somewhere Elmer had heard that a man buried in sand to his neck suffocates even though his head is in the open air. That is because each time he breathes out the sand closes tighter about him, and with the next breath he can only expand his chest to where it was contracted before. The silence of the woods was like that, closing in more solidly with each pause. And the thin, crackling whisper of their march was only a yardstick measuring the immensity of the silence. That was partly imagination, of course. On some other occasion they would have matched their voices against the stillness and blazed their way with a trail of sound. But in times like this there was always the chance of an ambush.

Governor Stevens had returned to his capital on the nineteenth of the month. From Camp Montgomery they had heard the thunder of the thirty-eight-gun salute. On that day the little Governor had taken charge of the war and was running it his own way, for better or for worse; and the volunteers were uneasy because of their mission.

The road through the big timber was only partly familiar, with everything muffled in snow. Ahead of their little column there were no foot- or hoofprints. The unbroken track met them with austere virginity. Elmer's mind was troubled by the thought that this world is many different worlds, and different times and seasons make strangers of familiar things. This was the well-known road only in the way of geography. It did not look the same in this deep snow, and travelling over it today had a different meaning. One way and another its past was buried, though some of it was still there.

Once Paul leaned out of his saddle and caught something from the underside of a snow-laden branch. Without saying anything, he held it out for Elmer to see. It was a bleached wisp of wild hay which had been hanging there since summer. The fragment called up the lost world to which it had belonged. A world of summer on the Nisqually Plain, with the sound of the creek and madly singing meadow larks; the clean wheels of the wagon rolling among bluebells which the scythes had missed; the white, twinkling tails of wild herds drifting in the sunshine, and Mount Rainier looking down from the sky like the tremendous white headland of another world. Dusk and the long drive home, with the dead deer and a handful of bluebells so newly cut off from life that they still kept its bloom and sweetness. Bluebells for Lisette who was going to have a baby; wild hay for the oxen at the prospering timber camp, and venison for the crew. The wagon with its spoils of summer lurching through the green twilight of the forest road; a branch snatching a wisp of hay from the load. A damp and bleached gray wisp caught from a snowy branch. The present becomes the past and the future becomes the past, and some of it never was. Dreams dissolve and leave you shivering on the wintry road. None of our crew is dead yet, but when will we log again; when will we cut hay on the Nisqually plain? When will we go on with our own lives?

When they came out into the open, there were caps of snow on the stumps in the timber camp, and the log which had been abandoned at the head of the skids was lopsided with a rounded top of snow. A deep layer covered the barn roof evenly, but on the cabin roof it was thinner; some of the shakes were bare at the fireplace end, and long icicles hung from the eaves. Across the still gray Inlet Elmer saw the snow deep and even on his small clearing and on the roofs of the house and shed; and it was piled three hundred feet into the sky, in diminishing domes, on the layers of branches of the fir forest. The shore looked asleep, or like a picture of an abandoned homestead, and the snowy forest gave it a feeling of overwhelming loneliness.

There was time to see that much, and then the big, wolfish
dogs came rocking and clamoring through the snow from the
direction of the barn. Uncle Jarvis came out, armed with a
shovel in case the dogs were attacking some one he cared about
saving. But when he saw it was a party of volunteers he leaned
the shovel against the side of the barn with the air of saying
it was a false alarm. The volunteers were in no danger while
they remained mounted because the dogs were tolerant of horses
and only snapped at the men's feet.

Uncle Jarvis had put on weight during the winter, and he
and his farm looked peaceful and in good order. He greeted
Adam almost affectionately, but without pretending to approve
of his efforts as a volunteer. Shaking hands, he said gravely,
"I want to speak to you about Mary."

Adam looked puzzled. "She's not sick, I hope?"

"She's getting old," Jarvis said, "and she's not as pretty
as she was some years ago, but I'm used to her, h'm? I wouldn't
want to lose her."

"What does the doctor say about her?" Adam asked.

"She's not sick. I was only putting in a word in case you
came to shoot her, h'm?"

"Shoot her!" Adam was aghast. Then he laughed, uncom-
fortably. "That's a hell of a thing to joke about!"

Uncle Jarvis stood with his coat unbuttoned, pulling at his
galluses. "I didn't know it was a joke. I heard Governor
Stevens address the Legislature the other day, h'm? And he
said every Indian caught on this side of the Sound would be
shot. He didn't mention any exceptions for age or sex."

"Adam said, "Mary's your wife; she's as safe as mine. That's
not what I'm here for."

"I'm not joining any volunteers, if you're recruiting." Jarvis
sounded as if he had said that many times before.

"That's not what I'm here for," Adam said. "We're ordering all settlers to leave their farms. Those are the Governor's
orders, Jarvis, and you're on my list. You have the choice of
going to Olympia or Montgomery Station or Steilacoom. You
are expected to comply in forty-eight hours."

Elmer heard the other men in the squad stir uneasily in their saddles, and he stirred uneasily and felt ashamed and angry, he didn't know at whom. Adam had taken his squad on this mission to make it as friendly as possible, but at best the order sounded bad. None of the settlers had taken the order kindly. Women and children had cried at the thought of going back to the nightmare of overcrowded blockhouses, and men cursed the Governor and said it would be ruin to abandon their farms.

But Uncle Jarvis heard it mildly. "Why should I leave my fa'm, h'm?"

Adam said, "Those are the orders, Jarvis."

"A month ago," Jarvis recalled, "settlers were encouraged to go back to their fa'ms. The troops were to protect them while they kept the country from going to ruin, h'm?"

"That was Mason's plan," Adam said.

"It worked."

"Governor Stevens has taken charge," Adam said. "His orders are for settlers to go to a blockhouse or the fort."

"Don't he give any reason for the order, h'm?"

Adam looked uncomfortable. "His reason is that no one is safe on his farm. Leschi and his savages are roaming the Territory, burning and plundering and murdering men, women and children without mercy."

"Am I supposed to believe that?" Jarvis asked.

Adam said, "That's the reason the Governor gave."

"I understand you." Jarvis stirred his rugged gray beard. "But it's shabby, h'm, when there hasn't been a settler hurt or a house burned south of the Puyallup?" Then he said, "When this trouble started, I cursed Mason for behaving like a fool. But he did his best, and he learned, and Stevens makes him look like a statesman, h'm?"

"I'm not here to criticize the Governor," Adam said.

Jarvis went on, "I'll admit that Mason's idea of protecting the settlements didn't work the way he expected. Leschi was too fast for you, h'm? He broke through on two raids without hurting a settler or a stick of property, and he only risked his life to ask for peace."

Adam said, "I'm not here to discuss that with you. I was sent with an order, and I've delivered it."

"Am I supposed to give you my answer?"

"You can please yourself," Adam said. "I wasn't told to bring one."

Jarvis said, "Leschi's done us a disservice, h'm, asking us to stay on our fa'ms. If he'd warned us to leave, the Governor would make us stay, out of spite."

Adam said sternly, "It ain't the time to talk like that, Jarvis, with a war going on."

Jarvis said, "When there was no war going on I was told it wasn't the time to talk because it might stir up dissatisfaction among the Indians, h'm. Isn't it ever the right time for a man to speak out?"

Adam said, "I didn't think you ever did anything else!"

It was cold and cheerless, sitting on horseback in the snow and listening to words. Some of the men were coughing, and behind him Elmer could hear the dry, monotonous cough which Miller had not been able to get rid of since Camp Misery. Adam seemed to have forgotten that Elmer had a wife at the house and expected to see her. But Uncle Jarvis heard the coughing and said, "You've done your duty, Adam, and we can at least agree on a drink. Bring your men in where it's warm."

Adam hesitated. "We should be moving on." Then he said, "Maybe for just a minute."

They tied their horses to the fence and tramped along the shovelled path to the cabin. It was like being home again, and it wasn't. Everything was familiar, but overcast by strangeness. Elmer had the feeling of acting in some strange, uneasy play which used a well-known place for scenery. The two didn't belong together, and neither seemed quite real. The other men in the squad felt the uneasiness, too. Bob was the only one who said anything on the way to the house. Kicking at a lump of snow, he said, "I wish to hell we could get back to logging!"

Elmer wished that, too. But that time seemed farther away than ever, with their crew scattered and the place itself ordered to be abandoned.

Uncle Jarvis paused with his hand on the latch and said to Adam, "Could you have your men leave their rifles outside?"

His voice wasn't lordly any more, and he looked anxious. "You don't want to scare Mary to death, h'm?"

"Lean them against the wall," Adam said quietly.

They leaned them there, with the butt-plates in the raw snow and the dark and polished old walnut stocks just out of reach of big drops falling from the icicles along the eaves.

Inside there were warmth and firelight, the skins of deer and cougars on the floor and warm brown-and-yellow Indian mats on the wall. There was even the luxury of the shelf of books, and one was lying open on the cougar rug by the fireplace where Lisette had been reading. The room was like a block of the comfortable and secure past which time had forgotten to destroy.

In one way and another, every one in the room was trying to make the past live again. Adam was talking about the battle with the Pikes at Rush's farm while he watched Jarvis pour whiskey from a gallon demijohn. Bill was talking about it, too, as he helped Adam watch the pouring of the whiskey. Bob and Paul were joking with Mary about all the *muck-a-muck* she would have to cook when they came back to the timber camp next summer. And Mary was promising them, with tears in her eyes, they could have whole legs of venison on their plates, and come back for second helpings. The men who were strangers to the house were being company for each other at the fire, and learning again what it was like to be warm. And Harland, the teamster, was explaining the kind of fireplace he was going to build when he moved to his own claim.

Watching the others, Elmer and Lisette sat on a bench by the front window, with their fingers twined tightly together. They too were trying to make the past live again: the past in which they had uninterrupted days and nights together. They could make it live only in their hopes in this uneasy visit after a long separation. It was hard to believe that there had been a golden age in the world, when people had the luxury of working as they pleased, and minding their own business.

Peace seemed farther away than ever, but Elmer found a disturbing kind of comfort in looking at Lisette. She was

thinner than when he had known her first, but she looked well.
Her eyes had got back their dark sparkle; her face was firm
and clear, and the color came into it beautifully when he told
her how pretty she was. When she blushed that way, meeting
his eyes steadily, he felt half crazy with desire. "Lisette," he
whispered, "I'm going to stay here tonight! I don't care what!"

"No," she whispered, *no!* If they made another raid, they'd
kill you. Some of the Nisquallys are still hiding. It isn't safe
for you to be out alone, ever!"

It was part of the nightmare face of the world that he risked
death where people so close to him lived without danger and
without fear. "I suppose they'd try to," he said, "but d'ye think
I'd let that stop me when I could be with you?"

She held his hand so tight that his fingers hurt faintly.

"Don't talk like that!" she whispered. *"Never!* If I begin
worrying about you I won't ever be able to stop! If I think
you aren't being ever so careful——"

"I will be careful," he promised, "always, Lisette!" He was
scared by her intensity, and he was afraid that he had already
loosened some terror in her mind.

"If you can be ever so careful," she said, "if you don't let
anything bad happen, we have all our life waiting for us.

"I'll be ever so careful," he promised, "always!" He felt
reproved, and he did not say anything more about staying.
Uncle Jarvis came over with a cup of whiskey for him. "There
weren't enough glasses to go round," he rumbled. "Drink it
like tea, boy!"

The other volunteers were standing about with half-filled
tumblers in their hands, and they looked strong and purposeful,
with their high boots and tucked-in trousers, the collars of their
red flannel shirts open over their coats, and young beards on
their faces. Adam was holding up his glass, and his older,
brown-bearded face was solemn as he proposed a toast: *"To
Washington Territory!"*

The volunteers responded with a muffled cheer.

Jarvis raised his glass, towering above the captain of volunteers like an untidy giant, with the words of his toast rumbling

out of the gray thicket of his beard: *"To Washington Territory; may she survive every noble effort to save her!"*

The volunteers hesitated, with their glasses in their hands, not being sure that was a proper toast. While they hesitated, Bob raised his glass and proposed, *"To the day when we start the logs rollin' again!"* That was acceptable to his late employer and to his captain, and the squad cheered. They drank and were warmed, and the room became noisy with friendly voices.

Elmer drank his cup of whiskey like water, but he hadn't wanted it, so it did not cheer him. Meeting his eyes, Lisette said with gentle suddenness, "Something has happened, Elmer! What is it?"

He told her about the Governor's new order.

"Will Uncle be driven out by force?" she asked quietly.

"I don't think so," he said. "Not by us, anyway! Adam was only ordered to notify him."

She looked at him, "Elmer, are you going to tell me I have to go back to the blockhouse?"

He sighed. "I made you go there once when you didn't want to go," he said. "I'm not going to order you around any more."

It was the nearest he had come to telling her he had been wrong, and that his insistence had brought nothing but misery and loss. It wasn't much of an apology, but her look of response was wonderful. "You're fine to me, Elmer," she said. "You were right to make me go because you thought it was right." Her voice was soft and broken. "I'd go back there now if you said I should. But I'm glad I don't have to."

"I know," he said.

She went on, "I can do some good here. Mary has taken this trouble so hard, and she's so afraid! She's seen volunteers hunting through the clearing with rifles to kill Nisqually Jim——"

He was aghast. "They did that?"

"They hunted for him," she said. "And it didn't make any difference that Jim wouldn't go with the Indians to fight because he wanted to stay with Uncle. They came here twice after the Governor said every Indian on this side of the Sound was to be treated like an enemy."

"Where is he now, Lisette?"

"On Fox Island," she said. "He wanted to stay, and hide in the woods when he heard any one coming, but Uncle knew they'd kill him. He had some terrible arguments with the volunteers who were looking for Jim. They were some of Nixon's men."

"They would be!"

"It was one of them that murdered the Hudson's Bay Indian, wasn't it?"

"Yes." He saw that she hadn't been told which one.

"He hasn't been punished, has he?"

"No." It was a bitter point with Elmer and with many of the other volunteers. They had expected that Joshua would be tried for murder when the Governor came back, but Joshua was the hero of the Pikes at Camp Montgomery. And Captain Nixon who had led the revolt against the arrest had been promoted to a major.

Lisette said, "Mary is so frightened by what's happening! She's so gentle, Elmer; in some ways she's like a child. When Uncle gets into these terrible arguments she thinks it's her fault; she thinks he's in trouble because of her, because she's an Indian. I have to talk and talk to her. Then after a while she's all right and doesn't worry any more. But I don't know what would happen if I went away. She needs somebody besides Uncle to tell her that she's one of us and that we need her and that she isn't making any trouble."

"You're fine," Elmer said, loving her hand with his. "I know Uncle values what you're doing."

She said, "I'm only doing what I want; I'm lucky. When times are like this you're lucky to have somebody counting on you. At the blockhouse, Dolly was happier than I was because she had somebody to take care of. I'm happy here because somebody needs me, Elmer."

He whispered, "You're finer than ever!" He didn't quite know how to say it, but trouble had changed her. When he knew her first there had been a kind of darkness about her. Something sullen that was afraid of being imposed on. Now it had changed to compassion for others who were imposed on, and she didn't think of herself any more. "You're lovely," he whispered.

She said, "Uncle and Mary are doing so much more for me than I am for them. Uncle's educating me, though he won't admit it. He says he don't believe in education, and hopes I never get to be a lady. But I'm learning to read books, and to understand a little why people do the things they do. It hasn't all been easy, but I wouldn't have missed it for anything. And I can see that trouble profits you more than good times."

Elmer said, "I'm glad you feel that way. Sometimes I've blamed myself for not taking you back in the *Maid*, where you'd have been safe——"

"Safe?" she looked at him. "Didn't Uncle tell you?"

"What?" he asked.

"Uncle had a letter from Captain Wallace a few days ago. The *Maid* was sunk at Buenos Aires."

"*Sunk!* Elmer was aghast. "Captain Wallace was always so careful——"

"It wasn't his fault," Lisette said. "A ship from Peru ran into them in a rainstorm on the Plate River. Two of the Sandwich Islanders were killed by a falling mast, but every one else is safe."

Elmer said, "It must have been a terrible blow to Captain Wallace. He'd never lost a man or a spar."

"Uncle was keeping the letter for you," Lisette said, "but he has troubles of his own."

"I'll ask him for it when I get a chance," Elmer said.

While they talked the volunteers were filing out, and in a minute there was only Elmer left with Lisette, and Adam having a final word with Jarvis. Mary was away rummaging in a cupboard. Adam's guarded voice was saying, "I thought it would be better to tell you privately. Governor Stevens said that every patriotic citizen is compelled to live in a blockhouse to save his life. He said that if anybody stays on his claim without being molested, it is proof that he is a traitor, and he will be dealt with as such."

Uncle Jarvis whistled. "That's laying down the law, h'm? And I can see what he's driving at: he's trying to make a war here out of a skirmish up north. But don't you think he'd do better to bring civil action against Leschi for not attacking settlers who mind their own business?"

Adam said, "It's no joke, by God!"

"He'd even do better to paint up you volunteers like Indians and have you scalp every one who's not in a state of panic, h'm?"

"Don't talk like that," Adam said warningly. "It's safe with me, but it'll get you into trouble one of these times. The Governor's wild against the Indians, and wild against any one who crosses him."

"God's little tyrant, h'm?"

Adam said, "I can't feel the way the Governor does about everything, but he's our Governor, and I've enlisted to see this trouble through."

"I'd call that tyrant thinking," Jarvis said, "making a traitor of every citizen who contradicts him by not getting murdered." He rumpled his thinning hair while his eyes gleamed with interest. "What d'ye suppose twisted his brain? What blight or pest got into the young crown, h'm?"

"I must go," Adam said, "my men are waiting." He was anxious to be on his way back to camp, but he hesitated as if he still hadn't said what he wanted to. "I'm your friend, Jarvis," he said. "I'm warning you to be careful because I don't want to see you in any trouble." He went out with Jarvis following him, rumbling on in his big voice.

"I suppose you have to go, too," Lisette said. She got up, still holding his hand.

"I suppose so." He got up and held her close in his arms, kissing her. "When will I see you again?"

"When it's safe," she said. "Not.any sooner." Then she said, with a sharp intake of her breath, "And not any later!"

It seemed to him that time stood still, conveniently, while he held her, and everything else went away. But it wasn't any use. While he was still holding her, time started on again of its own accord and the cabin came back. He let her go, with a groan. "It's no use," he said.

She said, "Oh, Elmer!" Her face was very dear and torturing.

Then Mary was there, and she was crying while she put a
half-filled flour sack into his hands. *"Tenas muck-a-muck,"* she
said. "You like to eat too much, Elmer." There were dark
tear-spots on her clean red calico dress, and she looked frightened and old and homely with crying, and as dear as his own
mother.

He put his arm around her and patted her shoulder. "Don't
worry, Mary," he said. "Trouble's almost over. I'll be back
soon."

"You be careful," she said. "Don't let the *cultus Siwashes
memaloose* you."

"Wake," he said. "I'll be careful."

Then she was clinging to him and rubbing her forehead
against his shoulder and weeping. "My two people!" she
lamented. *"Nika delate cockshut!* (I am all broken up.) I am
like a *pelton klootchman* in *Illihee Polakley!"* (A crazy woman
in the Land of Darkness.)

CHAPTER TWENTY-SIX

THE GOVERNOR'S order did not bring any settlers to the Montgomery blockhouse, and it looked as if it would be a failure. But Governor Stevens was a determined man. One morning an important-looking young man rode into camp and presented Colonel Shaw with an order. The boy officer called Adam, and the three of them conferred. After that Adam went back to his company, which was drilling, and told the first three squads to fall out and saddle up, and bring their rifles. Elmer's squad was one of them, and it felt good to be on the march again.

They rode north across the prairie, with Adam and the important young man riding together in the lead. And though everything had been done quietly and the expedition organized in a few minutes, word got around that they were going to evict the Muck Creek settlers. "They're English, you know," Bob said, "and they're in league with the Indians."

Elmer thought about that while they were riding toward Muck Creek, and he wasn't so sure about the settlers being in league with the Indians. All he had ever heard against them was that Leschi had visited the settlement on his first raid and told the people there that he wanted to make peace. That had also happened to Uncle Jarvis. And it was not true that the settlers were English.

In a way, Muck Creek was the oldest American settlement in the Territory. It even had the flavor of Revolutionary days. The settlers there had come out from England with the Hudson's Bay Company when the Territory was claimed by the British. They had later broken away from the company and from England to take up claims and become American citizens.

Some of them had come out in 1833, and all of them had been there before there were any white women in the territory. So all the men had Indian wives and half-breed children who were doubly American in a way. Elmer thought it was a pity that they had been picked out to be made examples of. And when the others spoke of them as traitors, it only left him cold and uneasy.

The settlement was about six miles from camp. It was along the creek which cut the prairie a mile to the west of the timber belt. Before reaching the first house, the volunteers had to go through several gates in zigzag fences, and a herd of bleating sheep where the ewes were heavy with lambs. There were good buildings of logs and split cedar, silvering with age, and behind the house there was a bare orchard with moss on some of the big apple trees. In a country so new that you hardly ever saw an apple tree bigger than a sapling, the moss of time was like a miracle. The three squads dismounted in the big, untidy yard, while Adam and the Territorial Secretary went to the house.

While they waited, the volunteers did not talk much. Elmer felt sharply aware of things around him because he was uneasy. Near him there was an apple tree, and by looking at it he could almost tell the age of the place. Not by the size of the tree, but by the things it had collected. Under the tree there was an old grindstone, and leaning against the mossy trunk there was a wheel from a light wagon or carriage, with the spokes wet and black with age. Hanging in the tree there were a broken scythe with the blade rusting away and an old horse-collar that was losing its straw stuffings. And in the top branches there was the broken skeleton of a kite. You could tell by the things growing on the tree that the place had been used for living for a long time. The place had old sounds, too: far away, the old, sad bleating of sheep, and the crowing of roosters, foretelling rain, the voices of children playing somewhere, and the sound of flowing water. Past the end of the house, Elmer could see bare willows along the creek, and a puncheon bridge over it. On the other side there was another carelessly prospering farm, with cattle and sheep in a field, and a parade of gray geese marching through the dooryard of a big split-cedar house, and smoke oozing from a tall smokehouse with green moss on the roof. While he looked, a girl on a white pony came along the far side of the creek at a lope. There was a sound of hollow, racing thunder as they crossed the bridge. It was startlingly loud, and it was over in a second because it was a narrow creek. The rider disappeared and came in sight again around the far side of the house, riding more slowly. She was a young half-breed woman with smoothly sharp features and quick eyes. Her black hair was arranged the way Lisette wore hers, and she was dressed like any settler's daughter, only more comfortably than most. She dismounted in front of the door and threw the bridle reins on the ground. Before going into the house, she said to the white pony, *"You stand there!"*

It was strange to hear an Indian girl speak such precise, clear English. From her Elmer could see a little why the Muck Creek settlers were looked on as suspicious foreigners. He had not seen any one else quite like her in the Territory. And in passing the volunteers who had come to evict her family she ignored them as coldly as if they were enemies.

After a while Adam and the Territorial Secretary came out of the house, with a massive, tired-looking settler. They did not look as if they wanted his company, but he walked beside the Secretary to where a volunteer was holding the horses. He had been silent, but when the young man was about to mount his horse, he said, thickly, "I have been here twenty years. I have been an American citizen as long as there had been American government here. I think one of my sons was the first American child born in the Territory. I have worked a long time to make this a good farm and to increase my herds so there will be something for my children. What would treason profit me? How can any man think I would fight the government I chose to live under?"

"I can't discuss that," the Secretary said. He mounted his horse, awkwardly. "We'll come back later."

Adam said to his men, "Wait here for us." He and the young Secretary rode around the house and across the creek. Elmer could hear the deliberate, hollow thunder of hoofs on the bridge. The settler sighed heavily, as if he were alone or did not care who heard him, and shuffled back to the house.

The volunteers waited a long time for their captain and the Territorial Secretary. They felt uneasy and embarrassed and talked only now and then in an undertone. And for a while they watched the white pony disobeying his mistress's order. He was edging away from the porch in search of grass, moving sideways to keep the trailing reins from under his feet. Moving that way he had the sly look of keeping one eye on the house. They watched him until he got careless and stepped on the bridle reins and got one foot through the loop. When that happened, Bob went and untangled him.

He was leading the pony back when the young woman came out and snapped the reins away from him. *"It was not necessary!"* She swung into the saddle in an angry flash and struck the pony with her braided rawhide quirt. He bounded away, and as the corporal came back, grinning sheepishly, Elmer heard the moment of angry thunder on the bridge. He knew it was a great comfort for the girl to have that sounding-board for temper.

After a while, a squad of children of all ages came through the barnyard, carrying pussywillows. They stood at a little distance, looking at the volunteers and their horses. They had Indian faces and brown Indian hands holding the dark, flowering twigs, but they were dressed in homespun linsey-woolsey, and when Harland spoke to them in Jargon they did not answer. At first none of them said anything. Then one of the smaller boys asked boldly, "Are you soldiers?"

Bob said, "Yes."

"I'm going to be a soldier when I grow up."

Unexpectedly, Bob said, "Ploughing is better."

"I can plough," a twelve-year-old boy said.

"He can't plough so good."

A girl with soft Indian features said hopefully, "I know all the presidents of the United States."

"No!" Bob said.

The boy who wanted to be a soldier said, "I'm going to have a pet lamb."

"It isn't born yet," the oldest girl said.

They would have been interesting children to talk to, but after a minute a young Indian woman came out on the porch and called them into the house.

When the children were gone, there wasn't anything to do but listen to the next squad arguing in uneasy, muffled voices. They waited a long time, and then their captain and the Territorial Secretary came over the bridge, with a hollow rumble, and rode into the untidy yard.

Adam looked quietly cheerful as he said, "Mount up, men! We're going back to camp."

"Governor Stevens will be furious," the Secretary said.

And Adam told him, "We can't help it."

Riding back to camp, the volunteers felt good again. The only thing that bothered them was the presence of the young Secretary. Adam was a good captain who told his men everything, but while the official was there they could not safely ask why it had been decided not to evict the Muck Creek settlers.

When Adam was able to tell them, they learned it was a matter of transportation. The settlers had big families and a great deal of furniture and household possessions, and there had been no way to move them. The orders were to make them load what they could in their wagons. But the Governor's Office had overlooked the fact that the Muck Creek settlers had already contributed their teams and wagons to the Volunteer Service.

That was remedied a few days later. Nixon's Volunteers were sent out with wagons, and the settlers and some of their possessions were dumped at Fort Nisqually. The Hudson's Bay Company did not want them, but it was the Governor's comment on citizens he found unworthy. He threw them back in the British lap with such supplies as they were judged to need for their families. The rest of their provisions and grain and herds were turned over to the Commissary to feed the growing army of volunteers.

CHAPTER TWENTY-SEVEN

EARLY in March Elmer wrote to his mother. He did not owe her a letter, but he had news to report. He wrote:

"Seattle was attackt by indians on the 26th last. The attack was hapily beaten off by a Volunteer Company and Marines from the U. S. sloop of war *Decatur*. The *Decatur* also was in action, shelling the indians in the woods behind the town from which they were attacking, and a cabin near the beach where some of the indians were eating the breakfast which the cookers had left to go to the block house. Some of the indians were from the River Country where they have been defying us so long. They riskt their lives plundering all the houses in town of food which they ate and carried away. They are said to be starving. The Citizens were warned by friendly indians and got to the block houses before the attack broke. The two block houses are inside a stockade and part of the same fortification. They have two stories, the upper one for women and children.

"The attack was quite severe, and two whites were killed. One was a young man who opened a window to get a better view of the attack. The other was also a young man who opened the stockade gate to get a better view.

"There are different acounts of how many indians attackt. Some say two thousand, some one hundred. Gov. Stevens was there before the attack. Usually he tells people there are Murderous and Bloodthirsty indians all around them and makes everything seem much more dangerous than it is. But when the people told him they were to be

attackt and asked for more troops to defend them, he said
they would not be attackt and there were no indians near.
While he was there the Volunteer Company was disbanded,
whether by his order I did not hear. But he went on board
the *Decatur* and told Capt. Gansevoort to depart immediately for Steilacoom because Seattle would not be attackt
and he was wasting his time there.

"Capt. Gansevoort would not leave and the Gov. went
away in high dungeon. Next day the guns of the ship saved
the city. Also the disbanded Volunteers who were still
in town and took up their arms again. A few days later
Gov. Stevens came back. When they told him of the attack
by the indians he was very angry and said there had been
no attack. He had said, by G-d, the town would not be
attackt and, by G-d, it had *not* been attackt! He is very
positive and will not let anyone contradict him.

"The Gov. was here two days ago and reviewed the
Companies in camp. He is quite small, at least a head
shorter than I am, and very swarthy with black hair and
beard and a firey way of speaking. He made a speech and
warned us against any talk of a peace treaty with the
indians. He would oppose any treaty with them because
nothing but death is mete punishment for their perfidy.
He asked us to pledge ourselves to carry on the war until
the last hostile indian is exterminated. When he finished
the cheers were deafening. I do not agree with his severe
attitude, and neither do many of the others, but he speaks
with great earnestness and in a way that draws men to
him.

"Last time I told you about Leschi capturing Fox Island
and inviting the indian Agent Swan to the stronghold in
the River Country. Col. Casey who is now in charge of
the Fort sent Mr. Swan to visit the hostiles when the Gov.
would not. He was there a week and reported the hostiles
very anxious for peace. They have suffered a great deal
living all winter in the swamps with their women and
children and had very little food for themselves or their
ponies and seemed low on amunition.

"Our Company is starting north this week. In some ways it will be a relief. We are very tired of drilling and going around telling settlers they must leave their farms when we would rather be back on our own. So far only the settlers living on Muck Creek have been removed by force and some of them have gone back. . . ."

Elmer's mother was getting very special news. The information about the Muck Creek settlers had not yet been reported; at least not by Elmer's squad. Scouting, they had seen smoke from a chimney which should have been cold and had gone to investigate, riding through fields that were empty except for manure left by confiscated flocks.

Near the barn they had found seven of the banished ploughing for a garden. A half-breed boy of ten was holding the handles of the plough. Shackled to the end of the beam was a rope knotted around bars of wood, and straining against the bars, pulling the plough, were six half-breed boys and girls. The plough was moving very slowly, and when they crawled, panting, past the halted squad, the children looked straight ahead. Their Indian eyes were sullen, but not like the eyes of slaves. They looked unconquerable. And the earth itself, the light gravelly earth of the prairie, rose and bowed down to them as the ploughshare crept on.

The squad watched them plough two short furrows, then Bob cleared his throat and said, "Well, let's get back to camp." He turned in his saddle with one hand on his hip, and looked at the squad, with his lower jaw pushed forward and his eyes challenging. "We haven't seen anything, have we?"

They said "No." And Harland said, "Hell no, we ain't seen anything!"

Bob said, "We didn't enlist to fight kids. We didn't enlist to drive people off their claims."

One way and another, Stark's Volunteers were glad to go up north where there were Indians to fight.

When they got there the war had gone ahead and everything was changed. At the crossing of the Puyallup, where the volunteers used to catch salmon, there was a big new blockhouse.

The blockhouse was garrisoned by regular troops whose blue uniforms had the scarlet trimming of artillerymen. The lieutenant in charge cautioned Adam about which Indians his men shot at, because there were two parties of friendly Indians being used against the hostiles. There were Chehalis Indians under Captain Ford, and Snoqualmies under Chief Pat Kanim, and they looked very much like the enemy. In fact, there were a few Snoqualmies with the hostiles.

The war was getting professional and complicated, and Adam was at something of a loss. "How are we going to be sure? We don't want to make any mistakes either way."

The lieutenant smiled in sympathy. "You'll get to recognize them," he said. "It's a safe bet that any Indians you see that don't shoot at you are friendly. The ones that shoot at you and you don't see are hostiles."

They crossed Vaughn's Prairie, in sight of Van Ogle's ruined cabin, and took the fearful road through the swamp where the brown domes of skunk cabbage were piercing the mud. In the way of geography, the war was about where it had started half a year before. But in other ways everything was different.

When they came out of the big timber and the swamp, they did not recognize Camp Misery. Instead of bark shelters, lashed by sleet, there were a big blockhouse and a log store house and army tents. And there was rare March sunshine on the prairie. For once the weather was not fighting on the side of the Indians, and the prairie was a busy, confident place, with soldiers and volunteers cutting wood and carrying water and looking after horses. Beside the blockhouse, soldiers were fencing a piece of the prairie for a garden, and others were already turning over the black earth with spades. There was something quietly triumphal in that. Adam and his volunteers stopped to watch, a little enviously. And Adam got some comfort by criticizing the work. He said to a soldier who was looking on, "Kind of early to dig such heavy soil. A week later would be soon enough."

The soldier to whom Adam spoke was a solid man, dressed in a flannel shirt and trousers tucked into high, spurred boots. The trousers were light blue with an orange stripe down the side. It was a combination Elmer had not seen before, so he did not know what service or rank it indicated.

"You're probably right," the soldier said to Adam. "But how are you going to stop men from digging in the soil when they get the feeling in the spring? I'm not God; I'm only a colonel."

"You?" Adam stammered, "You're Colonel Casey?"

"I am that," the soldier said cheerfully.

Adam drew himself up and saluted stiffly. "Captain Stark, with his mounted volunteers, reporting for duty!"

Colonel Casey shook hands with Adam, and then he sat on the unfinished fence and lit his pipe. He had a cheerful red face, smooth-shaven except for his big moustache, and friendly eyes, but he did not seem overjoyed by the arrival of Adam's company. "Who sent you?" he asked.

The captain of volunteers looked hurt. "Colonel Shaw," he said.

"Jesus," the colonel said. "I don't know what to do with you!"

Adam had come up with fine hopes of going into action, and now he looked terribly dashed. "But, Colonel," he stammered, "I understood——"

"Man, I'm not blaming you!" the colonel said kindly. "I keep sending dispatches to the Governor's Office that we don't need the services of any volunteers, and they keep sending us more."

"You don't need volunteers?" Adam looked bewildered. "But why——?"

"Because," the colonel said, "there are not enough Indians to go round. Look," he said, "west of the mountains, here, we have a thousand regular troops in the field. The Governor's called up a thousand volunteers, and most of them are on this side. And how many Indians do you think we have to fight?"

Adam said, "I've heard all the way from a thousand to two thousand, though I doubt if there are that many."

"Not a tenth that many," Colonel Casey told him. "I sent Agent Swan to talk peace with them. He was in their camp a week, and he figured two hundred at the most, not counting women and children. That means that for a thousand soldiers and a thousand volunteers we have two hundred hostiles. If you can call them hostiles: starving men burdened with their families."

Adam blinked and swallowed. "I heard there were anywhere from three to seven hundred Klickitats alone!"

Sitting on the fence, smoking, with soldiers behind him spading the garden, Colonel Casey said, "Swan counted nineteen Klickitats. Leschi told him there had been forty at the beginning. A few were casualties, and others went home. I've had the same figures from some of the Duwamishes who dropped out after the attack on Seattle fizzled."

Adam protested, "There were hundreds of Klickitats on this side during the summer, before the trouble started——"

"I believe that," the colonel said. "But the war started on their side of the mountains first. And they went home, naturally."

Adam was floundering like a man who had just discovered that his life work does not exist. "But, Colonel Casey, isn't there anything—? Can't you suggest——?"

The colonel took his pipe out of his big moustache, and said, "Actually, Captain, I have no authority to command volunteers. If I did, I'd have an order for you."

"What would it be, Colonel?"

"It would be, 'Go home and look after your own farms, and leave those poor devils in the swamp to the Army that's paid to look after such things!"

Adam was silent for a long time, then he said, "But we couldn't do that if we wanted to; we were sworn in for six months."

The colonel on the garden fence said, "Quite so. I can't give you any orders that would help in any way." He looked genuinely regretful.

Adam said, "I don't know what to do."

"Look!" Bill whispered, nudging Elmer. A band of forty or fifty Indians was marching on the blockhouse. Stocky blanketed Indians with eagle feathers in their hair, and some of them with painted faces, carrying their rifles any way. Undoubtedly they were friendly Indians coming in from battle with the hostiles, but Elmer felt more comfortable when they stopped short of the building and sat on the ground to smoke while their leader went in with a quick, hobbling gait.

"I didn't ask for them, either," the colonel said, indicating the Indians with his pipe.

Adam asked, "Who are they?"

"Snoqualmies," the colonel said. "The one who just went into the blockhouse is Pat Kanim." He spat, eloquently. "Know anything about him?"

"Nothing good," Adam said. "Years back he attacked Fort Nisqually. And before this trouble he was the only chief who ever threatened any of our settlements. I'd have expected him to be with the hostiles."

The colonel said, "He's a friendly Indian now, because the butter's on that side, but I'd feel more decent fighting him."

Chief Pat Kanim came out of the blockhouse with a young civilian, and they walked toward the colonel on the fence. The civilian interpreter walked, and the chief moved beside him with his strange hobbling, flitting gait. To Elmer he looked more like a woman than a man: a witch-woman flitting through woods at twilight, whispering evilly. His unbraided hair was gray, and he was wrapped in a dirty gray blanket. He was stooped, holding something under his blanket with one hand and using his long rifle in the other hand for a staff. But he did not give the impression of feebleness. In every move he made there was the suggestion of something evil and nimble and flitting. Talking to his companion in the throaty Snoqualmie language, his voice had a hoarse, whispering sound like the distant cawing of crows. He looked and sounded like an evil old woman, touched in the head. And he had the reputation of being the tyrant of his powerful tribe and the terror of his many slaves.

The young interpreter stopped beside the colonel who was sitting on the fence. "Colonel Casey, Pat Kanim has brought in a head and is trying to collect for it."

"I have nothing to do with that business!" the colonel said harshly.

"I told him, sir, but he insisted——"

"Tell him again," the colonel said, "from me!"

Pat Kanim flitted forward, saying *"Chickamun, chickamun!"* in a dry, whispering voice. He brought something from under his dirty and bloodied blanket and held it up before the colonel, by its graying, braided hair. It was a human head, with the eyes glazed and the jaw dropped so the mouth was open as if it were screaming. The head had been roughly severed, with part of the neck, and a little of the hacked windpipe showed when the chief held it up, asking for *chickamun*.

Adam and the volunteers near him shrank back from the trophy, while the colonel smoked and looked at it with distaste. "Tell him to take it way," he said to the interpreter. "It stinks."

The interpreter translated into Snoqualmie, but the chief kept up his wheedling croaking for *chickamun*. Dried blood was spattered on his dirty blanket, and it was caked on the stringy arms that held up the severed head.

Sitting on the fence, the colonel took the pipe from his mouth, and spat. "What's the matter?" he asked the interpreter. "Can't you make him understand?"

"He says it's a special head, worth ready money," the young man reported. "It is the head of his brother."

The colonel spat again. "Tell him to take it out of here. Tell him to take it to Simmons or Captain Ford, or to the Governor. I have nothing to do with that business. And get him out of here!" Looking at the chief, with his face suddenly red and angry, he shouted, *"Klatawa!"*

Pat Kanim put the head under his blanket again, and the hopeful, greedy light faded from his eyes. He went away with the interpreter, hobbling and flitting and complaining in his hoarse cawing voice.

"You see what I have to put up with," the colonel said.

Adam was staring after the chief, with uneasy fascinations. "What did he mean about it being the head of his brother?"

"Just that, I suppose," the colonel said. "His brother was with the hostiles."

"But, his own brother——"

The colonel said, "It's worth twenty-five dollars to him, when he collects." Then he went back to his own grievance. "How can I run this war decently? We're opposing men who fight decently and don't do more than take scalps. And the Governor sends in friendly Indians with orders to hack off heads; if they don't do it, they don't get paid. I can't run a war decently when men are encouraged to cut off their brothers' heads."

Adam said earnestly, "We're here to fight decently. We came up here in good faith. Now I don't know what to do."

The colonel stroked his big moustache. "You can camp here, if you like, though I haven't any shelter to offer you; not with six hundred men on this prairie. And if you need rations, I'm authorized to issue them to volunteers until the end of the month, not after that. If you want to look around and find yourself some Indians to fight, I can't prevent you."

"Thank you, sir." Adam looked a little more hopeful. "We came up here to fight. I'm not asking for any orders you can't give. But, Colonel, couldn't you kind of give me a suggestion of something that won't interfere with your men? I don't want to bungle in and maybe upset your plans."

Colonel Casey smiled and took the pipe from his mouth, and smiled still more. His blue eyes had a good twinkle in his red face. "Jesus," he said. "I'll have to think of something!" He got down from the fence, booted and spurred, like a man getting down from his high horse. "Have you ever been over the Military Road toward the Pass?" he asked.

Adam said proudly, "I was over there in the fall of 'fifty-three, going to the relief of emigrants."

"Good," the colonel said, "I'm going to suggest something up that way. And if all of you get killed, remember it wasn't an order."

"I'll remember," Adam said.

"More like you won't see anything but scenery," Colonel Casey said. "But there's just a chance it may give you the fight of your lives."

"Thank you, sir."

"It's like this," the colonel explained. "The war is over in the swamps, with all the parties we've sent in, and the Indians starving and low on ammunition. The thing is finished and it's just a matter of their admitting it. It was finished a month ago, except that the best peace offer they could get was hanging. But now it's over for fair because they can't go on. Any day now, they're going to give up or make a break. If it's a break, they have a choice of trying to get south where they can raid settlements for food. We're on the look-out for that. Or they can try to get east over the mountains. They can't do that, either, because the snow is still twenty feet deep in the pass, and with this warm weather, a horse or a man without snowshoes would go in up to his ears. They can't do it, but unless they surrender they have to try one thing or another that can't be done."

"You suggest that we cut off their retreat," Adam said.

"Quite so." The colonel looked pleased. "Not that they're going to retreat that way. Now, if you'll come into the blockhouse where we can look at the map——"

When the two had gone inside, the volunteers leaned on the fence and watched the soldier dig, and talked in troubled voices.

Paul said, "It's not fair that they can garden while they fight Indians, and we can't do either."

"If that colonel had his way," Bill said, "we'd be home on our own farms, and the soldiers would be looking after the Indians, like they're paid for. D'ye hear him say that?"

"I heard him," Harland said, "and I'm still thinking about it."

Bob had taken out his knife and was carving an initial, thoughtfully, on a rail of the new fence. "It's funny, the colonel telling Adam all that where we could hear." He glanced toward the blockhouse, and back to his carving. "He could have taken him there in the first place."

Elmer thought so too, but he was glad it had happened that way.

"It's not funny," Miller said with his voice going up a little. "It was because he wanted us to hear! He wanted us to know we're fools! All the time we were putting other people off their farms—" He was taken by a fit of coughing and could not go on.

The others looked at him in surprise or reproof. They saw his face pale and sweating and his eyes bulging while he coughed, and they looked away again, unhappily.

Paul put his hand on Elmer's arm. "Our six months will be up in April, Elmer. That's next month!" He spoke quietly, but his voice had the excitement of some shoot coming up in the spring. "I'm not going to enlist again, are you?"

Elmer had never really thought about that, because he had always been sure the war would be over before the end of the six months. But now he knew that whatever happened it would be over for him in another month. The knowledge filled him with a sober joy that went on and on. Out of habit, he said to Paul, "It'll be over before then, anyway."

"But if it isn't?" Paul insisted.

Elmer looked at his friend's earnest face, with its young, sprouting beard and gentian-blue eyes, shaded by a wide felt hat. "It'll be over before then, but even if it's not, I'm finished; I'm going home."

Bob said, "You boys are crazy; you shouldn't talk like that." Then he said, "If you're through, so am I. That ground smells nice, don't it?"

They leaned on the fence and sniffed the fine smell of the newly spaded earth. In his mind Elmer saw the unconquerable faces of the Muck Creek children who had harnessed themselves to the plough; he saw the prairie earth rising slowly and bowing down to them as the ploughshare crept on. And he saw the stumpy clearing which he and Lisette would be cultivating in another month.

CHAPTER TWENTY-EIGHT

*T*HE VOLUNTEERS spent two days and nights guarding the Military Road. The days were fine, but the two nights were enough for men who had been warned that they were on a wild-goose chase. The weather was kinder than they could have expected of March, and not every two days in June would have been as fair. But March was not the month for sleeping in the open, and the second night there was a heavy frost.

Camp was back in a burn, among a jumble of big fallen trees, where there was more than enough firewood for anything except to keep men warm in the open on a frosty night. The sentry post was at the edge of the bluff overlooking the White River. The place was strategic. From there you could look down into the valley of the river, eight hundred feet below. And you could look two miles downstream, where the Military Road went through the timber on the far side of the narrow valley. A quarter of a mile or so downstream, you could see where the crossing was, and above that, on the near side of the river, the road began its climb up along the side of the bluff from which it was notched. The road came up onto the bluff at the point where the sentries watched.

Paul and Elmer were on guard from midnight till four, and they had been there about an hour. They wore their blankets about them like Indians, and their breath was like white smoke in the moonlight. They yawned and shook their heads and walked about to keep awake. Elmer said, above the cold, plunging roar of the river below them, "Might as well crawl into the nest, Paul. Get a little sleep, and I'll call you in an hour or so." The nest was a place at the edge of the thick brush. It was sheltered on one side by a log, and there were fir boughs to lie on. There one sentry could roll up in his blanket and saddle blanket and get a little comfort while his companion watched the road.

"I'm not as sleepy as I was," Paul said. He stepped close to the edge of the bluff and leaned on his rifle, looking down into the river valley. "I think I'll always remember this night and this river. It seems to me if I looked long enough I could understand it a little."

Elmer stood beside him and looked. In the bottom of the narrow valley, eight hundred feet below them, the white water of the river raged in the cold moonlight. On each side there were gray-white boulders and blanched white logs, tangled with driftwood, and fir trees two hundred and three hundred feet tall, with moonlit tops and impenetrable black shadows. On the far side of the river, the wall of forest on the bluff deepened the valley to a thousand feet. And that deep canyon was filled with the cold, plunging roar of white water. Looking upstream, you saw the river raging, white, out of the blackness of the canyon, and looking downstream you saw it going away, tearing and foaming in the moonlight among white boulders and blanched white logs. Below the crossing there was one open space that looked peaceful and grassy between the white water and the blackness of fir trees. It looked like a park or garden, but one could not have any feeling of peace looking at it. The roar of the river filled the world with fierce insistence, and it filled the ears and emptied the heart of everything except cold and loneliness.

Paul's voice said, "It ought to be beautiful, but something's missing."

"It's because we're cold." Elmer drew his blanket closer about his shoulders, and stamped on the frosty ground. "You've got to be comfortable to enjoy scenery. Your mind has to be right."

Paul said, "It only makes me feel dead and gone."

"It's because you're cold," Elmer repeated. But he had the feeling of being in some lonely place outside the world where men were never intended to be. Like being lost on the moon. And far away, in another world, were the peaceful Inlet and

Uncle Jarvis and Mary in their cabin. There were Lisette and his own cabin, and the warm fireplace and the good bed. But that secure and friendly world seemed far away, and at moments like this he despaired of finding his way back.

While they watched the cold roaring scene and tried to make something of it, they heard a whistle close behind them, and turned with a start. Bob was there with a can which smelled of coffee, and something heavy slung in withes. "It's cold as hell," he said, "and going to be colder. I thought you might want something to warm you up. Take the coffee, while I put this in the nest."

"What is it?" Elmer asked.

Paul said, "It's a stone!"

"Right," Bob dropped it on the fir boughs with a thud. "But when you put your feet on it you'll think it's a damn good one!" In the gloom of the thicket, he covered it with more boughs. "It burned a hole in the bottom of the sack, and then in each side. Had to use willows on it. It ought to keep your feet warm till morning."

Elmer said into the coffee can from which he was drinking, "Your family'll be in luck, when you have one!"

Bob walked to the edge of the bluff and looked down into the roaring valley. "What a God-forsaken place!"

They admitted it was, but it did not seem as lonely with him there, and with hot coffee inside them.

Looking down the valley, Bob said, "There's only one good thing about the place: that river's so damn white that a pony fording it would show up like a black cow on snow."

Bob did not stay long, but when he went away through the frosty brush, some of his cheer remained. The post did not seem so desolate any more, or as remote from the secure and friendly world where the sentries longed to be. The corporal had given them a little of that world, out of his ingenuity and devotion. Elmer felt very sleepy and cold-footed, and he yawned a frosty cloud of breath. "You turn in, Paul. "We're not going to let that hot rock go to waste."

"You turn in. I'll watch a while."

"No, you first."

"You're falling asleep on your feet," Paul said, "and I'm good for another hour. Coffee keeps me awake."

Elmer yawned, "Nothing keeps me awake!"

"Turn in then. I'll call you if I see any Indians fording the river."

"That's right," Elmer said. "Call me, and I'll help you count them." He crawled into the nest and sat with his back against the log and his feet close to the hot stone which he covered with the edge of his blanket. At first the warmth did not go through his boots to his feet, but he could feel it coming up under the blanket, and there was a nice smell of hot evergreens, though there was frost on the boughs beside him.

Standing in the moonlight, with his breath like white smoke, Paul asked, "How is the stove, Elmer?"

"It feels good," Elmer said, "and it smells like Christmas. You ought to try it."

"I will after a while," Paul said.

"I don't know how long the stone'll keep hot," Elmer told him.

"Maybe I'll try it for a minute," Paul said.

Through the branches, Elmer saw him go to the edge of the bluff and stand there, looking down the river. He dozed and half woke and shifted one foot from the comforting stone as Paul settled down beside him. His mind thought weakly that he should not sit down in a comfortable place when he was on sentry duty. But the expedition was a wild-goose chase. Sometime they had to begin not doing unnecessary things——

He dreamed of cold, and horses fording white water. And he woke, cramped and cold, with Paul asleep beside him and the hollow plunging roar of the river going on unceasingly. Then his skin chilled and shrunk and his hair bristled.

Looking past the sleeping boy beside him, he saw a horseman crossing the moonlit strip at the edge of the bluff, not fifty feet away. The man was muffled in a blanket, like himself, and a wide felt hat concealed his face with shadow, and he carried a rifle, like any volunteer or settler. But Elmer knew he was an Indian by the way he rode, leaning forward a little, with his back in a straight, slanting line. And he was riding bareback on a horse so gaunt that Elmer was not sure whether it was real or something in a nightmare. It walked with a tottering lightness and its unshod hooves made no sound that he could hear above the hollow tumult of the river. Rider and horse disappeared toward the east, out of the boy's narrow range of vision.

Elmer took his rifle from where it was leaning against the log and laid it beside him while he shook his companion gently by the shoulder. *"Paul,"* he whispered, *"Paul!"*

Paul straightened himself with a jerk. "What is it?" he asked.

"An Indian! He went along the road, east."

"I slept!" Paul whispered. "I didn't mean to!"

"Sh-h-!" Elmer had heard the soft click of an unshod hoof against a pebble. Then the head and shoulders of an Indian and the head and gaunt neck of a pony appeared in the moonlight; the pony with his head raised, struggling weakly up the last of the incline from the river-bed. They came out into full view; an Indian wrapped in a ragged blanket, riding a starved gray pony; a horrible scarecrow of a horse with hipbones and ribs bristling under its shrunken skin. The pony's legs moved with spectral uncertainty, as if it did not know whether it was walking on the earth, or something dead in a dream. Elmer had a glimpse of the rider's face, and it was starved and fleshless as the tottering pony. They disappeared from his range of vision, toward the east.

"Did you *see*!" Paul whispered.

"Sh-h-!" Another pony scrambled up the incline, almost agilely, but it too was only a walking skeleton, and the swinging of its legs was like a dance of death. And in the moment of moonlight, the rider's skull showed through his tight-skinned face. They passed and disappeared toward the east.

"They're starving!" Paul whispered.

"Yes." For the last half of the winter people had been saying, with satisfaction, that the Indians were starving in the swamps. But starvation is only a word, until you see it.

"There's another coming," Paul whispered.

There were many more coming. A light mist was beginning to rise out of the canyon in the moonlight. As it drifted up, and the cold, plunging cry of the river went on and on, horseman after horseman came up out of the valley and passed like stalking specters; like an army of the damned coming up out of hell for a last parade.

"Listen!" Paul whispered.

There wasn't anything but the soft click of unshod hooves on pebbles as the next pony came up the incline. Then there was the thin wail of a baby. The next rider was a woman, with a light-colored blanket up over her head, like a shawl, and wrapped around something in front of her on the tottering scarecrow pony. Elmer heard her murmuring soothingly. As she passed to the east, toward the mountains, he heard the muffled wail of the baby. It affected him strangely and swiftly; it and the unearthly parade and the thin mist rising in the moonlight, and the hollow, plunging roar of the river going on forever. He was outside this world, in the night world of the Nisquallys, where the *ancuttie men* come back, and the living and the dead and the past and the present meet on equal terms. That was the wail of his own son, whom he had never seen; the little one who was lost in the shuffle of war. He was in this flight from the war that had killed him, and Elmer heard his passing voice as the Indians took him up to the mountains. . . .

It was a flash of old, impossible superstition. It passed almost in a moment, and with Paul gripping his hand he watched the march of wasted men on skeleton horses. Men muffled in tattered blankets; in pieces of blanket, or in old coats. There were a few more women, one of them big with child, or with a child already born in front of her on the spectral pony and wrapped in her blanket. And there were two small children on one pony, with the one behind embracing the other for warmth. His face was hidden, but the pinched face of the child in front had a goblin look of excitement, as if he knew this was an adventure to remember afterward, if there was any afterward.

More warriors passed, men in tattered blankets, and with no blankets; worn faces and grimly held rifles, and famine's horses stalking past toward the east and disappearing.

The warrior coming up the last of the incline had massive shoulders and head that caught Elmer's attention. He came up on level ground, riding a wasted skeleton of a horse. His massive, homely face was worn and sunken, but his head was raised proudly and he did not look defeated or changed inside.

"*Leschi!*" Paul whispered.

"*Yes.*"

And Leschi passed, on his wasted horror of a horse, with the look of some unconquerable dream burning in his worn face, which was turned toward the mountains.

After the horsemen, a few men on foot straggled past; men with bowed heads, and men with starved, grim faces raised in the moonlight. In wet moccasins and on bare feet on the frosty ground, they passed like phantoms and went away to the east. Then there was nothing but the moonlight and thin mist boiling up from the canyon and the cold, plunging roar of the river going on and on.

Paul was still gripping Elmer's hand. "Did you *see* them!" he whispered.

"I saw them, Paul." He was glad of assurance that he had not dreamed that march of phantoms.

"Those people, and those horses!"

"I saw them."

"Did you hear the baby?"

"I heard him," Elmer said.

"What are we going to do now?"

"Wait. There may be stragglers."

"I fell asleep," Paul whispered. "If I was awake I'd have seen them crossing."

"I'm glad you were asleep!"

"I am too," Paul said. "If we'd roused the company, and attacked them—! Those poor people!"

Elmer said, "They've been trying to make peace for months. I hope they find it on the other side of the mountains."

"The colonel said they could never get through; the snow's too deep in the pass."

"That's so," Elmer said, and he was sorry the heroic march would be for nothing. Then he remembered. "He said they'd bog down. It was warm weather then, and the snow was soft. Tonight it'll freeze like iron!"

"They'll freeze, too."

"I suppose so, but they have their chance."

"You want them to get away, don't you?"

"Of course," Elmer said. He was beginning to remember things. "I want them to get away on the Military Road!"

"I want them to get away, too."

"Leschi helped build the road," Elmer recalled. "He lent his horses for the work, and he did as much as any settler. He deserves something out of it. I hope the road takes his horses safely over the mountains!"

In the morning Stark's Volunteers broke camp and started back to Connell's Prairie. The grain they had brought for their horses was used up, and the country they were in provided nothing but unnourishing brush. And the volunteers had watched the road for two days and nights without seeing an Indian, which was just what they had expected.

On the way back they were surprised to meet a company of volunteers, riding hell-for-leather in pursuit of Indians. They met them on the far side of the river, where the road went through fallen timber in a burn. The volunteers were leaping their horses over smaller logs, notched for the wheels of emigrant wagons, and scrambling up and down logs of increasing and diminishing sizes which made rough wagon slopes over logs as high as a man, and they were ducking their heads for logs which bridged the road, resting on fallen trees which rested on other fallen trees.

Adam was much surprised to hear that the Indians had been defeated by the regulars the day before, and that a large party of them had retreated along the Military Road.

CHAPTER TWENTY-NINE

APRIL was a month of emergency, and the volunteers hunted their way through a country under martial law. The war in the west was over. Leschi was gone, and most of the hostiles had escaped with him over the mountains. The forty or fifty who were left were Quiemuth's men. They had broken out of the river country, to the south, and scattered in search of food and in flight from the volunteers who were hunting them down to kill.

That was an uneasy, frightening month, and sometimes the volunteers were made to feel like hostiles or a plague stalking through the country which they were trying to protect. They saw settlers and their families taking to the woods when they appeared, and sometimes they knocked at unresponsive cabins with barred doors and blanketed windows. When they went away and watched from cover, they saw the families come out, cautiously, and begin their interrupted lives again.

The volunteers were distrusted because of martial law which let them remove settlers from their claims by force. The martial law had started in Thurston County, with the Muck Creek settlers. After they had gone back to their stripped farms, Nixon's Volunteers had removed them a second time, and three of the men were put in close confinement at Fort Steilacoom, charged with treason. The settlers had appealed to the courts, and Governor Stevens had proclaimed martial law in the county. There was no evidence against the prisoners, but the Governor knew they were guilty. And under martial law he did not need to offer any proof. After that, martial law was extended to Pierce County. The reason for that was not clear, Adam thought

384

possibly because Colonel Casey had returned to Fort Steilacoom, declaring the war was over. The Governor believed it
was at its height, and martial law clinched his opinion.

April was the last month of Elmer's enlistment, and he encouraged himself with the thought that April is a short month,
with only thirty days. But April was a long month, with long,
anxious days. And Stark's Volunteers were no longer a real
company. They were like two different-minded companies
mixed together, one believing they had been wasting their time,
and only waiting for the end of the month so they could go
home, and the other convinced that they must go on and save
the Territory. Though politics was carefully avoided, they made
the others feel like fledgling traitors.

In the middle of the month they went back to Camp Montgomery for orders and supplies. They reached camp in a hard
spring rain which had pursued them all day, and the streets
of tents and the blockhouse and stockade were familiar in the
rain, but Elmer felt uneasy.

Paul did too. When they were coming back from the picket
line with their saddles, he said, "Camp don't feel the same, but
I don't see anything changed."

"I was thinking that too," Elmer said. "It's like the air had
changed."

"It's the same old camp," Bob insisted, tramping through
the mud and horse manure and wet straw in the rain. "The same
old camp, with the same Pikes fighting. You've just been away
from it for a while."

But even the voices of Nixon's Volunteers, quarrelling in
their tents, seemed changed. In the past, Elmer thought, the
Pike company had put some limit on its noise. The men had
never considered the ears or sleep of the company across the
street, but at least they had tried not to be heard all over camp.
Now there was no restraint to their racket. They shouted and
cursed each other and quarrelled and suddenly agreed, and
argued fiercely again because they did not take the trouble to
listen to each other. Their voices had the tone of unchallenged
ownership.

"The same old Pikes," Bob said, "drunk again."

But even that was not the same, Elmer thought. It sounded more as if they were drunk on neat authority or success. Maybe that was because their thick-bodied captain was a member of the court-martial board which had life-and-death power over every one within a hundred miles. For all Bob said, the air of camp had changed. Some men had become noisier and more confident, and others were uneasy and subdued.

"The same old camp," Bob said, untying the flaps of their tent. They spread their wet blankets on the dry hay, and settled down in luxury while the corporal brought out the iron pot and the flour sack of charcoal and kindling. "How about a lettle extry heat?" He whittled shavings into the pot and broke kindling across his braced knee. The sound of snapping wood suggested warmth. Then he struck a match on the side of the pot, and in a few seconds more thick, steamy smoke rose from the pot and burned away. Clear flame reflected on his square, devoted young face. Outside, the rain drummed on the thin tent, and inside the fire crackled in the pot as Bob added more kindling, and his face softened into a grim little smile of triumph.

In some ways, it was the same old camp where they had had good days. That was because Bob was part of the best of it, and he had not changed. And the squad had been lucky. All of them were there except Bill, who was no farther away than the blockhouse where he had gone to see Dolly. And all of them were well except Miller, who coughed a great deal. He was the only one Bob hadn't brought safely through the sleet storms at Camp Misery which had crippled a third of the regular troops and dozens of volunteers. Looking back, Elmer remembered the night before the Battle of South Prairie: Miller secretly taking off his shirt, and holding it out in the rain and sleet on the end of a ramrod, and afterward putting it on while it was still wet. That was because of Adam's kindly advice about washing their shirts before going into battle. They didn't know that being wounded is the last thing you worry about in an Indian war.

While the corporal was adding charcoal to the fire in the pot, Bill came in and the squad was all there together. But Bill did not stay. He said to Elmer, "Somebody to see you at the blockhouse."

Getting up, Elmer asked, "Is it Uncle?"

Bill said, "No." And when they were outside in the rain he said, "It's your wife."

Elmer couldn't quite believe it, though Bill never joked about anything. "But she didn't know when I'd be back!"

"She's living here," Bill explained. "She and Dolly are keeping house together."

It was like old times, with a vengeance, and it made the camp and blockhouse come alive to know she was there. But still he didn't understand. It didn't seem like Lisette to leave Jarvis and Mary and come back to a place where she suffered so much. "Has she been here long, Bill?"

Bill said, "I don't just know. I guess they brought her here when they arrested your uncle."

"Arrested him!" He heard his voice in a world that was suddenly hideous and unreal. "For what?"

"I don't know," Bill said. "They don't have to give any reason."

Lisette and Dolly were waiting for them at the door of the stable, with the rain pouring down from the eaves between them and their husbands. Elmer ducked through the cold sheet of water, and then Lisette was warm and dry in his arms, and her mouth was comforting. She looked anxious, but she was fine and well, and she made him feel that everything would be all right. Dolly was waiting beside Lisette, with her sharp, clear face and encouraging eyes. She looked as if she wanted to welcome and comfort him, too. He shook hands with her, and her thin hand was strong and warm. She said, bracingly, "You mustn't feel bad about your uncle. It's an honor these days. They even arrested a judge for holding court!"

"Let's go inside," Lisette said. "We don't have to stay here." They were standing near the open doorway, and there wasn't anything to see but a curtained stall beside them, and the mud and straw in the stockade, beyond a curtain of water falling from the eaves.

Dolly said to her husband, "We'll go for a walk, Bill."

"You're not going out in this rain!" Elmer said.

Lisette said, "Don't be foolish, Dolly."

"You want a chance to talk," Dolly said. Then she decided, "We can go to the cooking shed."

"Some of the home guards are there," Lisette reminded her. "And you want to talk, too."

Bill said helplessly, "There don't seem to be any place to go!"

"You're not going anywhere," Lisette said, "except to where it's comfortable." She led the way past the curtained stalls to her own, which was separated from Dolly's by the old patchwork quilt. "We can sit down here, anyway."

Dolly asked, "Shall Bill and I sit on your bed and listen to you, or shall we listen from the other side of the quilt?"

Lisette said, "You sit here. We need friends, and we all know there ain't any privacy here."

They all sat on Lisette's bed, which had been moved next to Dolly's, so that there was only the frame of the stall and the patchwork quilt between. The place smelled faintly of cattle and horses and wild hay; the rain made a dim, drumming thunder on the roof, and it was twilight in the stall where the four sat like conspirators.

"There's one thing about a war," Dolly said, sitting between Elmer and her husband, "you get to know people. Our families have got kind of mixed up." She almost sounded as if she liked it that way.

Lisette said, "It's the time to make friends, if only you don't have to lose them!"

Elmer was uneasy because they were talking about other things while he was still trying to realize that Uncle Jarvis was in jail. "What happened about Uncle?" he demanded. "Why did they do it?"

Lisette said, "They arrest anybody they please. Josh Sims and some of Nixon's thugs came for him."

"They're the law now," Dolly said.

Elmer had already sensed that.

"Where is Uncle?" he asked.

"He and Mary were taken to the fort." Lisette said. "I

wasn't allowed to go with them; there weren't any charges against me."

"What charge did they have against Uncle?"

"Treason," Lisette said.

"Everybody knows he's innocent," Dolly said.

Elmer's mind struggled with the nightmare which had moved into the world and taken possession. "Treason," he said. "Uncle Jarvis!" It was too monstrous.

Lisette said quietly, "Treason is anything Governor Stevens says it is."

Elmer remembered bitterly. "He said any one who stayed on his farm without the Indians killing him was a traitor!"

Dolly put her hand gently on his arm. "Don't talk too loud. There are people here who think everything the Governor does is necessary because of the emergency."

"What emergency?"

"The war," Dolly explained, "and the Indians murdering all the settlers and burning their houses and everything."

"The war is over," Elmer said, "and there's never been a settler murdered or a house burned within fifty miles of here— or anywhere else in the last six months!"

Bill said, "There's settlers on their farms all the way from here to the Puyallup. Some of them go to blockhouses at night and some don't, but they ain't as much afraid of Indians as they are of volunteers."

Dolly said quietly, "The Governor says there's an emergency, and he has martial law to back him up. You can't contradict him out loud."

"And you can't prove he's wrong," Lisette said. "The settlers on their claims are safe because they're helping the Indians and telling them where the volunteers are."

Elmer said, "It would be funny if it was a joke." But it was not a joke, and he felt sick.

Lisette said, "Uncle Jarvis treated it like a bad joke. When Josh told him he was suspected of communicating with the enemy, Uncle asked if that meant talking to Mary. He said a lot more that I don't remember. In some ways I guess he liked the chance to say what he thought of Nixon's hoodlums. Mary was the one I was sorry for!"

"She must have taken it hard," Elmer said.

Lisette said, "It was like the end of the world for her when they broke into the house and pointed their rifles at Uncle. She thought they were going to shoot him. She tried to get in front of him, and when she understood he was only being arrested, she begged them to take her instead. She offered to kill herself if they would let him go. It was terrible, Elmer, and pitiful!" Lisette drew a deep, shuddering breath.

Then she explained, "Mary couldn't get it out of her head that Uncle was in trouble because of her. Though I don't think that had much to do with it."

"I don't, either," Elmer said. "Without her he'd still have felt the way he did, and said the things he said."

"I'd almost made her believe that," Lisette told him, "and then they arrested the Muck Creek settlers. It wasn't any use after that, because all of them had Indian wives. Mary thought we were only trying to save her feelings—and then this happened!"

Elmer said, "This used to be a civilized world. I didn't know it could move backward."

"I'm sure Josh asked to have charge of the arresting party," Lisette said. "You could see him getting back at Uncle for that time at Rush's farm. I've always been afraid of him, but he's worse since he got to be a kind of hero."

"He got to be a hero cheap," Elmer said, "murdering a Hudson's Bay Indian cutting wood!"

Dolly said, "He killed a Squaxon Indian last week, in Olympia. They're allowed to go there for supplies. Joshua shot him on the porch of Sylvester's store, with women and children around."

"He can't help it," Lisette said, "he has to kill. They should have hung him before. Anyway, men like that shouldn't have power over everybody else."

"That ain't right," Bill agreed.

Elmer felt dull and sick. "And they didn't do anything to him?"

"The sheriff and some citizens followed him here," Dolly said, "but they couldn't do anything to Josh because there's martial law. Nixon arrested him and kept him in a tent until the sheriff's party had gone. Then he let him out and gave him back his rifle, and his men cheered him. Nixon boasted it was quick justice."

Lisette said, "Hush!" They heard familiar and deliberate footsteps, and got up as Adam stopped at their stall, with his hat in his hand. Bill and Dolly slipped away, and Adam said awkwardly, "I heard about Jarvis. I'm sorry it happened."

Elmer said bitterly, "So am I!"

"Won't you sit down?" Lisette said.

But Adam remained standing. "Jarvis is one of my best friends," he said. "I know he wouldn't do anything disloyal."

Lisette said, "We all know that, Captain Stark."

Adam said, "But you know how he was: too outspoken."

"Maybe there weren't enough other people to speak out in time," Lisette said.

"I don't think he'll be tried," Adam said, encouragingly, "there don't seem to be any evidence against him."

Elmer said, "I suppose they'll keep him a prisoner just the same!"

"During the emergency," Adam said. "I suppose so."

Elmer said, "The Governor could keep an innocent man locked up forever by saying it was an emergency!" Then he said, "I'm going to the fort now and see what I can do to help."

"You couldn't see him," Adam said. "He's in close confinement."

"I can try, anyway!"

Adam put a friendly hand on Elmer's arm. "Please don't." His face looked anxious in the dusk of the stable. "It would only make trouble."

"I'll take my chances," Elmer said.

Adam's lowered voice was almost entreating. "It might make trouble for all of us."

"I don't see why."

The captain of volunteers sank his voice still lower. "Colonel

Shaw is angry," he said, "because Leschi and his men got past us, somehow, and escaped."

Elmer said, "Oh!"

"God knows we did our best," Adam went on, "but Shaw thinks we could have been more vigilant. If you disobey orders and call attention to our company—I don't know what."

Thinking it over, Elmer said, "All right, captain, I won't go without permission."

"Thank you, Elmer!" Adam shook his hand warmly. "I knew you would be reasonable."

Elmer said, "I won't make any trouble for the company, but my six months are up on the twenty-ninth. I'm through then, and I'm going home."

"All right, Elmer." Adam looked disappointed, but he said, "I know how you feel. I won't keep you an hour beyond your term of enlistment."

"He's a good captain," Lisette said when they heard Adam's footsteps going away. "He's a good man."

Elmer put his arm around her. "Two more weeks," he said, and then we'll go home. And I'll be free to help Uncle."

She caressed his hand that was around her shoulder. "You'll be ever so careful, won't you, Elmer? If you got wounded now——"

"There won't be any more fighting," he said. "But I'll be careful. I've got you to come home to, and Uncle and Mary to help. I've got too much to live for to take chances."

She put her arms around his neck and kissed him with infinite tenderness and warmth. In the dusk of the stable her lips and her body against him and the dim roar of rain on the roof melted time and place. The same rain was falling on the roof of their cabin, which was only two weeks away, and for a minute he forgot that they weren't there already.

The next day he had a glimpse of how things were going on the home front.

Late in the forenoon, a messenger thundered into camp on a horse dripping with sweat. Ten minutes later, Nixon and his men were on their way to Olympia, riding like devils. At first it seemed that the city must have been attacked by Indians.

But Colonel Shaw explained that something more dangerous had happened. Judge Lander was trying to overthrow the government of the Territory by convening court.

The danger was averted, and that afternoon Major Nixon entered Camp Montgomery in triumph. He waved his hat, calling for cheers, and his hard, red face was alight with triumph. On a horse led between two of his men there was a man in a black robe, with his fair, defiant head bare to the rain. Josh Sims was carrying the court records, baled up with a piece of rope. The Circuit Judge was keeping his dignity, but he looked frail and hurt, and only a few of the volunteers shouted "Traitor!" and "Lynch him!"

Colonel Shaw took charge of the court records and treated the judge with respect, and he made Nixon responsible for his safety.

When Stark's Volunteers rode out of camp in search of Indians, the threats against the judge had died down. He was leading the quiet life of a prisoner in a horse stall in the far end of the blockhouse, and one of his guards was an unpunished murderer.

CHAPTER THIRTY

*I*N THEIR two weeks, Stark's Volunteers saw only one
hostile, and they had only one bullet fired at them. That one
was fired in panic by a starved boy who didn't know they meant
to take him alive.

So Elmer came through the Indian war without a scratch.
Adam had promised he could go, regardless of events, when
his time was up. And he was better than his word. He cut the
time by two days and sent Elmer to escort a wagon that was
going to Scatter Creek. Paul was the other escort, so the boys
finished their service together. Adam had fixed it up nicely so
they had only to report at Camp Montgomery when it was time
to be mustered out.

It was raining in the afternoon when they came out of the
woods onto Grand Mound Prairie, and the place seemed big
and lonesome. But it was spring and the ground was tufted
green with new bunch grass, and purple-dotted with violets;
violets that were numberless, with heart-shaped leaves. They
drifted away through the bunch grass, and where they were
too far away to be distinguished they gave the green prairie a
tinge of purple. Away to the west the prairie ended against
a wall of three-hundred-foot fir trees, gray-green and softly
ragged against the damp gray of the sky. There were signs
of a river or creek along the timber wall and following it, out
on the prairie, there were the cabins and barns of claims. Out
on the plain, on a rise of ground, there was a stockade with
two bastions at diagonal corners. The blockhouse had been
built only the autumn before, but it looked grim and ancient
against the sky, like a walled city on the plain. Looking at it,

Elmer thought of the windy plain of Troy. Only here everything was still and there was not enough wind to sway the
falling April rain.

Riding beside him, Paul said, "You've never been here
before, have you?"

"I was always going to," Elmer said, "ever since that time
at Rush's farm when you and Bob invited me to hunt with
you."

"That seems a long time ago," Paul said.

Elmer said, "It was a long time ago. But something always
interfered. Getting settled, and the timber camp, and then the
war."

"The war finally brought you," Paul said. "We're here
now."

"We're here," Elmer said.

Paul said, "I was thinking— It'll be noisy at home or the
blockhouse, wherever they are. Pa's so deaf you have to shout
and shout. Even then they'll never understand just how it was.
And you know how women are. I was wondering if you would
like to say good-by to Bob here, where it's quiet."

They stopped, and the volunteer teamster stopped the wagon,
and the spare horse behind the wagon stopped. The boys dismounted, and Paul lifted the tarpaulin. "We're here, Bob," he
'said, "the three of us."

Elmer bared his head to the falling rain. "Good-by, Bob. I
won't ever forget; our squad won't ever forget. You brought
us through safe. Because of you we were never hungry. You
found shelter for us in the sleet and snow when there was no
shelter. When things were worst you made life good. Now
you've made death not so bad because we have a share in it.
We're sharing you, Bob, and because we loved you we were
never afraid of places where you went."

While he was speaking, Elmer looked at Bob's face, but
he thought of it the way it had been in life. After he was dead
they had washed him and tied up his jaw and closed his eyes
with Elmer's last two Elaborate slugs of gold. They had done
their best, but even then his face seemed twisted with final
agony. The bullet fired by the cornered Indian boy had hit

him between the stomach and the lungs. He had died of pain, and his squad had to hold him down while he died.

When he reached Camp Montgomery the streets of tents were wet shadows in the darkness and rain. The camp itself was shadowy with outgrown meanings, and Elmer paused only to answer a sentry's challenge. He rode across the parade ground like an unmilitary stranger, and went into the stockade which was for civilians like himself.

Elmer had come to the end of his days as a volunteer and he was tired from a forty-mile ride and soaking wet and sad. But he also felt something new stirring in him on this dark spring night with frogs crying in all the wet places of the world. This night was the beginning of life, and he and Lisette were here to meet it. They were stronger because they had been battered, and they would value life more because it had been taken away from them for a while.

At the stable end of the blockhouse, he lit the lantern which hung inside the door and unsaddled his pony in a vacant stall. The judge and his guard were gone and the stable was peacefully occupied by settlers' horses and a few cows. While Elmer rubbed down its wet red-and-white sides with a handful of hay, the cayuse turned its head and nuzzled his shoulder, remindfully.

"I won't forget you, Spots," Elmer said.

The pony nibbled his ear with soft lips to tell him he had better not forget.

Elmer chuckled and put his arm around the pony's neck. "You monkey," he said. "So you'd eat me if I didn't give you hay!" He went around through the partition door, and Spots whinnied encouragingly at the sound of confiscated hay. Elmer filled the manger and threw some on the floor for bedding, and when he came back to spread it he brought his wet hat full of oats. He left the pony munching, and while he was blowing out the lantern he became conscious of the good sound of rain on the high roof. And when he went out into the dark spring night, the high, teeming chorus of frogs swelled from the direction of the creek. The same-sounding frogs, mad with

spring, would be crying from Scatter Creek, with their unceas-
ing chorus carrying out to the cabin on Mound Prairie, where
Bob had come home in the spring.

Once on the way home Elmer thought he would do a kind
of penance in memory of Bob. He would keep a last vigil in
the squad tent and burn charcoal in the fire-pot, and think
about the devoted lost corporal. But that idea had gone with
daylight, miles from the blockhouse. He had known then that
life does not pause that way. And more than ever, after being
close to death, he needed to be close to life. He needed life as
an antidote for death, and Lisette's compassionate warmth and
tenderness.

He unlatched the door at the far end of the blockhouse and
went in out of the dark and wet. There were the old peaceful
smells of cattle and horses and wild hay, faint as remembered
things, and there was the gentle thunder of rain on the roof,
saying he had come home. The lantern inside the door was
turned low for the night, and some one snored and a child
murmured earnestly in his sleep.

With his eyes accustomed to the dark, he went past dim
curtains, drawn for the night, and came to his own. He reached
inside and found the lantern, and heard some one stir in sleep.
But when he went in, with the light turned low, the stall was
vacant. For a moment he thought he had made a mistake, but
there was Dolly's patchwork quilt, dividing the stall from hers,
and there was Lisette's bed and the tawny Hudson's Bay
blanket with the bear-claw marks of the company and the black
band. The bed was neatly made, and in the other stall there
were the housekeeping things, nicely arranged, but Lisette was
not there.

At first it was a disheartening mystery. Then he decided
she and Dolly were sleeping together for mutual protection.
He could see that was only wise and it was no place for an
undefended woman to sleep alone. But he had not thought of
that on the way to the blockhouse in the dark and rain. Because
he had not thought of it being that way, it made his homecoming less perfect. He had only thought of Lisette welcoming
him in her warm bed, and her living comfort from the desola-

tion of the world. It had turned out less perfect than that, and to find her he would have to wake Dolly whom he did not want to wake or see.

He took off his wet coat and hung it on the partition while deciding how to wake Lisette, or whether to wake her at all. Then some one stirred on the other side of the patchwork quilt, and got up. The door curtain was drawn aside and Dolly stood there with her sharp, clear face softened by sleep and her eyes large-pupiled and blinking in the lantern light, like the eyes of a cat. Blinking and pulling up the top of her nightgown she whispered, "I thought it was Lisette!"

"She's not here!"

"I didn't really expect her," Dolly whispered. "She wasn't going to be back till tomorrow."

He felt empty and lost, and he was suddenly tired from his forty-mile ride, with nothing at the end. It had never once occurred to him that she might be away. "Where did she go?"

Dolly whispered, "I only saw her for a minute when she was leaving. Some relative of hers had died. She was going to the funeral. A messenger came for her with a horse." For one usually so sharp and clear, Dolly was vagueness itself when she was half-asleep.

Lisette didn't have any real relatives. If it was one of the Sims crowd, Elmer hoped it was Joshua. He hoped that anyway. "Where did she go?"

Dolly whispered, "I only saw her for a minute. Said she'd be back tomorrow."

It seemed to him he wasn't asking the right questions, if there were any. He felt dull and lost, and he was embarrassed by the cut of Dolly's nightgown, and by the single braid of reddish hair over one of her thin bare-topped shoulders. The whole braid would hardly have made one strand of Lisette's.

While he was thinking what to ask, Dolly began questioning him. "We weren't expecting you. How are you here?"

He told her about Bob.

"I'm sorry," she whispered, looking more awake. "He was one of the best of your company, wasn't he?"

Elmer said, "He was the best!"

She saw his look, and put her hand on his arm, with thin, steadying comfort. "Oh, Elmer, I am sorry! I didn't really know him, but I thought he was fine."

"He was fine!"

Dolly took her hand away, and asked, "Is Bill all right?"

"Yes, he's all right," Elmer said. "He'll be back tomorrow or the next day, with the company."

"That's good, Elmer." She looked at his unhappy face as if she would like to comfort him in some way. "Let me get you something to eat. There's some coffee left; I can heat it over the lantern while I'm fixing something——"

"No," he whispered. "No, I thank you."

She touched his arm again, with her thin, capable hand. "You're wet through, Elmer! Get into some dry clothes while I heat the coffee."

"No, Dolly; I don't want anything."

She looked at him, biting a corner of her lower lip. "You look so unhappy!" she said.

He did not deny it.

"You're lost because Lisette's not here."

"I suppose I am," he said. "Yes."

"I know you're disappointed," she said, as if it wasn't quite right for him to be. Then she said, "One night in a lifetime! She'll be back tomorrow. You'll take her home to your cabin. You'll have a good life and all the babies you want. And you're disappointed because you have to put it off for one night! You've got nothing to complain about."

Her quiet fierceness made him ashamed. "No," he said, "I haven't." But he still felt dull and lost.

"I wish I could do something for you."

"No, I thank you. I don't want anything."

She said, "I won't keep you up then; get some sleep. You have a comfortable bed, anyway."

"I'll go to the squad tent," he said.

"Don't be a fool," she whispered. "You have a comfortable bed here, even if you do have to sleep alone."

"It wouldn't look right."

"Right?" she whispered fiercely. "Do you think it's right

to make people live in a stable? You're lucky here if you don't
have a horse or cow next you!"

He said, "I think I ought to go."

She looked down, biting the corner of her lower lip. Then
she looked at him and said simply, "I'd feel safer if you stayed.
Usually Lisette and I are together. There's no telling who
might come in here."

He hadn't thought of it that way. "If you'd feel safer," he
said.

"Yes," she said. "Sure I can't heat the coffee for you, or get
you something?"

"I thank you, I don't want anything."

"Then I won't keep you up. Good night."

"Good night," he whispered.

She let the curtain fall, and he was glad to be alone since
he could not be with Lisette. But it was a fragile aloneness,
and while he was stripping off his wet clothes he heard Dolly
stirring restlessly in her bed on the other side of the patchwork
quilt.

He put out the lantern and slipped under the cool blankets
which warmed to the touch of his tired body. Rain drummed
softly on the high roof, and on the other side of the patchwork
curtain Dolly turned and was still. It seemed drowsily strange
to be sleeping so near her. Not right, either. But he was there
to protect a defenseless woman, and his long trip back from
Scatter Creek was being of use to some one.

He slept like the dead, and could not wake though he dreamed
Lisette had come back. The dream was persistent and almost
as strong as sleep. Then he came up a little from the fathomless
depths and found her there, warm in his arms. He was kissing
her with infinite hunger, and her body was responding fiercely
to his. More nearly awake, he was puzzled because Lisette
seeemed smaller, and too thin. And there was a difference in
her passion which was more taking than giving. When he woke
up and understood what had happened it was too late.

He went to the stable early and saddled Spots and led him
outside. It was not raining then, but there was mist close to

the ground, and in the trampled mud wet straws gleamed in the gray light of daybreak. This was the morning at the beginning of his life, but he felt that he had got there too early. He was cold and uneasy, and he did not know where he was going, except to find Lisette. He was not even sure he wanted to find her at once. Mostly he wanted to go away where he could think, and he was also hungry.

While he was riding across the enclosure toward the stockade gate, he heard the blockhouse door open. He looked and saw who it was and looked away quickly as he rode on toward the gate. But Dolly called after him, and when he stopped, uncertainly, he heard her feet hurrying through the mud of the enclosure.

She stopped beside him and said, "Elmer!"

"Well?" he said.

"You're not going away without breakfast."

He looked at her, and she was holding an old shawl at her throat with one hand and touching his stirrup leather with the other. Some one seeing them and not knowing would have thought they were parting lovers. Actually, he hated her, and he spoke roughly. "What the hell difference does it make?"

Dolly said, "You're hungry. You didn't have anything to eat when you got back last night."

He thought it was an affront for her to say anything about last night. He only looked at her sternly and said, "Well?"

She said, "When people are hungry they ought to eat." Her clear, sharp face had a drowsy bloom and softness which troubled him. And while he spoke roughly to her she was pleased and comfortable and triumphing over him quietly.

He asked, "Why did you do it?"

"Because I wanted to," she said.

He glared at her. "My God, and I thought I was protecting a defenseless woman!"

"I was defenseless," she said.

"You?" he said. "Against what?"

"Against nature, I guess. And it's spring."

"Really!"

"Yes," she said, "April's almost over."

He said, "You know I love Lisette."

"You'd be a fool if you didn't. I love her, too. But why should she have all the babies?"

"You know I don't love you!"

"I didn't love you," she said.

He said harshly, "People aren't cattle!"

"Then they shouldn't be made to live in a cattle barn!"

It was true it wouldn't have happened except for people living in a place like that. But he would still have expected them to behave like people.

Holding the stirrup leather, Dolly said, "You've got nothing to complain about. I haven't hurt you. You'll take Lisette home. You'll love each other and have your babies. Everything will be the same for you."

"No," he said. "You've spoiled everything!"

She looked as if she did not believe him. "You hate me, don't you?"

"I've reason enough," he said grimly.

Dolly said, "You've got no reason, if nothing comes of it. If it does," her voice was gentle and secret, "you won't hate me!"

He realized that was the secret of her triumph over him. And he did not hate her now, though he should.

Dolly said, "I'm going to make a fire now. I'm going to start some breakfast."

"Don't let me keep you," he said.

"Maybe you'll come back after you've had a ride."

"I don't ride for amusement!"

She asked gently, "What about Lisette? What'll I tell her if she comes back first?"

"You have a lot of consideration for her, haven't you?"

"Even if I haven't," she said, "you must. You can be as mad at me as you like, but you can't take it out on her!" She looked angry for the first time.

He felt ashamed, and thought and came to a decision. "Tell her I'll be back this afternoon in time to take her home. I'm going to see that everything's all right at the claim. Ask her to have things packed up."

Dolly said, "I'll help her."

"You like to help people, don't you!"

"Yes," she said, "even myself sometimes." She went ahead of him and opened the stockade gate. And when he was riding through, she said, "Good-by, Elmer."

He turned his head sharply and saw the look on her face: life which he could not control gently mocking him and triumphing over hate which he should feel, but could not. "Good-by," he said.

CHAPTER THIRTY-ONE

*H*E RODE at a gallop, taking with him all he was trying to escape: the ruin of his homecoming and the overshadowing fear that life had been mixed up forever. Everything was ruined, but the world had forgotten everything and gone back to the beginning. It was spring for those who could enjoy it; the rain was over and the weather clear. The sun was coming up behind him, and his centaur shadow stretched eagerly ahead, over the wet green prairie, spattered with violets. Death was gone from the prairie and bunch grass was growing up with a richer green through the skeletons of cattle and horses shot down at the beginning of the war. And once he glimpsed violets blooming in a cage of skeleton ribs, with the sun coming in to nurse them in the belly of death.

It was spring, for those who could enjoy it. Elmer could not enjoy it much, with his heart heavy and his belly empty, but he could not ignore what was everywhere. Dolly had reminded him it was spring. Damn the hussy, with her mysterious look of triumph! Flowers growing inside the barren ribs of death; life cheating death. Dolly cheating him, or maybe life cheating death. If he and Dolly should have a baby— But that didn't seem real or possible. They weren't married and didn't love each other, and people weren't cattle. Really it had nothing to do with him because he had not willed it. He hadn't dreamed of such a thing before it happened, and he would have to try not to think about it afterward. . . .

He rode at a walk through the woods, with Spots stepping daintily over logs notched for wheels. And once he reached out and caught something from the prickly grip of a fir bough : a few bleached and sodden straws that called up memories of summer on the Nisqually plain; Paul and Bob, and the lost *Maid* lying in the Inlet; going home to Lisette in the calm bloom of pregnancy. Dolly, damn her— No, Dolly whom he had seen a few times at the blockhouse but never really known. Dolly had said Lisette would have plenty more babies. And there would be other summers. It would be summer in a few more weeks. And summer would forget nothing of her own, even though so much of what he associated with summer was gone.

He came in sight of the Inlet, through the trees, and smelled good salt water. He had been away from salt water too long, and no good had come of it. Smelling it again and seeing the blue sparkling of it through the trees, he felt a wave of strength and well-being. The sick world was better and there had never been even a pretense of trouble here where he should have been all along. The smell of salt water sharpened his hunger and reminded him of the rations in his saddlebags. Getting home to his own claim and the prospect of food reassured him that the world was not ruined. It was in its youth of spring, with a fine appetite.

But he had learned that the world was not as safe as he had once supposed. When he saw a black bear on the other side of the little creek, he did not blaze away at it as he would have done earlier. The bear faced toward him for a moment, then wheeled and crashed away through the brush. As it went, he saw it was as lean as a cougar from hibernation, and he was glad he had not shot at it. While Spots paused to drink from the creek, Elmer admired the scooped black muck where the bear had been grubbing for skunk cabbage. It gave him a good feeling to know that useful business was still going on in the world, and to be close to where it was happening.

When Elmer came to the edge of daylight in his clearing Spots whinnied cheerfully as if he shared his master's pleasure at getting home. Then Elmer saw a bay horse standing in the shed, and smoke rising from the cabin chimney in noncommittal welcome. Letting down the top bars, he said, "Well, Spots, somebody's here," though he did not see any one about. But when he had jumped the pony over the lower bars, Lisette rose from behind a stump in the garden and hurried toward him, with a rifle in her hand.

They met in the middle of the clearing, and Lisette dropped her rifle to throw both arms around his neck. Elmer put his rifle down more gently and let Spots shift for himself, with the bridle reins trailing. Lisette felt infinitely good in his arms, and she was all that was real. In the morning sunlight of their clearing, in each other's arms, it seemed strange that once there had been a dark, unhealthy dream in which she was sharp and thin and greedy for life. She was all that was real, and all comfort and all generous things. He had once wondered how he would meet her, and what he would say. There wasn't any problem like that, because she changed everything, and she changed the hungry nightmare of the world into the beginning of life. And he did not have to say anything because they were kissing each other. Then she was saying between kisses, "You've come home, Elmer! We're home!" As if she could not quite believe it.

"We're home!" he answered in triumph.

Looking at him wonderingly, she asked, "How did you know I was here?"

"I didn't," he said. "I just came here to see that everything was all right for our coming home."

She said, "That's why I came here. When I'd got away from the blockhouse and had a horse to ride, I didn't want it to be wasted. I thought it wasn't any too soon to get started."

Kissing her, he said, "Then we're here because we were both thinking of the same thing!"

She said, "We always think of the same things! We always will, and we'll always be together." She sighed happily. "I'm so happy, Elmer! I was getting so afraid this would never happen. I was afraid something would spoil it."

He said, fiercely, "Nothing can spoil it!"

"Of course it can't," she said, "we're here." Then she said, "Last night, when I was here alone— I was a little afraid, and I kept wishing you would come home to me."

With his lips muffled in her hair, he said, "If I had known,

I'd have been here. I didn't get back to the blockhouse until late, but it wouldn't have been too late to find you."

"If I'd only known I would have been there to meet you."

"Yes," he said.

"I didn't know, Elmer. But I must have known, in a way, when I wanted you so much."

He said, "I wanted you more than everything else in the world!"

She said, "I dreamed about you."

"I, I dreamed about you, Lisette."

She looked at him, with her lips parted, and her eyes like dark stars. "We even have the same dreams!"

"Yes," he said.

"I dreamed that you had come home while I was asleep, and you were there, holding me, you understand?" She met his eyes while she blushed. "Was that wrong of me?"

"No," he said, "no! Because that's the way I wanted it to be."

She looked at him quickly, because of the way he sighed. "You look tired, Elmer."

"No, dear, not really."

"Hungry?" she asked.

"I'm starved," he told her.

"Why didn't you say so?" She was out of his arms and picking up her rifle. "When did you eat last?"

"Some time yesterday afternoon, I think."

"Mercy!" She was in a sudden panic of haste. "You tie your horse while I run and get something started. There's a fire— No, I'll take your rifle! You're not to do anything——"

He laughed at her, giving him orders with a rifle in each hand. And to show that he still had some strength left he picked her up in his arms, rifles and all. "You're not going to run and wait on me. We'll go together if I have to carry you."

"All right," she said. "Put me down, please!" Then she said, "You know I don't want to be away from you, even for a minute. I'd only be away from you to do something for you."

He kissed her and said, "You can do most for me by being with me."

Together they tied the pony in the shed, and Elmer took off the saddle-bags. "I've two days' rations here," he said. "That ought to be enough for breakfast."

"That's good," she said. "There's plenty of some things at the cabin, and none of others. I didn't bring any food with me because I didn't know I was coming here; not until I was on my way."

It was his turn to be concerned. "What did you find to live on?"

She told him, "Potatoes and smoked salmon. You must have noticed that when you kissed me."

"I didn't notice anything, except that you're sweet."

She said, "You love me a lot!" Then she said, "And there was coffee; there's some made. I can heat it for you while I'm fixing something."

"No!" he said.

Lisette looked at him in surprise. She had never known him to refuse coffee of any kind. But he had spoken by instinct, and he could not explain. He was even a little shocked that she and Dolly could speak in identical words. But he could not explain anything like that. So he said, "We're going to have breakfast together, and start out fresh with fresh coffee."

Everything in their house was safe and peaceful, welcoming them: the big berth with lockers under it, and the table and benches; all the things he had made with love. The earth floor was nicely swept, and the cougar and deerskin rugs had been put down, and there were the smouldering remnants of a fire which would blaze again. Here was peace and here peace had been all along, and they had found their way back.

Leaning the rifles against the wall, Lisette said, softly, "God bless our home!"

He took her in his arms and laughed at her because he was happy. "And you carrying two rifles! Were you looking for Indians?"

She told him gravely, "I was afraid I might meet a volunteer."

"You have met one," he said.

"That's so." Then she said, "You haven't explained anything.

How did you get back so early? Did you run away?" She was kneeling at the hearth, building up the fire, and she sounded sweet and capable, as if she would not be surprised at anything.

He said, "I'm here honestly. I was sent back with a wagon." He did not want to tell her about Bob now; not on the morning of their homecoming. Death would have to wait on life for a little while.

She went to the open door and threw out the cold coffee which he had refused, and rinsed the pot with a dipper of water. Outside, the morning had a fresh, misty sparkle in the shafts of sun that were coasting down through the great firs. The rhododendron was starred with magnificent, glossy leaves, long and curled, and robins were making brisk, satisfied comments on worms in the garden. Lisette filled the coffee pot with steaming water from the kettle, and put it on the brightened fire. "Elmer, you don't have to go back, do you?" Her voice was anxious and lovely.

"Not really. I only have to be back at camp the day after tomorrow to be mustered out."

"That's good, dear." Then she said, "We haven't much to cook in; there isn't even a skillet, and there's not so much to cook, either. And there's only one old blanket for the bed."

"I brought one," he reminded her.

She said, "Just about everything except ourselves is at the blockhouse."

"I can go for things after breakfast," he said, though he didn't want to. "We can go."

"That wasn't what I was thinking," she said. "I think it would be nice to·get along with what we have."

"Do you?" he asked gratefully.

She nodded, mixing flour and water in a bowl. "We won't starve, and we can keep each other warm. And we'd be sure of these two days if we didn't have to go anywhere."

He kissed her and said, "That's the way I feel."

"We always feel the same way," she said proudly. "Have you a knife to cut the bacon?" While he was slicing the ration bacon with his clasp-knife, she said, "I don't want to see the blockhouse again. I don't want to see any one there just now. Not even Dolly who was so kind to me."

"No," he said.

Lisette shaped the newly mixed dough into a cake. "We'll have bread if I can think of some way to bake it."

He said, "We can bake it in the ashes, the way the Indians do. It's not as messy as it sounds because you can blow the ashes off after it's done."

When he had put the cake in the ashes and was raking coals over it, she said, "Anybody'd think you had been hunting Indians to find out how they did things!"

Forgetting for a moment, he said, "Bob showed us how."

Lisette said, "I don't see how you could have got along without him."

"I don't either." But he didn't want to tell her just then that even this day together they owed to Bob.

Lisette said, "We can cook the bacon on sticks."

"Or on the shovel."

"So we could, if it was clean. It's like a skillet, isn't it? We could have baked the bread on it, if we'd thought."

He said, "We'll learn to get along with what we have." Then he said, "Only I'm afraid the heat'll take the temper out of it."

She said, decisively, "Then we'll do the bacon on sticks! We'll need the shovel for digging clams."

The water boiled, and she put the coffee in and stirred it with a big splinter, and set it aside. "Some of the things in the garden are almost big enough to use: radishes and lettuce. If we can wait long enough, we won't starve."

He had forgotten that she had planted a garden before she was taken back to the blockhouse. "I'll look at it while I'm out for the sticks," he said.

"I'll go with you," she said, "it's our garden. But you mustn't really take time to look. And with this sun, everything'll be bigger after breakfast."

So they only stood a minute to admire the little rows of tender green among the stumps: lettuce and radishes and carrots and turnips and beans. And Lisette apologized for the spindly look of the carrots and radishes and said that was because she had been weeding and thinning them, but Elmer thought they all looked splendid, and he had not known how rich they were, with a garden growing while it waited for them. Then he cut two willow switches for bacon, and they went back to the cabin.

After breakfast they went to the beach to dig clams, but instead they sat on a log and talked. And Elmer told Lisette about Bob. "I suppose I should have told you when I first saw you," he said. "But you were so happy; it didn't seem the time for it. And when you've been close to death, that way, there's a rebound and you want to get close to life."

"I know." Lisette held his hand with sober comfort. "That's just the way I felt. That's why I couldn't go back to the blockhouse, where everything stands still. I had to come here where things were growing, where I could do something to help our lives go on."

He was suddenly uneasy. "Dolly said you had gone to a funeral. Who was it, Lisette?"

She said, "Mary."

"Mary?" He stared, unbelieving, at the still cabin on the other side of the Inlet. *"Mary?"*

Lisette said, "She was buried at Steilacoom yesterday. They let Uncle Jarvis out of prison for the funeral."

"I didn't know she was sick," he said, trying to believe it. "She was never sick."

"It was very sudden," Lisette said. "Something she ate. The surgeon thought it was a kind of mushroom called the 'Destroying Angel.' She wasn't locked up like Uncle; she could come and go almost as she pleased. And she knew a lot about plants."

"But if she knew—" Elmer said. Then Lisette's words sank home, and he was horrified. "Lisette! You mean she killed herself?"

Lisette was looking past him, at the wet slope of the beach and the blue level of the outgoing tide. "Mary was the only one who knew, and she was dying when they found her. She didn't tell. But Uncle thinks she did it; so do I. You know she had it in her mind that he was in trouble because she was a Nisqually.

She must have thought she could free him that way. You know she'd have done anything for him; she wouldn't have thought that too much."

"No," he said after a while, "Mary wouldn't have thought it too much." Then he said, "I don't suppose it did any good?"

Lisette shook her head.

"Are they going to try Uncle?"

"He wants them to," she said, "but I don't think they will. There's nothing they can try him for. I talked to Colonel Casey, and he was very nice. He said his orders from the Governor were to keep Uncle and the others locked up until the war is over; until Governor Stevens decides it's over."

Elmer said bitterly, "That don't sound very nice of him!"

"Colonel Casey said he didn't have any choice because there isn't any real jail; he has to accept prisoners. But in most ways I guess Uncle has more influence at the fort than the Governor has."

"Do you really think so?" He felt a little hope and pride leavening his heaviness.

She said, "If it hadn't been for Mary, I guess he'd have enjoyed being in prison. And she's at rest now. He told me that when they locked up his body they freed his mind for serious work. He writes nearly all day to people he knows in the government, telling them what's happening out here. He said that maybe by the time the Governor decides to turn his prisoners loose he won't have enough power left to give the order!"

"I hope he won't!"

"Uncle said America's so big that it's easy for a man to set himself up as a little tyrant somewhere. But it's so American that tyrants can't last."

The thought made him feel strong and brave. "We won't let tyrants last!"

CHAPTER THIRTY-TWO

ONE SETTLER met them in his barnyard, with a pail of milk in his hand, and a black-and-white cat for company. The cat kept his tail straight up and rubbed against his master's leg to show what a good friend he was at milking time. But he stopped in alarm when his master shouted, "So you're a deputy sheriff!"

Elmer said, "Yes, sir."

"That's a hell of a joke! There've been two murders around here in the last month, and no end of cattle stealing, and not one arrest. Where've you fellows been?"

Elmer said, "The sheriff isn't allowed to act under martial law."

"Then why in hell are you here?"

Elmer said, "I have a capias to serve on you."

"What's that?"

"It says you have to be at the Steilacoom courthouse this morning at ten o'clock, with your rifle. It's a kind of order of arrest."

"This Territory has gone crazy! You can't arrest murderers, but you can arrest decent citizens!"

Elmer said, "If we can get the decent citizens together, we can take care of the other kind. You know Judge Lander has tried to convene court twice. The Governor had him kidnapped both times, and he's still locked up somewhere. Judge Chenoweth is going to try today. If there are enough of us to protect the court it'll be able to protect us."

"Suppose I tell you to go to hell with your warrant, or whatever it is?"

"You'll be liable to fine or imprisonment when the courts are working again. If they don't start working, you won't have anything to fear from the law. Neither will anybody who takes a shot at you, or steals your stock."

The settler looked less fierce. "Maybe I'm a damn fool," he said, "but if you want to save yourself some time, catch that little mare in the field while I get ready."

Another settler said, "I know what you're up to! You're trying to overthrow martial law. Governor Stevens wouldn't have it if it wasn't right. You can shoot me, but I won't go with you!" There was no use arguing with his kind.

At one cabin door, a sad, pleasant woman said, "My husband would have wanted to go with you, but he's away, trying to buy a cow. Both of ours were stolen while we were at the blockhouse. There's no one here but our sick boy." She lowered her voice. "He caught his death of cold with the volunteers, and he's begun to cough blood."

Elmer said, "I know him, Mrs. Miller; we were in the same squad. I wouldn't think of taking him when he's sick. But I'd like to be remembered to him if you don't think I should see him." He could hear some one moving about in the cabin, behind the door which the woman had closed. They were still talking when the door opened and Tow Miller came out. He was fully dressed, with his red volunteer shirt under his coat which was too loose for him. His powder flask and bullet pouch were slung at his side, and he was carrying his long rifle. "I heard what's up," he said, with his eyes bright and determined. "I'm feeling better today; I'm going with you."

His mother and Elmer both said, "No!" but he brushed their protest aside, passionately. "If I have done for myself," he said, "it was for nothing! I want something better'n that to remember. I can still use a rifle, and I'm going to march with you once more. This time it'll be for something." And they could not dissuade him.

So, with successes and failures, Elmer worked his way to Steilacoom at the head of a little, lengthening column of horsemen. Ahead there was another short column going into the town; another was coming down from the north, and on the prairie behind them a single horseman galloped like an express rider to overtake them. Men were on the move toward Steilacoom, but until they were close enough to express themselves there was no certainty whether they were enemies or friends. But because all the columns in sight were very small, Elmer felt sure they were the forces of justice.

The single rider overtook them near the fort, and reined up by the head of their column. *"Elmer!"* he shouted. *"Miller, Bill!"*

They all said, *"Paul!"*

Paul rode beside them on his sweat-dripping horse which was lathered with foam. He was wearing his red flannel volunteer shirt, and his jeans were tucked into his high boots, "California style," and he had his rifle. Riding beside Elmer and shaking hands, he said, "I'm here to join your squad."

Elmer gripped his hand. "Paul, you shouldn't!" He was thinking of Bob, dead under Grand Mound prairie, and the boy's parents. If there was any shooting today, and anything happened to Paul— "You shouldn't be here!"

Paul said quietly, "You'll need all the help you can get."

"It isn't even in your county," Elmer said.

"We have martial law in Thurston County, too," Paul said. "If we break it in one place, we can break it in another." Then he said to Bill, "This isn't your county, either, but you're here."

Bill said, "Some way Elmer and I are always riding together while our wives keep each other company. We got our families mixed up in the war and we can't seem to unmix them again."

Elmer said, "Seems like that." He hadn't wanted it to be that way, but that's the way it was. He felt discouraged for a minute. Then they were passing the fort, and he forgot to be discouraged. He smiled at the bastions above the stockade and said inside himself, "We're fighting for you today, Uncle!" It gave him a triumphal feeling.

They passed the fort and came into the town, with people turning to look at them, and faces appearing at windows. At first it seemed odd that people who had seen so many soldiers and volunteers should stare at a dozen armed men riding through the town. Then Elmer remembered that there were a dozen other deputies, and he would not be the first to arrive.

Probably no one had paid much attention to the first posse or the second. But with one small troop after another riding in all morning, it might be more exciting than the passing of a regiment, and it would give people that still feeling that something was going to happen.

They turned a corner and came to the courthouse, with women and children and a few soldiers watching from across the street. The unpainted wooden building was dingy in the sunshine; a dozen or so men with rifles were standing around in the yard, and a few more who had just arrived were leading their horses around to the shed at the back of the courthouse. Some of the men were white-bearded and some of them were only boys. The capiases had been served on every male of sixteen or over, and even then the results seemed disappointing.

The sheriff met them as they rode into the yard, and he did not look at all disappointed. "Eleven," he said. "That's good, boy! We can use them all." He was thin and straight and looked like a deacon except for the star on his frock coat, and an alert snap to his eyes.

Elmer said, "I wanted to bring more, but some were away, and some didn't have rifles, and some wouldn't come at the point of a gun."

"Eleven's the best any one's done out of town," the sheriff said. "You did well!" He caught Elmer's unhappy look at the handful of old men and boys in the yard. "Hell, boy, I got fifty armed men in the courtroom! That's all she'll hold. The rest of you'll have to stay outside. Tie your horses out back, and make yourselves at home."

When they came back from securing their horses, another deputy with eight men was reporting to the sheriff.

Elmer had imagined that defending the court would be a strenuous and dangerous business, but instead it was restful. When they did not feel like standing, the guards sat on the grass and talked, and pulled at dandelions. And it was comforting when they heard the sheriff's voice inside proclaim,

"*Hear ye, hear ye, hear ye! The Superior Court of Pierce County is now in session!*"

The men and old men and boys in the yard got up and cheered

in answer. Then they settled down to comfortable talk again.

Splitting a dandelion stem into curls, Paul said, "I used to think that courts were tiresome. I never thought about their meaning anything to me; I didn't know one could sound so good."

Elmer said, "I guess it's one of those things you don't miss until it stops."

"I didn't know the law could stop," Miller said, "not until this trouble happened. I thought you could count on it like the sun rising." He buttoned his coat over his chest and stopped talking as if he were afraid he might begin to cough.

Paul said, "That's the way I felt. I knew we'd had courts for hundreds of years, and I thought we'd always have them."

A settler near them said, "We could get along without courts if everybody was as decent as I am, but they ain't. The week we got martial law one of my neighbors on the prairie started stealing my sheep, just as if the skunk had been waiting for the chance."

Paul said, "They're stealing cattle down our way."

"One of my boys caught him at it," the settler went on. "That time I went to the sheriff, and he couldn't do anything because of martial law. When I got home, I said, 'Boys, we've got something as good as the law!' We laid for the skunk and caught him with another sheep. So we stripped him and tied him to a tree and I whaled the tar out of him with an ox whip, and gave him twenty-four hours to get out of the county."

Paul asked, "Did he go?"

"I'm telling this," the settler reminded him. "Next day I went back to make sure he'd gone, and he was still there, meek as a lamb. He said, 'How'n hell can I leave the county, while I'm tied to this tree?' So I cut him loose and gave him another twenty-four hours. I thought then we had something better'n the law. But the next week a stranger shot my oldest boy through the neck. You don't have to guess who hired him. And now I have two skunks to go after for murder because I couldn't get the law on one for stealing sheep."

Across the street there were faces at windows; people watched in a thickening crowd and boys were standing on the roof of a shed. The town had the look of watching a battle, but the court-house in the center of the storm droned on with the law's machinery, and it was peaceful in the yard.

Court had been in session an hour when the boys on the roof of the shed began to prance against the sky, and across the street women were hurrying their children away.

"They're coming," Elmer said, taking his rifle from the grass and getting up.

Some one else shouted, "Here they are!"

All around, old men and young men and boys were rising from the ground with new rifles and older rifles and long, lean rifles that had fought in the Revolution and crossed the plains. There was a sudden, swelling thunder of hooves, and a double column of horsemen galloped down the street.

"Nixon's Volunteers!" Paul said.

Bill said, "They're the only ones I ever wanted to fight."

One man shouted, "Murderers!" and shook his fist at the horsemen. Word had got around that Nixon's Volunteers had found thirty Nisqually women and children hiding on Mason River, and butchered them all.

Nixon's company came up with a dash and stopped short, the horses leaning back on their haunches and sliding as the men threw themselves off, with their rifles held handily. Nixon came towering into the yard, with his men behind him and the guards falling back a little before his confident march. Then he stopped, with the muzzle of a rifle touching his thick belly. There was no alarm on his hard-swollen red face, but he was respectful because the rifle was cocked. "Let me past, boy," he said, "I got business in there."

Elmer said, not very loud, "This is a hair trigger."

They heard the sheriff from the steps behind them. "You can't come in here, Nixon; court is in session."

"I got business in there," Nixon said genially.

The sheriff said, "You'll have your day in court, but this isn't it. There's other cases today. And the courtroom's so full of men and rifles you couldn't get in." Then he said, "You boys don't have to press him so close, unless he moves."

Elmer moved back a little and uncocked his rifle, but he kept it ready. Behind Nixon he saw the black-bearded face and animal eyes of Joshua Sims. And he couldn't decide which one to kill if there was shooting.

Nixon said, "I'm a peaceful man, sheriff, but I got orders to break up court."

"I have orders to protect it," the sheriff said, "and I have a hundred men to help me."

"I order you to let us in!"

"I order you to keep out!"

"I order you in the name of the Governor of the Territory!"

"I order you in the name of the law that was before the Governor was born, and will be after we're all dead."

Nixon stopped shouting and became genial. "You haven't any men in there, sheriff. All you got's out here. Your bluffing."

"Am I?" The sheriff went up the two steps and opened the door. The doorway was solid with men and rifles and old army muskets with bayonets fixed. Beyond them, in the courtroom, two men were shouting, and there was a hammering sound. The man with the loudest voice was bellowing, *"One moment, your Honor, I object! I object!"* The sheriff closed the door and the din was muffled and the armed men shut away.

Nixon made the gesture of spitting. "Listen to 'em," he said, "they can't even agree among themselves!"

The sheriff said, "They're here to disagree, and we're here to see they ain't disturbed at it."

"I'm warning you," Nixon said, "this is treason!"

"It's treason for a man to live on his farm; it's treason for a judge to convene court; it's treason for a sheriff to do his duty! What else?"

"The Governor says martial law must be enforced."

"I was elected by the people, not the Governor."

Nixon said, "I ain't going to stand here arguing, but we'll be back, and we'll call out the regulars if we need 'em."

"Go ahead," the sheriff said. "You try it; I hope to God you try!"

Nixon said, "It ain't far to the fort. We'll be back."

When they were gone, most of the guards were pleased with themselves and felt as if they had won a battle. But a few of them were anxious. One pale boy with an orange-freckled face wanted to know what would happen if the regulars were called out. "I aim to do my duty," he said, "but, goodness, we couldn't fight the army!"

The sheriff laughed and patted the boy's shoulder. "If the regulars turn out we'll be in clover," he said. "If they help anybody, it'll be us!"

After the encounter, the townspeople no longer looked on the court guards as men who were about to die. Small boys ventured into the yard and asked boldly and with regret why there hadn't been a fight. And when court recessed for lunch, women brought buckets of coffee and sandwiches and cakes and pies. One young woman who waited on Elmer's party was nice and friendly, and Elmer thought he had seen her before. After she had gone he remembered he had once asked her to marry him, though he couldn't remember her name.

The regulars did not appear to disperse the court or to help guard it. And Major Nixon's company did not come back. The afternoon was quiet for so long that a few of the guards slipped away to see the town. And because he was a deputy sheriff for the day, Elmer went to round them up, and he took Paul with him.

They strolled as far as the end of the street and looked at the Sound which went away from the foot of the hill in deepening shades of blue which darkened to purple in mid-channel. Across the channel to the north they saw Fox Island, steep-sided and high, like a land that has risen above trouble. The smoke of Indian fires was going up from the edge of the timber in straight blue columns, and a few Indians were fishing from dugouts close to shore. It was the island Leschi had captured on his raid in search of peace. He hadn't been allowed to find peace, and neither had any one else. Since then the Governor had extended his war to settlers and judges and courts. But to-day's small victory gave the feeling of peace coming back, and it was a good day to think of Leschi.

Paul was thinking of him too. He said, "That was a good sleep I took that night on the White River."

"I've always thought so, Paul."

"It's the only thing in the war that I'm proud of," Paul said, "and it's something I can't tell."

"You'd better not!"

"There wasn't any satisfaction in killing that Indian." He was talking about the boy who had shot Bob, while they were closing in on him to take him a prisoner.

Elmer said, "We couldn't have done anything else."

"Just the same, I wish we hadn't. It didn't do any good."

When they were on their way back, the church bell began to ring wildly, and an express rider dashed up to the court-house ahead of them, shouting some news. The men in the yard threw up their hats and cheered, and some of them fired their rifles. One of them embraced Elmer, shouting above the din, *"Martial law is ended!"*

It was a long time before Elmer got to talk to the sheriff. He asked, "Who ended martial law? How did it happen?"

The sheriff said, "We did! We did it when we kept the court going, but the Governor took the credit. He couldn't stand being beaten, so he proclaimed the emergency over."

Elmer didn't care who took the credit. "It was a good day," he said.

Standing beside them, Miller said, "It was a great day!" Fever spots were burning in his cheeks and he looked tired but grateful as he said, "This gives me something to remember."

Settlers were bringing out their horses and mounting up, and some were already riding away. The uncertain flame which they had shielded with their bodies was now burning securely and they were no longer needed.

CHAPTER THIRTY-THREE

MARY used to tell them about the Indian night which has no time. At night, she said, people who are not yet born walk the earth with the *ancuttie men* who came back from Mount Rainier. If Mary came back, they never saw her, but she was a gentle person who would never have troubled any one. Two others did come back.

They were in their clearing for the moonrise, which was part of their life. When they were first married, they had not taken time for things like that, but war and trouble and separation had taught them to value everything more. Now, when the moon rose behind the black woods to the east, they were in the clearing to meet it and worship its first light on their garden and on the rhododendron bush with its long glossy leaves and great clusters of pale, luminous blossoms.

Standing where the waist-high corn met the enchanted bush, Lisette said softly, "This is our life, Elmer: corn we've sweated over, and something magic like this." Then she pressed his hand and said, "But oh, how beautiful the corn is, too!"

He said, "I remember the first night I stayed on this shore, in this clearing. It was summer, and moonlight, like this. Only it was all brush and salal where it's garden now. But I knew this was where I wanted to be. The moon coming through the trees like that marked my place on earth."

"It marks mine, too," she said.

They were admiring the fine rows of potato plants among the stumps, when a boat grated harshly on gravel.

Lisette said, "It must be Uncle Jarvis." But when they looked from near the house, there was a very small dugout pulled up on the beach, and the stocky man coming toward them in the moonlight looked like an Indian.

Elmer called, "Who is it?"

The Indian called, "Elmer *tillicum!* Me Nisqually Jim!" He scrambled up the bank where both of them shook hands with him at the same time, and his flat, homely face looked as good as a familiar scene. Shaking hands, he said, "*Spose* we go logging soon, h'm?"

They laughed at his imitation of Uncle Jarvis, but Elmer was uneasy. "You have to be careful, Jim."

"*Wake,*" Jim insisted. "What-the-hell? Nisquallys belong this side of *salt chuck.*"

Elmer said, "The volunteers would shoot you, just the same."

"*Wake,*" Jim grinned. "No more. Nisquallys won the war."

"My God!" Elmer didn't know whether Jim had gone crazy or been deceived by some ghastly hoax.

Lisette patted the Indian boy's thick arm. "But, Jim, they didn't win! They were beaten and the volunteers are hunting them down! Leschi escaped over the mountains and Quiemuth gave himself up. He was killed by a mob in the Governor's office——"

Elmer said, "Slugia is the only leader left, and it would be better for the Nisquallys if he was caught! Sunday he and Hooit killed a settler coming home from church, and burned a barn. He's doing what Leschi wouldn't let him do and making things worse than ever for the Indians. Some one lied to you when he said the Indians won!"

"*Wake,*" Jim said, "we won." He tried to show them on his fingers how it was. "Nisquallys fought for land. The land Leschi said we should get. We got it. We won."

Lisette's face was strange. "You got the land Leschi asked for?"

"Sure," Jim said. "What-the-hell?"

"Who said you got it?"

"Governor Stevens."

Elmer sat down, unbelieving, at the edge of the bank, and

the others sat beside him. "When did Governor Stevens say that?"

"Today," Jim said, "at *sitkum sun*. He made a treaty on Fox Island. I come to tell you."

Elmer was beginning to believe the story, though he did not understand. "If that's so, the Nisquallys won the war, all right!"

"Not like Medicine Creek Treaty," Jim said. "At Medicine Creek Governor Stevens shut his ears and open his mouth. To-day he shut his mouth and open his ears. He was a *tillicum*. He sits on a log with Indians and says, 'Why do you Nisquallys fight us?' Old men say, 'You gave us *cultus* land: *halo chuck*, *halo* fish, *halo* grass, *halo* soil, *halo* everything. Only stones and fir trees. We *memaloose* there. That is why we fight.' Governor Stevens is like this." Jim sat for a few seconds with his face buried in his hands, like a man in deep thought or despair. "He says, 'What land do you want?'"

Lisette sighed. "Why couldn't he have said that the first time?"

Jim went on, "Old men tell him we want the land Leschi asked for. But they don't say 'Leschi.' They say eight miles of land on the Nisqually: prairie for horses, and bottom land, river for salmon and canoes to the *salt chuck*. Governor Stevens is like this." The boy sat for a minute with his big face buried in his hands. "Then he says, 'All right,' and his man puts it in the treaty."

"Is that all he said?" Elmer felt vague with wonder.

"That," Jim said. "'Why do you fight us?' 'What land do you want?' 'All right.'"

Lisette said, "We were so sure of it before the first treaty, and then everything went wrong. Now, when it seems as if it never could be, it happens like a dream."

Staring at the moonlit water, Elmer thought of frosty moon-light on the White River, and Leschi's ragged warriors passing like phantoms on skeleton horses. He recalled Leschi's face, raised toward the mountains with its unconquered look. Watch-ing, Elmer had not guessed that the starved band had held out to the turning of some invisible tide, and that theirs was a march of victory.

They sat on the bank and talked until they saw Uncle Jarvis's canoe push into the Inlet and head toward their shore.

"That means he's heard the news," Elmer said.

Lisette said, "And it probably means he's forgotten to eat. You boys fix the fire; I'll get something ready."

Uncle Jarvis had heard the news. Coming in, he boomed cheerfully, "D'ye hear the Indians won the war?"

Nisqually Jim grinned. "I told them; they thought I was *pelton.*"

"We're all a little *pelton,* h'm?" Jarvis kissed Lisette and embraced one of the young men with each arm, like a grizzly bear with two cubs.

Elmer said, "Maybe I am *pelton,* but I don't see why the Governor did it. Why did he nearly wreck the Territory to beat the Indians, and then give them everything they wanted?"

"Uncle Jarvis sat on a bench and took off his moccasins. "Maybe he had orders to give them land they could live on."

"Do you think so?" Elmer asked.

Uncle Jarvis pushed his bare feet toward the fire. "I shouldn't be surprised," he said. "We have a government in Washington, h'm? And the Indians held out long enough for some of us to call attention to their plight."

Lisette said, putting bacon in the skillet, "Leschi can start his people farming now, the way he planned long ago. We can all go on with our lives in peace."

"D'ye think the world could be that perfect?" He did not have the sound of contradicting her, only of wishing she were right, and not being sure.

"But Leschi will come back, won't he, Uncle?"

Jarvis said, "I wonder if they'd let him live in peace?"

"Why shouldn't they?" Lisette insisted. "The war is over, and Leschi was right all along."

Uncle Jarvis sighed and stirred his tangled gray mass of beard. "Suppose the Governor'll be able to forgive Leschi for being right?"

Elmer saw the shape of what his uncle feared. But he said, "He'll have to."

Lisette said, "He must!"

"We still don't know all of Isaac Stevens," Jarvis said. "But he's only five feet tall; that's a bad sign."

Lisette turned from the frying bacon with a puzzled look. "What has that to do with it, Uncle?"

"Everything!" Jarvis said. "Pride, vanity, the level from which a man sees this world. Look!" He towered up, six feet four in his bare feet, a mountain of a man, untidier than ever without Mary to look after his clothes. "If a man offends me I can look down on him, even if he gets the best of me, and my vanity's satisfied. But Stevens is five feet tall, and he has to look down on a man of Leschi's stature; his vanity demands it. And the only way he can look down on his enemy is to have him dead at his feet."

Uncle Jarvis was a little drunk and Elmer didn't know how literally to believe what he was saying, but he was uneasy.

The other night of *ancuttie men* had no moon. It was very dark outside Uncle Jarvis's cabin where Elmer and Lisette were spending the evening. The wolfish dogs had disappeared while their master was a prisoner at the fort, and they did not have the beasts' noise to announce visitors. Lisette was sewing buttons on Jarvis's shirts and hemming them where he had torn off pieces of shirt tail for gun-wads while hunting. Elmer was reading aloud from *Plutarch's Lives,* which Lisette had started during the winter, and Uncle Jarvis's shaggy gray head was bent over a blue bowl in which he was mashing Oregon grapes with a billet of wood. The grapelike berries were all skins and juice that ran out like purple wine when he strained it into a cup.

Elmer paused in his reading to watch, and Lisette said, "It looks good enough to drink!"

Jarvis dipped a pen into the liquid and touched it to his tongue, and his eyes closed and his beard bristled. "Corrosive!" He dipped the pen a second time and wrote on a sheet of foolscap, with the acid juice coming out red-brown and clear. "Turned into letters," he said, "it's guaranteed to eat the brass foundations from under a tyrant." While he was filling the ink bottle, Elmer went on with his reading aloud:

"For her actual beauty, it is said, was not in itself so remarkable that none could be compared with her, or that no one could see her without being struck by it, but the contact of her presence, if you lived with her, was irresistible; the———"

He stopped because the others were looking past him to where the door behind him had opened; he could smell the darkness outside and the pitchy smoke of a distant forest fire. And when he looked, an Indian was standing in the room.

The Indian spoke in Nisqually, and Jarvis pinched out the flames of the candle and grease lamp. Lisette and Elmer sat in silence while he went out and talked to some one in low tones. The room was in darkness except for some coals, like a dim sunset in the fireplace, and it was lonely with the smells of the night which had come in.

Uncle Jarvis came back into the room with their guest, and closed the door. "It's Leschi," he said. "Remember, you haven't seen him."

"We'll remember," they said, with voices as solemn as wedding vows.

The four of them sat around the fireplace, with Jarvis in the middle and Leschi on the far side. He was dressed in jeans and a hickory shirt and might have passed for a settler in the dark, but even in the twilight of the dying fire any one who had seen him once would have recognized his magnificent, homely face, with its tremendous forehead and piercing eyes. Some of the talk was in English, and some in Nisqually, but what the others did not understand Jarvis repeated afterward.

Leschi did not speak until Jarvis had filled a pipe and lit it and handed it to him. He smoked and said quietly, "It is finished. We have won." His voice sounded like the tired earth speaking after some tremendous upheaval.

"When did you get back?" Jarvis asked.

"Last night," Leschi said. "When one of our runners brought the news over the mountains, my heart would not let me fight any more. My heart said, 'You have won the land of the Nisquallys. Even if they kill you, they cannot take that away. If you go on fighting you may take it away from yourself.' I surrendered to Colonel Wright, and he did not kill me or keep me a prisoner. He said, 'You have fought a good fight, but we were too many for you. Go home to your own country and live in peace. You have nothing to fear.'"

Uncle Jarvis asked, "Did he give you anything written?"

"No," Leschi said. "He was a good man, and his words were enough. But when I got here I heard that Quiemuth had been killed in the Governor's own house after he had given himself up. I heard that thirty of our women and children had been killed on Mason River where they were fishing. I knew the word of one good man was not enough in a land where such things happen."

"You aren't safe yet," Jarvis said. "Don't see any one you wouldn't trust with your life!"

Leschi said, "I have seen the land we fought for and won, but I can only walk there at night. It is a good land. It is the land I dreamed of for my people, and it is like a dream because I see it only in the night. In the middle of the land I came to a good house by the river. My heart said, 'I would like to live in this house by the river and keep my herds on this prairie and cultivate these fields.' It was my own house, but I stood there like a stranger, and I did not dare go in. It was like being dead and still seeing and feeling in my heart. I walked in the fields, and I took earth in my hands, and smelled it. My heart said, 'I would like to grow food from this earth and cultivate these fields.' I came to a plough in the earth, and it was my own plough, in my own field. I went back and with my hands and eyes I found the furrow. It was grown over with grass and weeds, but it was there. I went along the furrow. It was crooked at first. In one place I had ploughed too deep, in another not deep enough. Then it was straight and steady—and I hit my head on the plough where it stopped when I heard the volunteers were coming to arrest me. I put my hands on the plough, and I could remember how it felt when I was going right. I had not forgotten; I could go on making a straight furrow. But my horses are gone, Quiemuth who drove them is dead, and I am a ghost, holding a rusted plough in a dark field. My tears fell when I thought that was maybe all I would ever plough: one crooked furrow that grew straight and stopped. Then my heart said, 'I used the sword to win this land for my people. Maybe the gods are angry or think that is enough and will not let me use the plough.' My tears stopped, and I took a little of the earth and put it in the pocket of my Boston clothes." He touched the pocket of his shirt. "I have it here."

The last twilight of the fire was gone when he said good-by. They shook hands with him in the darkness and did not know where he was going.

When they heard of Leschi again, he was at Fort Steilacoom, under arrest. His nephew, Slugia, had betrayed him to the Governor's men for a reward of fifty blankets. And instead of being treated as a prisoner of war, he was to be tried as a murderer.

CHAPTER THIRTY-FOUR

ON THE SCAFFOLD *he thanked me for my kindness to him. . . . He said he would not be the first man to lose his life on false evidence. If he was dying for his people he was willing to die; that Christ died for others.*

After he made his speech he turned and thanked me again for my kindness to him while he was a prisoner under my care, and said that he had nothing more to say and that he was ready. He died without a struggle.

It seemed to me he talked for fifteen minutes, but spoke very deliberate and slow: but he made very few gestures and had a dignified way that made a lasting impression on my mind. . . .

He did not seem to be the least bit excited at all, and no trembling on him at all—nothing of the kind, and that is more than I could say for myself. In fact, Leschi seemed to be the coolest of any on the scaffold. He was in good flesh and had a firm step and mounted the scaffold without assistance, as well as I did myself. I felt that I was hanging an innocent man, and I believe it yet. . . .

(Statement of Charles Grainger, executioner,
from Ezra Meeker's *Pioneer Reminiscences*)

CHAPTER THIRTY-FIVE

———

THEY KEPT UP a bright fire in Uncle Jarvis's cabin so he would have some comfort when he came home. Elmer did not have any comfort for himself, but Lisette had food and coffee waiting, and everything neat and clean-swept. She was in the calm bloom of pregnancy and she could not quite see death. Or if she did, it was overshadowed by the life she had to give. When everything was ready and in good order, she was able to sit quietly, with her hands folded in her lap.

Elmer did not want to do anything to disturb Lisette, but he could not sit still, or be in any one place for long. He went over to the window again and looked at the Inlet, strange with driftwood and masses of yellow foam and a floating tree with wild branches. And beyond the water, above the forest wall on his shore, Mount Rainier rode in the March sky, as old as Ararat and muffled and tremendous in new snow. At the left of the mountain there was the Military Road, deep under the snow of Summit Hill where starving men on skeleton horses had climbed in their desperate retreat. Try to think of them going up forever, unconquered. . . .

Behind him, Lisette's voice said, "Don't you want to go out and take a walk, dear?"

"I don't know," he said. He had the feeling that it was a dead world outside, without air, where he would suffocate. He went over to where she was sitting and stood close beside her for comfort. "I don't want to leave you," he said. But when he went back to the window, Nisqually Jim was walking slowly through the yard, with his head down. Jim had been gone since the day before. Elmer went out to meet him, and they walked back toward the deserted timber camp.

431

Elmer asked, looking at the ground, "Did you go to Steila-coom?"

"*Wake*," Jim said. "Nisqually."

They sat on the log abandoned at the head of the skids.

"Nobody sleeps last night," Jim said. "They only cry. Hooit came home when it was dark night."

Hooit was a murderer who was to die on the same gallows with Leschi. "He got away?" Elmer asked.

"*Wake*," Jim said, "they let him go to make us feel good."

Elmer groaned. "Slugia's friend!"

"*Halo*," Jim said. "He and Slugia kill White coming home from church, but *halo tillicums*. Hooit said, 'Come, we find Slugia!' We find him this morning."

"Where is he now?"

"On the beach," Jim said, "by the bluff, *cockshut, memaloose*. He falls three hundred feet."

"You shouldn't have helped," Elmer said, "you'll only get into trouble."

"What-the-hell," Jim's flat face was sad and sullen. "I think of Tyee Jarvis. This long time he logs no more, he ploughs no more. He writes and writes and goes away and comes back like a *tamanous*. He *memalooses* himself so Leschi can live."

"I know," Elmer said, "but you mustn't get into any trouble. We need you, Jim."

"All right," Jim said.

"Come and have some *muck-a-muck*."

"*Halo muck-a-muck*," Jim said, "my *tum-tum* is sad."

"Have some coffee, anyway."

"All right," Jim said. "Is Tyee Jarvis here?"

"He went to Steilacoom."

Jim said, "I was afraid."

"I wouldn't be there, either."

"Tyee Jarvis is never afraid."

"I don't know," Elmer said, "but he isn't afraid to be where a friend is."

Uncle Jarvis came home late in the afternoon. Elmer and Nisqually Jim met him at the barn gate. "It is over," he said.

His face was as gray as his beard. "It was like hanging a statue."

Jim took the horse, and when Jarvis was walking to the cabin with Elmer, he said, "It was far out on the prairie. Colonel Casey said they couldn't commit murder on army ground. And he made the sheriff a prisoner when he came to get Leschi."

"A prisoner! Why?"

"I suppose because he was fighting mad and couldn't bear to see an innocent man hung. The colonel had got to know Leschi while he was a prisoner, and he had fallen under his spell. So had the other officers who fought against him. And there was something about Leschi that caught the imagination, h'm?"

"There was," Elmer said, "there was!" After a while he said, "But I don't see what good it did to arrest the sheriff."

"It did no good." Then Jarvis said, "I can't be sure because we didn't try, but we might have delivered Leschi from prison. Some of his friends were there, ready to try. I talked them out of it, Elmer."

Elmer did not say anything.

"Leschi was innocent, and he was murdered. But it was judicial murder. If the army and his friends had taken the law into their own hands, God knows where it would have ended."

Elmer did not say anything. He was thinking Leschi might be alive, and he was dead because Uncle Jarvis had extinguished his last hope.

"We had martial law," Jarvis said, "and we broke it. We must abide by that. If we started our own martial law, there'd be another reign of terror. We can never undo the mischief of the last one, and the Territory can't stand another."

"I see," Elmer said.

"Leschi died for his people," Jarvis said, "but in a way he had to die for all of us, so we could go on with our lives in peace."

Elmer felt better after that, and he could see his uncle felt better for having thought things out. They went into the cabin and did not speak of Leschi's death any more.

Uncle Jarvis's face was still gray and worn, and for the first time he looked old. But he was almost cheerful, and he accepted a cup of coffee from Lisette. When he had rested a few minutes he went through his portable writing desk and burned some unmailed letters. He had been working for a pardon when the ground was cut out from under his feet. The Legislature in Olympia recognized Leschi's importance by changing the law so he could be executed before there was time to communicate with the President. That had been a bitter moment, but he did not have any look of bitterness as he burned the unmailed letters in the fireplace, and put his writing desk away under the bunk. Then he took off his moccasins and socks, and sprawled in his chair, resting, like a quiet and aging Titan, with his eyes closed.

They thought he would fall asleep there, but after a minute he opened his eyes and looked kindly at Lisette. "When is this baby coming, girl?"

She said, "Early next month, Uncle." She looked pleased because he was interested in something, and because it was the most important thing in the world.

"We must take good care of you," he said. "You must be well and happy and have a fine baby."

"I am well," she said, "and mostly happy. I don't worry."

"And you must have a doctor when the time comes, h'm?"

"We would like to have Doctor Tolmie," she said.

"I'll speak to him myself," Uncle Jarvis said. "And you'll want a woman to help."

"Dolly Slocum will be here," she said. "She made me promise I would let her help. Elmer thinks I should have a woman without a baby of her own. But she manages so well, and I tell Elmer he can watch her baby while she looks after me."

"I'll help him," Jarvis said. "We both need practice. This baby of yours is going to be spoiled."

Lisette said, "Not too much."

"As much as is good for him, h'm? And he's going to get a great deal of love."

Lisette nodded, smiling softly, as if she had known that all along.

"When he is older, too," Uncle Jarvis said. "We must see that he has a good life, and doesn't have to work hard while he is a boy."

Elmer said, "Only enough to make him strong."

"He can get strong playing," Lisette said.

Uncle Jarvis said, "Maybe we'll start the timber camp again this summer. We must be able to afford to give this boy a good life. He must have love and play and a garden of his own where he can plant what he pleases. He must have things of his own which no one can take from him, and he must not be anxious or afraid. He must not be made to work or study beyond his strength and hurt himself. Rather, he should set his own pace. Think twice, or ten times, before you are sure you know better than he. None of us knows very much. Remember, he is not growing himself; nature is growing him and knows better than you about many things."

Elmer had never heard his uncle talk that way before, and he was puzzled. When Jarvis had started talking it was an effort for him to say anything at all. He had started talking about the baby that would not be born until next month. But the baby had been born almost immediately, and it was a boy. Now he was quite a big boy, and Jarvis was lumbering about, excitedly, in his bare feet, planning how he should be brought up.

Jarvis caught his nephew's look and stopped in front of him, scowling earnestly. "I am not a *pelton man.*" He sat down, heavily. "Maybe I am a little *pelton* because these things are so important. I have been thinking of another boy, back home in Massachusetts, who suffered and had a hard childhood." He looked at his nephew with a kind of sad, rough tenderness. "You grew up on a New England farm, Elmer. You know it isn't all beer and skittles, h'm?"

Elmer said, "In most ways it was a hard life."

"This boy had a worse time of it, mostly because his father was crippled. While he was a young man a tree he was cutting down fell on him and shattered one leg. The bones never knitted properly, and he limped, in pain, through the rest of his life. On one of those stony little farms it's a race with poverty and death and taxes at the best, h'm? And a cripple is handicapped from the start. This one was grim Puritan stuff and he kept up in the race, or almost. But there wasn't any time for softness, and his wife didn't have much time to love her seven children, or means to indulge them, h'm?"

Elmer said, "I should think not!"

"The children worked as soon as they were able to walk," Uncle Jarvis said. "They were all in bondage to the gods for their father's shattered leg. The youngest child was puny and not expected to grow up, and there was no time to waste on him; mostly he was forgotten."

"The poor baby!" Lisette said.

"When he was three, his grandmother came to visit and found him still in his cradle; a puny baby forgotten in the grim race he wasn't expected to enter. The grandmother took him home, and in a week he began to walk and talk. When she brought him back, she said he was the brightest child she had seen; the most promising.

"His father took an interest in him after that. Here was one more small weapon in the fight against poverty and stony fields. He began preparing the boy for this grim life. Every morning he took him out of his warm bed and woke him by plunging him into the rain barrel——"

"*No!*" Lisette gave a cry of protest, as if she saw the thing happening and wanted to prevent it.

"It wasn't meant as cruelty," Jarvis said. "It was the father's idea of waking the boy to stern realities and hardening him. He wasn't brutish, and he wanted to make the most of the boy's mind. He sent him to school before he was five. When the boy learned in a flash and went beyond his teachers in some things, his father took more interest in him and urged him on.

"As he saw it," Jarvis said, "the father did everything he could for the boy. But the mother was a tenderer sort. She found time to give him a little love and comfort, and he loved her devotedly. But even that wasn't for long. The father was a furious driver; he had got into the habit of doing everything furiously, keeping up in the handicapped race. Once, driving home from Andover, he upset the wagon on a hill and the mother was thrown out on her head. She lived for two years in a kind of twilight, with the boy taking care of her when she should have been taking care of him. After she died the father brought home a stepmother who did not make any one happy.

"The boy had ideas of his own about special crops, and he wanted to try them in a garden of his own. But his father said, 'Not one foot of land for folly!' There were stepbrothers and stepsisters coming along by then, and nothing to spare of anything.

"That would have discouraged most boys, h'm? But this one said, 'If I can't have land, I'll make my own!' He carried stones to the frog-pond in the pasture, and filled in part of the pond until it was above the level of the water. Then he dragged soil from somewhere in a little cart he had made, and filled in over the stones. Mostly he had to work by moonlight or the light of stars. From long before daybreak until after dark he was doing chores and farm work and studying at school. You see the picture, h'm? Bare oak trees black against the stars of a New England spring; a million frogs crying from the pond, and a frail child dragging earth in a little cart to make a land of his own. And when he had finished, his father tore out all his plants and put in potatoes."

Listening, Elmer sighed. And Lisette said, "That was too cruel! No child of ours—" she couldn't go on.

"The boy was ambitious," Jarvis said, "and at 'Old Put's School' he went beyond his teachers. But his father urged him on to do still more. When he was ten, his mind was exhausted, and he had to quit school and go to work. He went to his uncle's woolen mill at Fall River and learned to be a weaver. The other weavers tended two looms, but he was ambitious, and learned to tend four. He worked from five in the morning until dark, and was paid fifty dollars for his year's work. On his way home, in Andover, he fell in love with some gingerbread in a bake-shop window. It was the temptation of his life, but he was resolute. He went home and handed his wages to his father. Then he asked for a penny to buy gingerbread. And his father said, 'Not one penny!'

"He had spent a year indoors, in the woolen mill," Jarvis

said, "and when he was helping his father with the haying, he worked too hard and got sunstroke. That almost killed him, but he got over it. Then next summer, when he was twelve, he was helping his father again, pitching hay into a cart. When he showed his father that he could lift as much as any man, his father encouraged him to do still more."

"That was wicked!" Lisette said. "A boy who should have been playing!"

Elmer said, "He might have ruptured himself."

"He ruptured himself terribly," Uncle Jarvis said. "It might have been the end of him, but he never accepted defeat. He heard of a doctor in Boston who was having success with ruptures, and he went there alone, holding his guts in with his hands. The doctor patched him up so he was able to go on."

Elmer said, "They couldn't kill him, could they?"

Lisette asked, "What happened to him then?"

Uncle Jarvis said, "He grew up, because they couldn't kill him. And where he was broken, he mended again."

"What happened when he grew up?" Lisette asked. "What did he do?"

"He became Governor of our Territory."

Elmer saw the world turned inside out. He had hated Governor Stevens and cursed him, and he had expected to hate him until the end of time. And now he didn't feel anything but tears. After a while, he asked, "But how do you know all that about him, Uncle?"

The big man sighed and stirred in his chair. "I've been fighting Stevens for a long time," he said, "tooth and nail. I tried to save Leschi, and I didn't leave a stone unturned. And I have friends in Andover." He stared at the floor, as if he were ashamed. "I've been over Stevens's life with a fine-tooth comb to see how he was put together and to learn his weaknesses— and to see if there was anything I could use against him."

After a while, Elmer asked. "Did you find anything?"

"Nothing," Jarvis said. "Only the indictment of poverty; the indictment of ruined childhood; the indictment of life!" He walked about, a gray and aging Titan, with a compassionate face. "I've told you all I found; all that matters. The making of a tyrant!"

Lisette said, crying, "But how could he be so cruel, when he had suffered so much?"

Jarvis said, "Because he had suffered and been broken, and mended again, a little crookedly, maybe. Everything he has done here was in his childhood; in his ambition to rise to where he would be safe forever from what he suffered. You remember his ambition to tend four looms; more than anybody else. Here he insisted on having three jobs: Governor, Indian Superintendent, railroad surveyor. If there'd been a fourth loom, he'd have tried to tend that, too. As it was, threads snarled and broke, and people died. He was ruthless in taking away the Indians' land. His own land had been snatched from him; the land he had made. He showed no mercy. He had never been shown any. He tried to crush every one who opposed him. He had learned that he had to conquer or die. He did what he had learned, and he wrecked the peace of a territory. None of that could have been changed because he had to be what he had been made."

Lisette said, "I can see it was his terrible father, being so cruel——"

"What else could he have done?" Jarvis asked. "He had to drive his family so they could live. He didn't drive any one harder than himself. And all the time he was hampered and gnawed at by the pain of his shattered leg. He got nothing out of life for himself; he asked nothing. He didn't even allow himself tobacco. Suffering and hardship made him hard, but he had to be cruel to the people he loved, so they could survive."

Lisette sighed. "If only his leg hadn't been broken——"

"Yes," the big man said. "you can blame it on a falling tree; blame it on the gods." He was standing at the window, looking out, and above and beyond his gray, massive head Elmer saw the light of sunset gleaming on the snows of Mount Rainier. Up there, to the left of the mountain, was where the Military Road went over Summit Hill. In the eyes of his mind he saw figures moving there: starved men on skeleton horses going up over the snow; Leschi, with the light of a dream on his face, leading his people safely to their promised land; and a frail child, dragging a little cart of earth. . . .

It was dusk in the cabin and dusk was falling on the water, but the light of sunset was on the mountain where the gods looked down on the little procession of men going to their destinies.